PATRICK GALE
Mother's
Boy

TINDER
PRESS

Copyright © 2022 Patrick Gale

The right of Patrick Gale to be identified as the Author of
the Work has been asserted by him in accordance with the
Copyright, Designs and Patents Act 1988.

First published in Great Britain in 2022 by Tinder Press
An imprint of HEADLINE PUBLISHING GROUP

1

Cataloguing in Publication Data is available from the British Library

Hardback ISBN 978 1 4722 5741 3
Trade paperback ISBN 978 1 4722 5743 7

Typeset in Sabon 10.75/14.75 by Jouve (UK), Milton Keynes

Printed and bound in Great Britain by Clays Ltd, Elcograf S.p.A.

Headline's policy is to use papers that are natural, renewable and recyclable
products and made from wood grown in well-managed forests and other
controlled sources. The logging and manufacturing processes are expected to
conform to the environmental regulations of the country of origin.

HEADLINE PUBLISHING GROUP
An Hachette UK Company
Carmelite House
50 Victoria Embankment
London EC4Y 0DZ

www.tinderpress.co.uk
www.headline.co.uk
www.hachette.co.uk

For Aidan Hicks

Watch your hurt heart when it wavers,
Keep your clay cool on the shelf.
Avoid other flesh and its flavours.
Keep yourself to yourself

From 'Never Take Sweets from a Stranger'
by Charles Causley, an early work excluded
by the poet from his *Collected Poems*

ATLANTIC – 1941

The ship was under attack and horribly exposed by a clear night and a full moon. Until a change in the weather brought fog or cloud, ideally both, all they could do was fight back and hope they were not outnumbered or outgunned. Sometimes an explosion would shake them from so close that Charles almost forgot, in his stifled terror, to feel sick. Sometimes the sounds of their guns going off or the shouts and stamping boots of their crewmates would stop long enough to let them hear the piercing cry of someone wounded.

Signals came through constantly so there was no time to do anything but deal with them, and certainly none to talk. Talk was impossible in any case because Dizzy had his headphones on. These meant that when he swore, as he sometimes did when the ship was especially badly shaken, he did so at the top of his voice, which made Charles jump almost more than the explosions did. Occasionally the speaker tube's thin peeping sound would summon Charles, to receive instructions from the bridge, or be asked to make a report on the latest signals to come through.

They worked at fever pitch in the hot little office, Dizzy barely turning from his console to flick signals he'd deciphered from Morse across to Charles so that he would decode them into something like English. Dizzy had said once that Morse was enough for him to focus on and that it would have scrambled his brains if he'd attempted to guess the meanings hidden under the second layer of code. He passed Charles neatly filled-out pages from his pad, lines of letters and numbers, always in groups of four.

Charles knew to resist the urge to interpret or anticipate. Accuracy was all. He decoded four letters or digits at a time and only read to check for sense once he had the whole signal down. Sometimes it would be gibberish, and he would know that Dizzy, or whichever wireless telegraphist was on with him, was tired.

In this case, he swiftly recognised the code shorthand for a powerful battlecruiser. He knew before getting two words further in the missive that this was one he'd need to take to the bridge in person at once, rather than shouting it to a junior officer through the voice tube. He tore the page off his pad, folded it neatly and tucked it into his pocket to protect it from spray. As he pulled on his duffel coat, Charles tapped Dizzy's shoulder and pointed upwards so he'd know he was heading to the bridge, then stepped out.

The cold on deck was a shock after the heat generated by all the electrical kit in the Signals office, but it was the painful intensity of the noise that momentarily confused him. The enemy ship they had engaged had approached from the starboard and they must have swung round to present a narrower target. Charles could see both forward guns blasting shells into the darkness. The weather was changing, thank God. Poor visibility might soon give them cover to slip away to the south. The swell was such that he was amazed the guns could be aimed with any accuracy.

2

Climbing to the bridge, he knew to avoid looking out at the sea for fear of making his sickness worse but, even so, he had to pause a moment before climbing further as a judder of nausea ran through him, making him dry-heave over the railings and break out in a sweat the Atlantic wind immediately chilled.

There was never mayhem on the bridge, but the sense of group focus was intense. It was known that because of the skipper's slight deafness, he would tolerate no unnecessary talk. Charles saluted, and handed over the signal. He waited to attention while it was passed to the skipper, who read it. Often there was a signal to send in reply, but this time the skipper simply shook his head, betraying nothing of the horrors he had just read.

'Back to your watch, Causley,' he said, then checked Charles's leaving. 'Causley?'

'Sir?'

'Did you know anyone on board?'

'Yes, sir.'

'I'm sorry. You know the drill, though. Not a word.'

Which was when an explosion lit up the night and caused several of them to lose their balance and grab at the nearest handhold. One of the officers swore.

'Off you trot,' one of them told Charles as the skipper calmly demanded damage reports.

The fire crew was tackling a blaze on the deck while the MO and his small team were pulling the wounded to safety. Everyone seemed to be yelling and one of the wounded was crying out in a thin, high voice as though astounded by the pain he was in. The MO was following two sailors, who were stretchering one of the wounded to the sickbay, when he cursed roundly and turned.

'Causley. Good man. Bring that for me,' he called.

Charles looked where he was pointing. It was a hand and part of a forearm, cleanly severed, smeared with oil, a dusting of golden hair on the skin. It wore both a wedding ring and a wristwatch.

Charles froze.

'Come on, man. We've not got all day.'

Charles picked up the hand by its wrist, averting his eyes the moment he made contact with the skin, and hurried it over to the stretcher where the MO received it on a napkin of bandage before heading inside with the shattered patient.

There was another terrific blast of shell fire as Charles staggered into the nearest heads to throw up.

A boyhood friend – his best friend, arguably – had been on the ship in the signal he'd just delivered, reported sunk in the Denmark Strait with only three survivors, and he could tell nobody. Now it seemed quite possible they were to be blasted out of the water as well.

Charles washed his face and hands, then sat on the heads for a moment, stilling his breathing. He conjured the greenish midsummer water of a small municipal swimming pool, the soapy smell of the rough beach towel beneath him, birdsong from surrounding trees, the artless chatter of the friend lying in the sun at his side.

TEIGNMOUTH – 1914

Laura was in the garden cutting a bay leaf and chives for one sauce and parsley for another when she heard the gate clang and, startled, turned to see him. He was tall – about six foot two – and dark, and smartly turned out in a plum-coloured drill waistcoat and had a matching cravat tidily tucked into a very well-laundered shirt. She took in no details of his face beyond that he was conventionally handsome – like an illustration in a library romance – because of the unconscious little boy held in his arms, who was bleeding from a wound to his head. The man looked so smart that it didn't occur to her to show him to the kitchen.

Without a moment's hesitation she said, 'This way, sir,' and hurried ahead of them to open the front door and lead the way to the parlour where she indicated the chaise longue below the bay window.

Then he said, 'What about the blood?' in a harsh Devon accent, and she knew him for a servant.

'I'll fetch towels,' she said, grateful, for the chaise was upholstered in silk. There was a lavatory off the hall, a room whose luxury still surprised her, with a mahogany throne, a pretty view across the orchard and a beautiful sink of blue and white china, which pivoted to tip its contents into a lead chute below. She fetched towels from the cupboard in there and hurried back to spread them over the chaise longue where he carefully laid the boy down.

'Is he dead?' she asked.

'I hope not. He ran out chasing his hoop and I couldn't stop the cart in time. We were on our way to a patient.'

She saw him now, his high-boned handsomeness and the way shock was turning him pale.

'I'll fetch hot water and bandages,' she told him, thinking she should bring tea as well. 'Afternoon, sir,' she added to Dr Butler, who had just come in. He was lame from a childhood illness and rarely strong enough to drive his own cart, much less carry a wounded boy. His black bag was weight enough for him.

'Good girl,' he told her. 'A palmful of salt in the water, please. Have you witch hazel?'

'Yes, sir.'

'That, too. I apologise for intruding but yours was the nearest house. The Frasers are out, I take it?'

'Yes, sir.'

She hurried down to the kitchen. It was Mrs Ashbridge's day off and she had gone to her sister in Exeter, leaving Laura to make a cod pie and a redcurrant fool. Her employers were still out for lunch in Dawlish, for which she was grateful. She swiftly gathered together all she imagined the doctor might need. She was relieved to hear the little boy groaning softly when she came back to the parlour.

'Concussion and a nasty cut,' the doctor murmured. 'He was lucky to be thrown clear of the wheels. Do you know him?'

She took in the pinched face, the too large boots worn without socks, and knew him for the cheeky scamp who sometimes followed her down the hill on her errands, singing saucy songs and asking if she had a sweetheart. She nodded.

'From the cottages,' she said, and the doctor sighed, knowing which cottages she meant.

'Are you squeamish?' he asked, and she shook her head. 'Good. This will hurt him and you'll be a comfort.'

So she sat with the boy's head on a towel on her lap and held his hand while the doctor cleaned out the wound, then threaded a needle and stitched it in several places to hold it closed. She watched, fascinated that skin could be stitched and stretched just like cotton, and thinking of the stitching on the back of her best kid gloves as the child clutched her hand hard. She murmured to him, 'It's all right, John. Soon be over. Brave boy . . .' Nonsense like that to keep him still.

And all the while she knew the other man's gaze was on her, like a lamp.

The hall clock chiming three seemed to bring the doctor to his senses.

'I must go to Miss Ramsay, Charlie,' he said. 'I can walk from here but you can collect me when you've driven our young patient home. Perhaps . . .?'

'Laura,' she supplied.

'Perhaps Laura can show you the way?'

'Of course,' she said, glancing up at the other man, now named, and realising he was her age.

'Dress the wound with this liniment,' he handed her a small jar, 'then make a dressing and a bandage. I doubt he'll

7

keep it on for long but at least it will give the wound a clean start towards healing. I'll see myself out.'

The boy was crying silently, from the pain and shock, she supposed. She used her handkerchief to wipe his eyes, then dressed the neatly stitched wound on his forehead, laid a pad of gauze over it, tapped it carefully into place, wincing in sympathy as the boy flinched. Then she bound it to his head with three turns of bandage.

'There,' she told him, 'you look like a right little soldier now, back from fighting the Boer. Cup of tea?' she asked Charlie. 'I think we all need one. You stay here with the patient and I'll be right back.'

She brewed a pot of tea and cut three slices of seed cake. Mrs Ashbridge always baked with duck eggs for the good rise they gave and the cake was butter-yellow from their rich yolks.

Everything was topsy-turvy, Laura thought, with her serving tea and cake to a fellow servant and an urchin in her employers' parlour, so she restored a measure of order by serving it on the sturdy kitchen china and using the brown teapot. Her employers drank tea from bone china you could see daylight through. She was so nervous of breaking it that sometimes she had to pause in washing it to step back from the sink a little and calm her hands. She had been raised to labour and her grip was as strong as a man's. It amused Mrs Ashbridge to pass her pickle jars to open.

The cake revived the boy, who sat up, taking in his fine surroundings with sly eyes. 'Are you going to be more careful where you chase that hoop in future?' she asked him, and he nodded. 'You are a very lucky boy. The kick that pony gave you might have cracked your skull.'

'If I'd died,' he asked slowly, 'would he go to prison?'

'Don't be daft,' Charlie told him. 'I kill boys like you every week. It's a community service, like rat-catching.'

Laura clucked at the harshness of his humour but the boy was amused and grinned.

'Come on, then,' Charlie told him. 'We'd best get you off and out before the bosses come home.' He scooped the boy up in his arms with a tenderness at odds with his humour and watched as Laura bundled the blood-splashed and muddied towels and gory cloths together and left them on the kitchen stairs to deal with on her return.

The pony and trap had been left in the sticky shade of the lime tree. He passed the boy into her arms while he turned the pony back to the lane.

'Uphill or down?' he asked.

'Up,' she told him, and handed him back the child so that she might climb up beside him. It felt exposed and unsafe somehow and she didn't like to have the boy on her lap so they wedged him on the bench between them.

The cottages weren't far, just half a mile away. Long predating the smart villas that were still going up along the valley below them, they were little more than a low roof. There were so few windows that people left their doors open for extra light on a fine day.

The mother looked not long out of childhood herself, in a much-mended dress cut for a larger woman. Leaving Charlie to turn the trap round again, Laura took charge of the boy and of calming his mother. She explained he had run out in front of a horse but did not say whose, as it was a small community and the doctor a charitable one when his patients were poor. As the child had suffered a blow to the head, she should try to keep him from sleeping until bedtime, Laura told her, and the bandages should be kept on as long as a little fidget would agree to wear them. Taking in the earth floor of the hovel where the young family lived, she held off from telling her about keeping the stitches clean. She had grown up in such conditions and knew both the extra labour they made of even basic hygiene and how house-proud they could make a person. Instead she simply handed back the boy's hoop and stick and said they were to call on the doctor to have the stitches taken out in a week, sooner if they began to hurt or if the wound felt hot, smelled bad or needed attention. The boy clung to her as she left and embarrassed her by having to be prised off.

'Go to Mother now,' she told him, and nervously told the girl, 'I gave him a piece of cake for being so brave.'

'That'll do it,' the mother said, and ushered him inside with no sign of tenderness or concern.

Charlie drove Laura the short distance back down the hill in silence and she wondered if, like her, he was haunted by memories summoned by the glimpse of poverty. But it seemed he was merely a little shy.

'Sorry we broke in on your afternoon,' he said eventually. 'You'll have a lot to do now, I expect.'

'A fair bit.' She appreciated the skill with which he drew the trap up so that it aligned neatly with the gate, and saw with relief that the Frasers were still out.

'When . . .?' he started, then faltered.

'You'd better go too,' she said. 'Dr Butler will be waiting.'

'He's seeing Miss Ramsay. That's never fast.'

Miss Ramsay was a rich invalid known to be a demanding employer.

'Poor woman,' she said. 'I expect she's lonely, with no family in that big house.'

'When's your day off, Laura?'

She thought again of the library romances that she'd started borrowing from Mrs Ashbridge until they became her regular guilty pleasure. 'By rights,' she said, 'you should call me Miss Bartlett.'

She was teasing, of course, but he seemed to take her seriously.

'Forgive me. Miss Bartlett, I was wondering when you are allowed out.'

She laughed. He was very handsome.

'When you get home,' she said, 'don't go putting soap on that bloodied cuff or you'll set the stain. Just leave it to soak in cold water with plenty of salt added. That'll lift the blood out. Wash it after that.'

'You think I wash my own shirts?'

'No, now you mention it. A man would never get them so white. But you'll be doing whoever washes them a kindness. Sunday afternoons. I'm free from after church until supper.'

'And what do you like to do?'

'Well, it's not enough time to go home to my family in Launceston so I usually just walk, if it's fine.'

'Might I walk with you, Miss Bartlett? If it's fine?'

She felt herself smile. 'Of course, Mr . . .?'

'Causley,' he said. 'Charlie Causley.'

She dropped him a mock curtsey and turned up the path to the house, hearing him click his tongue to set the pony in motion again. She had parsley sauce to make and red-currant fool to finish. She had made shortbread fingers for the fool that morning and allowed herself one now before she shook salt in the copper, pumped in cold water and set the bloodstained towels and cloths to soak for the night.

The shortbread was good, made with vanilla sugar, an exotic ingredient she had not encountered before coming to Teignmouth to take up her position.

⚓ ⚓ ⚓ ⚓ ⚓ ⚓

Her job was hard work, with long hours, and only Sunday afternoons and every fourth Monday free. The Frasers, a brother and sister, were not especially rich and could only afford two live-in staff – herself and Mrs Ashbridge. There was a local girl who came in to do the rough work every morning, clearing and laying the fires, sweeping and polishing, but Laura was somewhere between cook and housemaid. She performed the daily shop, to spare Mrs Ashbridge's legs, and did all the cooking on her superior's day off, but she was also charged with the household laundry and expected to answer the door to visitors and wait at table. Happily the Frasers lived very quietly and did little entertaining.

She had come to them at sixteen. This was the first position she had held so she had no points of comparison, but she heard stories of harsh employers and knew the Frasers to be considerate ones. She had been bitterly homesick on arrival. Miss Fraser had been especially kind when she once caught her crying after missing her brother's birthday, and fetched her a glass of Madeira 'as a restorative' and told her of her own unhappiness at being sent back to boarding school when their parents were weeks and weeks away in India.

For all the long hours and hard work and the homesickness, which continued to flare up if she so much as heard a Cornish accent, the position was full of comparative luxuries. As a child she had always shared a bed with one or two siblings. Before he was hired at the slate quarry, her father was a farm labourer, entirely dependent on the seasons, weather and fortunes of local farmers for his livelihood. If he was injured or fell ill the situation could rapidly turn desperate, for they had no savings or security with which to pay rent or buy food. Growing up in deep countryside, they all knew how to find food in the wild, from berries and mushrooms in season, to whatever rabbit, hare, pigeon or trout could be caught by her brothers. Here there were the comforts of a warm bed in a room of her own, with linen sheets that had never been resewn sides to middle to wring new use from them, of a well-stocked larder and bottomless fuel supplies. There were carpets and thick curtains and beautiful, interesting things to admire. She was allowed two baths a week in a proper modern bathroom with a gas-powered device called a geyser to heat the water. And although the attic had no lavatory, obliging her to use a potty as she always had at home, at least here she did not have to walk outside to empty it.

All cooks were called 'Mrs' out of respect, but Mrs Ashbridge was a real one. She had re-entered service as a young widow with money worries and she encouraged Laura to see the benefits of a servant's life.

'You'll never be cold or hungry,' she said, 'or have to worry about the roof over your head.' And she shocked Laura deeply by saying she was lucky to have lost her husband, at Laing's Nek, before he could make her a mother. Laura longed for motherhood, or thought she did. She had mothered her baby brother Stanley and been left with a kind of hunger for it ever since. She came from a large family. It had never occurred to her to question her own assumption that she in turn would have one; it was what the Bible expected of women, and those who didn't or couldn't were objects either of fun or pity. But as she taught Laura to make different kinds of pastry, or how to pour bone jelly down a funnel through the crust of a turkey and ham pie, Mrs Ashbridge made her see, through her countless anecdotes, that marriage could be a kind of slavery to women, and childbirth a downright danger.

It had never occurred to Laura that her mother had not wanted to have so many children or might have been better off an old maid. Imagining this, imagining a different reality in which she and her siblings had never been born was like trying to will smoke back into a log and it made her dizzy.

On her half-days Laura would walk along the seafront or cross the river by the footbridge to admire the pretty gentility of the houses across the way in Shaldon. And of course she would notice men and boys. How could she not? It was a resort, so there were always men at leisure, showing off their prowess at bowls or tennis or swimming. But it was also a busy port. If she walked west of the waterfront villas and terraces to the older, less gracious quarter, she would see weather-baked fishermen mending nets or hauling out creels of glistening fish, or the thick-muscled dock workers using stout hooks to hurl clods of clay quarried upriver from the decks of river barges into the holds of boats bound for the sea. And sometimes one of these would catch her eye or tip his hat to her or call out some comment to make her blush. And yet her fantasies were never about men and courtship, going dancing, being swept off her feet, risking heartbreak and disaster, for all that she loved reading about such things. Her fantasies were all about motherhood.

Laura liked nothing better than to find a space free on a seafront bench where a nursemaid was minding her growing charges or a mother was dandling her baby or adjusting the sunshade on a stately perambulator. If a baby smiled at her or a disoriented toddler grabbed her skirt to right its balance, she felt a warmth well up in her unlike the smaller surge she felt when a man winked at her or whistled.

Mrs Ashbridge had explained early on that what Laura did in her time outside the house was her affair, but that whether she got into trouble or got married, a man would lose her her job. Of course there were openings sometimes for a husband-and-wife team as cook and groom or even cook and butler, but it was not common. Pressed, Mrs Ashbridge said she supposed it was to do with innocence and loyalty. Unmarried people were held to be more innocent so less likely to gossip about their employers and they could give their employers their primary trust – be wedded to their jobs, in effect.

Laura's bosoms were a danger, apparently. Like her sisters and mother before her, she was what one aunt called 'made for babies' and another called 'stately'. 'All the Bartletts are stately, my girl,' the aunt had said, admiring Laura in her best black at a funeral. 'We carry all before us.' But Mrs Ashbridge was built like a tallboy, all thigh and bottom and smaller up top.

'I see you've a bosom on you,' she had said at their first interview. 'That'll make hard work harder.'

'Why?' Laura asked.

'Because of the extra weight,' she said. 'Still, I suppose you're used to it. But careful when you go out. Don't wear anything too tight or revealing. Men can be beasts, and bosoms bring out the farmyard in them.'

Laura had never been self-conscious before – her body was her body, healthy, serviceable, lacking in particular merits or flaws – but Mrs Ashbridge's way of regularly commenting on it, on her ruddy complexion, her admittedly wayward hair and the prominent nest of temptation in her blouse, made her so. The walk down to the shops and back, hat pinned on her, shawl tied or coat buttoned so as to reveal nothing to the beasts of Teignmouth, basket clutched close like a wicker shield, might have become a torment to her had she not learned to distract her thoughts by reciting in her head in time to her walking. 'Three yards pillow ticking. One pound sugar. Half a dozen eggs. Brisket. Dripping. Allspice berries. Reckitt's Blue.' But the rhythm of a shopping list was too irregular and could even cause her to trip if some item suddenly eluded her, so she tended to fall back on poems her mother used to have her recite for an elderly neighbour whose eyesight had failed: 'The boy stood on the burning deck' and 'I think that I shall never see a poem lovely as a tree'. Or the psalms and prayers they had been obliged to memorise and laboriously chant in school. The Benedicite worked especially well because of its constant repetitions and the stimulus of needing to remember in time what or who must praise the Lord next. That had been accompanied in class by a sort of march on the clanking piano by one of the unmarried ladies who ran the school, while the other led them in her rich contralto, and Laura had always rather liked its simple, unrewarding tune.

> O YE fishes of the SEA, bless ye the LORD:
> PRAISE him, and MAGnify him for EV-ER!
> O YE birds of the AIR, bless ye the LORD!

In no time, she would be in the bustle of Teign Street, rootling in her bag for her shopping list. Here the Frasers had accounts with every shop she was called upon to visit. Goods were handed to her or tucked into her basket tidily wrapped. There was a murmur of greeting and thanks and she left the shop. It was all beguilingly clean and easy. She knew most of the shopkeepers by name and many of the other servants by sight, if not to chat to. It was an un-spoken rule that servants shopped early, for food and mundane supplies, and their employers ventured out later for more personal things, like books, gloves, medicines or visits to milliner or dressmaker. There was a sense of two parallel Teignmouths not quite overlapping. Laura felt no resentment at it. She liked the town first thing, when the pavements were still wet from sweeping and rinsing down, and staff still energetic and friendly. She imagined the atmosphere changed later in the morning when it was all would Sir this and might Madam that.

Both sides came together on Sundays. For a small town, Teignmouth offered a big range of churches, from burning handbag Catholic to every shade of Protestant. The Frasers expected their live-in staff to attend with them but were not fervent Christians – one service a week sufficed, and they would discuss the service on the walk home afterwards with a keen interest more of the brain than of the spirit. Laura was glad they were Church of England and not too high or low. Adjusting to worshipping in a place with incense and statues would have made the change to living away from home so much harder. As it was, the weekly return to familiar words and ritual, to hymns she knew so well, felt almost like a visit home to Launceston. She drew comfort from the thought that her mother back in St Thomas's, with the river swirling past just outside, would be singing the same psalms, hearing the same readings and quite possibly lowering herself to arthritic knees at the same moments. It was like being just around the corner in the same room.

The church the Frasers attended in Teignmouth was more temple or circus than barn, being octagonal, almost circular, which took some getting used to as you had to work harder at stopping your gaze straying from the business in hand. Its thin, elegant pillars soared up to a lantern through which beams of seaside light slowly travelled around the

pale walls. There was no gallery, no gentry chapel or family
pews. At first glance it seemed as even and equal as Adam
and Eve's nakedness, with servants and masters entering
through the same door and being handed their hymn books
with the same welcome. By unspoken arrangement, however, the Frasers and their friends sat in the pews nearest the
altar, while servants ranged themselves in the pews to the
rear. Even the lame, like old Mr Potts, whose manservant
all but carried him in, and formidable Miss Ramsay, whose
hefty maid wheeled her to a pole position in her invalid carriage, were only joined by their staff to be settled into
position, handed rugs, prayer books, hymnals and so on,
then left among their equals.

Mrs Ashbridge always led the way to the same spot on
the far left-hand side because, she said, sun fell there in the
morning and at least gave the illusion of warmth, and
because they could easily see the Frasers from there should
they signal that they had need of anything. In practice, she
liked the way the pew gave them a fine view of any new
arrivals or people of interest. She knew all the principal
families by sight and, through her mysterious channels –
for she rarely went out now that she had Laura to do the
going-out on her behalf – was quick to find details of any
sons or daughters-in-law, births or deaths, attacks of gout
or arthritic hips.

Laura had never discussed religion with Mrs Ashbridge
but sensed that for her it was something she could put on
or off with her Sunday hat. Laura could never have been
the sort of person who talked boldly about it. She'd have
worried in any case that talking might cause it harm, like

bright sunlight on coloured fabric, but God for her was a daily presence, almost a constant one.

She knew that most people stopped saying bedtime prayers when they reached adulthood – she knew from growing up in a shared bedroom that her siblings had – but she did it still. She liked to kneel and close her eyes and open herself up like a book. It was reassuring and sustaining, somehow, like basking in a pool of sunlight. When they took their seats in a pew she always knelt in prayer for a few minutes to still her mind. Mrs Ashbridge never knelt. She said scrubbing hard floors had done for her knees long ago. For congregational prayers, she sort of slumped forward with her forehead on one hand, in a gesture that looked oddly like despair.

'Will you look at that?' Mrs Ashbridge murmured now as Laura returned to a sitting position. 'Now that is handsome.'

Laura followed her gaze and saw him standing in the very middle of all the gentry, gazing about him and looking as fine as any of them. He had on a Sunday suit, of course, and a white shirt even crisper than the one that had got the boy's blood on it, but he had added a dandyish dark blue velvet waistcoat and a silk tie the same candid grey as his eyes. He seemed taller than ever.

'It's Charlie Causley,' Laura told her, in a way she hoped sounded offhand. 'Dr Butler's man.'

'But the doctor goes to the Quakers. What's he doing here?'

'Looking for me,' Laura said quietly. 'I said he could walk with me after church. I didn't think—' She broke off.

20

He was holding his hat before him, looking about him.

Insofar as she had calculated at all, she had assumed he'd be driving the doctor to and from the Quaker meeting house, which surely was in Torbay or Exeter, for there was none she knew of in Teignmouth, where Quakers were as rare as Jews. So when she said walk *after* church, she meant precisely that, and with time for her to go home and change into something less Sundayish, certainly into her second-best boots, which were properly broken in so kinder than the ones she had on for walking any distance. But here he was and he had seen her and smiled and walked directly over just as the organ struck up for 'Praise, my soul, the King of Heaven'. Mrs Ashbridge nudged her, though for what exactly she had no idea. He reached them as they stood up with their hymn books and because his hat was already off, he made a gesture as though he had just that moment taken it off to greet them both and with a murmured, 'May I?' took the spare space beside Mrs Ashbridge.

He had a nice enough voice, in tune at least, although he did that comical thing men often had to of fumbling for lower octaves when the tune went too high. She caught his eye a couple of times before the last verse but then he stopped singing altogether and smiled broadly at her so she felt sure people noticed. She found it extremely hard to focus her thoughts on the service that followed or even to feel her usual sense of connection with her mother. He was so very spectacular – she could think of no other word – so unafraid of being looked at.

Mrs Ashbridge was a heavy-set woman with poor powers of concentration, much given to shifting in her pew and fiddling with cuffs or buttons, and yet, from that first hymn to the last, through the sermon and the Eucharist, Laura was constantly aware of his presence on Mrs Ashbridge's other side, like the confident rumble of a farm roller beneath the chattering of starlings. She avoided catching his eye or even looking his way again, but she could hear him in the hymns and in the mumbled responses, and when the time came to go up to the altar for Communion she stood aside to let Mrs Ashbridge out first so that she should be first back in and Mrs Ashbridge didn't think to let him pass in front of her as well for the same reason. So Laura ended up with him beside her in the pew for the final hymn and dismissal. Her mother had taught her always to kneel when she returned from the altar: 'It's a lovely moment and you don't want to fritter it away with idle thoughts.'

So Laura knelt as usual, even though she could see from the corner of her eye that he was sitting, like Mrs Ashbridge, and could feel his eyes were on her back. But she had the glow on her, a sort of flush from the drama of walking to the altar, the sudden sweet shock of Communion wine on an almost empty stomach. She rarely prayed at this point, merely hid her face and let her thoughts settle. Today they would not settle and she hoped, once the organ struck up and they all stood for 'Onward, Christian soldiers', that her face at least was calm.

She need not have worried, for naturally Mrs Ashbridge dominated the conversation as they walked slowly out to shake the rector's hand by the door and, through her fearless questioning, Laura learned things that might have taken her hours to uncover: that his family were from up the river at Trusham, that he was born in Canada (Canada!) and that Dr Butler did not always attend Quaker meetings but some weeks preferred, as he put it, to worship God in nature by taking a solitary walk instead. And that Charlie had in mind to walk Laura over the bridge to Shaldon for lunch.

'Have the crab savoury,' Mrs Ashbridge told her as she saw them off. 'It's famous and I want to know what goes into it so we can make it too.'

'You don't sound Canadian,' Laura said as they were finally alone and walking down through the streets towards the water.

'How does Canadian sound?' he asked.

'I dunno. Like American but politer?'

He laughed. He had such good, white teeth. All the men in her family – her uncles, her brothers and brothers-in-law – were missing one or two and had yellowed the rest with tobacco. Only her brother Stanley's were as white, but then he did not smoke and was what Mrs Ashbridge called 'exceptionally good-looking'. Charlie stepped between her and the gutter to shield her from the dust raised by a passing farm cart.

'I was born in Canada,' he explained, 'but Father didn't make a success out there, not like he'd hoped for, and we moved back to Devon before I'd formed any memories. All my memories are of Trusham.'

'My younger brother emigrated last year,' she told him.

'To be a farmer?' he asked. 'They're still offering free land.'

'Maybe, eventually. But he's a lumberjack at the moment. Timber's what he knows. Boys in Launceston either go

23

into timber, quarrying, slaughtering or tanning. If they're not on the land, that is. We were so glad when he went into timber. Father was killed in the slate quarry, and those other jobs, well, they make a man stink!'

She thought of Stanley with a pang. He was much her favourite sibling, to the point where she had harboured a guilty fantasy that he might send for her to keep house for him. She knew why he had gone; Launceston was too small for him and he was stifled living at home with Mother in her tiny house. Living away from home herself made it easier to forget he was no longer living there either, and when something reminded her he was now a vast ocean away, she felt afresh the pain of his leaving as if he had only just gone. She wondered what Stanley would make of Charlie. They were a perfect contrast, he blond and cream-fed where Charlie was black haired and sharper boned. Stanley would like him; he had it in him to like everybody and she worried he would be taken advantage of, with no sister to look out for him.

'Is your father still alive?' she asked.

He shook his head. 'He and Mother are both gathered. Worn out by work and grieving. He was a carter and market gardener in Trusham, at the end. He liked that. Liked what he did. How did your father die?'

'A splinter of slate was driven into his skull.' She could tell him quite dispassionately, having been only a child at the time. 'It wasn't even from stone he was cutting. It came from overhead, straight through his cloth cap. He was dead long before the men could get him on a board and carry him home to Mother.'

24

'How did she cope?'

'She worked,' she told him. 'Cleaned houses and took in washing, raised some of us single-handed that way.'

He whistled. 'No poor house for her, then?'

'She'd have died sooner.'

They had reached the middle of the broad bridge across the Teign and paused there to admire the dramatic view. The river dock to their left, where moorland clay was unloaded and shipped out all week, was Sunday quiet but a train whistled as it passed the dock on its way to the station and on towards Exeter. Older people still muttered about the noise and ugliness of having a railway line plough through the centre of the town and out along the old sea wall between red cliffs and beach, but the few times she had caught the train to Exeter, she had laughed at the audacity of it, especially where the line plunged through the rock before Dawlish. Ahead of them, the brown waters swirled around the town's promontory of fishermen's huts and pubs, past the little beach where the boats were hauled up and a few men were mending and checking nets, and out to the open sea. As they gazed and the smell of cooking lunch from some-where made her stomach rumble, she asked if he had brothers and sisters. Two sisters and a brother surviving, he told her: Maggie, who was like a second mother to him; and Dora and Lewis, who were younger. Two sisters had died: Hepzibah of meningitis when he was four and barely aware, lovely Edith more traumatically, when he was seven. They had been delivering a box of vegetables to the Trusham lime kiln when Edith's waist-length golden hair, a wonder of the village, somehow caught fire along with her dress.

'I beat out the flames with my bare hands,' he said, 'but my hands were still only small and she died that night all the same.'

'That's terrible,' Laura said.

'Yes,' he said. 'Sorry.'

'Don't be silly,' she told him.

'I mean I shouldn't have told you.'

'Of course you should. Let's walk on,' she said, and let him lead her on to Shaldon.

But perhaps he shouldn't have told her. The lunch was delicious. She obediently ordered the crab savoury and persuaded the waitress to tell her what went in it – crab, butter, cayenne, cheese, breadcrumbs, lemon and brandy – but whenever she looked at his hands she pictured them beating out the flames on a burning child and felt death was at the table with them.

Charlie put her at ease again by telling her about his work for the doctor and how he loved horses and found them easier to work with than pigs, cattle or sheep. And he said how the doctor was a great believer in education for adults and encouraged him to read more by lending him the simpler books from his library.

'He has me come to lectures with him sometimes,' he added. 'On history and fossils and that.'

'Does that interest you?' she asked, and he pulled a face, wrinkling his high forehead.

'Reckon I'm better at reading than listening. And my reading's pretty slow.'

She admitted that she loved reading but was always so

tired after work that she could rarely stay awake long enough to read more than a page or two.

After lunch they walked around Shaldon. Then he treated her to the little ferry back to Teignmouth where they strolled along the front, enjoying the Sunday crowds. There were children everywhere, as ever, and she realised she was watching to see how he'd react to them. Some men seemed to regard children as an irritant, to be ignored or brushed off like flies, but Charlie caught a small boy's wayward ball before it could bounce between the railings and on to the beach, and handed it back to him, ruffling his hair as he did so. Laura thought again of him beating out the flames engulfing his sister when still a child himself and she shivered, even though she was warming to him.

Thinking she was cold, he ushered her into a little pavilion to buy them each a cup of tea. She declined his offer of a bun. He ate the first half of his in a few swift mouthfuls.

'Sorry,' he said. 'I'm always hungry. Unless I've just eaten. Maggie says I have hollow legs.'

She saw how his expression softened when he spoke of his sister as it hadn't when he mentioned his parents, and guessed she had parented him in the way that happened in larger families, where grief or plain exhaustion could leave a mother slow to love a late child.

They spoke, as she imagined younger servants often must, of whether they would be in service all their lives. Each had felt the obligation to take the job offered to spare their families the cost of housing and feeding them.

'But Launceston must be a busy town,' he said. 'Could you not have found work there?'

'I tried,' she said, remembering the humiliating succession of visits to tradesmen's entrances and back doors in her funeral dress. 'But it's a tight sort of place where everyone watches each other and, well, I think people prefer to hire servants who aren't too local. They worry about gossip and trust. And my mother's place is small and she wanted me to fly the nest like the others. There was only Stanley still at home when I left and that made sense as he was working just up the valley in the sawmill then, and happy to be man of the house.'

'But he went to Canada after?'

'Yes,' she said, remembering as she stirred her tea to cool it. Stanley had found Mother's constant pressure on him to take a wife bothersome. 'I saw him just once more. The train he caught to get the boat from Liverpool stopped here and Mrs Ashbridge let me slip out to meet him on the platform and say my goodbye. It was awful. There was so little time and he had such a journey ahead of him. He's not a great letter writer. Neither of us is. But he sends a card sometimes, so I know where he is.' Her longing for Stanley, like homesickness, was always worse on Sundays because she had the leisure for it. It rose in her now like nausea. Charlie seemed to sense this and kindly changed the subject, pressing a last piece of his buttered bun on her and saying how he could never have stayed in Trusham. It was tiny and jobs were few. He loved horses but he was not a countryman, he realised.

'Town suits me,' he said, 'better than mud and rain.

Money was the challenge,' he added. He liked working for Dr Butler well enough as he was a kind and interesting man. The house was comfortable and the food more plentiful than he had ever known growing up. 'But in jobs like ours there's no progressing, is there? If we could progress that wouldn't suit our masters.'

'So what's your dream?' she asked him, and he said it was to run a little boarding house there for holidaymakers, maybe keep a horse and cart to fetch them to and from the trains and have a wife to run it with him.

'It'd be hard work,' she said. 'All those mouths to feed and beds to change.'

'Yes, but it'd be different when the work was for yourself.'

She wasn't so sure of that; dirty sheets were dirty sheets, and she imagined paying guests could be as demanding as masters, maybe more so, and possibly less considerate as they'd be moving on. She had not thought much of the future beyond imagining that Mrs Ashbridge might retire one day and she would take her place and have a country girl to train up in her turn.

She was mindful of all this and of Mrs Ashbridge's warnings when he walked her back up the hill behind the station and paused to ask what she was doing the following Sunday. Quite truthfully, she was able to say she was going to one of her sisters to celebrate their mother's birthday – a day she rather dreaded because her siblings all treated her like a child still. But he looked so crestfallen that she couldn't stop herself saying, 'But I'm free the Sunday after, Charlie.'

29

The birthday Sunday was just as she'd predicted. Her older sister Ellen and her brothers' wives patronised her in their married prosperity and gave her advice she hadn't asked for and monopolised their mother. But through the day, when she felt belittled or talked over, and as she endured the long hours of train journeys in either direction, she found she was drawing comfort from the thought of Charlie, like a secret warm stone in her pocket. When he dropped off a note during the week asking if she'd like to come home to Trusham with him the Sunday after, she readily agreed.

They met at the station – she had dissuaded him from showing up at church again – caught a train to Newton Abbot and were collected there by his stern younger brother, Lewis.

'He don't speak much,' he had warned her and, true enough, Lewis said nothing beyond an initial hat raise and how do. He fetched them in a pony and trap. Charlie helped her up into the back and climbed up there with her, so they sat facing backwards as the landscape spooled past them. Charlie made no attempt at conversation with Lewis so she didn't either, just relishing the sights and smells of deep countryside after weeks of town life.

Trusham seemed a world away both from the bustle of Teignmouth or the industry of Newton Abbot. It lay up one of those mysterious Devon coombes barely touched by modernity, a cluster of cottages slung between a church and equally ancient inn, everything dappled green by sunlight through trees and any sounds cushioned by layers of moss and leaf mould.

When they pulled up beside an old, low house just along the lane from the church, a little round woman wreathed in smiles was waiting to greet them. Her hair was as black as Charlie's but her face a sunlit version of Lewis's, her eyes black buttons, which almost vanished when she smiled.

'Hello, dear. I'm his big sister, Maggie,' she said, taking both Laura's hands in hers to look her over quickly. Feeling hands as work-hardened as her own, Laura liked her instinctively.

'Big sister,' Charlie said, chuckling as he bent his head to kiss the top of her head.

'Cheek,' she said, standing on tiptoe to kiss him back, then turned back to Laura. 'Welcome to Trusham,' she said, and ushered her through the gate where Lewis had led the pony and trap. The house kept its secrets from the road. Through the gate it revealed itself as an old farmhouse, forming an L shape with a little barn and washhouse-privy to one side. Its modest patch of land was set out as a market garden, with vegetable beds bordered by fruit trees and bushes. It seemed there was not an unproductive inch. The only flowers, apart from pea and bean ones, were on a climbing rose trained against the house, its base thick and gnarly with age, and a hedge of lavender noisy with bees. Chickens scratched and crooned beneath the bushes. All it lacked was a friendly cow, but one could be sure Maggie had an arrangement with a nearby dairy.

'Father's market garden,' Maggie said shortly. 'Lewis's little kingdom now, though Dora and I do our bits when he lets us and our hands aren't full of laundry. Dora, this is Charlie's friend, Laura Bartlett.'

A thin, rather mannishly dressed young woman with short hair ducked her head in greeting and darted back inside the house, scattering chickens.

'Shy,' mouthed Maggie with a grin, and sighed.

Lunch was leek and potato soup, and the delicious treat of a roasted chicken, Dora's home-made cheese on which she refused Laura's compliments, and a rhubarb pie served with yellow cream Maggie had clotted herself. The cream made Laura think of when they were small and still living in a farm labourer's cottage in the countryside. She knew how to make it and had offered, but the Frasers were faddish and believed thin cream was healthier, for some reason.

Laura found Lewis's almost aggressive silence and Dora's shyness made her fairly wordless as well, but Maggie's steady, salty conversation was like the crackle of a warm fire. Used to her younger siblings, Maggie respected Laura's reserve and soon gave up trying to draw her out, falling back, inevitably, on a soothing litany of reminiscence with Charlie, punctuated with abrupt bulletins about people they knew in common: who had died, who married, who had moved away and who had taken over whose cottage. Not being a talker, Lewis had eaten whatever was set before him swiftly and he left the table as soon as the pie had been dealt with, off to sit in the pub, apparently, where nursing two pints of cider was a Sunday ritual that would see him through to an early night. Dora washed up, a task nobody was allowed to help her with as she had her particular way of doing it. Laura had assumed they might sit on softer chairs to chat or that Maggie might let her see around the old house but Maggie was insistent Charlie show her the village.

'Show Laura the graves, Charlie,' she told him. 'And the wood. Our wood,' she told Laura, 'is something to see.'

So Charlie led her the short distance to the church and graveyard where, with a diffident sort of pride, he pointed out his various ancestors' graves, ending with the newest, where his parents lay beneath earth that had yet to level. She picked some oxeye daisies and set them in the little pewter cup on their grave, feeling suddenly abashed, as though meeting his mother's judgement in the flesh. It could hardly have been more different from her father's resting place. St Thomas's churchyard had the clatter of trains and industry all around, whereas Trusham's church was utterly peaceful, set on the ridge above the village with fields beyond it. The only sounds apart from the occasional voice raised from one of the cottages were birdsong and the insistent, excited barking of a tethered sheepdog she had noticed as they entered the village.

'I like Maggie,' she told Charlie.

'That's lucky,' he said with a grin, and began to lead the way away from the house and church and into the village, down a little side lane just wide enough for a barrow. Other households had also finished or were finishing lunch. They passed a man peaceably smoking a pipe in his garden while his wife scraped scraps from plates into a bucket for their pig. There were snatches of laughter, of conversation, a baby crying. They stopped to pet a ginger cat that rolled himself, saucer eyed and inviting, in their path and, as they walked on past more cottages and the inn, she wondered where the lime kiln was where his sister had been so horribly burned. She hoped he would avoid walking them past it.

33

But they left all buildings safely behind and climbed a stile on to a path that led them down a steep valley away from the inn and into a wood. It was still vividly sunlit in splashes.

'Next year I'll bring you here in bluebell season,' he said. 'Tis a sight would stop you in your tracks.'

'I love how their colour seems to float,' she said.

'Yes,' he agreed. 'And the scent's shy, like violets; you only get it in snatches. They say it affects some people.'

'Doesn't bother me,' she said, thinking of her poor employer, who was sometimes confined to a darkened room by her hay fever.

'No.' He nudged her. 'I meant in a good way. Makes them frisky, apparently.'

'Charlie Causley,' she said, because he was grinning at her from under the brim of his hat and looking so very handsome as he took it off.

And then he kissed her. It was sudden but she didn't mind because he didn't paw her but only cupped her face in his hands and kissed her lightly on the lips. Once, then once more. And he continued to hold her face as he looked at her a little gravely, gauging her response. And she found she wanted more. That small kisses weren't enough, and the minute gesture she must have made to indicate that was enough to make him kiss her again, more fully, encircling with his arms both her and the sapling she leaned against.

She closed her eyes, clearing her mind of warnings and common sense, of pastry and parsley sauce, simply enjoying the taste and clean warmth of him and the protective height of him and the intensity of the birdsong in the canopies of leaf above them.

They didn't speak of the kisses. He made no declaration of love and extracted no solemn promises, but when they broke apart and walked on down to admire the river at the valley's bottom there was an unmistakable sense of something between them having been settled. It was reflected back at them in Maggie's cheerful welcome and offer of tea and cake on their return. Even Dora afforded her a quick smile as she helped Laura back into the cart for their return ride to Newton Abbot.

Laura wouldn't have said she was a nervous person but she was industrious; her mind had long been a little motor, always powering on to enumerate the next task and the one after that. As they took their seats in the third-class carriage again and an understanding look passed between them, though, she understood that motor had been stilled, and it was he who had gently stopped its motion, as you might stop a clock's pendulum with one extended finger.

ST THOMAS WATER – 1918

People said Charles couldn't possibly remember back that far, that what he thought was a memory was simply something his imagination had confected from things he had been told or from old photographs he had been shown. But nobody had told him this or shown him a photograph. Mother could not possibly have owned a camera. The only photographs they had were rare studio portraits, to mark significant milestones, taken, after much tutting over clothes and brushing of hair, at Hayman's on Church Street. There was just one baby picture of him, captured once he was safely christened and reassuringly healthy, so that she could send it to Father at the front and Uncle Stanley in Canada and present copies to her siblings and Aunt Maggie.

In it Mother's dressed in mourning black, which is how he knows it's later than his memory, and he is old enough to hold his head upright as she holds him on her knees. Gussied up in the dazzlingly clean family christening gown brought over from Trusham, he stares with precocious curiosity, intelligence even, at the camera. Mother looks on him, meanwhile, with a hint of a smile and something like wonder. She is already rounded, the shape he will come to love and recognise in the distance, and looks immensely comfortable, irresistible to any child, a sturdy human sofa, and yet she holds him slightly apart from herself the better to gaze on him, perhaps, but also as though she is holding him for someone else and is not quite hiding her awe at the responsibility.

This memory is from before that, before he can sit up or even focus much. There is sunshine from outside, causing patterns and reflection to dance on the surfaces around him in a way that fascinates him. Close to are the wooden bars of his cot and, a little further off and directly above his face, the dark bar of an old roof beam. But even more entrancing than the dancing light are the sounds through the little open window where the draught is stirring a thin floral curtain. It's the sounds of fast-flowing water clacking pebbles as it passes, and the shouts of children at play in it. At such an age he cannot possibly know that they are water and pebbles and children, any more than he can identify the occasional helving of a cow or the labouring and whistle of a train or a clanging bell, which enter the air above his cot to intrigue him.

As an old man famous for his sensitivity, discretion, wit and discipline, he will secretly inspect this memory at intervals and do so with professional envy. The baby in his cot may be quite passive and vulnerable to the whims of others, but he is also quite safe and will never again be so receptive; he is all ear, all eye, no judgement, no defensive irony.

LAUNDRY BLUES – 1918

There was a good reason why women disliked laundry day. The key lay in the word 'day'. It took the best part of whichever day of the week you set aside for it, from filling the copper with water and soap and setting it to heat before breakfast, to ironing and folding dry linen at the day's end. It took more than a day, in fact, as ideally laundry had to be sorted by type and much of it set to soak with soda the night before. And stains had to be found, identified and treated with yellow soap or ammonia before that, as there were few things so frustrating as finding a stain only at the ironing stage and having to begin the entire process afresh. Laundry took method and planning, especially if there were men and children in a household to be fed or watched at intervals. It left little space for spontaneity or the unforeseen. Accidents happened. Visitors might call who weren't friends so couldn't easily be put off. And many women in Launceston also worked for a living, especially now so many were filling in for men away at the war. And others simply had chaotic lives, either through poverty or mental frailty.

Laundry had never been Laura's favourite part of her work for the Frasers, although she took a quiet satisfaction in it and knew she had the arms for scrubbing and was blessed with skin that didn't react too badly or crack up at the strong substances involved. Cookery was her real pleasure – the seductive magic of pastry and dough, the coaxing of richness from unpromising beginnings – and Mrs Ashbridge had recognised in her the useful balance of a desire to give pleasure with an instinctive sense of economy. When she let herself enter into Charlie's fantasy of running a seaside boarding house, she dared imagine paying another woman to rub the sheets so that she had more time to bake scones for tea and rolls for breakfast.

All that lay behind her now, no more than a sinking glow on the horizon. Just as dreamlike now were the all too brief succession of Sundays when she and Charlie were courting. From the moment, on their second walk in the woods at Trusham, when he had held her to him and kissed her and asked her to marry him, she had been wanton with time, greedy, urging the calendar on until they could be together. But of course now she realised those Sundays had been precious, as was the relative luxury of working for the Frasers and living in their pretty house, in a place where the only sounds were birdsong and the occasional clatter and clip-clop of a passing cart.

Charlie had enlisted, as Laura suspected most men had, without consulting his fiancée, for what girl in her right mind would encourage the man she loved to stand in the line of fire, whatever patriotic noises they made in public. Teignmouth was as caught up in war fever as anywhere, she imagined, with bands playing marches, entertainers singing ghastly songs like 'Your King and Country Want You', and young men not yet in uniform subject to mockery and worse. The doctor disapproved, as a pacifist, and not simply because he was losing his groom, but he still made the astonishing gesture of paying for Charlie and Laura to have a honeymoon weekend in one of Teignmouth's better hotels.

So they were married the February after they met, in St Thomas's in Launceston, with their small squadron of siblings present and Mother tearful with happiness and sorrow mixed, because Stanley was still in Canada. Charlie looked, Laura had to admit, what her sister Em called 'a catch', in his barely worn uniform, and she hoped she looked acceptable in the wedding dress both Em and Ellen had worn before her. Em had to let the sleeves out for her because of her muscles, and the bodice too, which convinced her she must look like a pudding in it, but the look on Charlie's face when he turned to see her walking up the aisle to him on her brother Willie's arm comforted her.

They had a deafening lunch, somehow squeezed into her mother's little house on St Thomas Water, where they had only ever gathered for weddings and funerals, then were waved off to Teignmouth on an afternoon train. Their room at The Royal had a sea view. They were still rather shyly taking it all in, especially the luxury of the little bathroom, also with a sea view, when a knock on the door brought a bottle of iced champagne from the Frasers, who had unexpectedly colluded with the doctor to track them down.

Laura was quite inexperienced – he was the only man she had kissed – and neither her sisters nor her mother had given her advice in the matter, but Charlie knew what to do. She had worried that, with three unmarried and rather unworldly siblings, he might be as virginal as she, but of course he was a well-turned-out, good-looking young man and Teignmouth a busy resort. She didn't ask him who had taught him to kiss, or to stroke her or nuzzle her in the ways and places he did, she was too busy being grateful he wasn't a brute the way Mrs Ashbridge had ensured she knew men could be, and then being astonished at the way the things he did revealed a completely different version of herself, insistent, greedy even, unladylike, tucked inside her like the Russian doll the vicar's wife at home had shown them once in Sunday school.

They paid another visit to Trusham on the Sunday, as newlyweds, and were solemnly handed significant gifts: a dead mother's cameo brooch, a dead father's pocket watch. There was talk of the war, silly talk she saw now, that it would be over by Christmas once the Boche had been taught a short, sharp lesson. And Maggie made her promise to keep in touch while Charlie was away and to visit whenever she liked. She hugged Laura in parting, as her own sisters never did, like a sister in a book.

They had one more wonderful, terrible night in which neither could bear to sleep for fear of speeding the coming day towards them. And then he was off to France in a great gang of other, fresh-faced boys, egging each other on to noisy bravado, and she packed her honeymoon clothes into the little suitcase that had been Mother's wedding present, and caught two trains back in the other direction to make a home again in Launceston and sleep again in the lumpy bed she had once shared with her sisters.

When she took her leave of the Frasers, standing shyly at the outer rim of the breakfast room's silk carpet while they ate their toast and kippers, and they congratulated her again on her imminent wedding, she had felt a pang at leaving their house and their calm good manners, and couldn't resist suggesting she might continue working for them while Charlie was away at war. Miss Fraser had responded almost as though she had proposed something indecent.

'Oh, my dear, no,' she said. 'He'll be home by Christmas. Everyone says so. And besides, you'll be a mother in no time.'

But the stupid war had gone on well beyond December, so it was a kind of mercy she had not been left pregnant by their weekend at the hotel. Officers were granted leave every three months or so – she seemed to be forever spotting one or other of the Williamses or the other local landowners' sons peacocking in their khaki finery and basking in the attention – but the Army was far less generous to the rank and file. Initially, when the assumption was that the war would be won by Christmas, no leave was granted at all. Once Christmas and a harsh winter had arrived without the promised victory, leaves began to be granted to other ranks, but then only every year or so. Poor Charlie had been out there for fourteen months before he was given home leave of ten days. As they each longed for this in their letters, it seemed a wonderfully long time. In practice, however, it cruelly included the two and a half exhausting days of travel at either end.

He came home to her, nut brown and so tired he could barely finish a sentence. He enjoyed a badly needed bath by the fire while Mother discreetly visited Em for supper next door, then staggered up to their room where he was soon asleep on the rug because he said the bed now felt too soft. She washed and pressed his filthy uniform, burning his underthings in the range as he slept because they were crawling with lice.

Tipped off by a friend at church, whose son had come home two weeks before, she had already nipped up the hill to buy him two sets of new ones in Treleaven's, one wool and one cotton. He had plenty of socks already – she had been knitting those for him constantly since he first wrote to her about how wet his feet were always getting. When she finally joined him upstairs after her mother had come back in and sighed over the cleaned up uniform, she was guiltily glad he remained sound asleep. She was tired from labouring over his kit after a long day of paid laundry work and cooking in expectation. All the same, she tugged the quilt off the bed to cover them both when she joined him on the chilly carpet and he stirred comfortingly as she slipped an arm about his bony chest. He drew her against him so that she could smell the soap on his neck.

He made love to her just twice on that first leave, once, very slowly and gently as they woke together on the floor in the morning, once more urgently that night, when her questions about the war brought tears to his eyes, which frightened them both. But neither time left her pregnant and when her monthlies started a hopeful three weeks after he'd left, she wept so bitterly out in the privy that her mother heard and came out to tap on the door to ask, mortifyingly, if she was all right.

His next home leave was fourteen long months later, in November. Laura counted off the months in letters, two sides of paper a week. She had not written so much since school. He wrote little back – penmanship was not his strong point – but he said he loved her letters, however mundane the details of her daily round or snippets of home news, because they were a world away from the daily horrors he was living across the Channel. She suspected he wrote a letter to Trusham in between the ones he managed to write to her.

She knew all letters home were censored, and knowing that would inhibit expression, but his letters were almost wilfully devoid of what she knew to be his lively personality. She didn't need the things the Army worried about – where he was on the map, what he was doing next, what his commanding officer was called – she needed to hear what he was feeling and thinking, if he thought of her and, if so, what details of her he called to mind. Had he made friends in his regiment? Enemies? Instead he told her what the weather was like and what birds he spotted and described in detail the horses he had to work with and the terrible injuries the poor animals suffered. And, like every English male made to live far from home, she imagined, he told her what he was getting to eat.

The only domestic work available when she moved back in with her mother was as a maid of all work at Werrington, the big house that lay in a huge park up the hill beyond St Stephen's, but that would have felt like demotion after her more skilful work at the Frasers' and she did not fancy joining many of her contemporaries brought in to hold down jobs for absent men in the local factories, mill and tannery. Instead she worked with her mother as a laundress. With double the hands, the workload was lighter and they could take on more. It also let her ease her mother's burden, freeing her to do the starching, ironing, deliveries and collections while Laura spent the days leaching out stains, scrubbing, washing and rinsing.

It was much harder work than she had faced at the Frasers' because it was so unvaried and relentless. Her back ached permanently from lunging back and forth at the tub or heaving bundles of wet sheets out to put them through the mangle, and the hours of contact with caustic soda and soap began to leave even her skin so raw she could hardly bear the feeling of sleeves and cuffs back around them at each day's end. But she was strong and growing stronger, and her skin soon toughened up.

The routine only let up at weekends. Saturdays were spent cleaning the cottage and baking bread – including the Communion bread for use in the church all week – shopping, which of course brought accidental socialising with it, a visit to the library, and cooking things like stew and heavy-cake to see the two of them through the week to come. Saturday night was bath night for them both, the tub drawn up cosily close to the kitchen range and the curtains tightly closed. Sundays truly were a day of rest, marked by wearing better clothes. There was church in the morning, and evening too if it was a notable feast day, a leisurely lunch, usually with one or other of Laura's siblings and their family, and an afternoon walk if the day was fine. Sometimes someone might come for tea, especially if there was to be evensong, as they were so handily placed for the church that they could hear the organ start playing and know to start washing and drying the Sunday china. Sunday evenings were quiet. Mother invariably went to bed early so that was when Laura wrote her weekly letters to Charlie in France and to Stanley in Canada.

Her weeks had become so undifferentiated she'd have had no trouble remembering anything unusual to pass on, but all the same she had fallen into a habit at the Frasers' of keeping a little pocket appointment diary in which she noted anything that happened. It not only served to remind her as she wrote letters but built up into an eccentric short-hand record of her year. 'Tuesday – cow bolted. Wednesday – birthday. Thursday – bad egg at breakfast! Friday – Brenda Titmus fell in river.'

Her mother's writing was not confident and a kind of shyness affected her when faced with a pen and a blank sheet, or when asked to do much more than carefully sign her name, but Laura always left her letter to Stanley unsealed so that Mother could add a sentence or two in the space she left for this on the last page. Stanley's letters were even rarer and less informative than Charlie's, but his last had horrified them both by announcing he had left his logging camp to sign up with the Canadian Expeditionary Force and was about to embark on basic training. Even kind people had become so ferociously, unthinkingly patriotic, egged on by stupid newspapers, that Laura found she was guarding her tongue, even at home. Neither woman dared put it into words but she knew they were both hoping the war would end one way or another before Stanley's battalion put to sea.

There had been weeks of rain recently so the river was in spate and threatening to burst its banks and flood the ground floor. The noise of it sucking and splashing was constant and so loud, especially in the dead of night when the trains and local industries fell quiet at last, that it was hard to believe it wasn't lapping at the foot of the narrow stairs. It did flood, of course, most years, but usually in the spring when the moorland could hold no more rain and turned the river the red brown of a Devon Ruby cow.

Charlie's troop ship was delayed and then so were the trains, so he had spent two nights travelling and was so exhausted he was wordless and then quite overwhelmed by the array of pie and ham and cheese and pickles with which they walled him in at the lunch table. The smell coming off him, a mixture of slaughterhouse and farm-yard, quite overpowered the spiced vinegar of Mother's pickled onions, which he ate like plums. His uniform was so stiff with mud and blood and God knew what that his hands were too weak to unbutton it and Laura had to help him out of it. She was used to the smell of men from the things she had to launder, but this was a smell with no man left in it, though it sat at the table with them like an unexpected extra guest.

Mother had made him a queen of puddings, a spectacu-lar one with a duck-egg meringue and bramble jelly, knowing it to be a favourite of his, but Laura found she could hardly taste it for the smell.

'You'll be wanting a nice long bath, my bird,' Mother finally told him, with a careful glance at Laura as she donned coat and hat. Then she took herself off to her brother Richard's for the night, where she had arranged to watch the grandchildren while Richard and Mabel went out for the evening.

Laura had supposed Charlie could smell nothing, like the women who worked long hours now in the tannery, but she was wrong, for he apologised repeatedly for it as she heated the water for his bath.

The comfort of the hot water loosened his tongue. She had been about to fetch his pyjamas and dressing gown and set his uniform to soak overnight but, like a child scared of the dark almost, he asked her to stay with him.

'I like your letters, you know,' he said. 'I live for them.'

She smiled, shy of his steaming nakedness. Then she noticed his left hand. The little finger was entirely missing.

'Oh my word,' she cried out. 'Charlie, your poor hand!'

'Have you only just noticed?' he said, holding his hand up a little proudly and turning it back and forth. 'And there was I thinking you were being polite. Your mother was polite; I saw her notice when I took the spuds from her.'

'Does it hurt?'

'Not any more. Hurt like buggery at the time. Sorry.'

'That's all right. How did it happen? Charlie, was it shot off?'

'Nothing so heroic. I was hitching up a horse to a gun carriage and a shell landed near enough to make him panic and somehow my finger got tangled in the harness. Doctor had to amputate it after a week as it went bad but, well, I'm just lucky it were only the finger and not the whole hand or you'd have me home again but useless.'

She thought of the legless veteran who sold matches from a little tray now, propped against the wall of the upcountry station. She had bought far more matches than she needed because she had learned he went to school with her and Em, yet she didn't recognise him or know his name. Whenever she passed him, she told herself how many boxes he must have to sell to be able to buy even a loaf of day-old bread.

'I can't think how I didn't see it,' she said.

'Too busy drinking in my handsome face, I expect.' He smiled to himself as he fell to scrubbing the dirt from his nails.

'Why didn't you write about it at the time?' she asked.

'You'd only have worried.'

'I worry anyway.'

'I dunno. If I started to tell you even half of the things that happen, I wouldn't know how to stop.'

'But—'

He left off scrubbing and looked her full in the face, not smiling now.

'Trust me,' he told her, 'it'd be like a scream on paper. These things are better in my head than yours.'

Unnerved, she took his uniform to the outhouse where she set it to soak with some soda. The clothes felt like him suddenly, even though they stank, a version of him she could reach and touch, and she wanted them clean and safe.

She heard him open the back door to tip away his bath water into the drain. By the time she had used the privy, washed her face at the sink, brushed her teeth and dabbed on a little rosewater, she had heard the floorboards creak as he settled into bed overhead.

He was asleep by the time she joined him but he woke just enough to reach for her before falling asleep again, leaving her wide awake and pinned in place. She lay there for a while until she felt sure she'd get cramp, but then a nightmare shook him awake with a gasp.

'Mattress is too soft,' he mumbled. 'I'll need to go on the floor again.'

She remembered what her friend Aggie Treloar had shocked her by saying, observing his first leave had not left her pregnant. 'It's no good waiting for 'em to offer, girl. Sometimes you just has to ask!'

'That seems a pity,' she said. 'Why don't we just try the mattress on the floor?'

There was just room, once they had moved the little nightstand out of the way. When she had turned off the light again she was surprised how bold darkness and determination made her. It was a fortnight to her next monthly so the timing was perfect. He was utterly shattered, she knew, but she also knew this was important to them both and found that a small, strong part of her didn't care. What if he went back to Flanders and died? Or came back like the station match-seller or worse? She needed this now and in a curious way she felt it was her due.

When he realised she had no intention of sleeping just yet, he made love to her and, once again, lit her up from inside so that she had to bite her lip in the effort not to shout or laugh. As they fell asleep he left one hand cupped protectively between her legs, which continued to please her in little waves as he began to snore softly at the back of her neck.

The next morning he made love to her again, when she took him up a cup of tea as a hint it was time to get dressed for church, as though the nearby bells and murmur of his mother-in-law's voice from the kitchen were not hint enough.

She tidied herself carefully before going back down but Mother said, 'He's happy to be home, you can tell,' which meant she had heard.

Once again he had arranged to spend his last night in Trusham, but this time, before she needed to hide her disappointment, he was turning to Mother, asking if Laura could be spared for a day so he could show her off. And her mother was all smiles and said a wife belonged with her husband. Laura knew Monday was the hardest day of their week so started putting things to soak before they left, with his uniform clean but still damp on a hanger.

Even though it was cold and wet out, the train carriage was well heated and it was good to be able to lean into him and hold his hand as they rattled along. Her mother's house only had chairs facing in politely from opposite corners. Maggie had no sofa either. Laura had never thought of it until recently but had begun to suspect that sofas were for the better off as their upholstery didn't last as well as that of armchairs. There was an oak settle at Trusham, though, across from the fire, from which Maggie evicted poor Lewis so they could sit together.

'Just look at you two,' she kept saying with a smile. 'Just look at you!' She knew Laura was pregnant days before Laura did, apparently. She said she was witchy that way. 'Dora can tell if it's going to rain, I can tell if a baby's coming and Lewis, well, whatever Lewis's gift is he keeps to himself!'

Naturally Laura wrote to Charlie once she was really sure. Her happiness was so intense she felt she ought to rein it in when writing to him – the state of his hand, the bloodied filth in his uniform, the violent gasps that persistently ruptured his dreams, told her all she need know about the grim weeks he was living through. Mother read her mind, though, and pointed out it was precisely the sort of news that would help him pull through. So Laura didn't hold back but told him everything, how sick she had been, how Maggie had 'known' on seeing them together, and how, if it was a boy, she thought it should be Charles after Charlie but a bit more serious. He took a while to write back, of course, or his letter took a while to reach her, but he had somehow found her a funny Belgian postcard picturing a bouquet of roses under the words '*mon amour*'.

'You make me happier,' he wrote, 'than I feel any man deserves to be. All my love, Charlie.'

That was all. Just two sentences on a postcard, but she knew it would be in her handkerchief drawer until her dying day.

She knew she ought to think of girls' names as well, and entertained possibilities as her mother and sisters tossed names this way and that, mainly girls' names they had always wanted to use and for which the opportunity had never arisen. But Laura knew it was a boy. Even before Mother had dangled her wedding ring over the still tiny bump on a piece of Laura's hair.

Pregnancy suited her as she had always known it would. The bouts of morning sickness soon passed, helped on their way by Mother's ginger fairings, and she found herself stronger and healthier than ever, proof against the almost constant hard labour of laundering and one of the harshest winters anyone could recall. But not against the cruelties of fate, for Mother died, without warning or illness, one evening in March.

Mother had insisted on being the one to go out on a filthy evening of driving rain to fetch down a basket of dirty linen from one of the larger houses in town. Nobody lived in the poorer part of Launceston without being used to climbing hills and if ever Mother heard someone complain about it she would repeat the saw that if you could survive childhood there, Launceston's hills would see that you lived to a healthy old age. The basket was one of the bigger ones, it turned out, like a wicker trunk, which she carried over her shoulders, held in place by a stout old leather strap one of the tanners had made her for just such tasks.

She hated fuss but she let Laura lift the hamper off her back for once and carry it out to the washroom while she slid the kettle on to the front of the range to boil for their tea. Laura was sorting the linen into the usual piles according to fineness of cloth and any stains needing special treatment, when she became aware the kettle was whistling persistently. Thinking that perhaps Mother had left it boiling while she took a message next door to Em, she went to make the tea herself only to find Mother slumped in her wooden armchair.

She had hung up her wet coat and scarf to dry, then sat down and had a heart attack on the spot. Laura hurried to tell Em, who worried the shock would make her lose the

53

baby so promptly took control, getting word to Willie, Ellen, Richard and Sam, and to the doctor and vicar. It was left to Laura to write to Stanley telling him, longing for him to say he'd come home for the funeral, though she knew that was quite impossible.

There were two surprises in the days that followed: that Mother had already paid for her own coffin and, a thing that had somehow been kept from Laura and Stanley growing up, that both she and their father had been born in Launceston workhouse, fathers unknown. The two were closely linked, Willie explained. Mother had a dread that any of them should fall into poverty, which must have seemed all too possible for her when their father was killed in the town quarry, and it would have been a point of pride in her to have died with all bills settled and enough money set by to pay for her funeral and headstone.

There was a freakish spring, with really heavy snow over Easter that blighted the fruit blossom. The hurried thaw that followed brought the Kensey over its banks for the second time that year and saw Laura, big with child by now, lugging chairs and rugs upstairs out of harm's way. The landlord agreed to her taking on her mother's tenancy. With Charlie away at the war and everything so uncertain but the looming fact of motherhood, it made no sense to move and it was a comfort to have Em in the cottage next door and have to walk only yards to put fresh flowers on Mother's grave.

The households that had given their washing to Mother now gave it to Laura. She even took on her mother's weekly duty of baking the Communion bread for St Thomas's. She had loved her mother and liked to think they shared a special bond by virtue of being so similar physically, and thanks to her having spent these last years living and working alongside her, but when she and the family had gathered to honour her after her wintry funeral the consensus was that her legacy to them was not love but work.

'Or perhaps,' she wrote to Stanley afterwards, 'hard work was how she expressed that love.'

With Charlie still away at the front and her brothers and sisters all occupied with their own work and families, Laura often felt as though her life was simply turning into Mother's, a harsh, unrelenting calendar of soaking, scrubbing, starching and pressing. Since that one high point of his floral postcard, Charlie's letters expressed so little of his hopes and dreams they did nothing to dispel this. What helped was the baby beginning to stir and kick, to become an insistent presence apart from herself. His daunting insistence on change helped.

And, harsh though it could be when her lower back ached or the soapy water scalded where she had already burned herself on the iron, there was an odd consolation for her grief in labour so intimately associated with her mother's voice and advice. There was barely a stage of her laundry routine that didn't call to mind a piece of motherly instruction and Laura became aware, as she had not been when her mother was still living, that in everything she did she still sought her mother's approval or judiciously measured praise. She continued to feel close to her again at church services, just as she had done in Teignmouth.

Charles arrived – because of course he was a he – on a deliciously balmy August day, the twenty-fourth, St

Bartholomew's Day. Laura managed to give birth at home, assisted by Ellen and attended by the old midwife from St Stephen's, who claimed to have delivered both of them in Father's old cottage in Langore. Charles roared when the midwife smacked his bottom but thereafter he proved an easy baby, a good feeder and regular sleeper, and much given to contentedly staring about him. It was impressed on Laura by both sisters and sisters-in-law how very lucky she was – most of theirs having been terrors at first, fretful or sickly or bad feeders. Em said it was because she was calm; that calm mothers had calm children. Laura thought it more likely that the baby was calm because he and his mother were so rarely apart. She went back to work as soon as she felt able and always had him in his cot where she could hear or see him unless she had to slip out for supplies, collections or deliveries. The advice was to set him to sleep at regular, strictly timed intervals, which she did in her room upstairs, where he had the sound of babbling water to soothe him and seemed to like the play of watery reflections on the ceiling when the sun was out.

And he was christened for the two men she loved best: Charles for her Charlie and Stanley for his uncle. There was no lack of aunts and uncles to serve as godparents. She asked Maggie to be a godmother, not just because she liked her so, but because some instinct told her neither she, Dora nor Lewis were likely to become parents themselves. By way of a Christmas present, she had a photograph taken of her with Charles on her lap, and sent small, portable copies to Charlie and Stanley.

This had not struck her as remotely strange until one of her sisters-in-law – Mabel – broke off from admiring the picture and how solemn and intelligent Charles looked in it to say that Laura being the only parent in it and wearing mourning still for her mother made it look as though she were a war widow. Silly woman. Her thoughtless words stung Laura and came back to her whenever she looked at the picture afresh, so that she moved it from the dresser downstairs to her bedroom, where no one else should look or comment on it.

Nothing had prepared Laura for the deep comfort and satisfaction motherhood had brought her. Beneath the daily exhaustion, beneath the sorrow for her mother and anxiety for Charlie and Stanley, which were like wounds forever made to bleed afresh, the pleasure she took in Charles was so intense that she felt it almost indecent, a thing she needed to hide. Her mother had warned her that a baby at the breast could hurt and her sisters spoke of nursing with a kind of revulsion, as a grim necessity to be borne with but brought to an end as soon as possible. So she was quite unprepared for the flushes of pleasure the baby gave her as he fed, not unlike the pleasure brought on in bed by his father. Unless it was his time for sleeping or she was out delivering or collecting laundry supplies, she had him near her constantly, either in his cot or strapped safely into a baby chair. He cried occasionally, of course, usually when she left him, but most of the time he just gurgled to himself and watched her, seemingly fascinated by her labours and any sounds they made: the splashing of water, the rubbing of sheet on washboard or nailbrush on collar, the hiss and clunk of the iron. And she talked to him, naturally, incessantly, glad of the company.

She had assumed she would stay put until Charlie came back. Perhaps the arrival of the baby had tempered a little his dreams of running a boarding house, for his last letter had asked her about work opportunities in Launceston, ideally involving horses. She was bringing in enough money to pay the rent on her own so with two of them working, they'd be able to afford somewhere a little larger, maybe even with a patch of garden. Despite the risk of flooding she liked the cottage for its view of the babbling water and proximity to the church, and having Em just next door so they could mind one another's children if need be.

But then Laura came upstairs to wake Charles from his nap one afternoon and was horrified to see a great brown rat with horrible yellow teeth sitting on the beam directly over his cot, quite as though planning to jump in and make a meal of him. She saw rats all the time outside, especially in the summer. They were drawn to the bins of stomach-turning waste at the tanneries and slaughterhouse, and children made great sport of hurling stones at them if they saw them by the river. But to see one in the house, and so close to the baby, filled her with deep disgust and also a sort of housewifely shame. She shouted, waking Charles, of course, and hurled a hairbrush at it so that it scampered along the beam and disappeared through a hole into the space beneath the roof. Ignoring Charles's cries for once, she stood on a chair and saw how the rat and its brood must have been coming in and out that way for a while, for the hole in the plaster was grey and shiny with the grease off their fur. She stuffed the hole tight with rags, although she knew rats would soon chew through those, stilled the baby, feeding him in a kind of fury, then set about finding them somewhere else to live.

She settled on a place barely two minutes' walk away up Old Hill. It was quite different, being one of four flats in a tenement, but there was a second bedroom for when Charles was old enough for a bed of his own, and it was raised above the threat of rats but still near enough to the street for there to be a familiar sense of town bustle outside. She liked that she could think of it as hers and not her mother's, and guessed that Charlie would as well.

Charlie was safe now. She thanked God for that in her prayers every night and remembered it every morning when she saw their wedding photograph as the baby woke her. She had lived with the dread for so long – had been shown the shockingly spare official commiserations other women received when their sons or husbands were killed – that her mind would not quite accept the good news and needed these constant reminders. There had been an unusually long wait since his last letter, to the point where she worried that continuing to write to him began to feel like nagging. Then she received a very short letter in an unfamiliar hand. It was from a nurse. Charlie had been hospitalised following a mustard gas attack. 'He is mending fast,' the nurse wrote, 'and has his sight back, which is a relief. But his lungs are still weak. He sends his love to you and the baby and says he'll write soon.' Then there was a scribbled PS from Charlie, which looked almost as though he had been writing in darkness. This said only: 'Invalided out! Hope to be home before much longer. Cx.'

But the weeks passed and no further news followed. Laura hoped that Charlie was right and that invaliding out meant he was spared any more fighting or danger, but of course now her restless mind fed off the few details. Mustard gas blinded and burned. He had his sight back but was he scarred? And what of his lungs?

She wrote to Maggie at once, of course, and for a few days her heart raced when she heard the upcountry train pull in. Then expectation was subsumed in routine and reason. He might need nursing for a few weeks yet, and as a mere invalid, not a hero on home leave, would be a low priority when it came to finding him a passage home.

It was only when Em came in to help her sort what to take with her or what of their mother's few things she might want to give to a sibling that it dawned on her she had no possessions other than her Bible, prayerbook, suitcase and her and the baby's (largely handed-down) clothes. And her wedding ring, of course, and a few necklaces and brooches.

Laura already knew all her new neighbours to chat to in the street and once they realised she had a brother who could get them cheap coal nobody complained at her need-ing to monopolise the washroom most days. One had a little girl only a few months older than Charles. Old Hill, or St Thomas Street as some called it, was effectively the town children's playground, along with the ruined castle at its top. Outside the hours of the nearby National School, children played along its steep length all day. She could hear their chatter and shouts, songs and skipping games even from the washroom behind the tenement as she had always heard the river at Mother's. It was hard now to imagine her baby as a harum-scarum little boy dodging the delivery carts to play cricket or piggy-in-the-middle, or to imagine herself being as relaxed as other mothers evidently were about letting her precious child out of her sight for hours at a time. But these houses were cramped and gardenless; where else could children let off steam?

The range was bigger than the one at the cottage, with a cool as well as a hot oven, so she could easily make rice pudding, bake potatoes or turn stale bread into rusks. It also had a useful rack built in above it, perfect for airing piles of laundry as she finished ironing it. If there was a part of the laundry routine that gave her any pleasure still, it was ironing. It was less hard work physically, provided she avoided burning herself it was kinder to her skin, and she liked the smell of hot linen and won a deep satisfaction from smoothing out wrinkles with heat and starch and seeing the steady transformation of a half-dry bundle to a crisp stack. And now, of course, she liked ironing because it brought her back into her own house, whereas the washroom, being shared, felt more like a workplace than the old one she and Mother had had to share only with Em.

She was there now, working her way through a small hill of napkins for the White Hart, letting the baby sleep on because he had troubled both their nights with a touch of colic. The upstairs neighbour was singing to herself as she swept. She had a stormy marriage. Laura had been made party to muffled arguments and yet, left alone, the woman invariably sang untroubled, even complacent love songs. She was still quite young, much younger than her husband, and always showed a noisy interest in Charles if they passed on the steps; perhaps childlessness, not lovelessness was the issue. Her singing was accompanied by rhythmic thumps from her broom. *By the light, by the light, by the light of the silvery moon thump thump thump!* It was odd to be doing housework in the afternoon. By an unwritten rule, Launceston's women seemed to do housework in the morning and then somehow change pace or even clothes for a more elegant afternoon, or at least remove their aprons or housecoats. Even the poorest households, and she knew of a couple that still had earth floors and had to fetch in water from the public pump, retained crockery and perhaps a teapot for best, in honour of some mythic teatime entertainment that never came.

Laura heard the sharp ping of a bicycle bell down below and set the iron safely back alongside the other reheating on the range before going to open the door. She was ever hopeful of letters from Stanley or Charlie, and had noticed how their letters often seemed to arrive in the afternoon post not the morning one.

Only it wasn't the postman but the telegraph boy. Well, they all called him the telegraph boy but the actual boy was away fighting and his stand-in was an austere, grandfatherly figure who somehow retained the strength in his shanks to ride his bicycle up the hill into town without either standing on the pedals or getting off to push.

'Telegram for Mrs Bartlett,' he said, respectfully removing his cap, his eyes the blue of a cold morning.

'She died,' Laura said.

'I know,' he said. 'It takes a while for news to get upstairs to the ministers. They make a lot of mistakes like this. Awful really.'

His voice was just like her father's, with the naturally querulous quality of the local men. She wondered if he had ever lived more than five miles from Mary Magdalene church. Perhaps he was old enough to have fought against the Boer?

She became aware he was holding out something to her and took the little envelope off him.

'I've never had one of these before,' she said, seeing her mother's name and last address typed on it. 'Well,' she added with a nervous laugh, 'I still haven't, I suppose, since this was for my mother. Thank you.'

She turned to go in but he cleared his throat. Was she meant to pay him something?

'I'm meant to wait while you read it,' he said. 'In case there's a reply to take.'

'Oh,' she said, and, flustered now, wiped her hands on her apron because they had become sweaty. She opened the envelope and smoothed out the little folded sheet of paper from the Post Office. It was hard to make out at first. It was carefully written by hand but the words were separated out into four columns rather than run together, presumably to ensure they remained legible. The first were 'Regret to inform you'. Her eyes misted over and she had to lean on the door jamb.

'There'll be no reply,' she blurted. 'Thank you. My husband's dead.'

'I'm so sorry,' he said, and made a sort of bow as she struggled out of his sight to close the door again.

The gas damage must have been worse than they thought, or he had succumbed to an infection. She had made herself face the all too likely possibility of him being blown apart by a shell, kicked to death by a terrified horse or downed by sniper fire. Charlie had told her sometimes you didn't know you were being shot at until you saw the undramatic little flick to the mud beside you as a sniper's bullet missed its mark. But the thought now of him dying in a clean, even comfortable hospital bed but far from home, with only some unknown nurse to witness his death and say a quick prayer under her breath if he was lucky, was almost worse than her battlefield nightmares.

She fell into a chair and made herself spread the thing out on the kitchen table, made herself read it properly. And of course it wasn't Charlie who had died, or it would have been addressed to her, to Mrs Causley, not to Mrs Bartlett.

'Regret to inform you, Stanley Bartlett, Railway Construction Corps died Thurston Harbour Hospital influenza and pneumonia 23.10.18.'

She read and reread the telegram as it dawned on her that Stanley had never even made it to the front. She and her sisters had been worrying about him all these weeks and he had come no closer to the battle than a harbour in Vancouver, to be laid low by an invisible enemy. She drank a glass of icy water at the sink to relieve the constriction in her throat. She could not let herself cry in the street. Then she pulled on her coat and a headscarf and was out on the steps before she remembered the baby. She turned back, ashamed. Having him with her would make breaking the news a bit easier.

He had woken already and was straining to look about him. Seeing her approach, he cried out with something like a laugh and reached a hand towards her. She kissed his tiny palm, then scooped him up, furling him in her shawl to hold him against her shoulder where he sucked noisily at her neck. She rocked gently from foot to foot, loving the warm weight of him against her.

'You,' she said. 'Oh, you.'

PENNY BUNS – 1922

Charles was only five but had already seen enough of other families to know that his father wasn't like the others. Other fathers were usually out doing things that made them smelly or dirty or cross when they came home. He had uncles who delivered coal, painted houses, forged metal. Charles's father was generally clean and tidy and was there all day, either in bed or on the bed or sitting at the kitchen table, or at the top of the steps if it was sunny or by the range if it was cold. He got so hot by the range that his tweed coat began to smell of wet dog and if you climbed on his lap, his jacket buttons were hot to touch. Sometimes he did useful things very slowly, like black-lead the range or polish the brassware.

He was home because he was not well. And it wasn't not well like when Charles suddenly got all hot and vomity, or woke up with a snotty nose or itchy spots. This was not well that made the other grown-ups either talk in whispers or, usually, talk loudly about other things.

Nobody was allowed to name it. He knew that, although he couldn't remember ever having to be told. He knew it the way he knew not to bang on the privy door when it was closed or never to say what he really thought in church. He knew the name nobody said aloud because it had only

66

two letters and he was slightly obsessed by numbers and the alphabet at the moment.

Mother sat him on her lap sometimes to read him Bible stories from a book with pictures, and Father regularly sat him on his while he read the newspaper. It amused him to read Charles stories from it or the best bits.

'Look, Charles. "Woman murdered husband with smoothing iron." Fancy that, eh? That'd take some doing. Or maybe not, if she was very cross.' Or '"The six to one favourite, Darcy's Fancy, was left far behind by plucky outsider Pirate Flag." And there's a picture, see? Pirate Flag. Lovely bit of horse, he is. He'd take you for a ride, eh? You'd like that?'

The pictures were interesting, as was having Father so close, but Charles found it was the letters that intrigued him, their patterns and repetitions. And then he found that he could read them sometimes, which made Father so happy he did it for him some more.

'Horse,' he said one day, and pointed at the paper.

'That's right,' Father said, and he pointed at the picture of a horse.

So Charles pointed again and said, 'Horse.' And again, somewhere else. 'Horse.'

It took Father a while to see he was pointing at the word 'horse' and he fetched Mother to show her. She was cross, because she was busy. She was always busy unless she was asleep, although she was excited, too. Also a little bit frightened, he thought.

'What does that say, Charles?' she asked, pointing at another smaller word.

'"From",' he told her, and she smiled and kissed him, and something shifted in the air between the three of them to make Jack, their little terrier, bark a quick question from his basket.

That night, washing him with a sponge as he stood in the sink, Laura taught Charles the alphabet song to the same tune as 'Twinkle, Twinkle'. Combining a melody with letters was almost too exciting and he had trouble sleeping afterwards because the circular song was like a roundabout going just too fast to get off. It helped, though. Now the letters hung on a sort of washing line in his mind, each a pinging note like a little bell, so when one of his older cousins, showing him off to a friend, said, 'Go on, Charles. Spell her name. Spell Bridie,' he saw B R I D I and E in his mind and heard their little notes ring out as he picked each one.

So then, of course, he began to read every word he saw, even when he didn't know what it meant and even though he was still overwhelmed by whole lines of them. He liked the big letters best, the ones on the outsides of books or on packets of soap flakes or salt.

'Saxa,' he told Father urgently. 'Oxo.'

Charles had heard the muttered letters 'TB' said out of Father's hearing by his aunts during a picnic and pictured them as ill-matched garments – a long sleeved vest and a bulgy b word garment like 'bodice'. The little book his parents kept had a long word on the front he couldn't make out, as nobody had said it aloud, but it was a bit like another word, 'consume', which he knew from church and which he liked for the funny thing it did to your lips. He made the link when he realised there were blank pages at the back with little boxes where Mother wrote down a number twice a day when she put the thermometer in Father's mouth for a minute while nobody spoke, especially not Father, then glared at it, turning it this way and that to catch the light before writing the number down. That was the first really long word he learned and it stuck in his head because it was said one way and written another.

'What are you doing?' he asked his mother, although he'd watched her doing it lots of times before.

'I'm taking Father's tempritcher,' she said. 'Look. We have to write it down here in these columns. "On waking. After lunch. After exercise. On retiring." See them? Tempritcher.' He looked as instructed and saw tem-per-at-ure, which you counted on four fingers whereas tempritcher took only three. But normally she shooed him off any involvement in this side of his father's life so he didn't risk asking. Every now and then she had underlined a number.

'What happened there?' he asked, and she sighed.

'Book says I must do that whenever it goes over where it should be – ninety-seven and a bit – and if it does that twice in a row I should call Dr Hart.'

'Only we don't,' said Father, 'as doctors are expensive and I'm all right in the end. See?' And he ruffled Charles's hair to change the subject.

He usually went very still and quiet while she took his temperature or when she made him go to bed early. It seemed to embarrass him, like having nappies changed or having no clothes on. The TB was also linked to his cough which, Charles noticed, made everyone else stop talking and look at their plates until it had passed, like a bad smell, and to the special creamy milk he had to drink after every meal and at bedtime, and to his Blue Henries.

There were two of these and they fascinated Charles because it was very important that nobody touched them but Father. Each day there was one *on the go*, which meant it was in his jacket pocket for when he needed it, and one soaking in a bowl of smelly disinfectant. (This was another word that was fun to say, especially loudly, as it sounded a bit rude, only you mustn't.) The Blue Henries were for the end of his coughs, when everyone else was looking at their plates or up at the ceiling, but Charles had seen and knew Father slipped thick stuff from his mouth into them. They were made of bright blue glass, like a Milk of Magnesia bottle, but had a wide mouth so he could easily dribble the stuff into them without spilling any. Charles had also seen how every evening, after his third glass of milk and before his bedtime, Father lifted the lid on the range and emptied the day's Henry on to the coals with a sizzle before rinsing it out under the tap and putting it to soak in the disinfectant.

Just once, when he had to stop and cough and use one on their slow afternoon walks together, he let Charles examine the shiny silver lid, which had the mysterious words on it: 'Beatson Clark and Co Ltd Rotherham', like a sort of spell. They must all use handkerchiefs when they coughed or sneezed, of course, and surrender them to Mother for a boil wash at the end of the day, but only Father had the awful cough that made people turn aside and that needed the Blue Henries.

Like all the children in the neighbourhood, Charles played outside all day long unless it was raining. It was expected as he would otherwise have been *in the way*. For as long as he could remember he had been fetched at some point most days for this by his cousin Gwennie, who lived down the road by the river and the cottage where he was born, but which they'd left in a hurry because of rats. He loved her unquestioningly although she was older than him so was apt to treat him like a long-suffering doll, to be tugged here and there, dressed up, undressed, told off and co-opted into complicated games. With the instinct of any small defenceless animal, he quickly sensed she was his protector as well as a major source of treats. If she did not come for him first, he would seek her out. Waiting patiently for her outside the nearby school gates, if it was a school day, he had become fascinated by the chanting, songs, shouts and bells he heard from within.

His mother and aunts kept saying he was *ready for school* in a weighted grown-up way whose full meaning he could not catch. Now that he had finally turned five, he would be allowed to start next term and could not wait as there were few children he cared to play with who were not already there.

Walks with his father were quite unlike playing with Gwennie and her friends. For a start, Jack the terrier came too. Since being found by him, shivering and alone on a Plymouth station platform, Jack only left Father's side when Father went to bed. Charles had given up persuading him out to play with him alone. When he did, the dog assumed a pained expression and glanced repeatedly over his shoulder until it was too much for him and he darted back to security and the man he loved best. Unless Father was having to be quiet in bed because of the thermometer, a daily walk was part of his day. Because he didn't have a job like other fathers, the daily walk was what he did. He could only walk very slowly, so he wouldn't get out of breath or too hot, but he did a lot of stopping to look at things and talk about them instead, so that the slowness was sort of hidden unless you knew to look for it. They had several routes. Downhill to the station to watch the trains and talk to the Matchbox Man. Downhill and then out to the Jubilee Baths and back, with a pause on the railway bridge if a train was going under on its way to the sea. Or, if Father was feeling very energetic, uphill into the market square where he might buy them secret penny buns.

Today they went up into town. They went so slowly that Charles did quite a bit of running ahead and running back so he didn't explode. He held Jack's lead so that Father could hold on to his walking stick and sometimes the railings as well. They took the quieter, back route, past the big red library and past the overflow gravy yard with the poisonous tree whose berries he must not eat. Then they came to the junction with Angel Hill, which Father said was called that because it was so steep Charles would take to the air if ever he ran down it, then they turned up into town and under Southgate Arch. Father bought them secret buns, which weren't really secret because they bought one for Mother, too, for later, and they ate them on the spot, with Jack making Charles giggle by snatching any falling crumbs before they hit the pavement, the way he caught flies in summer. And Father challenged him as to who could last longest without licking the itchy sugar off their lips, and won of course, however hard Charles tried.

Then Charles showed him what he had been shown by Gwennie and Bridie the other day. There was a statue of Mary Magda Leeny at the back of the church and if you could throw a pebble so that it stayed there and didn't just bounce off, you'd get a new suit. It was quite a distance from path to statue and he couldn't make his pebbles get anywhere near but he knew from their trips to the quieter stretches of the river that Father was clever with stones and could make them skip over the water like bouncing balls. Unlike Charles, Father wasn't from Launceston, hadn't grown up there and needed these things explaining to him just as Gwennie explained them to Charles. Once he understood, he fetched a pebble.

'So tell me again,' he asked. 'What must I do?'

'You have to stand just here and throw the stone so it lands on Mary Magda Leeny. It's no good if it just hits and bounces off. It has to stay there.'

'And if it stays I win a new suit?'

'Yes,' Charles giggled, sensing he was being humoured.

'And if I knock someone else's pebble off, do their new trousers suddenly disappear?'

'No!!'

'So I just throw it so it stays? Like this?'

And he threw a pebble very carefully so that it lodged tidily behind the statue's shoulder with a satisfactory click. Charles clapped.

'New suit!' he said. 'New suit!'

'Do you want one and all?'

'Yes.'

'All right.' And Father produced a second stone and tossed it and lodged it as neatly as he had the first.

Charles laughed. He felt slightly giddy, like when they'd been on the Golden Gallopers at the Shrovetide fair. He began to feel a little nervous as well, in case so much good fortune was not allowed, like taking a second slice of heavy-cake before everyone else had eaten a first one.

But then Father slyly produced a third pebble and raised an eyebrow. 'What do you think?' he asked. 'Best of three? Would your mother like a new suit? A nice tweed one, maybe?'

And somehow the idea came to Charles's mind of Mother not wearing the kind of suits ladies wore to church some-times, with a tweed skirt and matching jacket, but in a man's suit, bulky and baggy, and with a man's hat to match. And a pipe. And it was so outrageous a thing to imagine, there in a gravy yard with grown-ups clicking by on their business with baskets and parcels and serious faces, like Aunt Ellen's when someone burped, that Charles laughed so hard he may have wet himself a little. And then Father was laughing too, perhaps because Charles laughing was funny. But then he stopped laughing and had to cough.

Normally his coughs weren't so bad. He would splutter, tug out the day's handkerchief – some days he had more than one before bedtime – turn carefully away, cover his mouth and cough once, three times maybe. But this time he coughed several times so hard that it must have hurt, like when Albert from next door had whooping cough and his mother took him to breathe in the gasworks fumes every day to help it get better. Father had to grip a tomb-stone with one hand, bracing himself as the coughing shook him, and a lady made a clucking noise and stepped off the path to avoid them. Charles didn't know where to look. Everyone always looked away from Father when he coughed, and he knew it was rude to stare, but it was frightening and he couldn't look away for long. Finally the handkerchief was fumbled back into the suit pocket, but not before Charles saw a splash of poppy red on it. And then Father had to make a noise a bit like someone about to be sick – more tutting from passers-by – and made very tidy use of the day's Blue Henry.

He tucked the little bottle away in his jacket's outer pocket – where Mother made him keep it as she was fright-ened he'd forget it and sit on it if he kept it in his trouser pocket, took a few shallow breaths and leaned back against the tomb. He saw Charles and Jack both watching him anxiously and ruffled Charles's hair, which he knew he hated, and whistled to cheer Jack up.

'Sorry about that,' he muttered. 'We can go on in a moment.' Then he just stood there, leaning against the tomb with his eyes shut for so long Charles thought he might have fallen asleep standing up. Charles watched people stepping off the path to walk past them: an old woman with a lively little dog on a lead that Jack growled at; a man his father's age with a black leather bag; two pretty girls with parcels from the butcher, which were starting to leak blood; Edna the tramp lady, who lived in a hedge near the baths, of whom Mother always said mysteriously, 'You can tell she's clean underneath', and the vicar. The vicar looked as though he was about to speak to Father, then saw his eyes were closed, glanced down at Charles and visibly swallowed his words like a dry wafer as he walked past instead.

Finally Father stirred, but slowly, and led them on home by the most direct route. They were so slow that people kept having to step into the gutter to overtake them and Jack tugged on his lead. All the laughter was gone out of Father. All the words, too. He rested a hand on Charles's shoulder now and then as they walked, as though to re-assure himself Charles was still there. Charles knew better than to talk although, when he was nervous, his mouth got like sparrows in a bush.

They had to stop again at the top of Old Hill. It was steep – people sledged on it when there was snow – but it looked like a hill in a nightmare now that he saw it through Father's eyes. Somebody must have seen them because sud-denly Mr Wills was there and another man Charles didn't know and they said, 'Lean on us, Charlie. That's the way,' and helped his father slowly down the hill to home while Charles walked behind with Jack still tugging and Mother's bun in its bag.

There was a fuss when Mother saw them. She left her laundering, arms pink from the soap and heat, and took charge of Father, seeming stronger and bigger than him, thanked Mr Wills and steered Father up the outside stairs, his arm across her broad shoulder.

'You,' she said to Charles when they got in, 'sit there and be quiet. You know better than to tire him out like this,' which seemed very unfair as Charles was only just five and Father a grown-up who had fought in a war and galloped horses into battle, but he knew never to answer back and made himself small at the kitchen table while Mother bustled in and out, cleaning and changing the Blue Henry, tossing the bloody handkerchief into a pan with a fistful of carbolic acid and a splash of water.

It was some comfort that Jack felt himself in disgrace as well and made himself small in his basket after the necessity of a long, noisy drink from his bowl.

'We got you a secret bun,' Charles wanted to tell her, 'and Father won you a new suit,' but he remembered laughing at the idea of Mother in a suit so said nothing. When she was out of the room and he could hear her murmuring from their room and Father coughing again, he dared to fetch a plate and set her bun neatly on that by her chair with a cloth over it, the way she had taught him, to keep off the flies, and then he sat with Father's newspaper. He looked at the pictures and picked out the words he knew. And a few he didn't.

THE PORK-BUTCHER'S SON – 1925

On Fridays now, Laura worked at Werrington, the Williamses' big house. Like a lot of landowners, the family had hired local help while their male live-in staff were caught up in the war and when so many did not return had decided that using occasional outside help was fine. Fridays often saw the household preparing for a party of weekend guests and Laura could be set to cleaning, or helping assemble vast quantities of game pies and rhubarb fool for a shoot lunch. She appreciated the variety of the work after the monotony of laundry.

Today the family were away on their estate in Scotland, so she spent the entire day on her hands and knees scrubbing and then waxing and polishing the floor tiles that led from the big entrance lobby to the distant, leather-panelled dining room. The thoughtful housekeeper had given her some old sacking to kneel on, but even so, the floor was hard and cold, and her knees and lower back were sore by the time she had finished.

One of the reasons she liked working at the house was the longish walk to reach it, up the steep hill to St Stephen's, then over the hill's brow and down again along the house's back drive through the beautiful landscape of its park. The cattle grazing there were always superb creatures that looked as though each had been combed and polished for a show, and there were magnificent trees and exotic flowering shrubs of a kind she had seen nowhere else. At the end of a long day, however, the stiff climb from house to lodge was daunting. When her knees were sore, walking downhill was harder work than climbing, and the way home from the estate's lodge was all downhill. All she wanted was to sit in her mother's old armchair waiting for the kettle to boil and hearing Charles prattle about his day. Never at a loss for words, he could always be relied on to talk for two when she was too tired to contribute much. She knew he could be shy, but he took in everything he heard and saw, and would often come home bursting to tell her all he had packed away inside him.

It worried her that he had taken his father's death so calmly. Admittedly he had never known Charlie well and strong, but when the last horrible fever struck just before Christmas, laying Charlie low and sapping his strength so fast Laura summoned Maggie down from Trusham so they could take turns at his bedside when not napping in Charles's little bed across the landing, the boy's response had been watchful and oddly muted.

Charles loved his daddy, she knew he did, and was as capable of crying as any small, sensitive boy, but when Charlie's last hours were over and she and Maggie had wept quietly together and sighed and tidied themselves up and she had gone to find Charles and break the news to him while Maggie, bless her, washed Charlie's body and put clean pyjamas on him, all the child said was an oddly flat, 'Oh'.

She wished he had a sibling to discuss it with or one of the younger cousins like Gwennie. He remained an only, of course, although she and Charlie had broken doctor's orders a few times, and her sisters and brothers kept their children away from Charlie, fearing infection. She understood, but their withdrawal hurt Charles, she could tell. If she took him to visit any of them she pointedly washed hands with him on arrival. Her siblings were kind but she knew they were scared; TB scared people the way poverty did, or the workhouse, and they felt dirty by association.

There'd been no tears until after the funeral. Charlie was laid to rest with his ancestors in Trusham. Laura understood this, painful though it was to have him so far away; he had roots there and none in Launceston. Besides, the Launceston graveyard was hemmed round with the bustle of trains and industry whereas the Trusham one was a country idyll.

The service was a small, quiet affair, though with several friends of the family she didn't know, and Charles was the only child present. She had thought of leaving him at home with Em but he wanted to be there, he said quietly. Afterwards Maggie, who loved him dearly, suggested he stay on in Trusham for a few days of winter holiday so that Laura could sort things out at home, erase the traces of sickness by whitewashing the bedroom and so on. All seemed well. Charles loved Maggie back, although Dora and Lewis unnerved him sometimes with their staring and silence. He would enjoy playing with Jack in the snowy woods and sleeping in the tiny bird's nest of a spare room under the eaves.

After Laura kissed him goodbye, Maggie hugged him and said, 'Oh, we'll be all right. *He*'s my Charlie now!'

which finally brought on a great outburst of delayed grief from him, though it was expressed as not wanting to lose his mother, too. As the two women patted and reassured him, half laughing at the strength of his emotions, that it was only for two nights and that he'd have a nice repainted bedroom waiting for him when he got home, there was relief in both their voices that he was finally letting something out that might otherwise have poisoned him.

Charlie left Laura a hundred and thirty-five pounds, which he must have salted away in a Post Office account before the War, and she mentally earmarked it for Charles for boots and clothes and books. The women of the family had been very kind passing on unwanted clothes when he was really small, but once he started school, she told Charlie, she was determined no child of theirs would be dressed in hand-me-downs. She knitted him a jersey for every Christmas but his other things were to be pristine and bought at Treleaven's.

Charles had barely started school when it became clear he was very short-sighted and had to be kitted out with tiny wire spectacles so as to read the blackboard. Charlie had impressed on him that these were valuable and to be cared for like his boots, so polishing both before leaving the house had become a little ritual for the boy.

When Charles started school Charlie had told Laura off for being too protective. The boy had to take a few knocks to fit in, he reminded her. She had not forgotten the rough and tumble of the schoolyard and knew Charles was just the kind of boy to be picked on. Even without the glasses he was too keen, too trusting, too ready to speak. She was glad he had Gwennie and tough little Bridie in the seniors to keep an eye on him, but he lacked male protection and playgrounds were tribal in the way boys and girls separated out. If he continued to play with girls the way he always had, the boys would be brutal. Some of the girls would, too, in time. She didn't want him to change; she simply wanted him to be happy and to fit in. When he twice won top marks in a test she was thrilled and proud, naturally, but she was also fearful.

'Be careful with that cleverness of yours,' she warned him. 'Sometimes the clever thing is not to seem too clever.'

He looked quite shocked, peering at her over his spectacles like a much older man. 'You mean I should give a wrong answer on purpose? Wouldn't that be lying?'

She was baffled. To have produced the sort of child who came top of the class was so entirely unexpected and not at all in the family's sturdy tradition of muddling through.

'Just don't boast,' she said. 'Nobody likes a clever clogs.'

'All right,' he told her, but she could see she had troubled him.

She was relieved when he turned out to be only average at arithmetic but still hoped he would develop a love of kicking or throwing balls or catch the obsession with trains or cars that had reliably seized every small boy she had ever known.

That afternoon there were children out playing on the hill as usual, making the most of the time left them before the unofficial five-minute curfew bell rang out from St Mary Magdalene's. Laura was greeted by the skinniest two, to whom she regularly slipped buns before school when their desperate mothers weren't looking, and greeted a couple of others. Charles was not among them, not even with the small band of tough girls in Polly Venning's gang, who regularly co-opted him when they needed someone to be the man in their impenetrable games of make-believe. Sometimes she overheard one of them bossing him around, her mother in miniature, and was ashamed to realise how strongly she didn't want him to grow up to marry any of them.

Her hot feet were swollen and aching from the walk but she was then drawn into a chat with a neighbour who was using the washhouse, who needed her advice on how to remove a persistent fruit juice stain.

She knew something was wrong because Jack hadn't barked and run downstairs to greet her. Since Charlie's death the dog had transferred his primary allegiance to Charles, for whom he had been known to wait at the school gates on letting-out time, but he recognised Laura as the provider of food and mistress of the range.

Charles must have heard her talking because he already had the kettle heating and a teapot set to warm just as she had taught him. But instead of greeting her with the usual chat as she took off her coat and sank into her chair with a sigh, he kept his back to her at the table, deep in some book or other. The dog lay protectively at his feet and only thumped his tail in greeting.

'And how was your day, Mother? Oh, fine, thank you,' she said. 'Though I spent it on my knees.'

But he said nothing and turned a page. She saw his face was only inches from the paper.

'Where are your spectacles, Charles?'

'In my room,' he murmured.

'Well, you can't read with them up there. You'll ruin what's left of your eyes squinting like that.'

'It's fine.'

'It is not.'

He read on, hunched low over his book. The kettle boiled. She pushed herself back to her feet and noticed, as she went to pour it on the tea he had already spooned into the pot, that he shifted his angle as he read, to keep his face from her.

'Charles?'

'It's nothing. It's fine.'

'If it's nothing then you can show me. Charles?'

With a heavy sigh he took his hands away from his face and looked at her.

One eye was so puffed shut from bruising it was a wonder he could read at all. He must have been using one hand to hold it open. The other eye was blackened as well. There was every sign his nose had been bleeding and there was a nasty cut between his eyebrows.

'I fell,' he told her.

Leaving the tea to brew, she ran a basin of cold water, added some salt and soaked a flannel in it for him.

'Press this across your eyes,' she said. 'It'll help the swelling go down while I find the witch hazel. So what happened to your glasses?'

'They fell off and someone trod on them. By mistake.'

'Ah.'

Her hand shook as she reached for the witch hazel. It wouldn't do to let him see that she was upset. As she turned from fetching the cotton wool as well, she saw him carefully wet the flannel again, wring it out, fold it very precisely then lay it back across his eyes. It was a gesture somehow heart-breakingly adult, like watching him solemnly polish his shoes or make his own bed with hospital corners. He had learned both things from Charlie.

She poured them each a cup of tea, putting sugar in his for the shock. Then she pulled up a dining chair beside his and soaked a little pad of cotton wool with witch hazel. She had no idea if it had any medicinal powers beyond being mildly antiseptic but she had always believed it was good for bruises and the smell of it – fresh and clean – seemed to have stored up in it the precious moments of comfort and intimacy from her girlhood, moments when her mother was able to stop her labours and briefly focus lovingly on Laura.

'Here,' she said. 'Let's clean you up, my bird.' She lifted the flannel off his eyes and gently dabbed at the cut on his brow, seething at whoever did this to him. She had a good idea who. 'Might sting a bit.' He winced a little but let her continue. 'Brave soldier,' she said, discarding the dirtied pad and making up a new one he could hold there in its stead. 'Bit better?'

He nodded. She had already become so used to his little owlish glasses that he looked defenceless without them.

'Are you hungry?'

He nodded.

'I'll get something on then,' she said. 'Just how bad are they, the glasses?'

He looked thoughtful. 'They can probably be bent back

85

into shape,' he said. 'But one lens is cracked and the other is scratched.'

'Could you see the blackboard without them?'

'Not very well.'

She sighed. 'Well, we can't have that. Bring them to me and we can take them up to Mr Keast tomorrow and see what he can do.'

Charles fetched them with such reluctance she knew they had not been stepped on by accident. She showed neither her anger nor her sorrow, since neither would help him. That he had not cried and not told her all about it was a sign he preferred the matter dealt with discreetly.

She worried sometimes that his life was too quiet. His cousins, she knew, would often play games after supper but Charles was always content to sit quietly beside her with a library book, as he did tonight, while she knitted or darned or read as well. And she had to confess it was very peaceful and easy living with him. Once he began going to the library, which was only a few doors away, she did too, having never found the courage to before. While Charles was rapidly working his way through the few shelves of children's books, she was rediscovering the innocent pleasure of romance novels, finding their formulas and moral certainties soothing after a hard day.

⚓ ⚓ ⚓ ⚓ ⚓ ⚓

When Charlie collapsed after insisting on swimming with the others at the annual church picnic, she had realised he was not hers to keep. That night, and for his last year, she took to sleeping in the child's bed, not simply because Charlie's night sweats and restlessness made him impossible to sleep beside, but because she had accepted she now had to put the boy's health before her own happiness and be ever vigilant lest the TB be passed on to her or him. She still lay on the double bed with Charlie sometimes, but from that awful evening until the night he gasped his last, almost as the old year did, the balance of their little family shifted and she became closer to the son than to the father.

She knew this for a terrible thing, almost a sin, damaging to both of them, but could see no way to set things right again. And once Charlie died she and Charles became all in all to each other. Hints were dropped, of course, especially once she put aside her mourning. Well meaning, her sisters nudged other men her way – a tanner, a sawyer, an auction- eer's clerk, quiet Douglas from the Padstow line – all of them older, mostly widowers, but it seemed to her that any grown man who needed nudging, who couldn't shift for himself, was likely to prove just another person to tend and mend, like Charlie but without the balm of desire. For all that she relished romance on the printed page, her private dreams had never been of love and marriage.

The stamped-on glasses were the first thing Laura saw on waking, for she had left them on her bedside table with her library books and the ladylike travelling alarm clock Stanley had sent her for a wedding present. There were Saturday chores to be dealt with first – their own weekly laundry to be sorted and left to soak, and Sunday's Communion bread to mix and knead and leave to rise.

She took quiet satisfaction in the weekly baking of a loaf the two of them would barely taste, using the same tin, dimpled with a crucifix, her mother had acquired from the church baker before her. She liked the sense of contact it restored with her mother as she was kneading and liked that it was something she could do for the Church without fuss or show. It involved no meetings or committees and no going cap in hand to others. She baked the loaf each Saturday and left it, still warm and wrapped in one of two white linen cloths, prettily hemmed and embroidered with a small blue cross by the same old baker who had passed down the tin.

Charles's bruises had blossomed overnight so that from one side he might have been a highwayman. She told him that and he seemed pleased and went to admire the effect in the washroom mirror. He was coming to love disguises and dressing up.

His Saturday chore was to sweep and dust his room and put clean sheets on his bed, so it was easy enough for her to slip out to the road after setting the first lot of laundry to soak and have a quick word with one of the skinny girls there to confirm her suspicion as to who his tormentor was. She said nothing of this to Charles but simply called him to join her for a trip to the shops.

'Don't be embarrassed,' she told him when he dragged his feet. 'Everyone's seen a black eye before and they're not to know you didn't give as good as you got. Anyway, Mr Keast may want to see you in person when I take the glasses in. Come along, Charles. I've got things to do and we can go to the library on the way back. You know how you like that.'

She need not have spoken with the skinny girl. Charles's reaction as they neared the butcher's was confirmation enough. He knew as well as she did that Joseph, the butcher's son, helped out behind the counter on Saturdays.

On Charlie's first visit once they were engaged, he had been amused at how Launceston's tradesmen all resembled their Happy Families equivalents. The bakers seemed dusted with sugar and spice, the fishmonger's family shared an unfortunate appearance, fat of lip and rolling of eye, and Luke's, the butchers Laura favoured, in between the grand one, which seemed to charge extra for wrapping the meat in striped paper and counting the local gentry among its regulars, and the one that smelled of blood rather than sawdust and had a problem with flies, could only have been butchers. They were a ruddily healthy family, tow haired and red cheeked, broad of brow and loud of laugh, and given to jostling one another like so many bullocks at a trough. Regularly winning prizes for their bacon and sausages, they were handsome and had the daunting vitality of people who knew themselves popular. They made Laura feel shy. She knew the wife slightly from school where, as a slaughterman's daughter, she had always been at pains to be ladylike. She had the perfect job now, perched on a high stool, shielded by a window from the bloody business around her, taking people's money and smiling down on them as she passed them their receipts.

The shop had a fine position at the junction of the two streets looking down towards St Mary Magdalene and the Lower Market House. Through its windows, with their uprights like barley sugar twists, she guessed Mrs Luke enjoyed the sense that she was presiding over comings and goings; little escaped her beady gaze.

Charles enjoyed trips up to town with Laura, for all his reluctance to leave the house that morning. He was alert to any stories relating to the old buildings they passed. Now that he had realised the picturesque ruins where he often went to play or to read quietly in the sun were the remains of a Norman castle he was looking for history everywhere. But this morning he stopped chattering about the old gallows and executions as they came within sight of the Lukes' sumptuous window display. When he was very small, she had trained him to keep hold of her skirt when they were out together or, once he was older, her arm. She was touched that now he had outgrown such babyishness he still sometimes rested a hand on her elbow when he was talking of something that fired his enthusiasm. He had been doing that this morning, as they walked and he told her about dungeons and something nasty called an oubliette. So she noticed when he suddenly withdrew his hand and held back.

'I'll be waiting over here,' he told her and gestured towards the piano shop, which had always drawn him as other boys were drawn to traction engines.

There was only a short queue, so she had time to nod good morning to Mrs Luke and note that Miss Luke was becoming broad in the beam. She saw the son spot her in the queue and promptly look busy. He was a good-looking boy, like a Roman soldier in a church window, just the sort of boy any mother would like her son to befriend. Then she realised his father was waiting to serve her and she couldn't help picturing, as always, his huge forearms studded with cloves like a brace of Christmas hams.

'A pound of skirt, please, Mr Luke,' she stammered. 'And six of those Lincolnshire sausages.' In no time he had the beef and sausages wrapped in waxed paper for her. 'And half a pound of lamb's liver,' she added, aware of the women now queuing behind her and glancing across to see Charles watching her forlornly from across the street. She was glad he had stayed outside; he hated scenes.

'And your lamb's liver,' said Mr Luke. 'Anything else?'

The son was busying himself retrieving a rabbit from the game rack with a hook on a pole. With a speed and dexterity amazing in one so young, he chopped off its head and paws, then tugged off its skin like a glove.

'Yes,' she said, and made herself meet his father's babyishly blue eyes. 'I shall need these mending.' She clicked the spectacles on to the counter between them. 'Boys will be boys and Charles's bruises and cut forehead will soon heal but on the little I make and a war widow's pension I can't afford new spectacles more than once a year.'

There was a tutting sound behind her. Then one of the other women said, 'Look. There he is. Poor little mite. Looks like a badgern.' And everyone in the shop turned to look across the street at Charles, who was gazing, oblivious, at a piano being tuned in the window.

91

'What do you have to say for yourself, Joseph?' Mr Luke asked.

Still clutching the rabbit and looking as though he might cry, Joseph said, 'I'm sorry, Mrs Causley.'

Mr Luke thrust the broken glasses under his freckled nose. 'These come out of your pocket money,' he said, and slapped the back of his head with his other hand so violently the rabbit flew out of the child's grasp and was caught in her basket by the customer waiting for it.

This caused a burst of laughter under cover of which Laura said, 'Please don't. It's hitting him has taught him to hit others. I'll take these to Mr Keast, then.'

'Have him send me the bill,' Mr Luke said, handing her back the ruined glasses.

'Thank you.' She turned back to the boy. 'He didn't tell me,' she said. 'He kept quiet. It was one of the girls. He's half your size. It's not his fault he comes top in a test or two.'

'Sorry, Mrs Causley,' the boy repeated.

Mrs Luke took Laura's coins with studied politeness and a glassy lack of focus and Laura wondered whether she might have to transfer her allegiance to the butcher's with the blood smell and the flies.

She told Charles nothing of what had passed in Luke's but joined him at Hayman's shop window where they watched the tuner play a final flourish before fixing the front back on the piano to hide the workings that had so fascinated him.

'What did you say?' he asked.

'A pound of skirt, please, and six Lincolnshire sausages.'

'Are those the herby ones? I like those.'

'Which is why I bought them. Come on. Into Mr Keast's before he shuts for the weekend.'

Mr Keast, a kind man, took one glance at Charles's face and didn't need to ask why the glasses needed mending. As the lenses would need a few days to make up, he fitted Charles with what he called 'emergency' ones. They were tortoiseshell, more expensive than the simple wire ones he'd be repairing. 'If you're getting into any more fights,' he said, 'I'd appreciate you folding them carefully back into their case first. Can you do that?'

Charles nodded and smiled, opening to any fatherly kindness as he always did, like a flower to sunlight.

All errands run, they called in at the library. Laura's new book was easily selected. There was a shelf marked 'Romances' and she picked one she didn't recognise, but Charles was suffering his usual agonies of indecision as he was allowed only three books and they had to be the right ones.

'Can I leave him to browse?' she asked the librarian, assuming she'd say certainly not, and she was surprised to see a smile break out on the woman's careworn face.

'Oh, is he yours? He's no trouble. Not like some of the tykes we get in here. In a year or two we'll be offering him a job. Is he an only child?'

Laura nodded. 'How could you tell?'

'Well, he always comes in on his own, but also there's nothing childish about the way he talks. However do you cope?'

Laura saw the way the woman glanced at the romance she had chosen, at her roughened hands, but chose not to be insulted. She smiled. 'Oh,' she said, 'I just feed and house him and leave the rest to school and you.'

The two of them looked across to the children's section, where Charles seemed to be making a pile from which to select his difficult final choice. He would never be like his cousins. She had to accept and embrace that. He would always be different, and less trouble in some ways and far more of a worry in others. He would, she realised, probably never be like everyone else, never be normal, and the butcher's boy would probably not be the last to be maddened by his brilliance.

SUNDAY SCHOOL PICNIC – 1927

Life, Charles was coming to see, rarely offered her pleasures unmixed. The delicious pudding would be preceded by tubey pig's liver, the history lesson followed by a maths test, blackberries had savage thorns and Christmas carols were full of stabby little reminders of the horrors of Good Friday. Sunday school picnics were no exception. It was a treat to have a day out with his mother and he always enjoyed a trip in one of Sam Prout's charabancs. It was funny, too, seeing men and women he usually saw being all respectable in church becoming ever more unbuttoned on a beach. The picnics were always wild feasts, in their way, because all the women made a bit too much, thinking all the others might be stingy, but somehow it all went, even the tongue sandwiches and the seedcake, which were nobody's first choices.

There were games and competitions and relentless urging to join in, however, so that his eager anticipation was shot through with dread. He still couldn't catch and didn't think he ever would; his eyesight was all wrong for that. And he hated football and rugby and cricket because he was always too busy worrying his glasses would be sent flying and trampled to be able to care much about chasing a ball or scoring or avoiding being offside. He knew the rules, however, better than anyone, so he could understand what other boys were talking about and could always keep score in his head or act as a referee.

In the classroom Charles felt safe, happy even, depending on the subject. He had a reputation as a swot – he knew this because it was often what boys said before they thumped him. He wasn't especially clever – really clever children didn't have to work so hard – but he paid close attention. You were never asked anything in a test you hadn't already been told; the trick was to pay attention and he had discovered he was naturally attentive. Most boys were as easily distracted as puppies. If one looked out of the window at something happening below the school in the Willy Gardens, they all did. If one farted, all laughed. Charles, by contrast, found it very hard not to stick with the lesson in progress. He never gave up; Mother said his middle name was Relentless. Words held his attention like so many fish-hooks. If they were being told a story from the Bible or from history, he found he became quite unaware of anything else in the room. Maths held his attention out of simple necessity. Maths was nothing but instructions and rules, and if you didn't listen carefully, it was like walking through a strange place in a blindfold.

Girls were easily distracted, too, but seemed to have a better system in place for sharing information. He was used to being roughly accosted by other boys demanding answers or help and to having everyone around him copy off him during tests. At least while boys wanted something, they were less likely to thump him. He had only once made the mistake of writing wrong answers to a test on purpose then speedily correcting them all at the last minute before handing it in.

When they went to Polzeath, the picnic always happened on and below the same cluster of huge rocks on the left side of the enormous beach, not too far from the road for the unloading of baskets and handy for when anybody needed the public conveniences across the way. Anyone who had established themselves on the rocks already tended to melt away as the Sunday school group represented quite an invasion.

Although it was called the Sunday school picnic, it was actually the reverse of Sunday school. Miss Bracewell, the vicar's daughter who took Sunday school, was present but strangely eclipsed for the day. The unmarried daughter of the family, she was rumoured to have lost a fiancé in the war but she never seemed that bothered by it. (She was often referred to, he had noticed, as 'Poor Miss Bracewell'.) She lived with her widowed father, which might have been tiresome, but they had a cook and a maid, so she wasn't his slave.

On Sundays, she drew children from their parents into the parish room after the first hymn and returned them just in time for them to file up to the altar to be blessed by her father. It was an interval apart from the church service, apart from the rest of their weekday lives, with no punishment or rewards, during which she was in charge. The instruction was nominally about God and goodness but because it took them away from church, and because it involved a woman without children taking them away from their parents, it could feel like a holiday from all that. Miss Bracewell was very direct and kept her language very plain. When she spoke, you felt her words were like a well-chosen tool or a blade whereas when her father spoke, in what Mother called his 'pulpit voice', you felt his words were a screen he hid behind.

On the Sunday school picnic, however, it was Mr Bracewell who took over, noisily umpiring a game of rounders before lunch. Rounders, like cricket, might have been designed to humiliate Charles, since he invariably missed the ball when asked to hit it and failed to catch it when fielding.

Mother understood, he knew. 'But you still have to play,' she said. 'Everybody does.'

The handful of fathers who came joined in, getting competitive and shouty, like Mr Bracewell. The mothers busied themselves combining all the picnics into one huge feast across the rocks, which they then had to defend against seagulls and dogs, of course. Charles asked in vain to be allowed to keep score instead. He got through the batting with three humiliating failures to hit the ball, provoking yelps of incredulity from Mr Bracewell and groans from his teammates, then took himself off to a safely distant position when it was his turn to field.

Joe Luke was on his team, scored triumphantly in bat, of course, and was loud among the groaners when Charles failed to hit the tennis ball. Charles passed him on his way out to field and he surprised him by saying, 'Don't worry. Any come out this way, I'll catch them for you,' in a voice that was almost considerate.

'Thanks,' Charles told him but didn't risk saying more since they never spoke as a rule.

Since the Day of the Glasses, as Charles thought of it, Joe had never hit him again, although cronies of his did things like trip Charles up or send his books flying to curry favour. Joe was popular because he was big for his age and athletic, and because his father ran a thriving business and was a town councillor. Joe was good at mental arithmetic but his attention often wandered in classes and it amused Charles to help him out by occasionally whispering the right answer to him or by letting him copy his test responses. The terrible matter of his being upbraided in front of customers and made to pay the optician's bill from his pocket money lay unacknowledged between them and Charles could never decide if it was an unexploded bomb or a still-wrapped present.

Polzeath beach at low tide seemed especially huge and it was hard to stay focused on the game when there were so many people and dogs to catch his eye. The receding tide had left hard little ridges in the sand like the furrows in a field and it was tricky to see how breaking waves could leave behind an effect so delicate and regular. He was examining them and enjoying the feel of the ridges under the arches of his bare feet when a tennis ball smacked down in a sandy pool beside him and he became aware of shouting.

'Charles! Quick!' Joe Luke yelled, and held out his hands. Horrified, Charles grabbed the ball and threw it his way. For once his throw did not go way off-beam or land pathetically short and Joe was able to catch it and hurl it back to the centre of the game. He turned back immediately after. 'See?' he said. 'Not that hard.' And to Charles's amazement he winked. The vicar blew his whistle soon after that, ending the game and summoning them all to eat.

Almost more than the rounders match, Charles hated the moment at the end of every Sunday school picnic when the vicar climbed up on to a rock, big, black shoes slithering on the seaweed, and thumped his fist on the lid of a cake tin for attention. He loved attention, Charles realised. He could never say as much to Mother, who had unquestioning respect for the Church and its officers, but watching Mr Bracewell now, red faced and a bit sweaty, beaming around him, Charles understood that when he read lessons or conducted services, a part of him was showing off and enjoying it.

'The time has come,' he boomed. 'Gather round, children.'

'Go on, Charles,' Mother said. 'Don't want to miss out.'

Charles reluctantly got to his feet, instinctively taking off his glasses and folding them away into their case. Other children had none of his fastidiousness and were already clustering in tightly around the vicar's boulder, some of them knee deep in a rockpool to do so. At ten, Charles had started to dislike being called a child, lumped in with other children as though they were all the same age, though he knew this was unreasonable, that there was no other word to describe them. He stood towards the back of the crowd, embarrassed, avoiding looking at Mother, whom he suspected disliked this ritual of the vicar's as much as he did but would never have said so.

'Did you all have a good lunch?' Mr Bracewell called out.

'Yes!' everyone shouted.

'Oh. So you've no room for toffees?'

'Yes!' everyone shouted, and 'Toffees!' Everyone except Charles.

'Ready?' Mr Bracewell called, lifting the lid off the tin and drawing out the moment before he was no longer the centre of greedy attention but merely the vicar again. 'Steady?' He shifted awkwardly, clearly nervous of losing his balance.

Joe Luke, Charles noticed, had also positioned himself on the edge of the group, as though too old for such things now. His eyes caught Charles's and for a second Charles fancied they understood one another.

'Toffees!' shouted Mr Bracewell, and hurled the contents of his tin into the air so vigorously that he did finally lose his footing and had to drop awkwardly to his knees to steady himself. A swarm of brightly wrapped toffees flew up around him, a sort of riot broke out as fists lunged and palms swiped and children shoved each other aside so as to capture as many toffees as possible. The children in the rock pool were snatching sweets from under the weeds and water. The bigger, fiercer children, the hungriest too, perhaps, were scrabbling up the most as usual. Joe Luke had a fistful, Charles saw. Parents were cheering and laughing. Several of the smaller children were loudly in tears, either from hurt or simple disappointment.

'Well, get in there, Charles!' he heard Mother shout.

It was surprising how long it took for every toffee in the tin to be retrieved. Charles liked toffees, especially the ones made with dark treacle or the ones flavoured with peppermint oil, but he could not bear being made a spectacle of or being made to fight for food.

There was one, red-wrapped toffee that had landed between his feet. He saw another boy, Jim Garth, a rough,

101

weasel-featured lad who often had ringworm, see it at the same moment and lunge for it. Charles shocked himself by speedily stamping on it and simultaneously snatching up one of the dark ones he liked, which Slow Eunice had dropped from her hoard as she lurched in another direction.

The charabancs would not leave for home until four so there were still at least two hours to use up. Charles wandered back to the picnic rocks where Mother was chatting with Miss Bracewell. They had both tweaked up their summer dresses a little so as to enjoy the sun on their legs, he noticed. Mother's legs were strong and sturdy ('I'm good in a high wind,' she liked to say) whereas Miss Bracewell's were as thin as a wading bird's. Though with the knees the right way round. He knew he ought to offer Mother his spare toffee but guiltily kept it in the pocket of his shorts.

'Have you eaten enough, Charles?' Miss Bracewell asked. 'We saw you didn't get many toffees.'

'He's too polite,' Mother said.

'Well, that's no fault.' Miss Bracewell lowered her sunglasses and looked at him with an interest he rarely saw in grown-ups.

'Take an apple,' Mother said. 'Lighten our load. And take one for a friend.'

'Thank you,' Charles said and took two red apples from the cloth-lined basket beside them.

'Are you going for a paddle?' she asked. 'You look a bit hot.'

'Maybe,' he said. 'Or maybe I'll walk round the headland to St Noddy.'

'Oh, that would be lovely,' Miss Bracewell said, then sighed, 'but it's so good just lolling.'

'Isn't it?'

The two of them chuckled and Charles sensed he had interrupted a conversation they would take up once he was gone. He already had his costume on under his shorts but picked up his rolled towel.

'We've been plotting, Charles,' Miss Bracewell said. 'How would you like to come to me for piano lessons?'

'But . . . we don't have a piano,' he told her.

'You can practise on the church one,' Mother said, 'when there's no one in there, of course. Seems your legs are still a bit short for the organ.'

'Oh.'

'It's quite a long way to the pedals,' Miss Bracewell added.

'Yes, please. But how will we . . .?' He faltered. It was bad manners to discuss money in public.

'We've come to a ladies' agreement,' Mother said.

'And in return I want you to join the choir.'

'All right.'

'Charles,' said Mother, 'you're meant to say thank you. We don't all sing in the choir.'

'I was listening in as we sang in the charabanc on the way here and you've a nice true treble,' Miss Bracewell put in kindly.

They'd sung all the way from Launceston to Polzeath and would sing all the way back. 'Green Grow the Rushes, O', 'Early One Morning' and 'Blow Away the Morning Dew'. On the way home 'Trelawny' and 'Lamorna' would

103

be sung because they were Cornish and it was a tradition. 'Lamorna' could get a bit rude.

'Thank you,' he told her. 'That would be lovely.'

He put his glasses back on as he walked away towards the shoreline. When he wore them he felt the glasses were all people saw and not the awkward boy behind them. He had never felt like this on the beach before, but this year he was acutely aware of bosoms and bulges, of muscles and hair; it was all at once fascinating and appalling, and what he really wanted was to be alone in a quiet graveyard with a book.

The nice librarian had introduced him to Robert Louis Stevenson and he had devoured *Treasure Island* and *Kidnapped*, thrilled by the way they had young boys swept up in dangerous adult goings-on. Now he was reading *Dr Jekyll and Mr Hyde*. The librarian said it was 'for grown-ups really' and it did suggest darkly adult things he couldn't quite grasp, but it was compelling all the same. But Mother said they were not to bring library books to the beach as sand would get in them and possibly traces of picnic.

'You'll just have to talk to people, Charles,' she said in the teasing, slightly mischievous way she sometimes had.

Sometimes he felt she knew him too well. Other boys had fathers and brothers and sisters, which meant that their mothers' attention was divided several ways, so giving them more privacy. He had no one but Mother and she had no one but him, unless you counted the aunts and uncles and cousins. Sometimes it was a bit much.

So he had no book, just his glasses and a tightly furled beach towel amidst all these noisily happy, half-naked people. Disappearing out into the sea was a way of hiding, of course, or becoming just a bobbing head with no body, at least, but he had yet to learn to swim, to his shame, and could only look with envy at the boys diving through the waves or confidently swimming out on wooden surfboards.

The water was cold but deliciously so, breaking around his bare feet and splashing his calves. For a while he enjoyed standing there with the foam licking around him as he gazed at the breaking waves and beyond them across the mouth of the bay to Trevose Head and its lighthouse, but then he worried people would think him odd for just standing and not swimming so he started to walk parallel to the shore as though on his way to meet somebody. A yellow dog ran in front of him and launched itself into the water close enough to splash him.

'Charlie?'

It was Joe Luke. Nobody called him Charlie apart from Aunt Maggie. Joe was the sort to shorten everybody's name instinctively. If they spoke at school he called him Charlie Boy as a piece of mockery. Charles glanced around but saw none of Joe's usual cronies. In fact few of them had come on the outing as their parents were largely Methodists. Joe stood up. His costume did not look home-made, unlike Charles's, and had a striped navy-blue and red top. He was so much bigger than Charles, although they were nearly the same age. He even had muscles from carrying carcasses for his father. Charles often looked at the photographs his mother had of handsome Uncle Stanley, who died before he was born, and of his father, whom Charles sometimes worried he was forgetting. They were both big, handsome men – at least Father had been before the war got him. Charles wouldn't have minded taking after either of them but at the moment he seemed to have hatched from an egg.

'Aren't you coming in?' Joe called, as Charles feared he would.

'Isn't it cold?'

'Not really. It's lovely. Come on.'

'I was going to walk round the headland.'

'So? Swim first, then walk.'

Joe had walked out of the surf to join him. He seemed to radiate heat even though he was wet through.

'Aren't you cold by now?' Charles tried in faint hope, for Joe's teeth were chattering slightly.

'Nah. Anyway, it always feels warmer if you come out then go back in again. Come on. Get your togs off.'

One of the reasons Charles hadn't rushed to paddle properly was his costume. It was navy blue and in two pieces, like most people's, but Mother had knitted it to save money, reusing the wool from something else, and it was baggy on his thin frame, even when dry. She said it left room for growth and would do until he started to grow in earnest, but he had a horror of the trunks sliding down with the weight of water in them as their drawstring was untrustworthy and never seemed to sit above his hips as it should. Joe's costume had a smart white belt you could be sure would never let him down.

'Nobody's going to steal your things,' Joe added as Charles continued to dither.

It had never occurred to Charles that his discarded clothes and towel might not be safely left, but now Joe had added a whole extra burden of anxiety to the afternoon.

'Go on, man. Don't be such a maid.'

That clinched it. To be called a girl was the worst insult in Joe's armoury and was often the precursor to a thump. Almost as much as he wanted to be left in peace to read, Charles longed for Joe to accept him. He set his towel on the sand several yards back from where the surf was reaching, tucked his glasses safely inside and folded his trousers and shirt on top of it.

To be fair Joe didn't laugh at his baggy costume but merely called, 'Good man,' as Charles walked gingerly in to join him. 'It's coldest where it's still shallow, because of the wind,' Joe said, and led him into water deep enough to cover the shaming lower half of his costume.

It was thrilling to stand there and feel the swell lift you bodily off the sandy bottom and set you back down. He had never ventured into water so deep. When Mother was with him they did no more than paddle and jump over the smallest waves.

'This is the life,' Joe said, trying to sound older than he was. 'We live too far from the sea. Imagine if you could come here every day.' And all at once he dived down through an oncoming wave and was lost to view. The wave was large, and Charles felt a momentary thrill of terror as it lifted him and took longer than usual to set him down. It carried him out of his depth and he scrabbled frantically with his feet until they felt a rock and then sand again. He was just beginning to pace slowly back towards safety when a second, much bigger wave came in. All around him people were whooping and laughing in expectation as the water level sank then dramatically rose. But they were swimmers and surfers. All Charles could do was helplessly try to run for shore as a sudden current sucked his feet and the sand beneath him sharply backwards and what seemed like a wall of water rose behind him and then broke over his head. He lost all sense of up or down, back or forth. His nose and mouth filled with brine and he was tumbled like a piece of driftwood. Lashing out, his feet kicked somebody and then strong hands were on him and he fought against them. The water cleared briefly and as he gasped air he saw it was Joe and realised he had lured him out with a view to drowning him, so fought even harder.

'Hey. Hey!' Joe shouted, half-laughing, and again pulled him out of the water. 'It's all right. I've got you.'

'I can't swim.'

'I can see that. You should've said.'

'You should've asked.'

'Here. I've got you.'

For a terrifying moment Joe seemed to drop him back into the deep water to swim away but then he caught him behind with an arm around his chest and tugged him high over another big wave and back into shallower water. Being held like that, suspended in water, powerless yet safe, was confusing. It felt so good yet was somehow also deeply shaming, making him the most maidenly of maids. He hated Joe for so exposing him but also didn't want to let go of him once his feet were securely back on sand and his shoulders clear of the water. Joe adjusted a shoulder strap of his costume that Charles's tugging had pulled away.

'Can you not swim at all?' he asked.

'No,' Charles said, adding in his defence, 'I've never learned.'

'It's easy. Here. Take my ankles.'

'What?'

Joe tipped himself on to his back in the water – floating seemed to come naturally to him – and thrust his feet in Charles's face. 'Take 'em, then.'

Charles grasped an ankle in either hand.

'Now kick with your feet. Left right left right!'

As he spoke, Joe launched himself backwards, pulling Charles with him so that his feet left the bottom again. He kicked as he was told, fighting to keep his face out of the water. Joe laughed.

'That's it!' he shouted, and swam with his arms so that, for one glorious minute, they moved through the water together. Then a young woman on a surfboard came between them and Charles had to let go. He wanted to try again; he liked holding Joe's ankles and it felt safe being towed along and just splashing with his legs. But Joe said they had to change ends. He told Charles to paddle hard with his arms while Joe took hold of his feet, but that was an uncomfortable disaster as Charles simply sank head first, then panicked and kicked Joe on the chin.

He was getting cold now and wanted to get out and retrieve his clothes. To his surprise Joe didn't want to carry on swimming or return to the group, where another game of rounders had started up.

'Where are you walking to?'

'St Noddy,' Charles told him. 'It's a little church that was buried in the sand for hundreds of years.'

'Can I come?'

'Of course.'

Joe didn't change out of his wet swimming things so Charles didn't feel he should change out of his, although the wet wool was saggy and itchy and feeling rather cold now they were out of the water. He slavishly copied Joe, however, who took off his stripy top half and wrung it out before putting it back on.

'Soon dry in this breeze,' Joe said. 'Which way?'

So, clothes furled in his towel, from which he'd retrieved his spectacles, Charles led the way over the rocks to a footpath on Tristram Cliff and around the headland, past where a very few bungalows had been built.

'Imagine living in one of those,' Joe said, and Charles was startled to find himself picturing Joe mowing the lawn while he pegged out their washing in a stiff seaside breeze.

One house was still being built and, seeing nobody was about, Joe led them over to peer inside. Though only on one level it was a palace compared to Charles's home. There was a big hall that was just that: a hall to connect the other rooms. There was parquet floor being laid everywhere, which Joe said was expensive as the wood blocks came all the way from India or Africa. The kitchen was just a kitchen, not a kitchen where people also lived and ate. There were two inside lavatories and, most impressive of all, a proper bathroom with tiles up the walls and the bath plumbed in.

When Charles exclaimed over this Joe asked didn't he have one, and Charles remembered that the Lukes lived in a house all of their own on a street in the better part of town and not over their shop. He admitted he and Mother had a tin tub and that it took a while to fill and was heavy to empty. He didn't tell Joe that Mother always bathed in his water when he had finished with it, because it took fuel to heat water and money didn't grow on trees.

They hurried on because a woman was coming with a big dog and soon the lovely beach at Daymer Bay came into view. They didn't come there on Sunday school trips because it was a long walk from where the charabanc would have to drop them and because people liked big waves. Charles preferred this side. Opening on to the Camel estuary rather than the Atlantic meant the beach had only gently lapping waves rather than breakers, and there was a lovely view of the hills and fields on the western side of the Camel.

Pointing out Padstow in the distance, he told Joe the story of the Doom Bar, the sand bar raised as a curse to Padstow's sailors by a mermaid a fisherman had humiliated.

'How did he humiliate her, then?' Joe asked.

'He showed her off in the market with the lobsters and the crab,' Charles said, and went on to point out the little crooked spire of St Enodoc, which had been all but buried in shifting sand dunes but whose vicars had still claimed their money by climbing through the roof on a ladder once in a while to take a service by lanternlight.

111

'How do you know all this stuff?' Joe asked as though he might be about to call Charles a maid again.

'I dunno,' Charles said. 'I read a lot. I like reading and the library is just up the road from us.'

'Is that why you need glasses?'

'I'd need them anyway, I think. But I couldn't read without them.'

Joe admitted that he liked reading but was rarely given time. 'I have to help get the shop ready before school and help out there straight after. And Saturday's a full day and on Sunday it can only be Sunday books.'

Charles pulled a face and admitted that Sunday books were the worst.

The trick with Sundays, Joe said, was to go to bed in good time as Sunday reading in bed didn't seem to be covered by the same rules.

'If you could be anything when you grow up, what would you be?' Charles asked him.

'Not a butcher, that's for sure. I mean, it's a good business. It does well and people will always want meat, and I know I'm very lucky but . . .'

He fell quiet. Charles thought he was going to say nothing further but then glanced over as they walked and saw Joe was frowning in thought. Maybe this was something he had never told anyone?

'Sometimes it's like being in a corridor with no doors or windows. Fishermen and farmers' sons probably say that too, and they're facing real danger whereas I'm just facing, you know, something completely unsurprising. And working in the same room as my parents and sister until they retire or die.' He had picked up a stick of furze wood and now used it to lash out at some nettles. It was fragile, and snapped immediately, which gave him no satisfaction. He threw the stump of the stick hard out over the edge of the low cliff. 'You're so lucky,' he said.

'Me? Mother's a laundress. I'm not doing—'

'No, stupid. I mean you can do anything. You're clever. Everyone can see that. You'll work hard, do well, go to Horwell's, then to university and make something of yourself. You're not held to being the same as your dad.'

Charles had given no thought to grammar school, much less anything beyond, although recently he had thought it might be nice to be a librarian. But perhaps only slightly fierce ladies could do that? He had certainly never thought of himself as lucky to have no father, or as especially clever. It was as though Joe had thoughtlessly flung wide a window in what Charles had taken for a blank wall and left him feeling a bit dizzy. As did having a popular, bigger boy confide in him.

They started down the sandy path on to the beach. There were people picnicking and swimming here too, but far fewer of them, and Charles saw a woman on a smart tartan rug stare at them challengingly over her sunglasses, as though they had strayed into somewhere they were not welcome.

'Do you want to swim again,' Charles asked, 'instead of walking to the church?'

'Of course. Do you want another go at holding my ankles?'

'Yes, please.'

Joe scoffed. 'You're so polite, Maid.'

'Sorry.'

The water felt warmer, perhaps because it was shallower and coming in over warm sand. The waves, too, were negligible, which made it less daunting to wade in. Charles was slightly embarrassed by the presence of a lot of very small children and their mothers – this was evidently regarded as the nursery beach compared to Polzeath. Joe dived in ahead of him and swam some way off then stopped on a sand bar, turned round and beckoned, calling out, 'Come on, Charlie. It's great!' and grinning.

Charles waded out to him, even making a couple of attempts at doggy paddle, shamed by the game efforts of smaller boys. Then Joe lay down in the water, offered him his ankles again and soon was towing him along once more. Again, he suggested they try reversing roles and again Charles sank.

'Why don't you float?' Joe asked, irritated. 'Just breathe normally and you'll float. I think you're sinking because you pant like a dog. Here. Try this. I'll hold you.' He persuaded Charles to lie back while he supported his back and bottom on his hands. 'Now breathe.'

All Charles could see was the blue sky and Joe right beside him. He breathed. He filled his lungs properly as though about to sing. And he floated. Or sort of floated.

'Open your arms and legs out like a star,' Joe said.

The sensation, just rocked by the sea rather than knocked flying, was so new and so delicious that it took him a moment to realise Joe was no longer supporting him. Then Joe floated too and soon they were playing a game where they touched their feet, sole to sole, and each tried to push the other. Other boys played games like this all the time, pushed each other around, wrestled, chased balls or chickens or dogs or one another. When not obliged to sit still in class and listen to a teacher they seemed to spend their days like so many puppies, tumbling over each other, testing their strength, establishing who was leader. The simple, playful sensation of Joe's bigger feet pressed against his acted on Charles like a stolen teaspoon of Mother's liver salts, and brought on a kind of fizzing in him.

This unfamiliar sensation, he realised, was friendship, a thing he had witnessed and read about. Joe might come round to his house after work sometimes now, or on Sundays. He would involve Joe in his historical exploration of the town's ruins and churchyards. Joe would teach him to catch. He would shield Charles in the playground. Just when Mother and Miss Bracewell were about to make him fit in even less, with the admittedly bewitching prospects of piano lessons and singing in the choir, fate had intervened so that Joe could help make him like everyone else.

Tiring, becoming cold too, they thrashed their way back to the shore where Charles offered Joe his towel before using it himself.

'Thanks,' Joe said, and rubbed his hair and top half with it before suddenly, shockingly, stripping bare to step into the sandy clothes he had dropped any old how. Red-faced on his behalf, Charles became more flustered still in the complicated dance of removing his sagging trunks and pulling on his shorts while fighting to preserve decency

115

under a towel. Joe watched him with a surly sort of grin, though, which made it all right.

'We can go back by the lane,' Charles called out as Joe started to leave the beach. 'It's quicker.'

Neither of them wore a watch. Charles had inherited his father's, which was special because it had been to war and back, but he wasn't allowed to wear it yet, only to look at it and keep it wound, but Launceston was full of clocks, its air alive with bells and whistles from dawn to curfew, summonses to school or factory, church or chapel, as well as simple markers of the passing hours. So Charles had a strong sense always of what time it was, and he worried now that they might be late. A charabanc would wait for them but the disgrace of keeping people waiting would be terrible.

Joe seemed oblivious, however, and strolled up the narrow lane to Trebetherick beside him, thwacking at stinging nettles and foxglove stalks with his striped costume and, once or twice, thwacking the back of Charles's legs with it. Charles lacked the confidence to thwack him playfully back with his towel, so walked a little faster, which then became a not terribly pleasant game as Joe chased him up the hill.

'What are the baths like?' Charles asked him, panting, as they reached the top and could see Polzeath stretched out below them. 'They're so close but I've never been.'

'They're great,' Joe said. 'Bit green sometimes. But better for learning to swim in than the sea. You should go. They're best just before closing time. The water's a bit warmer then and they're not too busy.'

'Is there somewhere to change?'

116

'You worried about walking through town in your saggies?'

Charles nudged him. Joe nudged him back harder but it felt good.

'There's a changing shed,' Joe said. 'Men's and ladies'. And privies.'

'Could we, maybe . . .?' Charles wondered how best to say it. 'Could we go there together?'

Joe stopped walking a moment and looked at him with a scorn that felt worse than the fiercest slap.

'Don't be stupid,' he said. 'I mean, look at you. Four-eyed maid!' And he ran ahead down the hill to where Charles could see their group was clustering around the two charabancs.

He decided not to run too, to do nothing to betray that he and Joe had just spent two precious hours together. He took off his glasses, which his damp clothes and the climb were steaming up, and rubbed them clear on his handkerchief. He had a fresh handkerchief every day on dressing. Today's was as yet untouched, still ironed into a tight, soft square. It was like holding Mother in his hand, or a part of her. Clear. Fragrant. Tidy.

He put his glasses back on and walked on, naming plants to himself as he passed them: lady's bedstraw . . . tree mallow . . . betony . . . He glanced up and saw Mother had seen him. He carried on spotting and naming plants; better she should think him dreamy and absent-minded than the boy other boys shunned. Navelwort, he told himself. Policemen's buttons . . .

STAINS – 1928

The church's laundry bundle was where it always was, in the vestry of St Thomas's. As always, though, having once been falsely challenged over a missing lace bodice, Laura untied the bundle and went through it, carefully itemising everything in a dated entry in a notebook she carried for the purpose. Altar cloths, just like tablecloths, had to be ironed carefully and then folded in a certain way and never pressed in those folds so that their appearance would be smooth when opened out again, but the moment they had been used they were bundled up for her, wine stains, crumbs and all, as though they had no significance. After noting everything down, Laura refolded them with something more like reverence, then buckled them into her hamper, slung it on to her back and let herself out.

Her next call, as always on a Monday, was at Treloar's. Aggie Treloar, like the church, had her busiest time at weekends and always a pile of dirty linen come Monday. Aggie ran a rough little boarding house a few doors up the hill from Laura, between the library and the dosshouse.

They had known each other since school. Even then, Aggie had a reputation for boldness and for treating boys like so many farm animals. The girls' privies in the far corner of the playground were directly uphill from the boys' ones and shared an open drain – little more than a

118

glazed terracotta gutter sunk into the earth – which ran between the two. Boys could shout saucy messages to the girls, the sound passing through the narrow opening at the bottom of the wall where the shared drain flowed. Livelier girls had been known to sail paper boats the other way, sometimes with messages scrawled on their sails, listening for the guffaws on the other side when they were scooped out of the piss and read. Out in the yard or in the classroom, fraternising between the sexes was at once frowned upon and stifled by the dread of gossip, but the frank necessities of the privy arrangement and the inability of one side to see the others' faces encouraged boldness. Sometimes things got out of hand in there and a member of staff would burst in, flinching at the smell and quivering with embarrassment. When boys were caned, it happened in their half of the privies and girls would secretly cluster on their own side of the wall to listen and flinch, excited when a boy proved his manliness by not crying out.

Once, Laura had dropped her precious coral bracelet in there and cried out as it was swept away and under the wall. Quick as a flash Aggie had barged into the boys' half and insisted a boy retrieve it for her with his bare hands, agreeing to a quick kiss in exchange provided he kept his hands behind his back. It was a courageous double sacrifice, of reputation and pride, and Laura's startled gratitude had quietly warmed to friendship long after the bracelet had been outgrown and handed on to a baby niece.

Aggie's life had been tough. Born in the workhouse, often coming to school with bruises she was too proud to cover up, she saw her fortunes change when her mother married Mr Treloar, who owned the house outright and had made good money as a seed merchant. Both parents died when the same flu pandemic that had carried off Stanley crossed the Tamar. Aggie promptly turned her house into what Laura persisted in calling a boarding house. It was said Aggie had landed a licence to sell alcohol through favouritism shown to a couple of councillors, one of them quite possibly the boy who had obediently thrust his hand into a latrine on her command. Whatever people said, and envy of Aggie among 'respectable' women was usually disguised as disapproval of her slovenliness or unchecked fertility, Laura chose to recognise only that, like herself, Aggie worked extremely hard for modest returns. If men of the town liked Aggie's company more than that of their pinch-mouthed wives, it could only be because she offered something the wives withheld.

'Come in, my dear. You'll have some tea.'

Aggie was unrecognisable as the bluish, skeletal girl of their youth. She had blossomed with her first unchecked pregnancy and retained what she called 'a pound of comfort' from each of the babies that followed. When women and preachers hissed the term 'whore', they thought of scarlet silks, corsets and all that nonsense when the truth, far more formidable, was that Aggie's ample hips and bosom worthy of a ship's figurehead made her as much mother as temptress, as unjudgementally comforting to the men she entertained as apple pie and custard.

Heedless of the grubby children who had clustered around her skirts, she turned to lead Laura to her kitchen. To Laura's knowledge only four or five of the children were Aggie's, but there were always strays there, drawn to the household's warm and unregulated atmosphere by day as many of their fathers would be by night. If a parent met with an accident or was locked up in the cells, the child would know it would be fed and safe at Treloar's, if not washed or made to do homework.

Laura did not only launder bedding for her but clothes, so she had some idea of the splendour of Aggie-by-night. Aggie-by-day usually received her in the sort of front-buttoned housecoat many women wore to do their household chores. Aggie called hers her *peenwar*, as though to emphasise she was a stranger to dusting.

To sit down in the afternoon of a working day and be offered a cup of tea and a piece of gingerbread was a rare treat, even with children running riot overhead and a tap dripping loudly into a sink of neglected washing-up.

'Hard day?' Aggie asked, stirring sugars into her tea.

Laura sighed and took a bite of gingerbread. She had not been raised to complain. 'My mother always told us life was hard work but that it was the only life we have,' she said.

'Price of independence,' said Aggie.

'I'm not independent,' Laura told her. 'I'm just a widow, which means I have to work twice as hard.'

'Do you miss your Charlie?'

'Yes, but I wouldn't want him suffering like that again. I'd only want him back again well.'

'Of course,' Aggie said, pulling a face to warn off a child that was trying to come in. 'Would you consider marrying again, Laura?'

Laura felt herself blush. 'I'm not exactly swept off my feet with offers,' she said.

'I bet you don't give them time. Always so busy and then young Charles . . .'

'What about Charles?'

'Well, anyone can see he's your all-in-all.'

'I don't spoil him.'

'I didn't say as you did.'

Laura's sisters thought she spoiled Charles, because he was an only and had no father. She knew she was defensive about it.

'But any man who wooed you would have to woo him too, wouldn't they?'

Laura snorted at the thought of some man wooing Charles. 'He can be very – what's the word? – judgemental,' she said. 'Anyway, it's not going to happen.'

'Because you're independent! You see?' Aggie laughed and nudged the gingerbread plate towards her. Laura resisted temptation, though it was stickily delicious and studded with rum-soaked sultanas. She had work to get back to and Charles's tea to make. 'Some women,' Aggie went on, '*most* women, don't seem to feel complete until they've got a man to boss them around and complain about. But some of us don't really feel ourselves until we *don't* have to share a bed. Don't you love waking in the morning, girl, and stretching out like a starfish?'

'It is quite nice,' Laura admitted, although she never lingered in bed unless she was ill. 'Did you have to share when you were small?'

'Of course. Until we got out of the workhouse, I was always in with Mother. You?'

'Three of us girls,' Laura said. 'I'm amazed we slept at all. If one rolled, we all rolled. And too hot in summer and never enough quilt in winter. Having a bed to myself when I went into service was a luxury.'

The children burst in again and she seized the moment to get on. The littlest was still at the saggy-drawered stage, stomping after her siblings, her face smeared with a mixture of dirt and jam.

'The picture of her dad,' Aggie said, reaching for a wooden spoon to scratch an itch between her shoulder blades, quite as though Laura weren't there.

Laura realised just in time that she had been on the point of exclaiming at Aggie knowing who all the fathers were. Of course Aggie knew who the fathers were. For all Laura knew, so did the fathers, and were made to pay up. From the year she became a mother herself, Laura had fallen into the habit of checking any child that crossed her path, making instinctive comparisons. Were they more or less well-fed than hers, more or less healthy? Were they happier for having two parents? Aggie's little tribe was grubby but showed no signs of neglect. They certainly had none of the frightening listlessness she knew for a sign of chronic hunger; none of them was as skinny as Aggie had been in girlhood.

The two women giggled when they noticed Laura was leaving without having picked up what she actually came for.

'A bit more than usual, I'm afraid,' Aggie said, loading her up. 'Market day was extra busy. Price of beef must be up, I reckon.'

'I can cope,' Laura said.

'Course you can. You're a good woman, Laura Causley. That's for last week's.' Aggie handed over a plump brown envelope of cash, then watched placidly as Laura crouched in the hall that smelled of the previous night's beer from the bar and noted so many sheets and pillowcases and two lacy nightdresses in her notebook, before strapping the dirty things into her hamper with the altar linen. There were more than would fit in, so she tied the remainder into a tidy bundle, discreetly checking there were no obvious stains on display as she rolled it.

'Heppy can carry that for you.'

'Honestly, it's not far.'

'Zackly. Heppy?'

Heppy was summoned, a striking, dark-haired, bold-eyed girl all of nine. She scooped up the bundle and walked ahead, apparently enjoying the temporary importance of running an errand.

'Thank you, Heppy,' Laura told her, grateful as the hamper was full to heaviness. She stepped carefully as they came down the steep hill. It had been raining heavily and she was wary of slipping when laden and off-balance. 'Are you enjoying school?'

'Not much, Mrs Causley.' The child had her mother's frankness.

'Oh dear, because you'll be there a while. Is it the maths you don't like?'

'No. The maths is all right. It's all the religion.'

'Mrs Causley? Mrs Causley!'

Laura's heart sank. She was behind on her work already and it was Mrs Netley, one of the churchwardens, who was never short of talk. Laura paused, leaning the weight of her hamper against the wall of the nearest house while she waited for Mrs Netley to catch up. It was odd that she should be attached to St Thomas's as, although her husband owned one of the tanneries, they lived high on the hill, away from the source of her good bags and shoes. Laura feared it was because she had felt looked down on at St Mary Magdalene so had transferred her attendance to a church where she felt able to look down in turn.

'Heppy, you go on,' she told the child. 'Just leave the bundle in our washhouse and tell Charles he's to give you a bun as thanks.'

'What if he's playing the piano, Mrs Causley?'

'Oh, don't mind that. Just knock and walk on in.'

Visibly perked up at the prospect of a bun, Heppy sauntered on down the hill just as Mrs Netley came up it and drew level. Laura usually went out of her way to avoid her. She could never see her without thinking of her mother's expression, 'eyes everywhere'. Within seconds she felt the familiar twinges of self-consciousness, almost like nettle stings, as Mrs Netley's slightly protuberant eyes flicked over her hamper, her hair, her hands, her shoes, to Heppy, then back to Laura's hair.

'I thought I'd catch you at the church, Mrs Causley, but you always give me the slip.'

'Oh, yes?' Laura adopted her usual defence with such

people, honed at school, which was to affect an air of placid stupidity. Charles, who had long been old enough for nothing to escape his notice, called it her 'cow at a gate face'.

'You picked up the altar cloth?'

'Oh, yes.'

'And you were just in . . . in . . .'

'In Aggie Treloar's boarding house, yes. I do her laundry, too. Were you . . . lying in wait for me, Mrs Netley?'

'I wouldn't put it like that. I just happened to see you go in and, well, Mrs Causley, it's rather a delicate matter.'

'Oh, yes?'

Again the eyes went flickety-flick.

'How do you wash the altar cloths?'

'Why? Has one of them not been clean? I'm sure I always take the greatest care.'

'No, no. I'm sure your work is perfect as always.'

'Oh, well, good. It's just white linen. I deal with any stains, soak it overnight, then wash it with the other whites of the day tomorrow.'

'So the sheets from . . .' Mrs Netley's eyes flicked uphill to Treloar's.

'Are in the hamper here with the altar cloth. And they'll all be checked over and soaked tonight.'

'Together?'

Was the woman simple? 'I've only the one tub, Mrs Netley.'

'Yes, but, well, you don't think there's something wrong in mixing them up?'

'A stain's a stain in my book. Now if that's all, Mrs Netley, this hamper's heavy and I need to be on.'

'Yes, yes. Of course you do. But . . . I suppose what I'm saying is that I'm surprised a woman in your position has anything to do with . . .' Again the eye flick.

Mrs Netley was tall, but Laura was wide and this was her neighbourhood, which she felt gave her strength, and the hamper on her back lent her weight.

'Aggie Treloar pays me,' she said. 'Well and promptly. The laundry and baking I do for the Church I do for love, as my mother did. I wouldn't dream of expecting to be paid for it. But, like many of us on this street, I work all the hours I can, and I need to.'

The sound of piano playing reached her. Charles was home from school and practising, as he did every evening. He had been working all week on the same, joyful little piece, which Laura had learned was by Bach. She saw Mrs Netley had heard it too and been thrown.

'Does someone down here play the piano?' Mrs Netley asked. 'Or perhaps it's a radio?'

'That's my Charles,' Laura told her. 'It's a two-part invention. Good afternoon, Mrs Netley.'

'Now I've offended you and that wasn't my intention.'

'No? Well, I'm not offended at all. You were worried that sin in Aggie's bedding would somehow make its way into the altar cloth in the wash. Well, it may do, but I can assure you that I apply the same soda and standards to both and everything is thoroughly rinsed.'

Her sense of triumph was fleeting. As she walked on towards home, seeing Heppy walk past her munching her hard-earned bun, she went through Mrs Netley's words again and felt the anger rise in her she had been at pains to

127

tamp down. *A woman in her position.* What had she meant by that? A laundress? A widow? Or did she mean that to be a church baker and washerwoman was somehow a prestigious role, akin to churchwarden?

As always now, two or three children had gathered on her steps to listen to Charles's playing through the open window. Charles didn't like her telling him they were there. He said it stopped him doing what Miss Bracewell called 'proper practice' and encouraged him merely to perform for the street instead. But he had opened the window, she noted, surely aware of how the sound would draw his little audience back. One of them, a girl, ran off but Douglas, the railwayman's painfully polite little boy, who was there most days, lingered. Everyone called him Ginger, although his hair was mouse not red. Younger than Charles, he trailed around after him, evidently content to be beneath his notice.

'Hello, Ginger,' she said, and he smiled but apparently didn't like to speak over the music. She set down her hamper in the washhouse, paused to stretch out her back. Supper was oxtail pie. The tail pieces had been quietly stewing all day with a bottle of stout and a couple of the bay leaves Miss Bracewell let her take from her garden, and Laura had made the pastry for the lid earlier; it only needed rolling out. She could set it to bake, then have time to come back out to treat and scrub any stains and set the wash to soak overnight. Mr Bracewell could be clumsy with the wine. Once he had spilled almost a full chalice.

She let herself in past Ginger, tapping his shoulder to show he was welcome to stay put. She brought him out a bun, and milk in one of the tin picnic mugs, then put on the

kettle, called out hello to Charles over the music, although
or because she knew it made him teasy, then took the pastry
from the meat safe and rolled it out. Pastry work, like
kneading bread or prayer, was one of those activities that
made her remember her mother. She cut a little chink in the
circle she had rolled out to let the pie bird peep through and,
as she tucked the lid across the nicely stewed filling, remembered Mrs Ashbridge saying pastry was like a shy young
girl: it didn't do to overhandle.

Charles had the piano in his bedroom. They had only
managed to fit it in there by pushing his bed right into the
other corner beside his wardrobe. She had known the
arrangement was eccentric, that most people had their
pianos in sitting rooms or music rooms, but all she and
Charles had was their bedrooms and the kitchen. The
kitchen became a sort of sitting room when she wasn't eating or cooking or ironing, but there was simply no space
there for even the smallest upright she could find. Also, she
worried the often steamy atmosphere would send it out of
tune. Besides, she knew he liked it in his room, where it was
unambiguously his, and he could play for hours when the
mood was on him, which it often was. It was, she explained,
his inheritance as she had paid the deposit and first year of
instalments with the savings left by his father. It pleased her
that it was entirely her labour that fed, housed and clothed
him, but that it was Charlie, who would have been so proud
of him, who had paid for this outlandish ornament to their
otherwise simple life.

As for the lessons, Miss Bracewell gave him those in
exchange for Laura's doing her laundry and cleaning her

cottage one morning a week. (Mr Bracewell had unexpectedly married again, to a woman as fond of attention as he was, and his daughter had wisely made good her escape to a place of her own.) Charles knew about the laundry, though she took care never to dry or iron Miss Bracewell's undergarments when he might see them, but the cleaning she kept secret as he had a ferocious pride on him. The trips to Miss Bracewell's tiny house up in the town, with its watercolours and antiques and pretty walled garden were, she knew, a high spot of his week. From the first visit he made there, he had itemised, with the artless cruelty of childhood, the many ways in which it was superior to their tenement.

None of his cousins learned the piano, although plenty of them sang. She didn't want people thinking she was setting him up for some terrible disappointment later by giving him ideas above his likely station. All she dared hope for Charles was that he would be happy and safe, that no war should take him away and that he might have a job at a desk, using his brain, not one that might kill him or leave him ill or maimed.

She nudged open his bedroom door and set a tray with tea and bread and butter on his bedside table.

'Thank you,' he said, breaking off playing.

'I put the pie in,' she said. 'It'll be ready by six o'clock. I'll be finishing off downstairs. How's it coming? Have you done your homework?'

'I'll do that later. This is really hard.'

And he started the Bach piece again. He would drink the tea cold but at least it was there for him.

Outside, Ginger jumped up to let her pass.

'Don't stay there too late, Ginger,' she told him. 'Your father'll be worrying.'

Back in the washhouse she picked over the sheets and altar cloth. There was indeed a wine stain on the one and there were the usual stains on the other. As she soaked the wine stain briefly in her usual chloride of lime and soda mixture, she picked her way through Aggie's bedding, scrubbing gently at the stiffened or stained patches with a nicely dried bar of lavender soap and was briefly angry again at stupid Mrs Netley.

The Bible was full of references to stains and washing. She could not think of these marks as signs of sin; signs of human weakness, perhaps, and a challenge to a laundress sometimes, they were no less deserving of her best soap than the clumsily splashed altar cloth. Charles's playing had followed her in and she caught herself attempting to hum along with it, only it was too complex, and she could no more keep up with it than she could mimic a blackbird's song by whistling. Perhaps, after a while, Miss Bracewell would let him learn some dance music too?

PENTAMETERS – 1931

'In this morning's double period, I want you all to write a poem.'

There were groans around the class, especially from the back row, where the bigger, sporty boys all sat.

'Of course if you'd rather translate me two pages of Cicero . . .'

'Please, sir, no, sir,' someone said, and there was laughter.

There was often laughter in class, Charles had noticed, but it had nothing to do with affection or even amusement. It simply registered a kind of nervous relief.

'It must be at least twelve lines long. You may write on any of these themes.' Mr Sleep, who inevitably was nicknamed Weary, although his manner was always frighteningly alert and critical, used his chalk wiper to clean the blackboard, raising a little halo of dust about him. Then he wrote swiftly: 'Greed. Heroism. Regret.' 'I shall award marks for traditional rhyme schemes, terza rima, sonnet and so on, but I do not insist you use rhyme so long as the lines of your poem scan. Do you remember what I mean by scansion, Luke?'

Joe shuffled in the desk behind Charles, from where he would often, gratifyingly, nudge him for answers. 'Er, metre and so on, sir,' he offered.

'Metre and so on,' Mr Sleep repeated witheringly.

'Dactyls and trochees, sir,' another boy offered.

'Yes, quite, but I didn't ask you, Clarke.' Mr Sleep preferred the cricket and rugby players to the swots, even though it was a grammar school. Charles had to make a constant effort not to seem too keen.

Charles reached down to scratch an itch beneath his sock with a sharpened pencil. They all wore long socks, folded down just below the knee to show a regulation two stripes, and all wore flannel shorts and blazers. When he started at the grammar school and was taken for a photograph with Mother, Charles had been immensely proud of the uniform. The striped tie and cap he had glimpsed on Horwell boys around the town seemed the height of adult sophistication. A couple of years on and he detested them. The cap, in particular, was an invitation to rough, less clever boys to jeer and shout insults, and since puberty he hated walking around with bare knees. At least he was still relatively slight for his age. Bigger boys like Joe were straining out of their shorts, which were not designed with rugby player thighs in mind; Charles felt embarrassed on their behalf.

'Causley, how does a sonnet differ from a limerick?'

There was a young man from Australia, Charles thought. 'A limerick rhymes its first, second and last lines, sir, which are three feet long, and then has a second rhyme for its central couplet, whose lines are two feet long. A sonnet,' he said, thinking, *When, in disgrace with fortune and men's eyes* and trying to see it laid out on a page in his mind, 'has fourteen lines, rhymes them abab cdcd efef, then has a final couplet, gg. But—'

133

One of the big boys whinnied and received a withering glare. 'But?' Mr Sleep had never been seen wearing anything but a black suit. He was known to live with an equally severe sister out towards Callington so, unlike some of the masters, you never saw him around the town on a Saturday or in the holidays. He simply materialised at the school with his personal thundercloud.

'But,' Charles admitted, 'I'm afraid I've forgotten the required metre.'

'Shakespeare, boy. What's Shakespeare's favoured metre?'

Flights of angels sing thee to thy rest, Charles thought, counting off the beats on his fingers. 'Five, sir. Pentameter, sir.'

'Get there in the end, Causley. Head not completely full of your mother's soapsuds.'

There was the expected laughter.

'No, sir,' Charles said obediently.

'The best of today's offerings will win this crisp new copy of Shakespeare's immortal and often wildly misinterpreted sonnets. The author of the worst will be expected to memorise three of them over the weekend and recite them for our delectation on Monday. Any questions? No? Good. Off you go. You have your themes. You have your rules.'

Poetry appealed to Charles only for these bones that lay beneath it: metre and rhyme schemes, a system, something to unlock. But it was not where he saw himself. He didn't mind being called to recite it, because he had found he was a natural performer, but his secret self-image involved being brilliantly witty in a silk dressing gown in a way that rendered people helpless somehow. Not necessarily with laughter but certainly with awe.

Moving up to Horwell's Grammar from the National School, he had gone from being the senior boy known for never having been beaten by Daddy Lee, the headmaster, and called upon by him to play the harmonium at assembly, to being a scrawny boy of no sporting ability and therefore of no consequence in a much bigger crowd.

Life had changed in other ways as well. Mother and he had moved house from the tenement home he had always known, to a terrace all their own on Tredydan Road. It had a little garden backing on to the North Cornwall Line and, as though that weren't bustle enough, had a black-smith and all the traffic that attracted just next door. The privy was still outside – a chill visit on winter nights and frosty mornings – but there was a proper bath with taps and an Ascot over it, whose gassy firing up seemed to Charles the height of luxury. Mother no longer had to share laundry facilities with neighbours and had her own washing lines at the back, where she complained, charac-teristically, of smuts landing from passing trains when the wind was in the wrong direction.

Ginger lived a few houses along. His father worked on the railways and it was through him, Charles believed, that the house had become theirs to rent. Even though Mother wasn't a railway employee or the widow of one, some sort of favour had been called in or old obligation fulfilled. The town, which was coming to seem intolerably small to him and narrow minded, thrived on a network of such favours and obligations.

They had a front room, reserved for entertaining, and his piano was put there. He had tried to persuade Mother to call it the Music Room but she told him not to give himself airs and said he would have to stop his piano practice in there if ever she had company.

There was company quite often now, as though people had never called round before because they had felt awkward sitting in a thinly disguised kitchen. And Mother had taken in a lodger now that they had a spare bedroom, a young woman called Vera. Vera had a job typing invoices at the cattle auctioneers. Charles did his best to resent her at first, for her vivacity and her way of teasing him, and the scent she trailed behind her, which made his nose itch. The bathroom was haunted by her rose talcum powder and Dr White's towels and, even more mysteriously, her razor. If Mother used such things, she had always hidden them away, but it made her seem less feminine or simply older and unglamorous, which he resented on her behalf. Vera's femininity reached into other rooms, as flowers, both real and artificial, magazines and fur pieces, and the words to silly love songs, which she was forever singing under her breath, or at full voice if she thought to tease him.

He knew Mother thought Vera's presence was somehow good for him, had overheard her say as much to Aunt Em and Gwennie when she thought he wasn't listening. Puberty and its unnerving alterations had arrived as a private cataclysm Mother barely acknowledged beyond taking to washing his pyjamas once a week instead of once a fortnight, and having a quiet word with the barber, who then assured Charles that, in the absence of a father, he would teach him

136

how to shave *when the time came*. She also saw that he was confirmed, quite as though spending several Thursday evenings in confirmation classes with Mr Bracewell could halt the inevitable changes to come. There was just one excruciating evening, when confirmation was only a week away and they had finished working through the Creed one clause at a time, when Mr Bracewell sent the two girls in the class to talk to Mrs Bracewell in his drawing room, then spoke vigorously and bafflingly to Charles about the dangers of self-abuse and the importance of precautions.

'You have forty minutes left,' Mr Sleep announced. 'Then your masterpieces will be read aloud.'

Charles stared at what he had begun to write. It was, he hoped, in what he thought of as a poetic voice, part Tennyson, part *Hymns Ancient and Modern*. In his mind the city in its background was a *1001 Nights* version of Launceston, with the castle glorious, not a ruin, and the city walls impregnable. He wrote about a Jew counting his money, because Vera had told him that's what Jews did, and that they were untrustworthy and prone to doing immoral deals that tripped up trusting Christians. And he had read *The Merchant of Venice*. Mother had said Jesus and Mary were Jews, of course, and St Paul, but that they were different, and had changed, as though being a Jew was a phase you could put behind you. Like self-abuse. He had heard other boys talk about 'dirty Jews' and use other, harsher words for them but, so far as he knew, the nearest Jews lived safely in Exeter and Plymouth. In his head the Jew in his poem, counting his coins like a child with a broken-open piggy bank, was simply one of the many merchants of the town, cash drawer beside him, tidily inked ledger on his desk. In fact, in his head they probably weren't Jewish at all, but simply a shopkeeper. Unlike a lot of boys, he never had pocket money. Mother always said, 'If you want money of your own, you'll need to leave school and start working for it,' which they both knew wasn't fair as he had no choice in the matter. But money was never taken for granted and, from an early age, he had known, when asked to run errands for her, the exact value of the coins in his pocket. He had always known the town's shopkeepers guessed this, seeing him carefully doing sums in his head and weighing up the relative value of sausages and bacon. If he had always instinctively thought of them as the enemy, it wasn't entirely because of those early thumps from a butcher's son.

Since they both started at the grammar school, he found Joe had mysteriously become a sort of friend. Or, at least, not a person who threw his books in the urinals. Now he was a cricket and rugby star, he had less to prove and seemed to have adopted Charles as a harmless eccentric, and Charles had found that things he said in class often made him laugh. If he spoke up in class now, it was with the sense that Joe was his audience.

Probably because of the lack of girls there, who always seemed to be his natural supporters, the move to the grammar school had brought home to Charles the harsh truths that he was not popular and unlikely to become so. Popularity was not bestowed as a result of scoring well in tests, only in matches. Popular boys tended either to be handsome or built for battle and he was neither. Popular boys never wore glasses, and he was blind without them.

And, in a school where snobbery was rife, popular boys were never poor or on scholarships.

The fate to be dreaded was becoming one of the actively unpopular. These were usually what Miss Bracewell called 'unfortunate-looking' or unhygienic. Many such boys seemed incapable of keeping their uniform clean and tidy. This gave the masters a reason to mock or upbraid them for disrespecting the school, which in turn gave their class-mates a cue to attack them. He knew from Mother's often daunting example that his Christian duty was to stand with these outcasts or even try to befriend them and he was ashamed that his charity extended no further than never joining in the mockery or baiting but merely watch-ing, wincing inwardly from the sidelines, grateful the ugliness had passed him over for another scapegoat.

He had learned that the way for him to thrive was a stealthy one: to work hard yet draw no attention to him-self. The trouble was that there was an exuberance in him he could only imagine came from his father's family as there was none of it in Mother's hard-working, stoical kin. When he was sent to stay sometimes for a few magical days with Aunt Maggie in Trusham, he felt himself claimed by the streak of individualism in her and her siblings' eccentricities. But the side of him that liked to show off had a way of leaking out in the classroom, when he knew the answer to a question or couldn't bear to hear someone get something wrong. It came out outside the classroom too, in waspishness, so that the moments when he most wanted to draw admirers were usually those in which he drove people away.

Miss Bracewell understood. In her quietly singular way, she had divined his need of an audience at the same time as she spotted his musicality, but even she had under-estimated the stolidity of their community. 'When you get to the grammar school,' she used to say, 'you'll find your kindred spirits. You'll find your tribe.' But now he had been there a couple of years he felt more than ever an oddity.

There was only Ginger, who had started the previous September, being a year younger, but would be catching up fast as he was so clever. And it did not do to be too friendly towards younger boys, even your younger relatives. Charles was not even sure a spiritual kinship with Ginger was something to be desired. The boy was as faithful as a spaniel, even though Charles spoke cruelly to him more often than he was kind. Ginger's widowed father came to their church and Mother said Charles must be kind to Gin-ger because even she knew that people weren't. He had always been called Ginger, even in the National School, despite actually being a Gordon. But when Charles had commented on this and asked Mother why it was, she had pulled a face and muttered, 'Some stupid reason.' And yet even she called him Ginger. They all did.

Ginger was one of the unpopular boys, of course, his books regularly sent flying, but he seemed impervious, shrugging off teasing like bad weather. One of the reasons people picked on him was that it was well known he had kept house for his father since his mother's death. Charles had never said as much, but the idea of this fascinated him – a son doing the things for a father a wife usually did, baking him pies, washing his clothes and bed linen. He

knew Mother wanted the two of them to be friends –
evidently regarding motherless boys as far more needy
than fatherless ones – but her occasional complaints that
he didn't do half as much around the house as *poor Ginger*
did around his did not help the cause.

Safely away from school and out of its uniform, the two
of them would sometimes go for a country walk towards
Egloskerry or out past Werrington towards Holsworthy,
and during the summer they had often fallen into long chats
at the baths. But he would far rather have done either with
Joe, and at school he barely acknowledged Ginger, just as he
knew older brothers ignored younger ones. There was something about Ginger that made Charles feel unmasked, as
though Ginger's harmless chat shone an unwelcome light
on him. In church, though, they often sat in the same pew,
two half families coming together to resemble one. Recently
he had even asked Mother if she'd marry Ginger's father if
he asked. Her indignant response, telling him off for cheek
and saying Charles's father had been *husband enough for
her*, whatever that meant, suggested she had at least thought
about it as well.

He had begun to piece together thoughts about sex,
beyond the obvious farmyard facts of it, thanks to Vera.
Like him she visited the library at least twice a week but
she favoured titles in which passion, adultery and even
murder often featured, and would sometimes slip them
into his room before she returned them, knowing their
lurid vision of the world fascinated him as much as the
flickers of silent glamour they enjoyed at occasional film
shows in the town hall. The stories were often painfully

141

emotional, in ways that were almost unbearable. *Stella Dallas* affected him deeply and he read it over and over until Mother found it under his pillow and told Vera 'not to corrupt the boy' even though the book left him more baffled than corrupted. Finally he had asked Vera about it.

'Vera, you know *Stella Dallas*?'

'Yes . . .?' Vera gave him one of her teasing smiles. She was powdering her nose at the time, a process that usefully occupied her gaze so she wouldn't stare at him and see him blush. Mother didn't own a compact. It seemed to Charles to symbolise everything complicated and unknowable about girls and women. The seductive little click it made when she closed it was like the turning of a tiny gold key against his understanding.

'Well I don't understand. What is it she does that means she has to give up Laurel?'

'She's a—' Vera began, then checked herself. 'She's a bit like Ma Treloar. You know?'

'Ah yes,' he said, and went away just as mystified since Ma Treloar had felt no need to give up any of her children, who all had her surname as though she had made them all on her own just by wanting. Several, like Heppy and Tobey, had been at the National School with him but, though perfectly bright, had not come on to the grammar school but melted away, old before their time, to go into service.

'Five minutes more,' Mr Sleep said, walking slowly up the aisle between the desks. He always wore his black academic gown to class and Charles hated the musty smell it gave off as it swished by. He put down his pen and read his poem through one more time. It would have to do. It was,

142

he hoped, no better or worse than the ones being finished around him. He wanted it to be as irreproachable and just as dull as a tidy uniform.

He glanced to his right and saw a poem barely five lines long, full of crossings-out. He glanced the other way and was relieved to see another boy, like him, had found time to write a fair copy to make reading out easier, even though their poem, too, looked little longer than a limerick.

Reading round the class followed an invariable pattern, starting with the boy nearest the door and winding back to the boy nearest the radiator in the far corner. When they did Latin translation they followed this route, and when they read Shakespeare or history books. Only maths classes saw questions peppered across the class like unpredictable bullets. On this occasion Mr Sleep followed the usual route but made the torment worse by having each boy walk to his dais and read his poem from there, while he gave nothing away with his unvarying scowl and made cryptic notes in his ledger.

Shakespeare aside, Charles was not a great poetry reader, although he often read the hymn book discreetly during sermons as the verses there tended to be more interesting and dramatic when divorced from their tunes. But he knew the poems he was hearing were pretty terrible. Several had interpreted greed as gluttony and droned on about favourite food. Several were full of empty rhetorical questions. Several boys had metre that limped or tripped their readings up entirely and many of the rhymes on show were so bad they raised a laugh, at which the readers grinned too, reassured that they were indeed not at risk of being poets. Charles's turn came all too soon.

He approached the dais, took a breath, looked to Mr Sleep for the weary nod that said he should start, and read. He had to concentrate because his lines and sentences were quite long and he was careful not to gabble the way several boys had done. But nobody tittered or groaned and nobody cheered after. He returned to his desk in silence, feeling slightly dizzy from the attention and grateful it had moved on.

When they were all done there was not much time left, luckily, for Mr Sleep to tear their work apart the way he did when handing back essays. He said they were all to hand in fair copies by the end of the day and that for the most part their work had been poor, shoddy and 'as easily forgotten as your formless faces. Especially your disgraceful offering, Bailey, which was barely recognisable even as doggerel. You'll be reciting the first three sonnets from memory here on Monday.' There were loud cheers for poor Bailey, who grinned. Mr Sleep silenced them with a dusty hand. 'Just one of you has understood the challenge you were set and for that boy I am going to do something I have never done in my long career at the school. Causley, you get full marks, as well as a copy of the Shakespeare Sonnets. Very well done indeed, that man. Applause for Causley, boys. Very good. Yes, yes. That's enough.' And he swept out for the mid-morning break.

Usually Charles left the classroom after most, using tidying his desk as a pretext for letting the rowdy boys out first, but on this occasion he was mobbed, given back slaps and hair-ruffles and somehow swept out by the crowd quite as though he had scored the clinching try or thwacked

144

a cricket ball clear over the heads of the crowd at a match. Old Weary never gave top marks, yet somehow Causley had swayed him! As they moved along the corridor, other boys were told the story and his fame spread.

Even the headmaster heard and came over to shake his hand, having never even spoken to him before, and said, 'I gather congratulations are in order, Causley. Well done. Keep it up. We must print the poem in the school magazine.'

Ginger was fleetingly before him and said, 'Bravo, Charles,' embarrassingly using his first name, which nobody ever did in school time.

And then Joe came over. 'Well done,' he said. 'I never read poems, but can I read yours?'

'Of course,' Charles said, and let him carry off the fair copy to read during maths.

The fuss soon died down. Maths had its usual deadening effect on his confidence and spirits and only a couple of people mentioned the poem at lunch. Even routine tries were celebrated for longer than a top marks poem. But the news continued to spread because Mother had heard and welcomed him home with a proud hug and a lemon curd Victoria sponge. She also demanded to read the poem. Even as she was reading it, moving her lips as she did when reading required concentration, he registered an odd shame because she so wanted to say the right thing and didn't know the poem meant nothing to him. It had been an exercise, nothing more, no more imbued with honest feeling than a page of quadratic equations. He felt this even more excruciatingly when Vera insisted on reading it when she came home from work, and she repeated lines back at him and said, 'Very strong, that.'

And yet, making himself reread it on his bed that night, he saw in some way he was present in the poem, all his thoughts and feelings of that morning, about Ginger and Joe and popularity and *Stella Dallas* and how very much he did not want to live all his life in a small-minded, interfering place like Launceston. They had studied some basic codes in maths when starting algebra: substitution codes and so on. The poem was a piece of code, he realised. It didn't expose him directly, as writing a story or essay might, not like writing anything in the first person singular, but it locked his thoughts and feelings safely in a place where only those granted the key would ever access them.

NEW SUIT – 1933

It was extremely hard to keep secrets from Charles; he was far more observant than men usually were. Nothing escaped his notice: not a shoe in need of repair nor a loose label on an overcoat. They were not people who touched, it seemed, but he couldn't let Laura leave the house without reaching out to correct a collar that wasn't sitting right or picking a stray hair off her shoulder. His close observation made her almost nervous.

Laura wouldn't have minded had he not grown up so secretive himself. She had always believed that motherhood would guarantee her one person she knew as well as she knew herself, a loving confidant who told her all their thoughts and worries as she had done with Em when they were small. Since starting at the grammar school, however, or maybe even before that, Charles had begun to hide himself from her. Always good at tidying and cleaning his own room, he deprived her of any pretext to open his door, and she would never have opened his door when he was there without knocking first.

Before she got married to her chap and moved away, Vera had been a great help as she had grown up with a host of brothers. 'Once they start shaving,' she said, 'you'll know and hear nothing unless they're hungry or want something washed or mended.'

When Laura wrote to Maggie that she worried Charles was shutting her out, Maggie wrote a surprisingly forthright letter back saying, 'Thank heavens for that. You really don't want to know the things that go through a young man's mind, Laura. Besides, did you tell your mother anything at his age?' She had been quite right, of course. Laura had loved her mother dearly but perhaps more later in life than when growing up. She had certainly never confided in her, or in her older siblings. Em had briefly gone into service at fifteen and from then until Laura left for Teignmouth, Stanley had been the keeper of her secrets, such as they were, and had taken them with him to Canada and his early grave.

So, corrected by those who knew, she did her best not to fret when she suspected Charles was worrying about something and not telling her. He had a loyal friend in Ginger, who hung on his every word. The small age difference between them seemed to have lessened as they grew older. He had even a friend of sorts in Joe Luke, which she would never have predicted. She taught herself not to complain when Charles said that although he still came to church because he sang in the choir and enjoyed that, he wasn't sure he believed any more and reserved the right not to take Communion if the mood wasn't on him. She tried not to be querulous when he didn't want to come for a walk with her on a nice day, or chose to shut himself in his cold bedroom with one of his precious books rather than sit with her when she had gone to the trouble and expense of lighting a fire.

She took his smart new suit off its hanger in her wardrobe, where she had been hiding it for weeks now, folded it carefully with some tissue paper she had saved especially, then wrapped it in some smart striped paper she had found at Brimmell's. Her slyness in taking his latest measurements to Treleaven's, so the tailor there could ensure the fit was perfect, had almost shocked her.

She chose a dark, hard-wearing worsted with a nice texture to it and, for the cut, nothing too fashionable, lest it date. She paid for it, as had long been her intention, with the very last of Charlie's legacy, which had been quietly earning interest in a savings account. They would not know themselves with Charles finally out of school and earning as well, and being paid considerably more than her, even on his starting salary.

She had kept that news a secret as well, which had been even harder than the suit secret because the excitement of it made her feel like a boiling kettle whenever he was around. She had never known what it was to have a husband bring home a pay packet and had always listened with an uneasy mix of envy and curiosity when married women let slip details of being given 'housekeeping' and even 'pin money' from their husbands' wages. Even more interesting were those who expected to be handed the entire pay packet and then counted out of that spending money for the husband. Certainly this seemed the norm among her siblings in their marriages; the husbands were the primary earners but the wives ran the household finances, settling bills, placing orders and usually being better informed than their men, especially now that times were so hard, of what the essentials of life should cost.

As it was an important day, effectively the start of his life as a man, Laura had splashed out on a non-essential and treated them to a shop-bought cherry cake, one of his favourites, which she had gussied up with a nicely tart lemon glaze. The Padstow train pulled out of the station and she glanced instinctively at her watch and then at the kitchen clock to check they agreed. Now that the summer holidays were starting, the North Cornwall line would soon be busy with visitors heading to the coast. They often stretched their legs between the two train journeys, walking up the hill from the stations to look at the castle ruins, consulting guidebooks and exclaiming loudly in harsh, unfamiliar accents and pointing, or even laughing, at the locals quite as though they were visiting a zoo. Only the other day an upcountry woman had pointed a camera at Laura as she lugged her laundry basket down the hill from Miss Bracewell's and told her to stand still for a moment. Told her, not asked her.

'I'm sorry,' Laura had muttered. 'Basket's far too heavy for that,' and the woman had laughed and said, 'Oh, I *love* the way you *speak*!'

Aggie would have thought of some sharp retort, but Laura just stumbled past, hot in the face.

She set the kettle to boil again, moved the teapot to the shelf at the back of the range so it could warm. It was hot out. Perhaps she should have bought ginger beer instead? But Charles was no longer a child. And why on earth was she so nervous? Almost jumpy. She realised she was still wearing her housecoat. She took it off, hung it on its peg by the brushes behind the kitchen door and was just smoothing out her dress when she heard his voice as he let himself in. Ginger was with him.

'Hello,' she said, meeting them in the hall. 'Hello, Ginger.'

'Hello, Mrs Causley.'

'You two sit in the front room and I'll bring tea in.'

'We can sit in the kitchen, Mother. It's only Ginger, not the mayor.'

'It's a special occasion,' she said. 'You go in there, Ginger, and pay him no heed.'

Charles opened his mouth to object on principle, but she saw him relent as he relished a special occasion and might be pressed to play something on the piano. It was funny that she knew him so well in a host of small ways and yet found whole chambers of his nature closed against her.

She had bought a brown loaf along with the cake. She continued to bake their white bread but had never mastered the art of producing a brown loaf as fluffy as the baker's, so brown had long been their weekend treat. Sure enough, as she was setting cups and saucers on the tray beside the cake and plates she heard Charles strike up a dance tune. She sliced and buttered half of the loaf now, seeing that Ginger was there, and spread the slices out on a plate. She didn't have the patience to keep up with the latest songs the way Charles did, but she recognised this as one she had heard several times recently. They couldn't afford to keep buying records like some people, although they had a wind-up portable gramophone her brother Dick had given her when he and Mabel upgraded to a fancier electric one in a mahogany cabinet. She much preferred having Charles play the piano, not least because she didn't have to keep getting up out of her chair to wind him up or turn him over. He picked up the latest tunes as sheet music, often borrowed from friends, and had only to play them through a few times to have them off by heart. It was a gift he had.

Ginger was standing behind the piano stool as she entered. He had one hand on Charles's shoulder but took it off seeing her come in. Charles broke off playing and they both sat expectantly at the table as she sat across from them and cut slices of cake while waiting for the tea to brew.

'Cherry cake!' Charles exclaimed. 'And you iced it too. What's the special occasion?'

'The end of school, of course,' she said. 'Did you all celebrate?'

'We sang the school song at Assembly,' Charles said lugubriously.

'Nothing else? Didn't the headmaster make a speech to send you on your way?'

'Oh, yes,' said Ginger, 'but he's always doing that.'

She poured their tea and passed them bread. Ginger thanked her. He had lovely manners but then the poor lad had been standing in for his dead mother for years and was probably used to smoothing the way for his father socially. Douglas was a nice enough man but quiet to the point of awkwardness.

'And then we had our end-of-term marks,' he added.

'How did you do?'

'Ginger came top,' Charles said.

'Well done. That's quite something when you think you're nearly a year younger than most of that group.'

'Well I have to work hard. I want to get to medical school.'

'Good for you. No such dreams for Charles.'

'I have dreams, Mother.'

'Yes, but not practical ones. Nothing that'd pay the bills.'

'Yes, well . . .' Ginger put in loyally. 'Charles is good at things other than science.'

'Indeed he is,' she agreed, remembering it was Charles's big day. 'Help Ginger to a slice of cake, Charles,' she said. 'I just need to fetch you something.'

Too late, she regretted the silly touch of wrapping the suit up like a present when it was, after all, what he'd be wearing for work. She had not forgotten his terrible disappointment on his fifteenth birthday as he unwrapped the practical woollen dressing gown she had bought him in place of the silk one she knew he wanted, like no other fifteen-year-old in town.

She did her best to set the parcel on the table beside him as though it was just another plate of bread and butter.

'Is it your birthday?' Ginger asked. 'I didn't know.'

'It's not my birthday,' Charles told him rather sharply, and looked across the table at her as she poured them all more tea. 'You know very well.'

'Well, don't keep us all in suspense,' Laura said, nervously adding, 'It doesn't have one of those silly fashionable

153

cuts like Jimmy Cagney's that will date while there's still wear in it.'

Charles looked across at Ginger, seeking an audience in his pain. 'She always does that,' he said. 'Spoils the surprise.'

'Sorry,' Laura said. 'It's the tension. Just open it.'

'Oh, very well,' he said, and opened the wrapping the way she had taught him, carefully, so that the paper could be flattened and ironed and used again.

'Very smart,' he said carefully.

'Mr Treleaven had all your measurements but you'd better check. He said they can always alter it if need be.'

He stood, took off his school blazer and pulled on the new suit jacket, seeming to age five years in the process.

'Oh, Charles,' Laura sighed. 'You look so grown up! It fits perfectly. Bend your arms.'

He bent his arms at the elbows, revealing just enough cuff.

'Perfect,' she said.

'So why a suit now?' Ginger asked.

'Yes, Mother. Why a suit now?'

She felt herself smile at the relief of finally unburdening herself of secrets. 'You've a job,' she said. 'I got you a proper grown-up desk job working for Mr Finn.'

'The builders' merchant,' Charles said.

'No, the undertaker's. Yes, of course the builders' merchant. He'll pay twelve and six a week, more than I make, even for your starting wage, and he's said you needn't start until Monday week so you can have a whole week of summer holiday rather than jump straight into it.'

'So, you're not carrying on at school after all?' Ginger asked.

'Of course he isn't, Ginger. Whatever for? It's not as though he's burning to study engineering or to be a doctor like you, and this house needs a man who earns his keep. And you are a man, now you're nearly sixteen. Oh, Charles, I'm so proud of you. Mr Finn knew exactly who you were from the choir, of course, and said you were a *very bright, polite boy* and exactly what he was looking for to deal with orders and invoices. Aren't you happy? Charles?'

But Charles had snatched up the suit trousers and his blazer and walked swiftly from the room. There was a brief thunder of shoes on stairs before his bedroom door overhead was closed with an unmistakable slam.

'Should I go after him?' Ginger asked softly after a moment.

'Best not,' she told him. 'That room's private. Nobody goes in without an invitation.'

'Ah. Lovely cake, Mrs Causley.'

'Thank you, Ginger. It's only store-bought but it's his favourite. Another slice?'

'Better not. I should be getting Father's supper ready,' he added, but didn't leave, lining up the cake fork on his plate just so. 'Did he not know he was leaving school and starting work, then?'

Laura sighed. 'Well, Ginger, I thought he did. He's never spoken about staying on. He's never talked about university.'

'Maybe he's been telling you in his head just like you've been telling him about the job so often that you both felt you'd had the conversation? That often happens to me. My head is a noisy place.'

'You're a good boy, Ginger.'

He stood, clearly uncertain how to respond to what she'd said. 'Well . . .' he said.

'You must get on,' she told him. 'And so should I. I'm sorry about Charles. It was good to see you all the same.'

And to her astonishment he gave her a very quick peck on the cheek, light as a bird, and let himself out.

She stacked the tea things back on to the tray, took them to the kitchen and paused there after washing her hands at the sink, as for one awful moment she thought she might be about to cry. But the feeling passed, with just a brief stinging in the tip of her nose like a threatened sneeze that came to nothing. She gathered up her empty hamper and headed out and up the hill.

Miss Bracewell lived in an elegant little house in the heart of the oldest part of town, a stone's throw from the one surviving medieval gateway. It was like the doll's house of a little girl's dreams, with a neatly clipped pocket hand-kerchief of a garden beyond its white painted railings and a pretty fanlight over the front door with a lantern in its middle. Charles no longer took lessons with her because she said she had taught him all she knew, but he went to play duets with her sometimes. Laura continued to do her laundry, though, because she liked her. She had felt a little sorry for her, too, ever since her father had left . . .

When Charles called to play duets he would use the front door but Laura preferred to use the tradesman's entrance. The land fell away steeply behind the house towards Angel

Hill, allowing for a second, more private garden. The tradesman's door gave on to this and a brick path that led past a few gnarled fruit trees to Miss Bracewell's kitchen and what estate agents called Other Offices, which lay in a lower ground floor at the house's back.

There was a peremptory bark as she closed the garden gate. Miss Bracewell's life was ruled by her imperious Pekinese, Lady Shonagon, who invariably sat on an old silk cushion in one of the streetward windows, disdainfully judging the human passers-by and growling at any dog or cat who dared pass before her. For some reason she had always liked Laura and Charles, or accepted their homage at least. Sometimes she even greeted Laura with a sort of dance, alternately dragging back her front paws and kicking out her rear ones as though rearranging imaginary snow.

Several months before, amid suitable drama and awe-struck murmurs, she had been delivered of an appropriately small and exclusive litter. All the puppies had swiftly found homes and when Laura had last met her, Miss Bracewell had been, by her cool standards, almost emotional at having just handed over the last.

Laura let herself into the outside washhouse, where Miss Bracewell only did the most basic laundry herself, boiling up what she called duster soup in there and, Laura assumed, washing and drying her stockings, which Laura had never encountered. As always, the laundry had been neatly folded into a basket. She transferred it, piece by piece, to her hamper, writing it all down in her notebook as usual. Then she went to let herself in at the kitchen, thinking at least to say hello as a courtesy if Miss Bracewell were nearby.

To her surprise one of the three puppies was shut in there. He immediately let out a little squeak, for all the world like a child's toy, and ran across to greet her, first doing a version of his mother's occasional dance, then tugging at the lace on one of Laura's shoes.

'Well, you little scamp! What are you doing here again?' She set down her hamper and he immediately jumped on top of it to get closer to her. So she sat on one of the wooden chairs and he jumped on to her lap and settled down there, facing outwards, suddenly calm as though her lap had been all he was waiting for.

There was another peremptory bark followed by Miss Bracewell's soft voice saying, 'Now, my lady, please!' She called her that: 'my lady', quite as though she were the little dog's servant, not its mistress. She had explained once that the real life Lady Shonagon had been a lady-in-waiting to an empress but quite grand in her own right and a famous writer. Charles had borrowed a translation of *The Pillow Book* from the library but Laura had done no more than glance at it, fearing, from the title, that it might prove indecent. Miss Bracewell could be startlingly broadminded.

Miss Bracewell let herself into the kitchen, swiftly closing the door against Lady Shonagon, who could be heard growling on the landing above. The puppy remained on Laura's lap.

'Oh, Mrs Causley, look. He's chosen you!'

'I thought you'd homed them all,' Laura said.

Miss Bracewell sank into the other chair. Normally spry, she looked wrung out. 'I had. And all was well but then it turned out Wang had taken against the husband.

Possibly Mrs Felstead's fault for letting him sleep in their bedroom. Apparently every time Mr Felstead came to bed, Wang would growl and bark and finally he bit him, so that was that.'

'You'd never think to look at him. Butter wouldn't melt.'

Wang turned his liquid eyes on her, coyly cuffing one of his tasselled ears with a paw.

'As I say, he's chosen you. Evidently he had not chosen Mr Felstead. Pekinese are imperial dogs, very haughty and particular. Their sincerity can be daunting. And that's the trouble.'

'What is?'

'It's Lady Shonagon. You'd think a mother would be happy to have her son return to the fold, but she's furious. Mrs Causley, would you like a ginger beer? Non-alcoholic and so refreshing. I'm having one.'

'That would be lovely.'

Miss Bracewell fetched two of the familiar earthenware bottles from a crate in her pantry. The ginger beer was delicious. Brewed locally by Eyre's, it was not a thing Laura drank regularly as she worried the sugar would make her stouter than she was already, but she associated it with treats and picnics. She took a second sip and remembered how Charlie used to sink their bottles in a stream to chill.

She wasn't aware she had sighed but suddenly Miss Bracewell asked, 'Is it a problem you'd like to share with me?'

'It's nothing really,' Laura said. 'I'd planned a little celebration for Charles finally leaving school and getting a job and it didn't go off as I'd hoped.'

'He's left school?'

159

'Yes. You're the second person today to sound surprised about that.'

'But he's so bright that I assumed . . .' Miss Bracewell let her words trail off. 'It's really no business of mine.'

Lady Shonagon barked again closer to, and scratched twice at the kitchen door. Wang sat up on Laura's lap and barked back.

'Oh, do be quiet, both of you,' Miss Bracewell called. 'I'm at my wits' end.'

'Would it help, Miss Bracewell, if I took him in? Just until you can find a new home for him?'

'Are you serious?'

'Yes.' Laura looked down at the little creature on her lap, who now had his chin on her wrist. 'The house has felt a bit empty since dear Jack died and Vera moved out. And . . . And I think it might help.'

'For Charles not to be the only pebble on the beach, you mean?'

'In a way. But it would probably do me good as well. Do they need much exercise, though?'

'Heavens, no. It's not like having a springer spaniel or a pointer. What they need is company and attention.'

'And what do you feed them?'

'His mother has about half a lamb's heart a day. I just braise them until tender with a little stock, then chop them up. Always have fresh water down for him, of course, and do watch out for him in hot weather. They can find it very hard to cool down once they overheat.'

'Of course. Is he house-trained yet?'

'Oh, yes. He's quite clean. He'll make it very clear if he needs to go out.'

'You must let me know if Mrs Felstead changes her mind.'

'Mr Felstead won't.'

'I'll bring him to visit when I call back with the laundry.'

'Best not, Mrs Causley. My lady has made it quite clear they must have separate kingdoms . . .'

Laura had finished her ginger beer so Miss Bracewell fetched her the puppy's delicate lead – a thin strap of plaited tan leather – far smarter than the spliced rope one that had always done for Jack – and so Laura took her leave. Luckily the laundry load wasn't large so she could hold the hamper across her shoulders with one hand and Wang's lead by the other.

Jack had always been Charlie's dog, even when Charlie was ill, walking with Laura only on sufferance, and she had felt a little shy alone with him as she might have done with any male friend of his. Making her way back down the hill with Wang, stopping to introduce or explain him to people she met on the way, she felt quite different. She was protective and a little defensive too. She knew people were amused at the sight of a largeish working woman being led along by a self-possessed, grand little dog, but found she didn't care. She knew, as Charles almost certainly would, that people found his name smuttily suggestive, especially when she explained that it was the Chinese for monarch. (She settled on always remembering not to add to the accidental ribaldry in this context by saying 'monarch' not 'king'.)

161

Had they been friends of the kind to use first names, she would have told Miss Bracewell how worried she was that she had done the wrong thing for Charles, tying him down when she should perhaps have been setting him free, how she increasingly worried that he was growing into the sort of young man whom a small town like Launceston could never make happy. She might even have confessed her fear that a secret, small-minded part of her had wilfully ignored the hints that he wanted to carry on at school and was clipping his wings to punish him for wanting to leave her. She had said none of this, of course, because they were Miss Bracewell and Mrs Causley, client and laundress, but something in the giving of the dog, the giving disguised as grateful acceptance of a favour, made her feel that they had in fact had the conversation and that Miss Bracewell had both understood and offered her a true friend's comfort.

TRUNKS – 1938

As was usually the case in hot weather, the water in the Jubilee Pool had turned a bright emerald green. Charles had swum earlier. The water had been deliciously cold but quite soupy and he could smell the pondy traces it had left on his skin. A midday train passed up the valley towards Padstow, sending a line of white smoke puffing up beyond the pool's high wall. Soon they would hear bells striking noon. On the grass to his right Ginger fiddled with the contrasting belt on his new swimming trunks. He had sent off for them from a catalogue and claimed he worried they were too sheer, although he was obviously proud of the effect.

'You mean too revealing?' Charles had asked, when Ginger insisted on modelling them for him in his bedroom. 'They are, fairly.'

'They're made of something called Lastex. They're meant to cling,' Ginger insisted. 'They do on Johnny Weissmuller. But I don't want to be indecent.'

One of the small ways Charles had marked financial independence had been finally buying a pair of trunks not knitted by his mother. They were nothing as sleek or flashy as Ginger's striped pair, being in a serviceable navy with a waistband that covered his belly button and legs that reached to mid-thigh, but they kept their shape when wet and never slipped down unexpectedly the way the knitted ones had done.

To Charles's left, Joe sighed and turned a page of *Homage to Catalonia*. Charles had discovered Orwell through someone in the Left Book Club, a boy from school who had been laid off at the printing works and been trying in vain to stir up some kind of direct action among Launceston's barely unionised workforce since. They had read all the Orwell they could find, Joe even talking about wanting to run away to fight for the socialists, although he couldn't speak Spanish or Catalan, and had never been further afield than Bigbury Sands, where an aunt had a cottage. More than any of them Joe seemed tied, doomed almost, as the son of a thriving local business. He read the books in secret, often here at the pool on their precious days or half-days off.

Joe sighed again, scratched absently at his chest hair. Charles's chest went in where Joe's and even Ginger's went out. He had complained about this once to Mother, who scoffed and said it was worse for girls. A girl with no chest might as well just give up.

'Give up what?' Charles had asked, but she had only scoffed again and said, 'You know very well,' while brushing a crumb off her own impressive bosom.

Joe sighed a third time. 'Right-oh,' he said. 'Quick dip to cool off before work.' He tossed the book back on to his towel, crossed the grass to the pool and dived in with a lack of hesitation Charles could never muster, particularly when the water was so murky.

'You hang on his every move,' Ginger said lightly.

'I do not.'

'Charles, I know you better than you know yourself. When he was scratching just now, your mouth could have caught flies.'

'Piffle.'

Charles turned a page and promptly lost his place because he had only turned it for effect. He was appalled it was that obvious. Familiarity and friendship had done nothing to dim his . . . this thing he would not name even to himself.

He was reading Auden, although poetry was not really his thing, because Ginger had urged him to.

'What do you think?' Ginger asked.

'It's all right. He can write.'

Actually it was a revelation. Compared to any poetry they had read in school, Tennyson and such, Auden wrote like a man speaking. His tone was direct, conversational and witty, yet the poems managed not to be doggerel or that dread thing, comic verse. It was so unlike the poetry Charles had read before that he kept catching himself reading it for pleasure and then would pull himself up short and turn back a page or two to make himself reread analytically. He was intrigued by the conjuring trick and wanted to see how it was done.

Charles had written several plays now, one of which had been published by a firm specialising in the big market among amateur companies for one-act works with single sets. He had not dared tell a soul yet in case it didn't happen, but a radio producer had asked him to send scripts to the BBC for consideration. He knew there was a barely disguised version of himself in everything he had written to date: a sharp-tongued young man who played the piano and was not all he seemed. He also recognised that his work to date was artificial. Set in a fantasyland of Kensington bohemia, a place he had no more experienced than he had the South Pacific, a world of artists and people who spoke about art and passion, not people who spoke about the price of skirt or skirting board. He hoped they were witty but when a long day of making out triplicate invoices for bricks and cement and gravel had left his out-look bleak, he admitted they were dishonest. Auden seemed as honestly present on the page as Donne or Pepys. Charles could only imagine writing in such a revealing way if life were quite different, if he lived in New York or Berlin.

He was aware of Joe returning from his swim and standing over them, briefly blocking out the light as he towelled himself dry, laying confident claim to other people's physical space as Charles could never do. Charles was determined not to look at him, to prove Ginger wrong.

'I'll see you both at the dance tonight, then,' Joe said.

'Oh. Are you coming?' Ginger asked.

'Ann'd kill me if I didn't. Though of course I'd rather stay home and read. Course I'm coming. You?'

'Sure,' Ginger said. 'Someone has to dance with all the poor Janes and Joans pining after Charles.'

'Shut up, Ginger. Work hard, Joe.' Charles let himself look up in time to see Joe finish towelling his hairy armpits before heading indoors. They were all scrupulously mod-est about changing in the little, cobwebby changing cabins.

It was only on trips to the beach – to Widemouth or Crackington – that Charles was reduced to that tantalising, silly dance of tweaking pants up damp legs under a sandy towel, with which Joe and Ginger never bothered.

'Plans for the rest of the day?' Ginger asked Charles. 'Children are already arriving.' They were agreed that children greatly detracted from the pool's quiet, manly pleasures, which was why they either came there first thing or half an hour before it closed at dusk.

'I told Mother I'd walk with her and Wang. She complains she never sees me.'

'Doesn't she see you every day?'

'Yes but . . .'

'Couldn't you walk with her tomorrow afternoon? I thought I'd take my swimming things to Plymouth and enjoy the Lido for a bit. And go to the bookshop, of course. There'd even be time for a slice of cake at Goodbody's before you had to be back here.'

Charles was tempted. His supremely tedious job at Finn's was only made bearable by regular escape, either mentally, through the still novel experience of the Tower Cinema, where they watched everything shown, not uncritically but nonetheless with greed, or through shutting himself away in his room to write or read, or physically, in long walks (ideally without Mother and panty Wang) or his occasional evening job as pianist to a local dance band.

This last threw him into the company of women his own age, as five of the band's eight musicians were girls, which was interesting and educative. It saw them called to hotel ballrooms and village halls from Callington to

Padstow. It created the illusion of an active social life, even though in practice he was sitting at a range of often battered pianos watching other people have a social life and, through the occasional booking at a hunt ball or a private house grand enough to entertain on such a scale, gave him a deeply provincial version of what his mother mockingly called his 'silk dressing gown life'.

Going to Plymouth, a proper city, was a pleasure apart. Not only did it have a museum and art gallery, and bookshops and libraries large enough to browse in without some assistant pestering to know what you wanted, but there were department stores that made a good fist of impersonating the ones in Hollywood films, with glittering escalators and lifts and revolving doors. Best of all, every step away from its station into its bustling heart was a step nearer anonymity, a state that was still a precious thrill after growing up in a place where everyone was known. In Launceston locals couldn't relax on meeting a new person until they had *placed* them, reassuring themselves the stranger was not strange at all, being Boy So-and-So's cousin. To live and work there was to know yourself constantly observed and reported on.

'It's not sinister,' Mother would say. 'Curiosity's normal.'

'It's oppressive,' Charles would retort.

To which she'd smack right back with, 'It's human nature.'

'I'm not sure,' he told Ginger, because he had never ventured as far as the city's Lido and wasn't sure he liked the idea of appearing in even a shop-bought swimming costume in the sophisticated city. He went to the city to become someone else temporarily, anybody else, not to be irreducibly his pale, concave-chested self.

'Let's let your mother decide,' Ginger said. 'It'll be like consulting the oracle at Delphi. If there's even a whisper of unhappiness you can stay to walk with her, and I'll go alone.'

'Oh, but you need someone to keep an eye on you,' Charles said.

'Which is just what I'm counting on her saying. Your mother likes me.'

'Yes,' Charles said. 'It's very galling. I've tried telling her you're not the blue-eyed, daddy's boy she takes you for, but that only makes her like you more.'

A year ago now, he and Ginger had experienced what the girls in the band called 'a moment'. Looking back, he now realised Ginger had engineered the situation from the start. Drawing Charles up to his bedroom on the pretext of offering to play him some new dance records he had brought back from a trip to relatives in Bristol, he persuaded him to hold him close to demonstrate the steps of the foxtrot and then had taken advantage of the moment to kiss him full on the lips while doing things with his tongue Charles was fairly sure never happened on screen to Claudette Colbert. Charles had never kissed anyone before so went along with it for a moment or two before saying they should stop at once, that it was a sin and against the law and everything. Ginger said yes, of course it was and he didn't know what had come over him. And then they had gone to evensong as it was Feast Sunday and they were both singing. But ever since then his manner towards

Charles had altered subtly, as though they shared an understanding, quite as though they shared a secret, though the secret was all Ginger's and Charles was merely keeping it for him. Most of the time he chose to ignore it, maintaining a lifelong practice of treating Ginger as a sort of necessary irritant, like a moth or daddy-long-legs. But just occasionally, when he and Ginger were unobserved by people who knew them, Charles caught himself entering into Ginger's delusion that they were alike, and the effect could be as pleasantly giddying as one of the less violent funfair rides.

Mother was ironing curtains when they let themselves in, Sunday's Communion bread rising on the shelf at the back of the range. She was oppressively industrious, working through a list of tasks around the house when it wasn't one of the days when she took in paid work for other people. If ever Charles had come back during the day and found her sitting down and doing nothing, he'd have assumed she was unwell. Even when she did sit, after supper had been washed up and crockery dried and put away and the kitchen swept of any crumbs Wang hadn't licked up, her hands could not abide idleness so there would be a pile of darning to work through or a knitting task to progress. She loved reading but regarded it as an indulgence for after she had gone to bed, which made him feel guilty for having passed judgement on her reading choices all too often.

Once Wang had gone through his usual performance of barking then doing a stately dance of apology, Laura greeted Ginger fondly as usual and asked after his father and the sciatica that had been troubling him. He complimented her on her thoroughness in washing curtains – a thing it had never occurred to him to do, then slyly asked if she could possibly spare Charles to come to Plymouth with him as there were things he'd promised to show him in the city's art gallery.

'Of course,' she said, always glad when Charles spent time with Ginger rather than Joe, or even the girls from the band, whom she thought 'high spirited', which was Mother-code for easy. 'Charles and I can walk tomorrow afternoon. Supper's only a chop, Charles, so it can keep till you're back. Give me your wet swimming things.'

'Actually Ginger promised to show me the Lido,' Charles said.

'Really?'

'After Charles has shown me the Turners in the museum.'

'Oh, but your towels will be wet.'

'Mother, it's fine. It's a hot day. We can dry them on the luggage racks.'

'Can I bring you back anything?' Ginger asked her.

'No, bless you, Ginger. I've got all I need up the hill here. But you boys have fun. Hurry now and you'll still catch the quarter-to.'

As Charles had suggested, they spread their towels and swimming trunks to dry across a couple of the overhead luggage racks. It was a glorious day and there was nobody around them to complain about smuts blowing in, so they opened the windows around them wide and their end of the carriage soon swirled with late summer scents of ripe barley and mown grass. They both fell to reading, but

Charles was soon distracted, first by wondering at how travelling deeper into Cornwall felt like an adventure, but heading east, in his mind at least, and crossing the Tamar into England always felt like escape. Then he was distracted by the repetitive rhythm of engine and carriage rattles and fell to pondering Auden again.

Perhaps the trick was not to think of poetry in terms of heightened or special language? Perhaps one had only to recognise the natural metre in so much spoken prose? *We're going to Plymouth in the train*, he thought. *We're GOing to PLYmouth IN the TRAIN. Not a CARE in the WORLD if it DOESn't RAIN!* Perhaps, he thought, he could attempt a verse drama? It could be just another domestic comedy, about ordinary people for a change, farmers and fishermen and builders' merchants' clerks, but the difference would be to have them all speak in verse, only in such a way that it sounded like everyday prose. You'd only know for sure it was verse if you saw it written down. But then, what on earth would be the point?

'Terrible about Spain,' Ginger said suddenly. 'How were the refugees?'

Charles had recently been in Delabole, where a group of local churches had worked together to take in women and children fleeing the Civil War.

'Desperate,' Charles said. 'Frightened and isolated and short of clothes. And a lot of them in shock and mourning, of course. It felt so useless that only one of us, a teacher from Wadebridge, had any Spanish, so we mostly spoke to them in slow English, as though they were simple.'

'Joe still wants to go and fight.'

'Yes. He won't, though. Too cowed by his father, or too dutiful. He'd have gone by now, if he were going.'

'Hmm.'

'I reckon his father thinks Franco's doing a good job.'

'You'd probably find half the Chamber of Commerce does. They admire Hitler too, though only among friends.'

It was an accepted litany between the three of them that it was impossible to be properly, actively left wing in Launceston, that liberal was as left as Cornwall dared lean, such were its feudal loyalties and civic pride. They read of men and women whose writing or work they admired actually joining the Communist Party as of people walking on the moon. That was part of the relief, Charles realised, in coming to Plymouth: you looked out of the carriage window and saw not a castle and church on a hill and dirty factories below, but valleys and hillsides covered in thousands of terraced houses housing thousands of workers and voters. In a city like this it was easier to believe that things might change and that the tenacious will of ordinary men and women might bring it about, by ballots and votes and, if necessary, by industrial action.

Sometimes he felt nothing in Launceston would ever change; the grandsons of butchers and railwaymen and tanners would do what their grandfathers had done. A world war seemed to have changed little, from what Mother said, and neither had a stock market collapse and widespread redundancies. From what he could gather from the bookkeeper at Finn's, the business was starting to borrow more than it took in. He hadn't breathed a word to Mother yet, but he had guilty fantasies in which he came home, final pay packet in hand, to announce that he had no option but to seek steadier employment in Bristol, or even London.

Charles and Ginger had certain rituals on visits to Plymouth. One was always to call in at the City Art Gallery on arrival, as it was close to the station and held such treasures it always made Charles feel a little as he imagined pilgrims did on visiting a great cathedral. And they always called in at the same North Hill tea rooms for tea and a slice of cake. This meant that the unfamiliar thrill of then walking down crowded streets with multiple vehicles and wide pavements, gawping at the latest fashions in huge window displays or admiring cars and gadgets that had yet to cross the Tamar was heightened by the hum of sugar coursing through their veins. Even without cake, Ginger was excited by crowds. He liked playing games like Beard, where the first one of them to pass ten men with beards of a given colour was the winner and got to pronounce a forfeit on the other. Possibly because of his nickname, he was fascinated by redheads and would appal Charles by engaging them in conversation, brazenly playing the role of shy country bumpkin new to the city. Once he had made them both almost hysterical with nerves and laughter when he devised a game whereby they had to follow a redhead wherever he went until he happened to pass a second redhead they could follow instead.

Today his quarry was more specific.

'Look, Charles,' he said as they emerged from Goodbody's. 'Sailors!'

'Well, yes. Plymouth is a major naval base, Ginger.'

'Yes, but lots. Look.'

He gestured to where a quartet of sailors was strolling ahead of them, arms around one another's shoulders, which only emphasised the snugness of their uniforms. There were, Charles saw, sailors everywhere today, shopping like tourists, staring up at high buildings, clustering at the doors of pubs.

Ginger darted ahead before Charles could catch his sleeve and, in his sprightliest manner, engaged the foursome in conversation. They surrounded him as he chatted, which Ginger clearly relished. Charles saw him mime reluctance with a shrug and point at Charles, and fancied he saw the four glance at him as they might at some killjoy landlady before they entered a pub, unable to coax Ginger with them. Ginger darted back.

'There are three ships in,' he said. 'Destroyers. They say we'll find most of the crews up on the Hoe so it's lucky that's where we were going anyway.'

He didn't explain why sailors rather than policemen or men with golden moustaches were suddenly that day's game, in both senses, and this was a relief. When things were left in the realm of the implied, Charles did not feel compelled to pass judgement and assume a contrary position on moral grounds.

Sure enough, there were more and more sailors on view the nearer they came to the Sound. Their blue and white uniforms were so distinctive, so athletic and cheerful compared to the bagginess and predominantly drab colour of men's suits, that seeing them en masse gave the illusion that the streets were brighter, even decorated. The happiness of the sailors on being ashore again, too, was infectious. He wondered how it must feel to live in a place subject to such friendly invasions. The nearest Launceston had was the start of the tourist season, but the tourists were often fractious and bad tempered after long journeys, and Launceston's castle inevitably less spectacular than many had been led to expect.

Ginger smiled broadly at a huge sailor with tattooed forearms like furry logs, who smiled broadly back because Ginger's essential innocence had that effect on the most unexpected people.

'They're not just happy to be ashore,' Charles said, demanding Ginger's attention as he was still looking over his shoulder at the one with the arms. 'I think they're enjoying each other's company. You'd think after months at sea they'd be sick of each other or racing off to find women, but just look at them taking such pleasure in each other!'

Ginger snorted and disguised it as a wet sneeze.

Of course there were women and children and civilians here and there, and barking dogs and feasting seagulls, but the overriding impression, as they climbed the steady hill from the shops and up on to the broad flattened hill-top of the Hoe, was of entering into a kind of naval jamboree. Everywhere there were groups of sailors, sitting on benches, gathering in chattering circles, sprawling on the grass to sunbathe, eat ice creams or simply gaze out across the Sound to where other ships were manoeuvring. Charles didn't think he had ever felt so buoyed up at being surrounded by men. It was how he imagined attending a really big football or rugby match must feel, only happier.

The Tinside Lido was only a few years old and was still spoken of as one of the wonders of the South-West, but Charles had never been, partly out of loyalty to the leafy smallness and relative peace of the Jubilee Baths at home, which was only two minutes' walk from his front door, and partly from a late learner's fear of large expanses of deep water. Ginger only now admitted he had been a regular visitor without him. As they each paid their penny entrance fee at the turnstiles he explained that, initially, the Lido's main pool had been ladies only, because it was felt a modest bathing space was needed away from all the nude bathing that had long gone on in the older tidal pools nearby. Almost at once Charles felt his apprehensions about the place were well founded. With so many tiled and concrete surfaces, the noise inside was deafening, every laugh and shriek magnified, but then they emerged on to the succession of open-sided terraces of washrooms and changing rooms that gave out on to the main pool, and he had to lean on a balustrade to take it in. The pool was vast, at least the size of a rugby pitch, and had three big fountains in it through which fresh sea water was being driven up and where swimmers had clambered up to sit, laughing in the cascades.

'Do we just change and go in?' he asked, hesitant in the face of Ginger's greater experience. With bars and tea salons, the Lido was all so sophisticated it made the Jubilee Baths look like something dug out by slapdash labourers in a farmyard.

'If you like,' Ginger said. 'Or . . .'

'Do you have other plans?'

'No. You're right,' Ginger agreed. 'Let's change here, then we can wander around and see what's on offer.'

They changed and walked down to the main pool. The effect looking up was dizzying, as the structure and the paths radiating on either side were dug into the Hoe above them. With so many passers-by, and so many sailors among them, walking out on to the terrace around the main pool felt like walking out into an amphitheatre.

'We're on stage, Ginger!' he murmured.

'I know,' Ginger said, adjusting the belt on his new trunks. 'Isn't it bliss? If you lose track of me, I'll be in the Lion's Den,' he added airily.

'What's that?'

'Oh. Over there.' He gestured to the Lido's left, where a curving wall created an effective screen for whatever lay beyond. Just the top of a diving tower was visible. 'It's the men-only bit. Slightly, you know, more private. Come on. Race you to that fountain!'

He jumped in and began to swim through the crowded water. Charles jumped in too and was momentarily taken aback by the extreme cold after the sun-soaked warmth of the Hoe and south-facing terraces. The soupy water in the Jubilee Baths was never as clean as this, and there was surely a link between the way it warmed up in the course of a hot day and its tendency to bloom emerald with weed and algae. Actually being able to see other people's legs and costumes underwater was a novelty and distracting, and by the time he had dodged two women powering through competitive lengths and apologised to a man who had reversed into him while teaching his toddler to swim, he had lost sight of Ginger.

People tended to forget how short-sighted he was without his glasses but swimming in them, he had learned the hard way, was an impossibility.

He swam to the fountain, thinking he'd find Ginger there, but there was no sign of him. Perhaps he had meant them to aim for a different fountain? Being freshly charged from the sea, the water around it was even icier than elsewhere and close to it felt disturbingly industrial, more like a potentially dangerous area in a factory. A gang of young women was sitting on it. They glared at him territorially like girls on a prized playground bench, so he turned around, teeth chattering, and swam back the way he had come.

He retrieved his towel to rub himself down, as he was cold, then made his way cautiously towards the enclosure Ginger had indicated. An attendant was sitting on a chair scowling at a cluster of giggling children who were asking, in broad Janner accents, if they could just slip past for a peep. Charles had expected to be challenged but the man only gave him an incurious glance as he passed.

There was a rough, modest concrete pool built into the rocks and a diving board beyond that to let people dive into the open sea, which was sloshing over the walls it must breach each high tide. Beyond the noise of the water, though, the atmosphere was peaceful, almost churchlike. Some men were swimming but others were basking on the concrete shelves above the pool, shielded from the view of anyone up on the Hoe by a concrete half-canopy. Some were reading, some smoking, some talking quietly to their neighbours. And almost all were naked.

Charles's immediate impulse was to turn on his heel at once, like someone who has begun to leave the lift on the wrong floor of a department store, but he didn't because, he realised, he had made no mistake. He was nervous, though, and embarrassed, so he did the obvious thing, which was to spread his towel to dry on a sunny ledge and climb down for a swim. To reach the water he passed by two men not much older than him, but hairier and more athletic. One, who glanced his way as he passed, had kept on his sailor's hat to shield his head. His friend had a discreet anchor tattoo on one arm. The water seemed less cold than in the main pool, either because this pool was so much smaller so able to be warmed by the sun, or simply because his earlier dip had acclimatised him. He made himself swim underwater for a few strokes, while he gauged how deep the pool was, then surfaced to tread water for a while and gaze about him. To his relief he saw two other men still had their costumes on. Even without his glasses on he could see that the nudists were all shapes and sizes. A couple nearby were properly old, their pubic hair a shock of white. One very muscular man had red fur all over, like a sort of bear, while another, trailing his feet in the water, seemed as smooth and white as a Victorian statue.

Against the rear, he saw, there were doors let into the cliff, presumably for more changing rooms or lavatories, but the feel of the place was rougher than the new lido beside it and had some of the improvised feel of the Jubilee Baths.

The two sailors he had passed by stood just then and went together through one of the doors at the back. The one with the hat on glanced quickly around before closing the door behind them but nobody seemed to be paying attention. No one but Charles. A new young man arrived and Charles glanced up in case it was Ginger, but he had the wrong coloured trunks on. Then another door at the rear opened and a large man came out. He only had his bellbottoms on, but Charles recognised him at once as the one they had passed on the way up to the Hoe from Goodbody's, the one with the arms like logs. Charles watched, marvelling at his simple physical confidence, as he stooped to retrieve his shirt and hat, which he put back on before leaving, lighting a cigarette as he went.

Too cold to stay in the water any longer, Charles swam back to the pool's edge and tugged himself out. He was just towelling himself dry again when Ginger emerged through the same door the big sailor had, saw Charles and waved. Charles had never seen him so merrily relaxed. Happily, he had kept on his trunks as well.

'Sorry,' Charles said. 'I'm blind as a bat without my specs and I lost you out there.'

'That's all right,' Ginger told him. 'I lost you, too. Charles, your teeth are actually chattering.'

'Bit cold,' Charles stammered. Whether from nerves or cold, his whole body was juddering.

'They do nice cocoa at the café at the top. Let's go up there and sit in the sun.'

They dressed again, then headed back upstairs to drink cocoa until Charles had stopped shaking, then lay on the grass in a sea of basking sailors.

They talked about Ginger's hopes for medical school, Charles's next play, anything but where they had just been and what Ginger and the sailor might or might not have been doing that was suddenly making Ginger loll as though he wasn't wearing cricket whites but a clinging metallic evening gown.

'You do know,' Charles wanted to tell him, 'that what you were doing, or what I suspect you were doing, could have you up in the courts in Bodmin and wreck your prospects, even send you to prison?' But he said nothing about it because what he longed to do was ask questions instead, and he knew the answers Ginger might give would change the dynamic of their friendship for ever in ways for which he wasn't ready. Not yet.

They lost track of time so then had to rush across town for a train that wouldn't involve them missing supper and making Charles late for the dance. On the train they fell silent until they had stopped at Tavistock and Lydford.

Then Ginger asked, 'If there's a war, as Joe seems so sure there will be . . .'

'Yes?'

'Will you fight or object?'

'I'll fight. I mean if they'll have me. I've thought about the other, but this time I think there's a proper enemy, not just someone the papers want us to hate. Besides, I'm not sure I'm brave enough to be a conchie. Can't you imagine how people would be at home?'

'Mrs Netley would hand you a very public white feather.'

'Leading Girl Guides with drums and fierce expressions.'

Ginger laughed then fell back into thought, staring out of the window as they gathered speed. 'Army, Air Force or Navy?' he asked quietly.

Charles sighed. 'Well I've always promised Mother I'd not join the Army because of what it did to Father. And we stayed with a cousin of hers once near Crownhill Fort on the far side of Plymouth and you could hear how they shouted at the new recruits, drilling them into obedience or whatever. I don't think I could do that . . . And the Air Force is a non-starter because of my eyesight. Anyway, this is all academic. Who's to say Joe's not wrong?'

'Hmm.'

'Apparently in the Navy, clever boys can be something called a reader. Or perhaps it's a writer?'

'That sounds peaceful and undemanding.'

'Yes.'

'Navy it is, then.'

They fell to staring out of the window again and Charles pictured himself sitting in a chair surrounded by sailors in various stages of undress, held rapt as he read them Robert Louis Stevenson. Then he imagined himself at a cosy mess table writing letters home for an inarticulate young gunner who looked like Joe but with red hair.

He had been keeping a diary since the shock of leaving school. It was a pointless exercise really, a not terribly scintillating conversation with himself. He did it, he supposed, as an act of quiet rebellion against the tedium of his job at Finn's and against the increasingly stifling limits of the conversations he had with Mother. It wasn't a great literary outpouring, not written for posterity, not even written as an aide memoire of witty thoughts or interesting observations he might otherwise forget. He didn't even write in the sort of page-to-a-day diaries that were published for the purpose, but in tiny pocket appointment diaries of the sort to allow barely two square inches for each day's entry. And half the time he wrote in pencil, so that his entries faded and smudged, and he might as well have written in invisible ink.

The entries were truthful, that was the thing, even if the truth was dull. Every walk with Mother, or talk with Joe, every film he saw with Ginger at the cinema or party he played at with the band was recorded. Nobody reading them in years to come would have much idea what the playwright Causley thought of world affairs or whether he believed in his heart when he knelt in church with his mother, but they would know that he'd seen *The Bride of Frankenstein* twice and attempted oddly unsustainable not-quite romances with young women whose names always seemed to begin with J.

That night, after he returned, brain fizzing and fairly drunk from a long evening of playing with the band for a dance at Egloskerry, he opened the latest diary and wrote, 'Went to Plymouth with Ginger and sat in the sun on the Hoe. There were sailors everywhere. Oh, how I wished I could draw!' He had written it in ink, he realised, so couldn't rub it out. He thought of crossing the entry through, or just the last sentence, which might have been shouting from the little book, but he left it, set down his pen and slid the diary back into its hiding place. It was true, after all. He could not draw at all. But when he had put on his pyjamas and tumbled into bed, the pictures in his head were as vividly coloured as the new season's postcards before the summer faded them.

NATIVITY – 1941

In the summer of the previous year Councillor Netley had been required to call round at every house to note who had spare rooms that might be used for evacuees in the event of the cities being attacked by poison gas, which made it clear that the threat might become reality. He had been eagerly assisted by his wife, who clearly relished the chance it gave her to peer behind front doors previously closed to her. And to wield influence.

Although anyone taking evacuees in was to be paid, via the Post Office, for their board and lodging, not everyone was keen on the idea, not least those old enough to remember how the last war had been promised to take only months, then had ground on for years. And people didn't like the idea of not having a choice in the matter. Laura, and occasionally Charles, had already helped out in the effort to rehome families fleeing the civil war in Spain, so it was shocking suddenly to be asked to do the same for English families. Of course Laura hadn't demurred in showing the Netleys her small spare room where Vera had lived while she was their lodger, and where Maggie slept when she came on visits from Trusham. And Charles had been at pains to make sure such notorious gossipmongers knew he had enlisted in the Navy, and that his bed would also be available once he was called up.

'What about when you're home on leave?' Laura asked him, startled, momentarily forgetting Mrs Netley with her pen and notebook.

'It won't be for long, or that often,' he told her. 'The sofa will be comfy after a hammock.'

Laura could imagine few things worse than entrusting a small child to the care of distant strangers, or more upsetting than to have to be sent away from home while still little, so she set about redecorating the spare room to make it more welcoming. The official packing lists issued only covered clothing, and she suspected the poorer mothers would have trouble fulfilling even those meagre requirements: *a warm frock as well as two cotton ones, six handkerchiefs, one pair Wellington boots,* etc. She asked among friends whose children had outgrown them for a teddy, a doll, jigsaw puzzles, children's books and so on, to make the little room more welcoming. By the bedside table she hung a print from her own room she had always found immensely comforting, of a shepherd on a hillside at sunset with a rescued lamb in his arms.

Only then she learned that her evacuee was to be Gertie from Hackney Wick, who was fifteen, so was too old to need to go to school, and would possibly be old enough to help Laura around the house or even to find a paying job. She thought at first she should clear some of the toys out, lest they be thought babyish, but Charles said they'd still be comforting but why not add things a fifteen-year-old might like? He rustled up a stack of fairly recent copies of *Film Weekly* from the girls at the office and Laura found a hairbrush and mirror set at a church jumble sale, which cleaned up well.

She could not remember a time when she had felt so pinned against the wall by officialdom. They were issued with identity cards and ration books and there was a flurry of indecision as people had to decide which grocer and butcher to patronise until further notice, and then register with them and shop nowhere else. They had to queue up at the Congregational Sunday school to be fitted with gas masks, and provided with little boxes on straps in which to carry them at all times.

Inevitably there was much talk about gas bombs and terrible reminiscences from any men who had experienced gas in the trenches. An exercise in which the local volunteer nurses, doctors, air-raid patrolmen and ambulance drivers had to act out their responses to a horribly realistic air raid involving incendiary and poison bombers, driven inland from a raid on Plymouth, put the fear of God in everyone. Laura had never seen the church so full outside of funerals and Christmas.

War was finally declared on a September Sunday. The first evacuees left London on a series of trains on the Monday. The logistics were mind boggling, with an army of volunteers from the Women's Voluntary Service at every station west of Liskeard, and bus and van drivers standing by to ferry the children destined for outlying farms and cottages.

'Just think of it,' Laura told Charles. 'They're mobilising bossy women everywhere: a whole army of Mrs Netleys bearing down on you!'

Entire schools were coming, complete with teachers, she heard. But perhaps Launceston was thought to be too close to Plymouth, a likely bombing target, to be considered safe, and most of the evacuees were settled in farms and villages deeper into the country.

Entirely characteristically, the Netleys saw to it that Launceston's evacuees were sorted along class lines: children with smart little overcoats and shiny buckle shoes were taken uphill to the smarter households where, as Mrs Netley put it, 'they will feel at home', and humbler boys and girls were scattered around the households nearer the stations and the town's dirtier industries.

Laura had not realised how intense her anticipation of Gertie had become until she was waiting for her on the station platform, as WVS women shepherded children away around her, and she felt a lurch of shock when the rather tall, shabbily dressed girl stepped forward to name herself to Mrs Netley, clutching a very new baby. Mrs Netley immediately started to make a loud, insensitive fuss about 'nobody having mentioned a baby', but Laura swiftly intervened, saying there was plenty of space and that it would be a delight to have the baby as well.

Little by little, bun by sugared bun, Laura coaxed the shreds of Gertie's sad story out of her, learning that her parents had delivered her to a mother and baby home when she proved unable or unwilling to name the father, and assumed she would agree to give the baby up for adoption. But Gertie was determined to be a mother, however young a one, and had seized on the evacuation call as her and Fred's escape route. She was no trouble, didn't eat nearly as much as Laura felt she should, and was at pains to keep out of Laura and Charles's way most of the time.

Tonight was the last night of the Nativity play. Charles had written several short plays already, two or three had been published and one had even been on the radio, so that lots of people had heard it. But this was different. It wasn't grand, although the local papers covered it in detail, and he wasn't being paid, but it was a commission from the community, for an event where the audience participated as much as those on stage. Half the people cramming into every available seat in St Stephen's community hall had been involved in some way, from lending props to making animal masks or gluing feathers on to angel wings. An immense amount of work was involved considering there were only a few performances but that, people kept saying, was the point. The country was at war, everyone was on edge and this gave a focus and a temporary diversion.

Laura had been buttonholed after church one day and asked to starch the white dresses for the angelic choir – Gabriel and the rest. These had to be really stiff so their folds would stand out. The job had taken up two whole days when she couldn't do any paid work. And then she had sewn the robes for one of the kings, Caspar, from curtain fabric donated by Hart's the drapers. It was a good green brocade that could be turned into some nice cushion covers afterwards, she pointed out, though it wasn't clear what would become of any of the costumes once the play was done, or to whom they would belong.

Charles was very secretive about his writing, as he always was, telling her only, 'Well, I can't change the story, can I?' and complaining that the director wanted at least some of it in verse.

189

'I suppose that's to make it more solemn,' she said, which was plainly the wrong thing to say as he pulled that face of his, as she told Aggie, that made her feel she was back in service and had been accused of not smelling quite clean.

She would sooner die than admit it to anyone, but she had rather fallen out of love with Charles in the last two years. When Finn's went bust, around the time when several firms did, she managed to land him a job at the Electricity Board in Market Square for better pay and in an environment that was less dusty and more sociable than a builders' yard. He took the job but with an ill grace, and then was so taken up both with the band and with his clever, pinko friends that he seemed to have no time for her and barely came home to eat and sleep. The most she saw of him was when there was something he wanted to hear on the radio – he had bought them a good one with his staff discount – and then she was obliged to sit in silence across from him, listening too, and darning or knitting.

Great rages would burst out of her sometimes, that she was barely fifty and could have done other things with her evenings than wait in for him and wash and mend his clothes, that other sons were grateful for such a sacrifice and so on. But these rages made him contrite in a ghastly, pitying way, so that she knew he knew, had somehow guessed, that she was reaching what stupid women called 'a difficult age'. She had never admitted to wanting a second child – fathering one had clearly been out of the question in Charlie's condition – but the few years of having Vera as her lodger had awakened in her a painful, pointless longing for a daughter. She dreamed of a daughter

190

who would understand her, work alongside her, marry a good man but still appreciate her, then give her grandchildren like so many of her friends were already boasting of. And, just recently, as her monthlies had begun to stutter to the point where, last month for instance, the lateness and meagreness of her bleeding, a cruel parody of early pregnancy, had brought savagely home to her the foolishness of such fantasies. Having Gertie arrive, complete with baby, sometimes felt like a compensation.

And of course, her temperature had gone haywire. She had been warned by Em to expect the sudden heat rushes at night, where she would sweat so hard it woke her and she would have to leave her sheets and nightdress draped around the bedroom to dry when she got up. She could cope with those easily enough as she slept alone. It was the hot flushes by day she found excruciating. She always sweated when doing laundry – there could be no nonsense about laundrywomen merely *glowing*, for it was hot and vigorous work. Her mother had taught them each in turn always to keep a small towel handy in case someone called by when you were at it, pounding sheets or whatever in the boiler, so you could at least mop your face and armpits and not be caught 'looking unnecessary', as Mother put it. But flushes when she was shopping or in someone else's house were a thing to be dreaded. She was convinced they made her smell, so took to using lavender water for her own ironing, until Charles said she was smelling like the sweeter old ladies in church.

And while she suffered, Charles was either out at his play-reading club or rehearsing with his dance band or

191

drinking beer with friends, or else he was shut in his room, stabbing away at his typewriter, or listening intently to the radio, as often as not to some programme about the international situation and politics, which made her head spin if she tried to follow it, and telling her to knit more quietly.

She knew she had no right to complain, not really. He brought in money now and handed half his pay packet to her for his board and lodging and the rest. He was as clean and tidy as she had raised him to be. He was kind to Wang – although he also laughed at him – and took him for walks after work if she was working late. He even looked after the goldfish he had won her at the fair. But she felt herself excluded and found it hard to bear. She knew she was unjust. She had always hoped for a clever, special boy and he had grown into a clever, special man, which meant he could be prickly and difficult and knew exactly how best to wound her with his sharp tongue. If he had been ordinary, or what Miss Bracewell called 'low wattage', he'd have been married by now, like several of his contemporaries, and lost to her that way, and probably risking his health in the iron foundry, sawmill or tanneries.

There were often times now when she looked at Charles, or more often at his firmly closed bedroom door, and remembered the tale of the foolish woodcutter and his wife whose magically granted wishes all came true but in unexpectedly wrong ways.

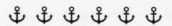

In this last year, although his job at the Electricity Board was no more exciting for him than his job at the builders' merchant's, Charles had become quite the local star. First he had played Frederic in *The Pirates of Penzance*, then he had one of his short plays broadcast by the BBC. Laura had kept a copy of the *Western Morning News* with the headline, 'Cornishman's Play to be Broadcast!' and been sent two more clippings by proud relatives. She had been impressed that Charles was paid twelve guineas simply for the right to broadcast and extra for adapting his script to make sense on the radio. And of course it was gratifying having so many people stop her in the street to tell her how proud she must be, and how they were going to be listening in.

'Wherever does he get his ideas from?' they asked, and, 'Is it all about the two of you?' Silly things like that.

She had assumed he'd have arranged to listen with his friends, the ones he discussed books with, and the play-reading group, but the evening came and she made a mutton pie she knew he liked, then realised he wasn't going out, so they sat and listened together after supper. So as to give it her full attention she did no mending or knitting, although her fingers itched to be busy. Charles paced nervously about the room, interrupting now and then to laugh or to complain about a line said wrong.

It was very strange. Because there was nothing to watch, her mind's eye saw the play happening right there in their front room at Tredydan Road. When the excitable young hero played the piano it was Charles she saw playing just across from where they were sitting. He even played one of

193

the pieces Charles often played, a classical piece, not the dance tunes he was always having to learn for the band. And when the young man's comic landlady came in and flirted and fussed, she saw herself doing things with food and tea things she often did, but saying things she would never say, and in a would-be genteel accent, like the waitress in Goodbody's Charles and she had chuckled over. There was a girl in the play, who sounded pretty and no better than she should be, and another young, rather graceless young man, who was performing in a band with the two of them. The hero was in love with the girl who was meant to be engaged to the other man.

Try as she might, however, Laura couldn't see her as any of the girls in either of the bands Charles played with, who could be vivacious but were all thoroughly sensible, hard-working local girls. The few girls Charles had ever asked out to the cinema with him had only been briefly mentioned and then dropped from conversation soon afterwards. When she had dared ask him about one of them and enquired if he was seeing her again he said, shortly, 'She said I was too sarcastic,' which sounded so likely Laura had forgotten to offer any words of motherly reassurance. He could be terribly sharp. Sometimes she worried he didn't really like women very much and that it might be her fault.

Having started as a merry enough sort of comedy, the radio play took a very odd turn. It became evident that young Benedict, the pianist, harboured dark secrets. He made some strange references to repression and how much strength he took from it and then, for all his protestations of passionate love, he was revealed as a murderer on the run from a lunatic asylum.

'Well,' she said. 'Well done, you. Were you pleased with how they did it?' which was the right thing to ask as he then spoke about the performances and didn't ask her what she thought. She remained unsettled by the play because the identification between Charles and its frighteningly out of control, yet oddly gifted hero felt like a sort of warning.

She wasn't the only listener to be at a loss for what to say. 'Who'd have thought it?' people told her in the days after. 'A murdering lunatic and he seemed so friendly.' Or else, as she had done, they simply said, 'Well!' then asked, cautiously, 'Was he pleased?'

The unpaid commission to write the Nativity play came soon after the broadcast. She was very pleased that he had said yes. With all the doubting, questioning books he had taken to getting through his Left Book Club, and which she occasionally picked up and read herself, she was worried he might scoff and say no. He hardly ever came to church with her these days and had taken to asking her impossible questions like where was God in Hitler's Germany, or what good had prayer done the victims of Franco? But he had taken the commission very seriously indeed. It should happen after Christmas, though, he said, and deal with the kings and Herod and the escape into Egypt as that spoke more to the arrival of evacuees and the horribly unstable state of things than the usual story of Joseph, Mary and the shepherds.

And then, of course, they had edged ever nearer war breaking out so that people started to ask her, 'Is Charles's play still happening?'

'Yes,' she told them all. 'Of course. We need it more than ever.' But when war was declared she began to have doubts too. Surely, she thought, people would have more important things to do than dressing up? And when the director was called up it looked as though the project might founder, but Charles agreed to direct it, as well as playing the piano in its band. So now not only was *The Coming of the Magi* more 'Charles's play' than ever but, by a kind of community magic rare in a town so divided into clans, clubs, churches and classes, it came to represent something far more important than a mere nativity. People who never normally got involved in such things came forward to help. Charles said the interest shown was a bit overwhelming and the performers were being made nervous by it. There was such demand for tickets that an extra performance had to be laid on.

⚓ ⚓ ⚓ ⚓ ⚓ ⚓

Laura had chosen to come to the play on its last night, not wishing to burden Charles with any need to look after her on the first night, when he assumed she wanted to come, and knowing he'd be involved in a cast party tonight when it ended. She could slip off home alone afterwards if she didn't enjoy it and wasn't sure what to say. It was often hard to say the right thing with him, especially so when she was nervous of saying the wrong one. Gertie had been offered a ticket too, of course, but had chosen to stay home with Fred, who had not been sleeping well, and Laura was guiltily glad of having no company on the excursion.

It was strange walking up the steep hill to St Stephen's and not heading on to Werrington, where she still worked occasionally. She only came to St Stephen's on the rare occasions someone she knew had their funeral there. Used as she was to feeling, even obliquely, part of the home team down the hill in St Thomas's, she felt stupidly nervous coming there. She hoped she would see familiar faces but knew most of her friends and family had been already, and she had been obliged to listen patiently while repeatedly being told all about it. She was very glad she had decided to wear her best navy coat and felt hat, as the first thing she saw on coming in was how many of the audience were in evening dress, quite as though this was a night at the opera, not a Christmas play in a small Cornish town.

She gave her name to the very upright couple running the box-office table, who insisted her ticket was complimentary and then, to her horror, had her shown to a seat in the very front row. Her instinct would have been to sit in one of the side aisles towards the rear, as she did in church, where she could enjoy looking about her but not feel on display. As it was, she felt exposed, so close to the stage; she couldn't change places as the seats were reserved and she knew the performance had sold out. She concentrated on watching Charles and the band, who were playing a selection of carols, and tried to remember that most people would be paying no attention to her at all.

There was a slight commotion and a large group arrived, all in evening dress, and were shown to her row and the one behind. They had no idea who she was, of course, but she knew them for the Williamses from Werrington, presumably with guests still staying from their New Year party. Several of the men were in uniform, of course. Army. A tall young man turned politely to greet her as he settled in his place beside her.

'Looking forward to this?' he said.

'Very much,' she told him, adding, 'That's my boy playing the piano.'

She didn't know why she said that and not that her boy had written and directed the play; it was just what came out. Perhaps she didn't like to be thought a show-off?

'Marvellous,' he said, in that way upper class people did when they meant no such thing. 'Well, three-line whip for us. Have to support local talent and so on.'

But then his attention was sought by the woman to his other side and he left Laura in peace. They all stood in honour of the mayor and his wife, arriving in their funny furs and chains. The lights were turned out briefly, to silence everyone, then came on again and the band struck up 'God Rest You Merry, Gentlemen' and, with much shuffling and chat and hasty discovery that they all had the words on their programmes, everyone stood to sing.

She knew the story, of course: the three Wise Men alerted by the star and travelling to Bethlehem, via Herod's palace, Herod's terrible slaughter of children and the flight into Egypt, and perhaps because she knew it so well she didn't pay as close attention as she had to the radio play. With such a press of people in thick coats and with theatre lights shining, the hall because surprisingly warm but she was transported nonetheless.

The production had the probably rather clumsy charm of all amateur shows – she had never seen a professional one unless you counted the cinema – it was hard to take seriously as a king a man who sold you balls of wool – but then there were moments that took her breath away. The angel Gabriel was played by a young blonde woman of such striking severity you could believe she was more than human and knew things mankind could only guess at. And Charles, who had often said how he was haunted by the cries and shrieks of the poor animals in the abattoir up the road, had given speeches to ox and ass and sheep, whom she knew perfectly well from her programme were women she often saw in the queue at the post office or buying buns, and yet Charles's words, and the utterly lifelike animal heads someone had made, rendered them strange and commanding. Her grand neighbour, who had giggled audibly on occasion, was struck silent and then muttered, 'Marvellous masks. Marvellous,' when the scene finished, in a way that told her he was fighting tears.

She knew nothing of poetry apart from hymns, but recognised that Charles had reflected the social differences in the story by writing the Kings' scenes in solemn verse and the domestic scenes, the family scenes, in normal speech. And this was heightened by the Kings all speaking beautifully, like radio announcers, and the others talking with their familiar Cornish and Devon accents.

She would ask to read the script at home later. One moment of Charles's writing really struck her. Near the beginning, when the Kings were speaking, they said, 'We are the tired men of the stars, the thin moon, the glitter of other worlds in the tall sky.'

It made her think of those times when she'd been walking Wang along Underlane on a clear night, and how the stars seen through the winter trees had made the night feel colder and comfortless. How had he done that? You would never say the sky was tall, and yet when Charles did, it worked and cast a sort of spell. She liked, too, that he kept involving the audience by expecting them to sing along, and having the hall lights turned up briefly so they could read the words to 'I Saw Three Ships' and 'We Three Kings'; it made them feel part of the drama and reminded them there were still monsters like Herod, still young families forced to flee like the Spanish and now Polish and German refugees the Churches had been working to help and rehome. And the British evacuees, of course.

People enjoyed the villainy of Herod, who was wearing a turban made of a tablecloth Laura was sure she recognised, and they cheered uproariously after his curtain line, 'I will worship him . . . with my sword!' but it felt too real to her for laughter.

When the show ended with everyone on their feet to sing 'It Came Upon a Midnight Clear', she was almost overwhelmed and had to mime the words rather than risk singing and hearing her voice crack. As everyone was taking their bow, animals clutching their beautiful heads under their arms and looking slightly flushed with hair awry, there were shouts of 'Author! Author!' and Charles was duly led out from the piano to bow. He looked so

smart in his evening dress, but also about ten years old, and
Laura felt a great rush of protectiveness towards him as he
took little bobbing bows and had to lift off his specs as they
were steaming up with emotion.

There was a great babble then, and a rush for the door
and a simultaneous rush to press in the other direction to
congratulate the cast, so Laura stayed where she was.

'You didn't tell me your boy was the author and director
as well as the piano player,' young Mr Williams said, while
he waited for the rest of his party to leave their row. 'You
must be so proud, Mrs Causley.'

'Oh, I am,' she said. 'I am.' He had a kind face and the
dark, bushy eyebrows of all the men in his family, and she
knew he would have no inkling that she occasionally
scrubbed his hall floors or starched his napkins. 'Happy
New Year, sir.'

'Happy New Year to you, too,' he said. 'I'd better
just . . .' And he followed the others out into the aisle.

She wanted to congratulate Charles but there was such
a scrum around him and the musicians and actors, and she
knew she would see him at home later. Besides, she could
feel her face beginning to burn with a hot flush and imagined herself stammering before him and his clever
friends with her face running. She faced several more
congratulations on her way out, at least twice from people
she didn't know, then found herself back out in blessed
chill and anonymity under a canopy of stars. *The glitter of
other worlds in the tall sky,* she told herself, amazed that
she had somehow remembered the line. She could not have
said how, but she recognised it had a similar ring to some

lines in the Prayer Book that had always got under her skin like, *But thou art the same Lord, whose property is always to have mercy*; lines that felt they had power in them, spells to hold evil at bay.

Gertie had been sitting in the kitchen, she could tell, as she had left a copy of *Picture Show* on the table there, but had now turned in for the night. Laura hoped she had enjoyed having the place to herself for the evening and realised it would be a kindness if she found a way of going out somewhere one evening a week, to give her and the baby some space. She made a plate of brown bread and butter, cut thin the way Charles liked it, and a pot of tea, drank and ate a little herself, then fell deeply asleep in her kitchen armchair. When she woke, Wang was snoring on her lap and Charles was standing over her in his best over-coat and smelling of beer.

'Mother? It's past your bedtime.'

'I wanted to stay up,' she said, 'to say well done. Charles, it was so good. I was very proud. People kept telling me how proud I must be, which was silly really, as of course I was proud. But really. I was.'

He smiled and put a hand on hers, something he never seemed to do any more.

'I made you tea,' she said.

'Oh, that's long cold,' he told her, 'but this looks good.' And he sat at the kitchen table to eat the bread and butter. 'It's always so much better when someone else makes it. I didn't want it to end,' he added. 'The run of performances, I mean. It's silly but I felt they were holding off the war.'

'It will have meant that to lots of people.'

'I've got my medical tomorrow,' he said. 'In Plymouth City Art Gallery. Of all the places to have to drop my trousers.'

'You never said.'

'Didn't I?'

'Are you settled on the Navy?'

'Yes. Apparently I can be something called a writer, which sounds about right. I could never be a stoker like Joe. That takes brawn. And my maths and eyesight are too hopeless to man the guns like Ginger's going to do.'

'Ginger's a gunner?'

'Yes. Little Ginger firing huge guns!'

'I thought they'd want him as a doctor.'

'Well, he's not gone to medical school yet, so his maths is more useful, calculating trajectories or what have you. Come on. Bed. You look done in.'

'Yes.'

But she sat on there a while, watching him sing softly to himself as he riddled the stove and let Wang out into the yard for a pressure-reliever.

⚓ ⚓ ⚓ ⚓ ⚓ ⚓

Laura prayed guiltily that Charles would fail his medical but, despite his poor eyesight, he was declared A1 and told to expect his call-up papers in the post any day. They had laughed at him, he said, when he asked if he could be a writer. 'Oh, we'll find something just as suitable for you,' they said.

'All the way home,' he told her, 'I was saying to myself, "I'm a sailor, I'm a sailor," but it doesn't feel remotely true yet.'

'The uniform will help,' she said. 'And I expect you'll get training.'

She couldn't bear the prospect of losing him, let alone that of losing him with a capital L, as several families she knew had already lost sons with shocking speed. They treated each other with great tenderness, it seemed to her, as the days passed, then weeks, as they waited for the dreaded brown envelope to come. He included her in things, led her for icy walks along Underlane with Wang, took her with him to the cinema. It became more and more common to see boys and sometimes girls they knew in uniform. There were more and more uniforms around, and army vehicles, as camps were being built in the grounds of Werrington and on the other side of town at Pennygillam.

Charles bought her a watering can and spade for her birthday and helped lift the paving slabs at one end of their little yard to make a bed for growing vegetables in when the spring came, although neither of them knew a thing about gardening, so she would probably end up asking someone for help.

Typically Charles prepared for the Navy by reading a book: *Naval Life and Customs* by Lieutenant-Commander John Irving RN. 'Listen to the nicknames for all the jobs people do on board,' he told her and Gertie over breakfast. 'Posty, Lampy, Chippie, Bugles, Crusher, Slushy, Dusty Boys and Tiffy Blokes, Jimmy Bungs, Poultice Walloper and Salt Beef Squirrel! It's a poem!' And he took to testing himself on the naval slang for different food, from soddick and trap, to lobscouse and shrapnel, and insisted on calling a pasty a tiddy-oggy, although Laura detected the nerves in his hilarity so humoured rather than encouraged him.

He took her to see *A Star is Born*, even though he said poor Janet Gaynor's face was 'an odd mixture of sharp-featured and cake-like'. In the queue outside they met Joe Luke, home on leave, a new girl on his arm and looking even bigger in uniform and with the extra muscles he must have gained as a stoker. Laura said how pleased his mother must be to have him back for a few days, and Charles told him he was still waiting for his call-up papers and that it wasn't fair Joe getting all the fun. But then Joe told them how he'd been in the engine room when the *Mohawk* suffered a direct hit close beside them.

'The din was like nothing I'd ever heard,' he said. 'Like being inside a kettle drum. And then we all raced on deck to help haul survivors on board. Charles, you've . . . I didn't know men could be that injured and still swim!' His hands were shaking so hard his girl, who Laura recognised now as one of the Cocks girls grown all busty and barely recognisable in lipstick, folded them in hers like injured birds and led him gently away.

The film was almost unbearably moving, not at all the comedy Laura had hoped for. Charles had often been told off by the proprietress for disapproving out loud when he thought films were rubbish, but in this one he sat almost on the edge of his seat. Laura knew he was upset, whether by the film or seeing Joe in such a bad way or both, because he clean forgot his hat and had to dart back inside to retrieve it before the next screening.

'Poor Joe,' she said, as they began their walk back down

the hill. Gertie had promised to heat up supper for them all and she was suddenly hungry. 'Perhaps you should take him and Wang for a walk while he's back? Let him talk about it all.'

'Yes,' Charles said. 'Maybe. I was rereading some Orwell last night,' he added, 'when I couldn't sleep. He says war smells of excrement and decayed feet. Or maybe food. But decayed feet is better.' And he tucked her arm into his and drew her close as though he'd just murmured an endearment. 'Perhaps war at sea is cleaner?'

I AM A SAILOR – 1941

He had spent weeks and weeks in a shaming limbo during which more and more of his contemporaries vanished from the streets as though taken in the night. Mother felt compelled to keep explaining to people that, no, Charles wasn't a conchie or excluded on mysterious medical grounds, but simply awaiting his call-up papers. It was an eerie echo of being the last to be picked for a school football team. He was humbled that even Ginger had been called up long before him.

He was at work, in the first-floor office above the little Electricity Board showroom on the square where people could buy toasters and kettles and irons and so on. All the younger male colleagues had gone – none of them was a friend – leaving just Charles and the women and Mr Shuttle, who was already self-importantly busy in the Home Guard every evening and whose humourlessness made the rest of them giggle over their bills and invoices.

It had been rather fun. Sometimes their joking became quite saucy, especially when one of the girls took to reading aloud from a much-thumbed pornographic paperback she had filched from one of the soldiers at a battalion dance and gave them all nicknames from it. Mr Shuttle became Madam Lash and Charles, for his perceived innocence, was dubbed Little Milly.

'You'll get called much worse in the Navy,' they told him. 'You'll see.'

Six whole months had passed since his medical and they were enjoying a heatwave – Charles swimming every day at the baths, which had turned their usual midsummer creamy green, and playing with the otherwise all-girl band at stiflingly hot and noisy dances for soldiers at seven and six a time.

Mechanisation had arrived at the Electricity Board, causing bitter complaints that they were now expected to work twice as fast. The office had already been loud with the clatter of typewriters but now there were noisy adding machines as well as the hubbub from the street as they had the windows open wide in hope of any cooler air that might be stirring. Charles didn't hear Mother calling his name. It was Gladys Sampson, she of the smutty book, who suddenly looked up from her desk by the window and asked, 'Little Milly, isn't that your mother? She's calling up.'

Mother had hurried up the hill as soon as the letter came. She came in her laundering clothes, sleeves rolled up and red in the face from both the effort and making a spectacle of herself.

'Should I open it?' she called up.

'Of course!' everyone shouted. The atmosphere in the office was suddenly excited, almost celebratory, as though he'd won a scholarship or the football pools.

They misheard her at first.

'Sheerness?' Gladys said. 'Ooh, lovely. There's donkeys at Sheerness.'

But it was Skegness where he must report, which had no donkeys and was famously bracing. He was to be enlisted not as a writer but as an ordinary coder, which worried him as there was no mention of the rank in the book on the Navy he had been studying as homework.

Before the journey to the Lincolnshire coast Charles had to catch a train to Keyham and walk from there with a loose group of other new recruits to the Devonport dockyard and barracks. There he passed a hellish first afternoon and night in the Navy. Even on a hot summer evening it was a far cry from the scenes of sunlit enchantment he had witnessed on the Hoe all those months ago with Ginger. Devonport felt like a sweaty prison; a vast and confusing array of forbidding granite buildings behind a high wall and thick, well-guarded gates. Any glimpse of sea was obscured by a tangle of ships at anchor and ships under repair or construction. Everywhere there seemed to be the blinding flare of acetylene torches, the sound of hammers on steel and men swearing with a vigour and colourfulness he had not heard before, even in Launceston's rougher corners. He was kitted out in his uniform – square rig, as he already knew to call it.

'You've got no badge,' they told him, 'because coders are so new they've not delivered those yet. You'll get it later to sew on yourself. We reckon it'll have two big Cs for Clever Cunt.'

The uniform seemed so outlandish he wondered if he would ever muster the complexities of getting the arrangement of collar and lanyard on his own. It was also designed to make a shy man shyer yet, particularly the bellbottoms, skin tight compared to the baggy suit trousers he had been wearing most of his life, and with an alarmingly frank buttoned trapdoor arrangement in place of the usual decorous fly.

The New Entry Mess was run by a cheerfully potty-mouthed three badge AB, whose name Charles didn't catch in his new-boy confusion. 'See these,' he told Charles, pointing a thick, scarred finger at the red chevrons on his arm. 'Each of these beauties represents four years of what the top brass would call good conduct and what I like to think of as undetected crime. Your accent,' he added.

'Mine?' asked Charles, who until then had not thought of himself as having an accent. Certainly since starting at the grammar school he had striven to speak like a radio announcer, or at least like a schoolmaster.

'Yeah. You're local. You're a Janner. We should call you Jan. Pretty face like yours; it suits you. Eh, boys?'

'Actually I'm not from Plymouth,' Charles said. 'I'm from Launceston.'

'I'm from Elephant and Castle,' the AB said. 'You all sound Janner to me,' and continued to call him Jan at every turn. He bestowed similar nicknames on all the recruits, quite as though the titles were part of each man's uniform: Shorty, Lofty, Chalky. Curly for a boy who was dramatically hairless. Clarky for a boy whose surname was Gable. Charles was briefly offended. He had never liked nicknames, despite having known Ginger as such so long he had to work hard to remember his actual name. Then he found he had remembered all the recruits' nicknames and saw they had done the same, and that the names had swiftly made them a group as surnames would not.

They were also each given a number – their rating – starting with D for Devonport and, along with the uniform, a hammock, a thin mattress, a kitbag, shoe brushes and a kit for mending their own clothes and for Charles to use to sew on his badge when it came. It was called a housewife. It was days before Charles saw the word written down and was charmed that the Navy had retained its Elizabethan pronunciation. He tried to explain this to his messmates and was met with looks of blank disdain.

Before a feast of 'floaters in the snow' – sausages and mash – they were given a bewilderingly fast tour of the smoke-filled sheds, shown to another room where they all had to drop their new bellbottoms for a further medical inspection – for VD, Clarky said – and to another where each recruit had his teeth closely inspected by a dentist, who tapped them one by one like a wheeltapper checking the integrity of train wheels and axle boxes, listening for faults.

'No dentists on board,' their guide explained. 'Better to get any extractions done here under gas than by a messmate with only fucking rum and pliers . . .'

Then they went to yet another room to be issued with tobacco coupons and a Quarters Card.

As the evening progressed Charles became increasingly worried that there had been some administrative error and that the morning would see him abruptly embarked on a ship for war and not sent to Skegness for training.

'I'm to be a coder, sir,' he finally plucked up courage to say to a petty officer. 'I think there's training for that,' which gained him the same looks as when he had denied being a Janner.

'You're in the Navy now, Causley,' came the comfortless reply. 'First law of the Navy? Don't ask questions. You're in a system and there's a plan for you. Just button it and go where you're sent.'

They spent that night in a dormitory with cavernous ceilings and tall, curtainless windows overlooking the fiery labours in the dockyard. Hammocks had already been slung up, but it was a challenge to get into them and stay there unassisted. Bruised from tumbles, failing to sleep for what seemed like hours under a dirty grey blanket with his head on a canvas pillow that smelled of armpits and hair oil in a room alive with snores and mumbles, Charles felt desolation steal over him. Nobody would dare admit anything so unmanly but he wondered how many others among them were missing the simple privacy and comforts of home already; missing, in this harshly male environment, mothers they had been irritated by when they saw them every day.

It seemed he had no sooner fallen asleep than he was woken by the shriek of air-raid sirens and the thunder of raw recruits falling out of their hammocks. Word soon spread that the first air-raid attack on the city was under-way. There were already booms and crashes worryingly nearby and the clatter of anti-aircraft fire as they were noisily herded down to a fetid basement shelter where everyone complained loudly about not being able to see *the action*, and where Charles was just starting to nod off in a dark corner when the all clear sounded and they were just as noisily rounded back up the stairs to another bout of hammock tumbling.

Sure enough the Navy had not forgotten he was wanted in Skegness. After a cruelly early rousing with a bosun's pipe, a humiliating hour of being shouted at during PE in ways that made him feel every skinny inch the pen-pushing, four-eyed weakling the PTI said he was, and a huge and welcome breakfast, he and two others, a deputy bank manager and an accountant who had also suffered during PE, were told to pack quickly and head to the station.

The kitbag must have weighed three hundred pounds, and of course Charles had packed several books in his suitcase, along with jars of the piccalilli and marmalade Mother had insisted he take with him. Even though they were in the cooler, summer version of their uniforms, all three wore their coats rather than carry them or try to pack them, so fell into the London train breathless and sweaty. It was so packed with soldiers and sailors on the move that they had to stand for the first hour. Their conversation was stilted and limited. Charles managed only to establish that they had both confessed at their medicals to enjoying sailing and cryptic crosswords before the deputy bank manager, who had one of those inexplicable moustaches like a caterpillar, sternly reminded them to avoid careless talk. It was a relief at Exeter for Charles to let them find seats while he spent the rest of the journey sitting quietly on his kitbag in a nicely breezy corner, reading his guide to naval life.

Vocabulary was going to be his first challenge, he could see; the Navy seemed to function on over two hundred specialist words of which he could confidently use about fifteen. When his brain began to fog over with an excess of technical terms, he occupied himself with a small handbook of essential knots and a short length of stout twine he had packed for the purpose.

From Paddington they had to make their way on the Underground to King's Cross. They saw nothing of the bomb damage Charles had been reading about, but everywhere there was the acrid after-smell of burnt timber, and he noticed how the Underground platforms had a thickly human smell. The accountant said it was because of all the poor, unevacuated Londoners reduced to taking shelter in them overnight.

'Think I'd rather take my chances under a tree in Hyde Park,' he said.

Then they had to catch a similarly packed train to Grantham before changing to an almost empty branch-line service out through bleakly flat acres of summer cabbage to Skegness. There a lorry picked them up, along with several other sailors, and drove them to a requisitioned Butlin's holiday camp a short way up the coast to the north at Ingoldmells.

In what Charles imagined was a parody of what happened when holidaymakers arrived at the place, an unsmiling officer – he realised with a panic he had yet to memorise how to recognise the different ranks – read off a roll call of their surnames and numbers and when each answered, 'Here, sir,' told them their chalet number.

'You've missed the start of supper,' he said, as though this was their fault. There was to be an address in the ball-room at nineteen thirty hours. Late arrivals would be punished.

Charles's little blue chalet, one of many identical rows of thinly disguised garden sheds stretching into the distance from the central cluster of swimming pool and fairground, was at least five minutes' walk away and he once again regretted his mother's Kilner jars and the impulse that had made him think it a good opportunity to tackle *War and Peace*.

There was already a kitbag on the chalet's second little bed, an alarm clock with a very loud tick and a copy of *A Guide to British Birds and Continental Migrants*. As Charles hurried back towards the refectory, following the clamour of hundreds of men eating and talking, he called in, with sinking heart, at the nearest latrine block. The first three cubicles had broken locks. The fourth had a lock but no paper. The fifth had both but was filthy beyond words. He feared this was a portent.

They were in HMS *Royal Arthur*, a shore station or stone frigate, mostly to be trained for the brand-new rank of ordinary coder. (The badge, surely dreamed up at very short notice did, indeed, feature a big C beneath a pair of signals flags.) They would be there for five weeks, with the intensive coding course lasting a month, at the end of which they would sit an exam.

The senior officer who welcomed them spoke just like one of the landowners from around Launceston, with the same clipped vowels and absolute confidence that his words counted for something. 'Some of you will not prove competent,' he said, 'and will be reassigned elsewhere at the end of one week. Those who fail to score well in the exam will also be reassigned. You'll be learning to do a highly specialised job under extreme pressure and, as with any task on board ship, lives will depend on you.'

On the one walk Charles had taken back home with Joe before his January leave ended, Joe had warned him that the Navy would confirm everything Charles thought wrong with the country: the rigid hierarchies, usually along lines of birth not expertise, the flagrant inequalities, the sentimental acceptance, worship even, of upper-class authority. 'What you have to understand,' he said, thrusting his gloved hands deep in his duffel coat pockets to control the shaking his emotion was bringing on, 'is that most of the officers went to public schools and have been boarding since they were seven or younger. For them the Navy and its regulations are a reassuring continuation of life as they've known it most of their days: unfair, violent and emotionally stifled. But the rest of us have to adjust to it fast to survive. The ones who get it straight off are the ones who've been to prison or grew up in orphanages.'

'You will also be trained here in how to be sailors,' the officer continued. 'Several of you are older than most recruits and you are all notably cleverer than most, so you're probably used to doing your own thing and getting your own way. That has to change from tonight. A ship is a highly efficient man machine, but it can only function as such with unquestioning obedience to your superior officers, even when you think them inferior men. As part of that process we will be drilling you every day, giving you vigorous exercise, training your bodies alongside your brains. The booklet being given you by your petty officers now will tell you all you need to know about the regulations and timetables here. Make no mistake, HMS *Royal Arthur* may be a requisitioned holiday camp but it is run as one of His Majesty's ships, and the same penalties will apply as though she were ploughing the mid-Atlantic or braving Italian planes in the Med. Any questions?' He glanced around the refectory, then chuckled drily at his own joke. 'Fast learners.'

Charles's chalet partner, Newby, the birdwatcher, was a big-eared, raw-necked lad from Bridlington. He was painfully shy and clearly horrified at having to undress in front of another man. He was already in bed in his well-buttoned pyjamas when Charles came in that first evening, after a stroll around the camp to get his bearings in the moonlight. And in the morning, he woke Charles as he hurried out, still in his pyjamas but clutching his uniform and boots, presumably planning to change into them in a washroom cubicle.

'I'll be one of the ones they kick out early,' he told Charles gloomily. 'I'm a sparks by trade. I'd rather be a telegraphist or a radio operator.'

The speed with which he could identify any passing bird and provide its Latin name made Charles less certain. The more likely candidates for failure, he felt, were the crossword fiends, since it soon became clear that cryptic interpretation was less what was needed than blind obedience to a system. They were not to be code-breakers but coders, taking messages in and out of an agreed code as swiftly and accurately as possible. Incoming messages were doubly encoded, of course, being received in Morse. The boarding school element – being far from home, having to take showers in rowdy company, daily PE sessions and having to master the art of sitting on a filthy lavatory with one boot firmly against an unlockable door – might have proved less of a shock to the privately educated, but as soon as he was back in a classroom, Charles felt entirely at home.

They learned in classes of around twenty in Nissen huts still smelling strongly of creosote. They sat at school desks slightly too small for comfort for the taller men, and those not lucky enough to be seated near the end with windows had to squint in the dim light to read. Charles was saved having to learn *flag-wagging* (semaphore) or how to read a message delivered by hoisted flags or the flashes of an Aldis lamp, but everyone in the camp had to learn Morse as a basic skill, and in case a wireless telegraphist was, cue euphemism, 'out of action'. It was the first time since being expected to learn the basics of Latin on arrival at the grammar school that Charles could remember having to digest and memorise such blocks of information. At first it seemed impossible, but he was determined not to be demoted, as he already thought of it, to a different task, and the more the other men moaned and huffed, the steelier he found his determination becoming. It helped that their teacher was a kind older officer, not unlike the most effective grammar school maths teachers, who taught with patience rather than fear.

'You could learn Morse code in twenty minutes,' he said

MOTHER'S BOY

when they started, 'but I'm giving you a week, because you're human.'

They were to forget about the alphabet, he said. Instead they would memorise the code by use of mnemonics that linked the letters linked in Morse. So *FUEL* helped them remember that F, which was dot-dot-dash-dot was the exact opposite of L, which was dot-dash-dot-dot. On this principle *ATE I'M SO HOT* would remind them T and E were one dash and one dot respectively; I, two dots; M, two dashes; S, three dots; O, three dashes and H, four dots, followed by the three dashes of O and the one dash of T.

Other phrases they had to learn were *ANN BEE VEE, D'YOU FEEL GREAT WAR 'CUTELY* – which undoubtedly worked better in Newby's Yorkshire accent – and *KAISER PAX*. This last illustrated what were called the Sandwiches.

'We and our allies are dots and the enemy are dashes. Kaiser began the war and hemmed us in, thus K is dash-dot-dash. R is the end of the Kaiser, when we turn the tables, thus dot-dash-dot. P stands for peace, for which the enemy sued once surrounded by the allies, thus P is dot-dash-dash-dot. X, confusingly, is the end of peace (pax) with the allies in the centre sending the defeated armies home; thus X is dash-dot-dot-dash. Got it? You at the back, see if you can repeat all that back to me.'

The awkward buggers, the letters with no opposites, were C, Z and J. One memorised these as *SEIZE JEREMIAH*. C was dash-dot-dash-dot and Z, as an emphatic C was double-dash-double-dot. J was plain awkward. For that they

219

had to memorise *JEREMIAH IN THE BIBLE MOANING ON HIS OWN* to remind them that J was a dot and three dashes, as in the short vowel of Je and the three long ones of re-mi-ah.

After a few minutes of thinking these mnemonics astonishingly unhelpful, Charles found they had stuck in his head and won full marks when they were tested on them at the first lesson's end. Far harder were the numerals. Whereas he found he could accept the letters as a given, something about numbers made him expect logic.

'Pivot. Do you see? The single dot of 5 is the pivot,' their teacher kept saying. 'Before that it's 1, 2, 3 or 4 out of 10; after that it's 10 minus the number of dots. Easy, really.'

Charles's brain rebelled at this point, so he scored less well on day two and was riled to hear not so quiet jeers when it was heard that he hadn't made the top ten a second time.

The coding classes were smaller. Coders were dotted through the camp's intake but were under strict instructions never to describe their work to their messmates, even in the broadest terms. Their teacher for this was not an officer but a civilian from a ministry, Charles assumed. They all simply called him sir, although he could only have been thirty at most. He certainly hadn't fought in the last war, like their Morse trainer. The coded messages had to be decoded using complex substitution codes, which would be changed regularly. They were also given messages to put back into code the same way. The decoding and coding were relatively simple; what at first seemed impossibly hard was to do the tasks at speed. Just as the desired speed to reach for Morse proficiency was eighteen words a minute, it made sense for the coder working alongside the telegraphist to be able to work at the same speed to avoid a backlog of potentially important signals. They were introduced to code books. These were small, about two inches square, with a dull grey binding. Each page displayed a different date in the month above a grid on which letters in black were shown alongside their code substitute numbers. A Greek theta and an underlined R were also used. Signals, or messages, were inscribed on signal pads as they came in, which were divided into columns. The first letter in each signal told you which code book to use, the second, the page to use in it and so on. They were taught to recognise recurring patterns to save time. Ships, places, common phrases, all had their own four-letter codes, again to save time.

The pace of the coding classes was relentless and usually began with quick-fire mental arithmetic around the group. Much of them took place in a sort of frenzied silence at the end of which, as their work was checked for errors, Charles would feel his heart racing. At the end of each class every single scrap of paper written on was burned in the stove in the centre of the hut, while the code books were locked away in an attaché case their teacher brought in every day.

Each day began with some form of physical training before breakfast. Usually this was a run several times around the playing field or out on to the adjacent beach for punishing routes up and down the high bank of sand. There were also gruelling rounds of physical jerks: scissor jumps, press-ups, running on the spot with knees brought high.

Many of the recruits seemed to be weekend footballers or rugby players and relished all this. For Charles it was a humiliating torture but, just as at school, it helped him find his fellow misfits: the skinny, the bookish, the sharp-tongued outcasts. They would often sit together at meals and he soon found he wasn't the only one instructed to send home parcels of dirty laundry to his mother. He endured football, gym, endless drills in marching and in learning to ground and slope arms, and submitted to needlessly fault-finding kit inspections. He became sunburnt from all the hours outside in the bracing Skegness breezes without a hint of shade, and the blue serge of his collar dug painfully into his skin and stained it where his sweat made the dye run. His fingertips ached from endlessly slapping his rifle and from taking it apart and putting it back together again until he thought he could weep from the pointlessness and tedium of it all. The epilogue to every day was the melancholy cleaning and polishing of damp boots.

His chalet proved to be on the wrong side of the camp's sewage plant, so it reeked when the constant wind was in the wrong direction, and the summer heat and blackout blinds made it like a little oven long after sunset. Every night was broken by air raids, the shrieking siren Charles longed to ignore, then the hasty tugging on of dressing gown and slippers and stumbling trudge with all their neighbours to a horribly cramped and airless shelter. Sleep there was impossible for all the chat, the enthusiasts watching the high-up flashes and dogfights and providing running commentary, and the ceaseless round of dirty jokes and competitive farting. When he dared to complain he was told, 'You think this smells bad? Just you wait till you're living in a mess on board!' and 'Just pray you're not made a submariner!'

A sizeable group left Skegness after the first week, among them, Newby, his lugubrious chalet mate. This gave Charles the luxury of snoreless nights, which he dared not mention in case someone else was assigned Newby's bed. He was certain everyone was worrying and no one was letting on. He worried, too, that all the others were bonding, forming swift and easy friendships while he not only found himself inhibited by constantly remembering they were in competition, but also that they would soon be split up and scattered. There would rarely be more than two coders to a ship – possibly only one at first, as it was a newly created rank – so what was the point in friendships that could go nowhere? Charles knew that he was not popular. Just as at school, popularity seemed to go hand in hand with being good or at least fearless at games, with being able to climb the ropes in the gym without worrying about the height or being able to intercept and tap to a mate a ball kicked at cannonball speed. And being good-looking.

Still, quiet alliances of a sort developed, often based on something as simple as overhearing a Devon or Cornwall accent. His Devonport nickname, Jan, had mysteriously travelled with him, presumably spread by the two older, superior coders with whom he had caught the train and no longer seemed to encounter. He hated them for it, although

223

he did not feel compelled to correct its inaccuracy, as he had done before it was shortened.

They had evenings off occasionally and would catch buses into town, or walk there along the featureless beach, past the hospital for miners with damaged lungs. Skegness was a curious place. He found its lack of cliffs and utter flatness disturbing, though there was a bleak beauty to the sand dunes beyond the edge of town, where he could walk to the mouth of the Wash, and where the drama of the enormous skies reminded him of climbing Rough Tor. Most of the men headed straight to noisy pubs. Charles usually went to hide in the cinema, watching whatever was on just as he had always done at home, briefly losing himself in a tangle of narrative and newsreel, heady glamour and tawdry crimes. He fretted that his piano playing would be suffering; it was the first time since boyhood he had not been practising every day, and he was sure all the sloping of butts and bruising on sports fields would not be good for his hands.

One evening, he emerged blinking from a surreal double bill of *Rebecca* and *My Favourite Wife* and was caught up in a group heading to a nearby seafront hotel for a drink before the long walk home with their handful of carefully shaded torches. Unable to enter any of the conversations, his head still full of silk gowns and preposterous breakfast china, he spotted a piano in the corner of the saloon bar. Without thinking, he sat at it and played a version of 'Ah! Sweet Mystery of Life', which must have been slightly showy, as it earned a round of applause, and suddenly he was surrounded by beery messmates shouting requests. There were soldiers there from another camp as well, and a strikingly handsome one bought him a whisky and soda and shouted, 'There you go, Jack,' in a way that made Charles blush.

Out of the blue, in the week before their exams, they were sent home on leave for just forty-eight hours. They were issued with identity cards and a swift lecture.

'Liberty men, 'shun! Now pay attention, liberty men. Remember your leave expires at 10 p.m. back here in the camp, not on a train halfway across the country from wherever you've been. Look after your identity cards. They are your birthright. They are your property. Loss of your card is liable to land you in serious trouble. Carry on, liberty men.'

Most of the precious leave was eaten up in train journeys – to Grantham, to King's Cross, crawling out of Paddington at nearly 2 a.m. in a train grey with cigarette and pipe smoke, to Plymouth, then on to Launceston at eight thirty in the morning. Mother was hard at work when he arrived. Gertie, the evacuee, was hiding in her room with the baby, or not yet up. Charles fell asleep in a blissfully hot and soapy bath, then again in his bed, where Mother woke him to say she had lunch ready, and aunts and uncles and cousins keen to see him. Everyone said he looked fitter and taller, which might have been down to all the PT but was probably just the heels on his boots and the effect of wearing uniform. Then he was asked to play at a dance and Mother said to do it as it would be a chance to catch up with everyone. It was a public dance, crammed with soldiers, and she came along and sat happily at a table with her sisters.

Charles woke the next day in a kind of anguish at finding himself back in his boyhood room, even though the bed was shorter than the chalet one. Mother delayed starting work so as to enjoy breakfast with him. She must have used up her week's ration on the bacon, even though he insisted the one thing the Navy didn't stint on was food, and there was a sweetness to sitting with her, eating toast and hearing chat about who was doing what and what the soldiers got up to, and how poor Gertie didn't understand the countryside.

'Did you mean it about putting an evacuee in your room?' she asked.

'Of course,' he said, and told her he would empty his wardrobe into a suitcase under the bed for her before he left.

'Thank you, Charles,' she said. 'It will feel odd. You will write when you can?'

'Of course,' he said.

'And so will I,' Mother said. 'Though you know mine won't be clever. It'll be like when your father was out there.'

'Did he write?'

'Not much.'

She batted away a tear with the heel of her hand. She had cried when she saw him off the last time and it had been almost more than he could bear.

'When's your train?' she asked. 'Are you on the three o'clock?'

'I'd better go before that. I have to change three times and there are bound to be delays. It amazes me Plymouth still has a station to change at, with all the bombing they've had.'

'Don't.'

They'd been spared in Launceston, apart from a single bomb dropped without killing so much as a cow in a nearby field, but had been watching poor Plymouth's fiery glow in the sky night after night. Between sets at the dance he had noticed how older men, not in uniform, were keen to impress on him how close the war was getting. Asked about the Home Guard, Mother pulled a wry face and said it stopped old men's pride being wounded.

She insisted on making him a picnic for his journey, as it might take all day. She packed corned beef and pickle sandwiches, apples, slices of fruit cake and three bottles of Eyre's ginger beer to remind him where he came from, all of it wrapped in the waxed paper she always smoothed out and cleaned and saved when she unpacked shopping. Charles let her, because he knew she needed to be occupied.

'When will you go to sea?' she asked.

'As soon as they've done training me, I suppose,' he said. 'Assuming I pass.'

'You'll pass. You know you will. Boiled egg?'

'No, thank you.'

'Will you tell me? Just so I know. I know you can't give details but . . .'

'Yes,' he told her. 'Of course I will. Mother, I don't know when I'll get back here again.'

'Don't,' Mother said. 'Just . . .' She wiped the bread board and put away the knife with a click. 'Just come home safely when you do.'

He said goodbye in the kitchen rather than let her come with him to the station. She hugged him tightly. Wang left his basket and came wheezily over to them to turn slow circles, sensing emotion but too old to bark.

GERTIE

Waving Charles off for the second time felt far more painful than the first. The first time, less than two months ago, had been the first time in their life together they had parted for anything other than an overnight school trip to London or the short holidays he sometimes took with Maggie in Trusham. The first time, Laura had little idea what to expect. His second departure, after a cruelly short leave, felt like a bereavement compared to a serious illness. While he was in training, she entertained all sorts of unpatriotic fantasies that he would be found wanting and sent back home. She had hoped they would find him too weak, they would discover he had failed the medical after all but that the paperwork had been muddled or, all too probably, they would find him too insubordinate. But this second time he was in uniform and almost certainly bound for the sea and danger within days.

Laura had promised not to come with him to the station because she had found it hard not to cry when waving him off before and sensed he had found that unbearable. But then, after Charles had left, she realised she couldn't bear not to. If she followed him directly but only came on to the platform a few minutes before the train was due to leave, she could wave at him and he could wave back. He'd be gone, but at least she'd have blessed him on his way. What had begun to make her weepy last time had been the waiting together, the awful sense that he was having to make conversation to fill the void, the sense of her own flesh and blood feeling awkward with her.

She took off her housecoat, fretted that she had somehow picked up a streak of flour on the front of her dress, decided there wasn't time to change so pulled on her summer overcoat to hide it and was just wondering whether to take Wang as well, if he wouldn't make her too slow, when she heard weeping from the spare bedroom.

'Gertie?'

Laura walked back to the foot of the stairs and called up quietly, so as not to wake the baby. 'What's wrong, girl?'

The child opened her door and looked down, her pinched face all flushed, nose red, eyes puffed up.

'Is Charles still there?' she asked quietly.

'No, dear. You missed him. He's gone for his train. I was just going to—'

But her plan to catch him at the station was scuppered as Gertie broke down in fresh weeping.

'Here,' Laura said. 'Hush now. Come on down or you'll wake that mite of yours. I know he was up half the night.'

'Sorry.'

'Don't be silly. Thin walls is all. I'll make tea and you can tell me all about it.'

She made a pot of tea and set out bread, margarine and jam, which she had learned was Gertie's main form of nutrition. She heard many women complain in the shop queues about their older evacuees being dirty or lazy or rude, but had realised early on in Gertie's stay that problems arose when hosts tried to make their evacuees behave like them: rise, eat and wash when they did. Once it was clear that Gertie had a very different internal clock to her own, waking late and often coming down for a while in the middle of the night, Laura made it clear to her where to find food if she missed any meal. They agreed on bath nights and a laundry rota. Laura had Gertie's ration book and the one for little Fred. She had made enquiries of the WVS and secured a bundle of baby clothes for him, and a pram so he could be taken out for walks.

The hardest part of having Gertie in the house was resisting the urge to take over the care of Fred entirely. Laura regularly pushed his pram out for slow strolls with Wang to let Gertie sleep, and tended to clean his nappies more often than not, as Gertie had a tendency to leave them piling up in the soaking bucket until they were pushing off the lid and stinking. But otherwise she had tried to act like a good mother towards her, gently showing her how best to wash and change the baby and helping to still his cries when Gertie's impatience made the wailing worse. She said nothing about Gertie not coming to church, or appearing in her dressing gown when it was nearly lunchtime. She looked after the baby while Gertie went to the cinema, which Laura knew she loved, and taught her simple bits of cookery when they coincided in the kitchen, and the girl was in the mood to learn. But Gertie spent most of her days up in her room and was rarely talkative. She wrote no letters and received none, seeming utterly alone in a tiny family of two. Perhaps it was this that made

Laura feel for her so. She appeared to have broken entirely with her parents since they had parked her in the mother and baby home.

Gertie had made an effort when she finally joined Laura at the kitchen table, had brushed her hair and put it back under a velvet band, and dressed in her nice frock with the daisies around the hem.

'You look nice,' Laura told her truthfully, and poured her some tea and cut her a slice of bread, which Gertie duly spread with margarine and bramble jelly.

'Thanks,' Gertie said.

'What's the matter?'

A piece of bread had been halfway to Gertie's mouth. Her hand sank back to the plate.

'You'll think I'm so stupid,' she said. 'Promise you won't be angry.'

'Have I ever been angry with you?'

Gertie shook her head and looked down. She swore she was no longer a minor though she still looked barely more than fifteen. She was so thin still it amazed Laura she was able to nurse the baby.

'He went without saying goodbye.'

'Who did? Oh, Gertie, did you meet somebody?'

It was always possible. The town was so busy with soldiers now that even the homeliest girls were not short of dance partners if they wanted them. Laura had not managed to persuade Gertie to go to a dance yet, but she might well have met someone on a trip to the cinema. Last time she had gone with Aggie's girl Heppy, who had lost her job as a maid and was already said to be proving a handful.

'No,' Gertie said. 'I mean Charles.'

'My Charles?'

'Yes.'

As far as Laura knew, Charles had done nothing but complain about Gertie since her arrival the previous autumn. At least he complained about the baby's crying keeping him awake or stopping him writing. And he often seemed to ignore Gertie entirely if they coincided for a meal, or to leave a room when she came into it. But now she remembered a couple of occasions where she had come in from doing laundry to find Gertie sitting at the kitchen table with Fred on her lap, listening as Charles played the piano next door.

'I felt I should stay out of the way yesterday when you had family round to see him, but then you were both out at the dance all evening.'

'Oh, and I could have babysat for you if I'd known you'd wanted to go. I'm so sorry, Gertie. You've never wanted to go before.'

'No, no. Don't be. It's silly. All in my head, really.'

Upstairs the baby woke and started to grouse.

'I'll go,' Laura said, standing. 'You drink that tea and eat some more bread and jam. Get your strength up.'

The spare room was heartbreakingly tidy. Given the girl's youth and chaotic background, Laura would have expected heaps of discarded or dirty clothes, but the space was as tidy as a nun's cell, with everything put away, the inadequate cardboard suitcase with the broken handle tucked under the bed where Gertie had been using it as a laundry basket, and the stash of cinema magazines she never seemed to tire of examining neatly stacked by the tightly tucked bed. The magazines and the presence of the bawling baby were the only un-nun-like touches.

Laura scooped Fred up, stilling his cries by letting him wail then mumble into the warmth of her neck as she rocked him against her, delighting in the warmth of him and the indefinable smell, somewhere between rising dough and newly baked shortbread, coming from the top of his blond head. It was the smell she remembered from when Charles was that age, a smell nature had surely perfected for enslaving women over the centuries. Whenever she came across women who seemed offhand or even cold with babies, she always wondered if their noses were faulty.

She hugged the borrowed baby for a minute or two as his cries subsided to hungry gurgles, rocking slowly from foot to foot, holding him as she had missed holding Charles, and wondering if it would be so bad to acquire him as a grandson. She realised guiltily that she had never let herself imagine a wife for Charles in any detail, beyond being resolved to be a more welcoming mother-in-law than some she had watched at work. Her instinctive reaction was that Gertie would be quite wrong for him, too young, too uneducated; the child could barely sign her name. But what did she know? Perhaps Charles's apparent impatience had all been a front and there had been long, late night conversations over cocoa and biscuits about the film stars they adored, while she slept oblivious overhead? Perhaps he liked the fact that she was from Hackney, not Launceston, and couldn't tell a cow from a heifer or crimp a pasty to save her life? Perhaps he liked the thought that she had a passionate nature that had got her into trouble and saw himself as, somehow, her protector?

Fred had quietened but was plainly hungry, from the way he was mumbling at her neck, and he needed changing. She took him down, resolving to be supportive and hoping her face had betrayed none of her shock.

'He wants his mum,' she told Gertie, 'and a change . . .'

Although she knew she could change him in half the time, she needed to let Gertie do it or the girl would never improve her technique. She had persuaded her not to feel she had to nurse him alone in her room – that it was cosier by the range, where they could both relax. The nuns who ran the mother and baby home she had escaped from had been ferocious about *modesty*, apparently.

Still red of eye and nose, Gertie settled to feeding Fred while Laura washed up the breakfast things. Then Laura plugged the iron in to heat so she could smooth yesterday's wash. She turned the radio on as well as they both enjoyed it and Laura suspected Gertie was self-conscious about Fred's occasionally vigorous sucking noises. The girl grew calmer and happier as he fed, which was a relief.

The placid sight of the two of them, Fred's happily twitching toes, the delicious smell of hot linen as Laura began to iron and the happy music from the radio did not cast their usual spell, however. This young girl, for whom she had felt nothing but protective, even motherly sympathy since her wretched first appearance on the station platform surrounded by chattering children, now seemed sharp-faced to her, even feral. Where less than a day ago Laura had been looking around for possible work Gertie could take on once Fred was weaned, or at least able to be left with her and a bottle, now she found she could only think of how little she wanted her for a daughter-in-law.

She shocked herself. The poor girl had only admitted to what was almost certainly a hopeless and unnoticed crush.

'If you'd like to write to Charles,' she made herself tell Gertie, 'it couldn't be easier. We could always put your letter in the next one I send him. Or even just a picture of you and Fred? We could go up to the Square and have your picture taken together at—'

'No. I don't think so,' Gertie cut in. 'He'd think it was odd. I don't think he noticed me really. I was just being silly.'

'Of course you weren't,' Laura said. 'I bet he thinks you're lovely.' *What are you thinking, woman?* she told herself. *Hold your tongue!*

Gertie changed Fred soon after that, then, saying he was sleepy and that she was too, took him back up to her room. Laura turned down the volume on the radio only to hear her softly crying again. On and on. Combined with Charles's departure it brought on a creeping feeling of desolation that entered her like a chill and would not be shaken off. Finally, noticing the time, she unplugged the iron, folded away the cloths she used to turn the kitchen table into an ironing surface, hung up her housecoat and went to her room to put on a coat and hat.

'Gertie?' she called softly across the landing.

'Yes?' The response was characteristically limp. That's what was wrong with the child: she lacked vim. She sucked the energy from a room simply by entering it.

235

'I'm just heading up the hill to Mary Magdalene. I've remembered there's evensong today and I thought it would make a change. Do you want to come? We could leave Fred's pram just inside the porch.'

'Better not,' Gertie said.

There was a pause. A long pause.

'I'll see you later, then,' Laura said eventually. 'Lancashire hotpot for supper. It's all made so we can eat whenever you like after I'm back. And carrots from the garden.'

A stupid thing to say, but she felt she had to say something. She had never felt awkward with Gertie before, or felt the need to make conversation.

Walking would do her good; it usually did. She took the less direct route into town as there was time to kill, up the hill past the National School and the allotments that were always busy with Sunday gardeners since the command to dig for victory, and then turning left around the castle and along Castle Dyke to the church.

Laura loved evensong, even though its frequent references to rest and nightfall tended to make her think of death. Charles liked to say it was a poem from beginning to end, provided nobody spoiled it with a sermon. Attendance that night was high, as it had been in St Thomas's at early Communion that morning, because people were worried, she supposed, and in need of comfort. There were a surprising number of soldiers from the camps that were springing up on the edges of town. Miss Bracewell was there, looking sadly aged suddenly and walking with two sticks. She had been in hospital until just recently after a nasty fall, and Laura had not been to work for her for a few weeks. Miss Bracewell didn't see her; Laura was sitting near the back, by the memorial to the two men who had variously drowned in the West Indies and 'suffered a worse fate at the hand of ignorant savages'. That was a favourite of Charles's. She was always a little shy on the rare occasions she met Miss Bracewell out. They were friendly enough when Laura was collecting her laundry or cleaning for her, but on the street the differences between them inhibited them both.

Laura hoped her hip wasn't still too painful. She seemed to be walking with such difficulty it was hard to imagine her coping for much longer in a house with so many stairs. Perhaps she would move out to a bungalow on the edge of town, or even somewhere with a sea view, like Polzeath or Widemouth Bay? When all but the last collects ended and there was a moment to pray for others, Laura prayed for her, and for Charles and then for Gertie and Fred. And she prayed that she would not feel awkwardly towards Gertie for what the girl, in her sincerity, had blurted out.

As she was returning, coming by the more usual route down Angel Hill and past the top of the Zig-Zag, she heard the last London train of the day set off. It was a perfect late summer evening, the light golden, swallows on the wing. She saw the train's steam as it headed off and the second shrill of its whistle drew over her the Sunday evening sadness that the spell of evensong had briefly held at bay.

Charles had surely crossed London by now and would be heading out to the eastern coast again. Her sense of geography beyond Devon and Cornwall was imprecise but he had shown her Skegness on the school atlas at home, shown her the route the succession of trains there would take. She knew he couldn't keep sending her his laundry once he went to sea. He had explained how sailors were all expected to clean their own clothes, that laundering was inexplicably called dhobeying after the Hindi for washerman, and had asked her to demonstrate some techniques. She showed him how a nailbrush was his friend, how a nailbrush scrubbed first on a bar of soap would lift most marks before laundering. She told him to be sure always to rinse and wring three times, that rinsing not only lifted the last of the dirt but the last traces of soap as well, which might otherwise bring his delicate skin out in a rash. She taught him that woollens should only be washed in cold water, however dirty they were, to stop them shrinking or losing softness. Her last blessing to him was the trick of slipping a matchstick between button and fabric when sewing a button back on a coat or jacket, to keep it loose enough not to pinch and distort the garment. It had touched her to feel him paying her closer attention in the few minutes of these lessons than he had done in years.

The house was silent when she let herself in. Perhaps after their troubled night both mother and baby were sound asleep. Laura turned the radio on fairly low, thinking to wake them gently with it in time for supper, slid the stew to the front of the range to heat and chopped carrots and set those to boil too. Thanks to advice from neighbours she now had a good row of parsley outside. (The trick, strangely, had been to pour boiling water over the seeds in their narrow trench, something she'd assumed would have cooked them.) She went out to pick a small handful to chop over the carrots when they were ready. Gertie hadn't been used to vegetables when she arrived, and Laura had taken to making a special effort with them in order to tempt her. Young mothers needed iron, she told her, and vitamins, especially when nursing. With butter rationed to only two ounces each a week, and margarine and lard to four ounces, she tended to use marge for spreading, lard for baking, and butter, in tiny quantities, for making things like carrots and cabbage more tempting. She was seriously considering keeping a few hens for the extra eggs, as she yearned for sponge cakes and fluffy baked puddings. Heavy-cake and flapjacks no longer felt like an indulgence when they were all she could bake. Several people in the neighbourhood were doing this, while some enterprising lads had started keeping ferrets to catch rabbits for the pot. Leaving church just now was the second time she had been asked if she'd care to take out shares in a pig someone was fattening in their backyard, but she had demurred as she wasn't sure of the legality of this and had a horror of breaking the law.

She stirred the hotpot. It smelled good, if not very summery. She had carefully lifted off the disk of hard yellow fat from it before reheating, as that would do for roasting potatoes. Mutton fat had a stronger taste than most, but it didn't do to waste it.

There was still no sign of Gertie. Some woman on the radio was singing along with a band: songs by Ivor Novello. Laura found it a bit treacly but knew Gertie would love it. She responded to anything sad or sentimental, which was odd given how life had taught her such tough lessons so early. More than ever, Laura wished she could make contact with the girl's mother, partly to reassure her that mother and child were doing well but also, she knew, to shame her a little. But Gertie had balked at her repeated requests for an address. Laura couldn't bear to involve the Netleys so she had left well alone beyond making sure Gertie knew where paper, envelopes and stamps were kept, in case she wanted to write to her parents or to anyone else under her own steam.

'Gertie?' she called. 'Supper's ready.'

There was silence. Usually Gertie responded at once, even if only with a sleepy mumble. Laura climbed the stairs. She would look in, she decided, and let them sleep on if they were sleeping.

They had gone. The room was as tidy as she had seen it earlier, but the cot was empty and the little suitcase had vanished. She checked and found nothing in the chest of drawers or wardrobe. The girl must have left the house minutes after Laura had, presumably for the London train and with Fred bundled in a blanket in her arms as the borrowed pram was still in the hall. All she had left behind was a handful of nappies soaking in the bucket in the washroom.

It was only when Laura finally drew up her chair to eat a solitary supper, having turned off the radio as the music was making her more upset, that she saw the little card propped up against the small posy of wild flowers they had picked on a walk along Underlane in honour of Charles's leave. It was a postcard of Bude that Gertie must have bought earlier in the year, when buses were laid on to take the evacuees there for a day trip to the beach. The hand-writing was uncertain and impossibly small. 'Thank you for everything,' was all it said. 'Gone home think thats best Gertie'. There was no punctuation and the line of writing trailed downhill as though mimicking the writer's weighed-down mood.

The previous winter, just weeks after the evacuees arrived, but before air raids had become so frequent, there had been a crisis when many parents demanded their children return to them in the cities, or even sent for them, finding the sep-aration unbearable and believing all the precautions had been taken unnecessarily as the war was never actually going to get underway. Many children had gone from the Launceston area then. On one farm she knew of, where the childless couple had taken in six boys, only one remained. It was so bad that government posters went up and advertise-ments appeared in magazines and papers, showing Hitler murmuring seductively, 'Come back, come back,' to an uncertain mother, who was sitting with her baby beneath an apple tree as he gestured to the far distance where a city was in flames.

Gertie had agreed with Laura that people were fools and, like her, had worried about what became of the returners once the bombing started in earnest. For her to have taken herself back, now that London was being pounded night after night, gave a measure of how little she wanted to remain in Launceston. Assuming her family home was still standing, it was hard to imagine a warm welcome for her and the baby from parents who had abandoned her, rather than be disgraced. But perhaps they had given her up for lost when she ran away, had felt remorse and would run to meet her? Or perhaps there were friends or relations who would take her in instead?

Laura washed the sheets and aired the room and waited a day or two for news that never came, then braced herself to tell the Netleys that there was room for more evacuees should it be needed; extra room, even, now she had confirmed permission to make Charles's little room available for the duration of the war.

She wrote to Charles wishing him luck in his exams and sending a clipping from the local paper about a runaway cow, which she knew would amuse him. She told him Gertie had decided to return home but not the possible reason why Launceston should suddenly have become a place to make her unhappy. Charles's response to the news, or lack of it, would tell her all she needed to know.

SCAPA FLOW – 1941

The exams were gruelling but surprisingly short: from eight thirty to eleven fifteen for two days. They were on theoretical coding the first day and practical coding the next. Then came a day of anti-climax and worrying. Charles had duty class: sweeping and mopping, then fetching and distributing parcels and letters. He was walking back from delivering the last parcel when a gang of the heartier men came by, bouncing a football between them.

'You're all up,' one of them said, whom Charles knew hadn't sat the exams because he couldn't retain what he needed to. 'You're top, Jan.'

Charles muttered something non-committal, assuming it was a cruel joke, then hurried his pace to the notice board in the mess and found it to be true.

By one of those utterly pointless pieces of administration, he had to travel back to Devonport for two grim nights in a dormitory only then to be told that he had been assigned to a ship that he would need to join in Scotland. The journey, on a succession of trains by a route he could scarcely have plotted on a map, took nearly three days. On the last leg of it, heading ever further north, another sailor climbed up into his little box compartment, a big man with china-blue eyes and thick auburn hair. Charles guessed they were about the same age, only the other was clearly a far more experienced sailor as his uniform had a single red stripe for four years' service with good conduct. Also, the blue on his collar was faded from scrubbing. He offered Charles a cigarette, which Charles accepted, though he was still learning to smoke convincingly.

'*Starburst?*' he asked.

'Yes,' Charles said.

'First trip out?'

'Is it that obvious?'

The big man grinned and held out a hand that made Charles feel every inch the pen-pusher. 'Cushty,' he said. 'I know. You thought I'd be called Ginger or Red, didn't you?'

'No . . . I. Funnily enough, my best friend's a Ginger but his hair is mouse.'

'Is it now? No, I just say cushty a lot, apparently, so it stuck.'

'But what does it mean? Do you want a piece of cake?'

'Ta, lad. It means very good, I suppose. It's Romany but we're nothing fancy, just Scousers.'

'Well I'm Jan, as in Janner, because someone thought I came from Plymouth, though I don't.'

'Jan,' Cushty said, and looked at him a moment as he ate his slice of cake. 'Suits you,' he added with a wink. 'Did your mother make this?'

'Yes. Why? Is it cushty, Cushty?'

'Very much. If ever I meet her, I'll tell her so.'

Charles imagined Cushty at the kitchen table at home, cradling one of Mother's good teacups in his big hands as he charmed her. 'She'd like that,' he said.

'So what's the badge? I've been a gunner for a while but I've never seen that.'

'Coder,' Charles said. 'Ordinary coder. It's new. I'm told I'll be messing with the Signals men, telegraph, radio and so on.'

Cushty smiled to himself and Charles knew he had been sounding wet behind the ears. 'So you're clever?' he asked.

'No,' Charles said, 'just not sporty.'

'Gunners and stokers need brawn, it's true,' Cushty said. 'I'm not on the guns. I'm usually down below hauling shells up from the magazine. Shell after fucking shell. I used to play rugby so I already had the shoulders for it, I suppose. And the thick ears.'

'Have you seen much action?'

'A bit.' Cushty looked out at the darkening landscape beyond the window. There was more visible than there would have been, as blackout regulations had seen all the carriage lights replaced with very dim blue ones. 'A fair bit,' he added, and a sort of steel shutter seemed to come down on the conversation. Charles could think of nothing else to say so retreated into rereading his manual on naval life by the dim light of his torch. But then, just as they finally drew in to their station, Cushty stirred as though he had nodded off and said, 'No, you're all right,' in a low voice that made Charles feel he had been forgiven.

There were other sailors gathered at the dockside, none of them a new recruit like Charles. Most, like Cushty, had the resigned air of seasoned men used to saving energy. Charles had taken the precaution of stuffing his little manual deep in his duffel coat pocket before anyone could see it and laugh at him.

'This is Jan,' Cushty told them all. 'Our new ordinary coder.'

They were fetched in a motor-boat – a *larnch*, as their Morse trainer would have called it. The crossing seemed pretty bouncy, but the sailors laughed and even whooped when the boat rose and fell dramatically and Cushty seemed quite unconcerned. It was a relief, though, to realise they were slowing at last to pull up alongside the *Starburst*. As they embarked, hauled one by one over the alarming black void between boats, he was immediately singled out as Ordinary Coder Causley by a Scottish sailor, who introduced himself seriously as Signalman Disborough.

'But everyone calls me Dizzy and I gather we call you Jan.'

Dizzy gave him a quick tour. The ship was unexpectedly warm and dazzlingly well lit. The Signals mess was spotless, though small, and Charles was relieved to see it had little bunks rather than the hooks for hammocks he had been dreading. A radio was playing. Malcolm Muggeridge was saying something about belief and idealism, and Charles felt a keen nostalgia, not for home precisely, but for the distinctive smell of boot polish, cheese and apples in the neighbourhood corner shop. Dizzy, who he was realising had a wafer-dry humour and was probably one of those telegraphists who could solve cryptic crosswords without a pencil and paper, showed him 'the route you'll use most often, especially until you've got your sea legs'. This led from the signalmen's mess up a steel ladder, through the seamen's mess, which had just been cleaned and reeked of disinfectant and Pusser's soap, to the bathroom, with its tin basins and spotted mirror and past the heads. 'You'll be here a lot but it can get busy so . . .' Dizzy continued the tour past the wireless office, a hot, windowless box as brilliantly lit as a pre-war radio shop in the run-up to Christmas, past the galley to the ship's side. 'This is where you empty your gash bucket when there's no heads free,' he told Charles. 'Just be aware which way the wind is blowing; no one will thank you for getting it in their face. Any questions?'

'Yes. Which watch am I on?'

'Keen, eh? Four to eight tonight, so try to get some shut-eye after we eat. Then you're on mess duties. Not cooking tomorrow, just sweep and swab. Easy stuff. Now I should go and wash and brush up. Maybe shave? Don't want the mess thinking they've taken on a tramp.'

This was a good idea. The bathroom was empty and the water very hot. Shaving, while they were still at anchor was restorative after such a long and dirty journey. Sure enough, his messmates were bright and funny, not a scrum half or rowing blue among them. His nickname led to talk of West Country dialects and one of them revealing himself to be a linguist, who knew far more Cornish words than Charles. Another insisted on lending him a James Thurber book they had been passing round and, with much hilarity, Charles's copy of *War and Peace* was added to the two already in the mess library. Supper was pork chops, buttery mashed potato, Savoy cabbage and some emerald fresh parsley sauce followed by treacle tart and custard.

As ravenous as he was painfully homesick, Charles ate everything, even washing it down with a tin mug of strong, sweet tea made with condensed milk without blanching. Or not much.

'You get used to it,' the linguist told him, seeing him flinch. 'I was raised on very pale, milkless Earl Grey. Just don't think of it as tea but as condensed milk with tea flavouring. It's actually remarkably like the tea you get in Tibet where they put yak butter in it.'

There were groans at this – clearly a wilfully stomach-turning comment they had all heard before. Then a pipe announced the next watch and those on duty hopped to it.

'You'll have sailed before,' Dizzy said. 'Having eaten like that?'

'Er, no,' Charles admitted uncertainly. 'I've never been on a boat until today.'

With hindsight it seemed everyone stopped what they were doing to take that admission in, like the horrified figures in a Bateman cartoon, before going about their business.

'Sleep,' Dizzy told him, as the ship filled with new noises and vibrations and began to move.

Charles had never been seasick before, because he had never sailed anywhere. He had been sick from stomach bugs, which always seemed to spread through school in January and, once or twice, when he had caught too much sun and, more recently, when he had drunk too much beer. But in all these cases the eventual heaving up of whatever he had in him had brought such instant relief it was a wonder to him people did not vomit as readily as they coughed or yawned. This sickness, however, was without relief.

He had dutifully climbed into his bunk – by muttered consultation he was assigned a bottom one – and briefly actually fallen asleep, lulled by the chugging sounds from the engines, the clicking and murmur of messmates playing bridge and the soothing chat of the radio. But then he woke in semi-darkness, felt the ship seem to plunge bow first into a chasm and knew he was about to throw up. A messmate had thought to hang a gash bucket so that it would be close to hand when he sat up. He barely had time to yelp an apology before half-filling it, with a sound and smell that brought groans from the bunks around his. Then the ship plunged into a second hideous chasm and he had the bucket almost full. Somehow he stamped into his boots, not daring to lace them for fear of losing control of the bucket, then he made the challenging journey up the ladder singlehanded, bucket slopping in the other, heaved afresh in the seamen's mess, which earned him a round of furious curses along with raucous applause, before he staggered to the heads. These were indeed fully occupied so he lurched on to the galley and the ship's side where he tipped the bucket and watched, astonished as, against all laws of physics, its contents seemed to fly directly sideways rather than down. Until he realised that down was briefly sideways, and threw up again, directly over the rail, keeping a desperate hold of the bucket handle and hearing himself actually sob between violent gulps for air.

He started back the way he had come only to realise it was futile as his stomach heaved again, although there was

PATRICK GALE

nothing but acrid liquid left to bring up. Instead he edged
out on to the deck beside the rail and found a thing – a
seat, a bench, a shelf? He had no idea what it was called
but it was secured – and he could slump on it and hold
himself in place by slipping his arm around another thing
for which he had no name. Braced like that, with the gash
bucket hooked over a forearm, he spent what must have
been an hour or two waiting for a death that was never
merciful enough to arrive.

It wasn't just that he felt so sick, so constantly sick, from
the ship's relentless pitching and yawing that he wanted to
die, but that, he began to understand, he was utterly terrified. He was on a ship of which he could navigate his way
along just one short section, on his way to Scapa Flow,
whose very name sounded like a spot marked on a detailed
map of Hell by a vindictive Puritan, in a sea that seemed
utterly wild but was probably calm compared to how it
might be later, and with the prospect of coming under
enemy fire from air, sea or underwater. Surely neither sensation would ever pass. He found that whenever he closed
his eyes, he was picturing the bottomless chasm of water
beneath them over which they were so unnaturally travelling. It was like the sensation when he put down a foot
when swimming and found nothing there, only taken to
extremes.

'All right?'

He hadn't realised he had nodded off. Cushty was standing before him, steadying himself by clutching something
overhead. All Charles could manage was a soft groan.

Cushty grinned. 'I heard you had it bad. Here.' He held

250

out a mug of icy cold water. 'Don't gulp, mind,' he said. 'Just sips. You need to keep water in you, or you'll get a blinder of a headache.'

Charles took the mug, aware he was parched. 'Thanks,' he muttered.

'Christ, your teeth are chattering, man. Where's your coat?'

'Back on my bunk.'

Cushty undid the toggles on his duffel coat.

'But you'll be cold,' Charles protested.

'I was on first watch. I'm off to sleep now so don't need it. Why don't you sleep too?'

'Too sick,' Charles managed. 'And I'm on the morning watch. Scared of oversleeping.'

'No risk of that. Someone'll shake you awake.'

'I don't want to risk it. I just want to die.'

Cushty chuckled, took off his coat and held it out to him. 'Come on,' he said.

Charles set down the mug between his boots, made sure the bucket was going nowhere, then stood gingerly while Cushty pulled the coat around him. It held the other man's warmth and smelled of tobacco and comfort.

'Thank you,' he murmured, then an abrupt lurch made him sit swiftly down again.

'It'll pass,' Cushty said. 'It took me a week. Sip, don't gulp, remember.'

'How do I get this back to you?'

'My mess is in the same position as the Signals one, but on the other side.' He patted Charles on the shoulder as one might a frightened dog and walked away.

Other shipmates came and sat by him through the night, usually to smoke while waiting for a heads to come free. They all said they had been seasick when they started and variously prescribed looking at the horizon, avoiding looking at anything beyond the ship, lying down, standing up, moving to the bows (surely the most violently moving part of the ship?) and nibbling dry toast, but none offered comfort to match Cushty's duffel coat. Charles liked that nobody could tell the coat wasn't his, as they were all identical.

He dozed occasionally, already developing a sailor's birdlike instinct for gripping a perch even in sleep, and counted off the bells through to three in the morning, when he went to wash his face, use the heads and rinse out the gash bucket before reporting for duty in the wireless room.

He was on with Dizzy, which was good.

'You'll not be needing that,' Dizzy told him, indicating the coat and, sure enough, their little office was as hot as a bakery towards dawn. 'There's a hook for your bucket under the desk,' Dizzy added. 'You're not the first.'

The layout was exactly as they had been shown in a series of photographs during training. The code books in a safe, with the lead-weighted bags they were to toss overboard in the event of disaster, and the coding pads. The coder and signalman they were relieving left their posts with grateful glances, looking shattered, and Charles soon saw why. The pace was relentless, and he was keenly aware, as it was his very first watch as a coder, that he was completely unready for making the snap decisions required of him as to which signals were routine and could be filtered out and which must be passed to the bridge at once. The skipper was a bit deaf from shell damage, apparently, so didn't like them to use the speaker tube. Instead signals were to be relayed to him in person or on paper. Sometimes, if things were fairly quiet, as they mercifully were that first night, he would send a junior down at intervals to collect them. When things were busier, though, the coder was expected to ferry them to the bridge and Charles could only imagine the nightmare of being held up on such an errand, then returning to a backlog that only rapid sifting would clear.

He continued to heave at intervals, bringing up bitter bile and sips of water, but having to concentrate furiously on his code pad and slowly learning to recognise recurrent clusters of numbers, as in their training, at least took his mind off wanting to die. When his watch ended at 8 a.m. he was so drained that he had to be called back to take Cushty's coat and the unsavoury gash bucket with him.

Rather than head straight to the mess, he found his way round to the other side of the ship and down through the first mess to Cushty's one beyond. The air was ripe with the sailors' night smells combined with those of breakfast, and he was abashed to be faced with several cheerfully naked men, none of whom was Cushty.

'I . . . I brought back Cushty's duffel coat,' he blurted, glad he had at least thought to rinse out and stow the bucket on his way.

'Oi! Cushty?' one of them shouted towards the bunks. 'One of your fancy men's brought your mink back.'

There was a grunt.

'I'll give it to him,' one of the naked men said, taking it from his hands, and Charles fled.

He obediently nibbled dry toast and sipped brutally strong black tea for breakfast while all around him were feasting on fried eggs and asking if they could eat his share of sausages. Then he began to be sick again, while mopping and scrubbing out the mess. When he finally tumbled into his bunk, the air thick with the same disinfectant he had smelled the day before, he turned to the bulkhead in an effort to block out the light and the cheery chat of messmates, and craved the crisp, clean smell of Mother's ironing.

GIB – 1942

'Let's take it from the top again,' Charles called out, 'but this time try to take your time. It's a love song, not a school hymn. Try to relax.'

'I am perfectly relaxed,' Rusty told him, sounding as relaxed as a Home Service announcer.

'Good,' he said. 'Maybe try to show it!'

He played the introduction with an extra lilt he hoped might infect her style but once again Rusty sang 'Bill' like a head girl itemising the failings of a junior prefect, whereas the whole poignant appeal of the song, one of the reasons he'd chosen it, was that Wodehouse's lyrics celebrated ordinariness and would make all the ordinary men in the audience feel a little better about themselves and a little more hopeful romantically.

The audience would be almost entirely male as the population of Gibraltar currently was. The local women and children – the 'useless mouths', Churchill chillingly called them – had been abruptly and inefficiently shipped out at the start of hostilities so that the colony could become a garrison. Spanish women came over the border every day to work, of course, as cleaners, cooks and waitresses in the bars and, in some cases, on their backs in upper rooms with an impatient queue of men on the stairs, but Rusty was one of a tiny cluster of Wren signallers living in a well-guarded house, working punishingly long shifts in the tunnels high on the Rock. The population was so overwhelmingly male and loveless that these few women were in a strange, unenviable position: subjected to constant lewd advances from the men wherever they went and loudly accused of snobbery or lesbianism when they didn't respond in kind. They were regularly condemned for pip-hunting – only walking out with officers – but Charles could see no blame was called for if they did; a civilised evening's dinner and dancing at The Rock, the good hotel requisitioned as the officers' mess, was surely preferable to the mauling, or worse, any woman would get who braved the overflowing bars of Main Street.

As one of the few acknowledged pianists, he had been charged with throwing together a Twelfth Night fundraising concert for the Red Cross. Any of the women who could perform anything, from a song to reciting limericks, had been co-opted, along with the inevitable female impersonator, Taffy, a burly cook from Newport – who could have sung 'Bill' with far more kindness and emotion than Rusty's clipped manner could convey – and a tall, very camp messmate of Charles's everyone called Clara because his surname was Bow. Clara had been a choral scholar at Cambridge, where he was a star of the Gilbert and Sullivan Society, so was to give a couple of patter songs in his unexpectedly fulsome baritone. One girl was doing magic tricks involving an amazingly compliant dachshund and another was to play Handel's 'Largo' and 'The Sailor's Hornpipe' on a violin.

Because rehearsals in the Theatre Royal were throwing them together with Rusty and the others, Charles and

Clara and Taffy were subject to noisy envy from the other men and pestered with requests to *put in a word* or even pass on letters and photographs from the lovelorn. Charles soon realised the girls regarded them as no threat.

'Oh, you're all right,' Rusty had said on the first day. 'Anyone can see you're safe in taxis.' Her tone was dismissive, even by her head-girlish standards. She was used to telling people what to do and didn't like it when she realised Charles wasn't merely her accompanist but also her artistic director for the entertainment.

She was spectacularly attractive, a sort of Home Counties Ginger Rogers, tall and athletic with *legs up to here*, as Mother would have said, and he suspected that her singing would be largely drowned out by wolf whistles and drunken invitations to forget Bill and take up with Alf or whoever, but it was such a delight not to be coding for a change or swabbing out or chopping onions or delousing the beds. It was disconcerting, though, after uninterrupted months in the company of men, to be alone with an attractive woman and feel nothing, to feel himself, in fact, a kind of eunuch.

'Will you be a brick, Charles, and walk me back to the Wrennery?' Rusty asked once he'd realised no number of repetitions were going to wring a more heartfelt performance from her. 'I thought Diana or Bridget could scoop me up in the Jeep but they've had to go on watch early so I'm on Shanks' pony and defenceless.'

'Of course,' he said, although he was fairly sure a stinging rebuke from Rusty would have brought any leering mariner to his senses.

The freshness and light when they emerged from the old velvet gloom of the theatre was startling. It was one of the good days when the Rock hadn't gathered a heavy cloud above it. There was real warmth to the sun and a delicious smell of caramel and frying nuts was drifting from a nearby kitchen. It was said that several local men had succeeded in hiding wives or daughters in cupboards or secret rooms and were looking better fed and more contented than most of the servicemen. Quite apart from his daily relief at no longer being at sea, Charles rather loved Gibraltar. He had written to Mother that it was like an exotic version of Launceston, with the houses stacked up against the rock-face, the preposterous warren of alleyways and dwellings seemingly built one atop the other, giving the sense that everyone knew everyone else's business. Just as at home, there was the frequent smell of baking or laundry, and yet there were also marauding apes, orange trees, a beach with sand often too hot for bare feet, and a view of Africa. The place names bore testimony to a salty Englishness even as the weather and plentiful fresh fruit belied them.

'So how did you end up here and not at sea?' Rusty asked, cutting in on his thoughts. 'Friends in high places?'

'Seasickness,' he admitted. 'Everyone said it would clear up, but it didn't. We sailed to Scapa Flow, Iceland, Londonderry, down to Freetown, back up to Londonderry and it was still as bad as ever.'

'Grim.'

'Yes. Finally I dared to go and see the skipper about it since nothing the MO did was helping. I've never forgotten the shock, after months of our cramped little mess with its hard leather cushions and narrow bunks, of being admitted to his cabin and finding chintz armchairs and silver photograph frames. He seemed completely unimpressed but it turned out he'd recommended I be given a post here. Actually how he worded it was "unsuitable for small ships".'

'Oh, you were on a little one? They're the worst. You need something the size of a Cunard liner.'

'I'd rather just stay here.'

'You all get sent back to sea eventually,' Rusty said. 'It's just turnover. Christ. Here we go. Do you mind?'

She firmly took his arm as they turned the corner on to Main Street where there were already beery crowds spilling out of every bar and café.

'It's just if they think I'm yours, they're a little less likely to think I'm theirs.'

Her arm was strong – from swimming and playing tennis, he imagined – and he felt she was leading him as much as he, her.

The effect of Rusty appearing on the street was almost instantaneous. Every conversation seemed to break off. Every head to turn. Walking so close beside her, arm in arm, Charles felt the massed male attention on him as much as on her, or felt the stares pass through him to get at her. Then the comments started: 'Hello, darling', 'Try me on for size' and 'What's your poison, love?' It struck Charles the men didn't really expect her to respond – if she had, they might have been at a loss. Rather it was as though they needed to signal to each other that she was what they really wanted, that the company of men was always second best. It was an assertion of polarity as much as of desire. Every now and then a man would lurch out of his group and half-block their way along the narrow street, reaching for Charles's arm or shoulder, or Rusty's, with some stupid comment like, 'Are there more where you're from?' or 'What's he have that I don't?' and Charles would summon up a voice not really his and say, 'Now steady on,' or 'Show some respect, man,' as he felt Rusty's grip on him tighten still further.

They neared the Catholic cathedral and the pavement crowds lessened. Whether by accident or design, the bars were mainly clustered towards Casemates Square and the stretch from the Catholic cathedral past Government House to the Southport Gate was more genteel and residential, dotted with shoe shops, druggists, bakers and barbers. He felt Rusty relax beside him and at last she let his arm go free.

'Thanks for that,' she said shortly.

'It's a myth, then,' he said, 'that women like all the attention?'

'Some might,' she said, 'but they'd be braver than me. I hate it. I was in all-girl schools until three years ago. And I'm an only. The Jennies with brothers, like Bridget, are better prepared.'

'But you seem so confident.'

'That's just war paint,' she said. 'And years of riding and ballet lessons. The thing I really dread, the thing I have nightmares about, is that one day I might be in the middle of a crowd like that when there's an air raid. I think I'd rather take my chances out in the open.'

They were passing the chapel attached to the Governor's residence – the church of what had once been the convent.

'I love it in there,' Rusty said. 'It's like going into a village church back home. You almost expect to be asked if you'd join the flower rota or give some tinned peaches for the harvest festival.'

'I know what you mean,' said Charles. Although God had departed for him when they suffered a direct hit somewhere in the Atlantic. He had to take a signal to the skipper in person and came out on deck to a scene of carnage: not just wounded men, but pieces of men. 'But I think God has taken a leave of absence,' he told her. 'At least he has for me.'

'But surely you believe he's on our side?' Rusty asked, her little frown making her look more than ever like a symbol of home and glory, a poster girl for whatever it was people were dying for in such obscene numbers.

'Don't you think both sides have to believe that to keep going?' he asked, and her frown deepened. 'Did you go to the Nativity play?' he asked.

'We did,' she said. 'I sobbed. Hadn't registered how homesick I was until then. When we all had to sing "Away in a Manger" I couldn't get beyond "crib".'

'Well, that carol would undo anyone.'

'What was your favourite bit?'

He thought, remembering the crammed chapel, a delicious smell of tangerines cutting through the pervasive fug of under-washed men, tobacco and massed duffel coats and British Warms. He remembered being especially struck by the young recruits playing the angels, dressed in a dazzling combination of snowy white robes and gleaming silver breastplates from some regimental armoury or museum. 'The trumpet playing,' he told her. 'That was what undid me.'

There was a little café-cum-newsagent in the small run of shops between the Government House and the Southport Gate. He had developed a taste for the tarry little Italian coffees they served – infinitely preferable to the watery brew served up at the mess. These and extremely fresh oranges had become his two luxuries and he had taken to trading half his tobacco allowance with Clara, who boasted he was a professional smoker, so as to indulge himself.

The place was fairly busy but there were a few free tables outside in the winter sunshine.

'Can I get you something?' he asked. 'The coffee's good here. Have you time?'

'Why not?' she said. 'Perhaps a bitter lemon. Thanks.'

He installed her at a table and went in. The place was loud with sailors inside. Charles guessed they had just come ashore and not yet worked out that the bars proper lay further into town.

He had just seen a couple of faces he thought he recognised when a familiar voice said, 'Jan?' and he turned in the midst of being served to find Cushty standing right behind him, his left arm done up in a fetching navy-blue sling. Most reunited shipmates shook hands or slapped one another about the shoulders, but Cushty used his good arm to pull Charles into a hug that went on so long someone shouted, 'Leave it out!'

Charles could feel other people touching him on the back as though their reunion gave off a kind of good luck. He felt simultaneously flustered and deeply comforted.

They soon established that the *Starburst* had docked to refuel and take on supplies and that Cushty and the others would be shipping out that night or towards dawn.

'But your arm!'

'Ooph, it's only a burn. I'm walking wounded.'

'What happened?'

'A very close shave is what. I can still lift the shells when I need to, it's just less sore if I wear this and it gets me sympathy bevvies.'

'Well, there you go!' Charles handed him the pint he had ordered along with the coffee and bitter lemon. Cushty widened his eyes at the abstemious drinks. 'I'm on the next watch,' Charles explained, 'and I'm escorting a Wren back to her nest.'

'You're with that glamour puss?'

'It's not like—'

'Dark horse. We miss you, Jan. I miss you.'

'You don't miss me throwing up all the time. Anyway, I never saw you.'

But Charles knew what he meant. They would see one another on shore leaves when the tight tribal loyalties of the various messes slackened the further one went from the ship. They would walk and talk and drink, although he couldn't fathom what pleasure lay in it for Cushty. Mainly Charles talked, prompted by Cushty's questions, and his own slight nervousness that his increasing fondness for the man was a wild, even dangerous misreading of simple courtesy and curiosity. Cushty teased him and took mischievous pleasure in getting him drunk, but also liked to say he was 'better than school'. Weeks would pass between shore leaves but then, when they met up on the dock of Belfast or Freetown or wherever, it felt like the entirely natural resumption of a briefly interrupted conversation.

Cushty never tired of hearing stories about Launceston people, which of course Charles would embroider to make them funnier or more scandalous, and Charles in turn prised stories out of Cushty about his huge family in Liverpool, presided over by a tiny matriarch who kept his father's earnings in a teapot from which she gave him drinking money on receipt of his wage packet.

If anyone had noticed their curious friendship, nobody commented on it, at least not to Charles. It was one of the strengths of naval life that it had learned to compensate the men for an unnatural life without women, and far from home, by imposing on them an intense surrogate domesticity. Each mess was a miniature household with its routines of cleaning, feeding, socialising and sleep, as regimented as those for the watches and, deprived of choice, men swiftly adapted to and embraced them as the most natural thing in the world. Within those households there were friendships, sometimes more-than-friendships, tantamount to undeclared marriages, which were only challenged or acknowledged when booze-fuelled strife broke out away from the ship. In his own mess there was a pair of signalmen – a radio operator and a coder – who had adjoining bunks, always worked the same watches, and spent all their leisure time together, the one compiling cryptic crosswords, the other executing meticulous watercolours of seabirds, quite like two unmarried sisters. Assuming such alliances and loyalties were fairly common, they could only enhance the social cohesion and networks of mutual support on board. Cushty had an older brother who had done time for housebreaking and subsequently gone into the Merchant Navy, who assured him that prison life and shipboard life were not so very different.

Cushty followed Charles outside, presumably hoping to be introduced to Rusty. Charles had become so used to the willowy presence of Clara, who often joined him on excursions into town, that he had forgotten how walking anywhere with Cushty always felt like taking a dancing bear for a walk, only without the cruel chain. He never walked beside Charles but always loomed slightly behind, representing at once comfort, threat and responsibility. He was helpful now as in his short absence the other two chairs at Charles's table had been taken by sailors intent on chatting up Rusty, who cast a despairing glance Charles's way as he approached.

'Sorry, lads,' Charles said.

'Hop it,' growled Cushty, and the chairs were relinquished as they never would have been had Charles been on his own.

'What took you?' Rusty said.

'Sorry. This is an old friend from the *Starburst*, Cushty. Cushty, Rusty. Oh, look. Ha! You nearly rhyme!'

They both looked at him blankly. Then, having established that Cushty was shipping out that night, Rusty lost interest and Cushty fell to quizzing Charles about his life in Gibraltar and, rather touchingly, asking if he'd had any news from Launceston. Charles said that he'd heard nothing from Mother for weeks then had six letters from her in a bundle. He told him about her adventures with evacuees and rabbit pie, how the town's businesses were all thriving again thanks to all the soldiers flooding through. As they spoke, he found Cushty's craggy, familiar face and close attention were making him almost more homesick than the funny specifics and newspaper clippings in Mother's letters had done.

There was a sharp little cough from Rusty and Charles became aware that the evicted sailors and their friends had taken advantage of her tuning out of his conversation to gather round and try to involve her in theirs.

'Charles, we really should be going. If you can bear to . . .'

'Yes, of course,' he said, getting up. 'Sorry, Cushty. I promised Rusty I'd see her home.'

'We'll see you home,' one of the sailors shouted.

Rusty came round to Charles's side of the table, ignoring the men, and firmly took his arm again. Cushty stood politely. For a moment Charles thought he might be about to hug him goodbye as tenderly as he had greeted him, but instead Cushty made a sort of respectful bow and muttered to the men to show some respect for a lady. Charles wanted to explain but could hardly say it was duty, not pleasure in front of Rusty and, anyway, Rusty was tugging him towards the Southport Gate.

'So sorry about that,' he told her. 'I hadn't seen him since they put me ashore here months ago and you know how sentimental sailors get.'

'I'm learning rapidly,' she said, then added more kindly, 'Perhaps you could hurry back from the Wrennery to find him and carry on chatting. I feel bad now.'

'Don't be silly,' he told her, but as they passed the pretty little graveyard with the exotic trees and the gravestones for the dead from the Battle of Trafalgar, he glanced back and saw that, entirely characteristically, Cushty had turned potential confrontation into new friendship and was strolling slowly along the street towards the chaos of Casemates Square with the other sailors.

The Wrennery, formerly the old Naval Hospital, had been chosen because it was both on the quieter end of town and handy for the road that led past the officers' mess and on to the tunnels of the Rock where most of the Wrens were working. It was a handsome building with a garden and even a tennis court, Rusty confessed, though the blessedly cool courtyard was spoiled by a huddle of Nissen huts. 'And in the heat we'd happily have exchanged tennis for a swimming pool. We can't really enjoy Catalan Bay without being pestered.'

Rusty hadn't admitted that she had an arrangement for the evening. When they drew near an army major climbed down from a Jeep to greet her. He received Charles's salute and took Rusty off his hands with a muttered, 'I'll take over from here, thank you.'

Charles heard Rusty make a rapid excuse about the rehearsal having run on rather and needing to change, then she hurried inside without a backwards glance, embarrassed lest the officer had seen her on Charles's arm.

Gibraltar's naval dockyard had come as a benign contrast to the Devonport one. Smaller and friendlier, with its half-built motor launches like boy's toys, the buzz of its sawmill reminding Charles of home, the smell of its paint shop, its cobbles and a railway line like something a boy would play with on his bedroom floor. The Signals quarters were friendly too – a far cry from the huge granite walls of the Plymouth barracks. They were in low timber and concrete buildings which, especially on sunny days, reminded Charles of the flimsy-looking buildings in cowboy films. The quarters formed three sides of an oblong, with thirty cabins along each of the long sides. The central space was slung with dhobying on washing lines and dominated by a huge, precious and temperamental fridge forever being cosseted by the wireless operators and just as regularly catching fire or flashing violet lightning. The short side of the oblong housed the galley, the chief and petty officers' mess and the general mess, which contained an inexplicable spinet Charles coaxed into badly tuned life when persuaded. The tin roofs of the cabins made them hot and airless in summer and deafening when it rained. The cabins were cherished for having army cots rather than hammocks, although some, like Clara, reverted to their hammocks because the cots were on the short side and subject to regular louse infestations.

Charles gathered from Rusty that the Wrens' sleeping arrangements in the Wrennery were little more comfortable, squeezed into a row of extremely leaky Nissen huts. Added to which they worked their long watches in chambers carved into the upper Rock, where the damp from the clouds that regularly gathered there turned all their bedding soggy and musty.

He arrived back just in time to catch a plate of cottage pie and cabbage but had barely wolfed half when the deafening dockyard hooter warned of an air raid and sent everyone rushing for cover. Their officially designated shelters lay in tunnels in the base of the Rock, some two hundred yards away, so most men simply dived under bushes or pressed themselves against walls with some overhanging shelter. Clutching a slice of bread and butter, Charles raced over to his usual hideaway – a gnarled old fig tree that spread out from the base of a stretch of historic wall. He had lost none of his fear at the rumbling approach of enemy bombers, though, irrationally he knew, found it less terrifying than the shriek of diving fighter planes he had learned to dread during sea attacks. The target here was mainly the harbour, along with its fuel stores and any ships or submarines at anchor. The main risk to the signallers came when the huge home gun batteries let rip at the enemy aircraft and their shrapnel began to tumble. It was lethally sharp. Charles had seen a boy running for cover trip just in time to be horribly peppered with it down his back and legs, and had never forgotten how they all had to remain in hiding, listening to his screams, until the shrapnel shower ceased and they could drag him, too late, to shelter, where he bled to death among friends.

He heard it landing now, its deceptively pretty tinkling on the tin roofs all around. One bomb fell somewhere far off, then another closer to, and then the raid ended as abruptly as it had begun. A Levanter, the warm wind from the east, had started blowing and was bringing in the usual muggy ceiling of cloud to obscure the upper Rock, which presumably made it extremely difficult for bombers to work with any accuracy over such a tiny target.

As he headed to begin his watch, past the men with big yard brooms who were already sweeping up the shrapnel into piles, Charles thought of all the men in the bars along Main Street and around Casemates Square. He had only once been caught up in an air raid along there and the shelter had been unbelievably noisy and sordid, with men pissing and brawling in a dank space so overcrowded he felt the buttons of the man behind him pressed into his back. Perhaps Cushty had already re-embarked before the alarm had sounded, but he would be all right if not; Cushty never seemed unnerved by crowds as Charles was. He said it was growing up in a packed tenement in a city where all entertainment – football or drinking, basically – involved standing in noisy crowds and shouting.

The Signals Tower stood almost like a lighthouse in a clutch of balconied Spanish buildings at the southern end of the dockyard, only a short walk from the mess. It was spacious compared to the hot, cramped signals room on the *Starburst*, but housed over five times as many men, with sixteen on duty there at each watch. And unlike a ship's signal room, it constantly received and processed flag and light signals as well as wireless messages. Like the beehive it resembled, it was tiered and regimented. First there was the signal distribution office – a noisy flurry of telephones, typewriters and signal pads with such a constant whirl of paper from desk to pigeon holes and such an omnipresent fug of sparks and smoke from Spanish cigars and navy-issue cigarettes that the fire hazard barely bore contemplation, especially as Charles worked up at the top of a wooden tower above it all.

The way upstairs took Charles past a huge carbon machine where there was always someone churning away at the handle with purple-stained hands, duplicating every signal, however insignificant. The telegraphists manned a wireless office on the next level of the hive. Above them the leading signalmen and two or three juniors occupied a sort of draughtily glazed birds' nest from where they could officially communicate directly with ships at anchor, but also unofficially spy on locals through their telescopes and binoculars. In one corner of the room, they maintained a nest of mouldering flags on an antique daybed on which they would take turns to nap. Cups of tea were regularly requested from the telegraphist one floor down, who had a jealously guarded kettle and supply of condensed milk. The cobwebby voice pipe used to place the orders was also handy for the sharing of filthy jokes and any choice gossip gleaned by way of the misdirected telescopes. Charles worked in the cyphering office, along a little balcony. It was the only one of the top-storey rooms to boast a coal fire but also felt like a quiet refuge from the mayhem down below. When he came on watch in the small hours he was woken for it by the coder coming off duty and would arrive at the desk to a slightly panic-inducing backlog of messages awaiting decoding. Arriving on the kinder side of midnight, Charles was able to take the previous coder's still warm seat with no backlog, so the process felt calmer.

At sea he had to filter out the messages that were either routine or irrelevant. Here there was no filtering and every single message was decoded, duplicated and circulated. It was startling to discover that he could decode at a

271

respectable speed, keeping pace with the signals coming in, yet think of other things while doing it. At some miserably nauseated point between Belfast and his second voyage to Freetown, he had imperceptibly begun to memorise and recognise the forty or fifty commonest number clusters, most of them representing destinations, ships' names or words like 'proceed', 'refuel', 'attack', 'damage' or 'assistance'.

War had blasted all his old dreams to shreds. Despite agreeing to things like organising the Red Cross gala, Charles no longer thought of himself as a theatre animal waiting for his day to come. He had even begun to wonder if his playwriting, like his playing Frederic in *The Pirates of Penzance* and even his working in two dance bands, hadn't been a kind of metaphor in action: that what he yearned for wasn't to emerge into an actual spotlight to applause, for all Mother's teasing about silk dressing gowns, but to emerge into his true self. Whoever that might be.

He continued to keep a diary, all written very small, in tiny books, although he was fairly sure it was illegal for a serviceman to do so. He was scrupulous about leaving out all geographical specifics and any references to what his work involved, but he was aware that the process had become precious to him as the sole surviving thread of literature in his days. When he couldn't sleep – usually after a night watch when his brain was fizzing from code and the sugary tea at breakfast, and the Spanish sunlight was blazing into his curtainless cabin – he would often reach into the hiding place he had created inside his mattress and take out one of the earlier diaries to squint over and reread.

It was strange to encounter his younger self and find him already a stranger: so snobbish, so judgemental, so wilfully closed to Mother's good influence. But then he would stumble on something that made him smile: a dry account of 'the afternoon at the pool declining into a melancholy spitting match with the Cocks children' or 'an encounter with a pink, fishy young man from Sennen with false teeth' or read something that seemed queerly prophetic like, 'Oh, the letters I would write were I free! Or would I?'

After the things Charles had seen, his plays now seemed utterly self-centred and facile, the work of an over-indulged child. He knew he should be writing furious, Orwellian reportage and had made a few attempts, especially when he first arrived at Gibraltar with the scenes from life at sea still vivid in his mind, but what he now recognised as an arch tone kept creeping in. He burned the attempts, in any case, knowing they'd be even more frowned upon than the careful notes he made in his diary. He had tried writing short stories instead, boiling down incidents and people into terse narratives but time and again these threatened to turn confessional, leaving him too unambiguously exposed for comfort and he burned most of these too. Just one or two he carefully edited for the censor, excising anything specific, and posted them home to himself, disguised as letters and marked 'to await return' lest Mother wellmeaningly forwarded them back to him.

The mess always offered up the *Gibraltar Chronicle*, its news up to date but its pages shrinking by the week, thanks to paper shortages, which also left its heavily doctored reports ever more drained of colour. Then there was an array of local papers, all weeks out of date but sent with love from families back home, deeply reassuring reminders of the constants of life from Bradford, Caerphilly, Lowestoft and Kirkcudbright. Mother had several times added to the library of newsprint, with carefully ironed and folded copies of the *Cornish Guardian* or *Western Morning News*. There were months-old copies of the *New Statesman*, which Charles read far more assiduously than he had at home, and regularly, garishly printed in red or blue on paper so rough it often caused the pictures to bleed, there was a magazine called *The Rock*. Far trashier than the sober *Gibraltar Chronicle*, it was produced in the handsome Garrison Library, a civilised building, much as he imagined gentlemen's clubs in London must look, from which all women and other ranks were excluded. Its editor set no such limitations on inviting contributions. The writers all seemed to be servicemen and the numerous poems, inevitably signed only with an initial, had titles like 'Middle Watch Musings' and 'Home Thoughts from Alex'.

Charles read these poems with far more patience than he'd have shown a few years before, because he recognised the pain from which so many of them arose. He found himself analysing why so few of them worked. It was the tone, he realised. They were reaching, as he himself had once reached, for a high tone, like something in a hymn book, when what was needed was candour and directness. The sort of candour you heard any night in an air-raid shelter or bar. Without the swearing, naturally, but with the conversational directness the swearing would bring.

The few poems he had written since leaving school were heavily influenced by Spender and Auden and, he saw now, were often quite witty but as arch as his plays had been. Almost without meaning to, he had recently begun to attempt poems in his head. He kept them in his head on purpose, enjoying the discipline of holding and turning and refashioning a few lines while he scrubbed out his cabin or chopped onions for the Spanish cook, walked through the tunnel for a bracing swim at Catalan Bay or even as the other half of his mind deciphered signals. If the lines couldn't be remembered, then he felt they were lacking and deserved to be forgotten. It was fast becoming his equivalent of the old sailor's patiently whittled piece of scrimshaw or the intricate jigsaws or needlework fashioned by his messmates on the *Starburst*.

Tonight, as signals came through from his old ship reporting no damage sustained in the attack on the harbour and requesting a progress report on a boat they were to escort, he started to work up a poem about the frustratingly cut-short meeting with Cushty. As he flicked rapidly through code books and neatly deciphered signals about bunkering, about enemy sightings and engagements, and damage on either side, the other part of his mind, which he began to picture as the poet, shaped one line, then a second.

The poet was at work in a quiet room, perhaps one floor up still from this one, with a view of the ships at anchor and the oily reflections of the lights in the water. He thought about Cushty's dimple, the beefy arm rendered powerless by its navy-blue sling. He tried to make a link between the sling and the two misinterpretations he had felt unable to correct: both Cushty's and the army officer's assumption that there was more to Rusty's arm on his than simple support.

VALLETTA – 1942

Nobody in the Gibraltar signal station would have admitted to having begged to be there but plenty would have begged to be allowed to remain. From the resentful conversations Charles sometimes overheard in washhouse or mess, some would gladly have picked a colleague to go back to sea in their stead. The summonses to rejoin a ship arrived with the swiftness of calamity in an old play. Sailors were profoundly superstitious, even enlisted ones soon became so, and whenever there was news that so-and-so had been called back to sea, an unseemly hilarity often broke out for an hour or two among those who felt they had been stroked by the black wingtip but spared the talons.

When the *Starburst* was safely out of harbour, any anxiety Charles felt for his former shipmates was shot through with shameful relief at not being with them. Nowhere in the theatre of war was safe. Air raids were almost daily events and everyone was aware that, caught between the enemy in North Africa and the not-quite-enmity of Spain, Gibraltar might be snuffed out by a concerted effort, but working there was an idyll compared to being strafed in the Med or torpedoed in the Atlantic. Being able to loll on the broiling sand of the beach or gorge on fresh oranges in the Alameda Gardens, or standing in a cloud of cigar smoke outside one of the countless barber-shops on Main Street to watch a mule train bringing in barrels of Rioja and sherry to the bars meant it was some-times easy to forget the war was still all around.

Spring rapidly unfolded into a long summer. As the war progressed, Charles began to work regularly in the Government House, in what was formerly the ballroom. Chandeliers and mirrors had been bundled up against air-raid damage, royal paintings left to glare down on the assembled desks and tables. On the first floor of the house, facing the street, it was mercifully shady compared to the coding room on top of the Signals Tower, which became like a greenhouse in the August sun. He knew from the signals he was decoding that something big was in the offing, involving several ships, mercantile as well as naval, but hadn't pieced together the details when, quite suddenly, the *Starburst* was back, having failed in a mission to escort a supply ship safely past the Italians. Within days Charles's long summer idyll of coding and beach trips was shattered and almost a third of the signallers and coders found them-selves summoned back to their ships, including him. Missions were always carried out on a need-to-know basis, with mariners, stokers and even gunners often barely aware of where they were going or why until it became obvious. Men only had to cast an eye across the ocean around them in the dawn light following their departure to appreciate the scale of the operation underway.

Charles hoped against hope that time would somehow have cured his seasickness or that the Mediterranean would prove kinder than the Atlantic had, but a keyed-up dread had seized him the moment his transfer papers came and was made worse by his panicky claustrophobia on returning, after two years of fresh air and open skies, to a world of clanging metal, diesel fumes and sweating paint-work. And though the sea was indeed a little calmer at first, they were soon back in the all-too-familiar plunge and clank, plunge and clank pattern, and he was back at the coding desk with a gash bucket between his thighs.

Several of the faces in the signalling mess were unchanged and he was welcomed back with the usual mix of mock-ery and affection. He soon learned, however, that his replacement, by all accounts an outstanding coder and linguist, had died of wounds during the attack that had recently sent them limping back to Gibraltar. The sense of filling a recently dead man's shoes, and indeed his bunk, was horrible.

The days that followed their departure were the hardest Charles had known, so frightening, so relentless that, despite the rigid keeping of their allotted watches, he lost all sense of night and day or even of how many days had passed. They were a small part of a great convoy escorting essential food and fuel supplies to Malta, which had effec-tively been under Italian siege for months. If Malta could be brought to surrender, the Axis powers would be that much closer to seizing control of the Mediterranean, so it felt as though the combined might of German and Italian forces had gathered to stop any relief getting through.

The noise during attacks was beyond belief, the din of the *Starburst*'s own guns seemingly magnified by the ship's steel plates and made more alarming still by the yelling and sometimes screaming of men and the stamping of boots. Then there was the terrifying shrieking of diving aircraft and the sickening vibration of detonations in the water or direct hits on boats nearby. And all of this came to Charles in the ferociously hot, windowless little Signals office where the only way of knowing what was happening was from the signals coming in or going out, or from bulletins stammered out by swearing visitors on errands from the bridge. All of this while feeling constantly sick and struggling to fix the fraying thread of his concentration on his coding and decoding.

He knew they could all die at any moment. He had sat through long conversations with Cushty and the others about best and worst ways to go. Having seen first-hand the maiming injuries of survivors, he sometimes thought he'd like to die swiftly if he must, to be so directly in the path of a landing shell or line of strafing fire as to have mere seconds or half-seconds in which to register what was happening. The unlucky were scalded alive or roasted in flaming fuel. Drowning alone in the ocean scared him, especially drowning in an effort to avoid burning oil on the surface – he had given this all too much thought – but he had agreed with Cushty that the worst would be to be trapped on a sinking ship, unable to free yourself for whatever reason as the water level rose around you and the structure groaned as it began to plunge. This, they had decided, was the very worst fate, as it combined drowning with the horrible powerlessness of being buried alive.

He came off duty in what felt like the dead of night because he longed for sleep but was actually just before dawn. Heading to empty his bucket over the side, he found an inferno on deck. A great chunk of the boat had been blasted by a shell and men were still fighting the fire in the jagged crater left behind. Miraculously neither the fuel tanks nor Cushty's magazine had been hit, but the air was acrid with smoke from whatever had been burned. Simultaneously around sixty men had been hauled on board from another ship in the convoy that had been less lucky. Those that could walk were being led to the messes or found spots where they could sling hammocks. The numerous wounded were being tended by the exhausted MO and his short-tempered number two.

Charles offered to help.

'Can this one have your bunk?' the number two asked. 'Sick bay's overflowing now.'

'Of course.'

'Good man,' said the MO. 'Cotter? Help Causley with the stretcher, would you?'

The figure on the stretcher looked little more than a boy, he was so slight, though it was hard to tell as his face was so heavily bandaged, as were both his hands. Burns, presumably. He had the unmistakable porky smell of a recent burns victim.

'He's had morphine,' the MO said. 'So he'll sleep like a baby. At least I hope he will, for his sake, poor kid.'

Charles had never carried a stretcher before but Cotter was about his height, so keeping the patient level wasn't too great a challenge.

'What do we do when we get to a ladder?' he asked Cotter.

281

'Fireman's lift, I suppose,' Cotter said.

Charles had no idea how to give a fireman's lift to someone conscious, much less to someone dead to the world, and knew, too, that to clamber down a ladder with the boy over his shoulder would have been beyond him. But his messmates were all prepared, along with several rescued marines draped in borrowed towels and blankets, and the bandaged boy was neatly slid from the stretcher on to a kindly bed of outstretched hands and borne, with only one heavily drugged moan, to Charles's bunk.

In his shattered, sleep-deprived state, Charles thought the graceful motion of the boy through the dimly lit cabin, and the tenderness with which the men laid him on the mattress and tucked a blanket over him, one of the loveliest things he had ever seen.

Cotter and he helped carry four more wounded men to borrowed bunks, then joined the others at the Signals mess table for an impromptu feast of bread and butter, tinned ham and the beefy condensed milk tea he was coming to depend on to keep him alert, despite his jittery stomach.

Even with the tea, however, and for all the chat around him, he fell fast asleep where he sat. When he came round, his neck stiff and his face crumpled from being pressed into one of the mess's leather cushions someone must have given him for a pillow, it was to find he was being summoned back on watch, just as another air onslaught was getting underway. To judge from the signals, the same enemy submarine suspected of torpedoing their neighbours earlier was now being fought off with depth charges.

It was only as they finally limped into Valletta harbour, what remained of the convoy greeted by cheering crowds, wildly rung bells and the hooting of tugs, that the sorry state of the *Starburst* was revealed. As well as the blast Charles had seen already, there was a gash on the other side, which had been taking in water as fast as it could be pumped out. The prospect of shore leave was welcome, but the excitement was shot through with the threat that all, or many of them, might be assigned to other ships if the repairs could not be made swiftly. Supplies to the island had been so choked off by the enemy that no one seemed entirely sure of the capacity of its dockyard to mend so many ships in need. Still, they had got off more lightly than one of the supply ships, which had to be rescued by tugs and was already low in the water as crews raced to unload her cargo.

The washroom was steamy bedlam with so many men keen to wash and shave in readiness for Valletta's welcoming nightlife. Relief at a safe arrival lent a manic edge to the usual horseplay in there. Charles found the washroom made him shy at the best of times and he couldn't face all the joking and buffeting when he was so sleep-deprived and feeling stripped of protective layers even without peeling off his stinking uniform, so he retreated back to the Signals mess to let the eager get ahead.

When he came down the ladder and found the MO in there, sitting on the edge of his bunk, he realised that since the drama of getting the boy into bed, he had given no further thought to him. The MO was checking the lad's wrist then neck for a pulse before glancing at his watch. He didn't look round but sensed he had an audience. Charles stood quietly to one side as the MO noted the lad's rank and serial number in his little book and drew the blanket up over his face.

'Probably for the best,' he said. 'Wouldn't have been much of a life after those burns. We'll take him ashore to the mortuary with the others once you're all gone. Are you all right, Causley? You look done in.'

'Just tired, sir.'

'Get a shave and shower. Fresh uniform and a good night's sleep will sort you out.'

'Yes, sir.'

It felt all wrong that the death had happened among them so quietly and quite unnoticed. Charles didn't know the boy's name and had never even seen his face but felt compelled to pull up a chair and sit beside him, quite as though keeping watch at a sick bed. The ship lurched abruptly, tugging at her anchor perhaps, and the boy's left arm, the one the MO had briefly checked for a pulse, fell out from under the blanket, the bandaged hand slapping quite hard against the floor. He still wore a wristwatch, a cheap-looking one, a boy's birthday present. The dial was misted over from his time in the water but, now that Charles could see it, he realised it hadn't stopped ticking. Perhaps it would continue to keep obedient time long after its owner had been slid into the mortuary dark. He realised he had no idea what happened to the possessions of dead sailors and soldiers. Perhaps some painfully slow bureaucracy saw to it they were removed from the body and posted home to loved ones still numb weeks after receiving the dreaded telegram? He imagined bodies were buried on the nearest dry land. Malta, to which the boy almost certainly had no ties, would receive him into some sun-bleached military burial ground his family might never visit, just as Mother would almost certainly never travel to Canada to lay flowers on Uncle Stanley's grave.

Hearing loud voices approach, he reached down to lift the boy's arm by the wrist and tuck it back beneath the blanket. To his shock, the flesh was still warm and yielding, cooling but warm.

Two messmates clambered down in their towels, clutching washbags and smelling of hair oil, faces pinked back to innocence from shaving.

'He didn't make it,' Charles told them, watching how his words killed their laughter. 'MO was just here.'

The men swore softly. Like Charles, neither had known the boy. Perhaps for that reason, his face blanked by bandages, he stood in for all their friends who had died or gone missing, or for their brilliant coder friend, who had also died of wounds so very recently in that very bunk. Then they set about dressing, and Charles, about undressing, as there was nothing to be done and there would be a gharry to catch to shore for a respite from Hell.

He caught what must have been one of the last boats taking men ashore, even as repair crews were getting busy fixing what they could of the ship until she could be towed to a dry dock. There was nobody he knew on the launch. Most were officers and he was content to be ignored. He felt afresh, as he had on boarding, that his time ashore in

Gibraltar had estranged him to the crew. He had no arrangements to meet anyone in this place or that, though it was an article of navy lore that Strait Street was where one went, or ended up, at least. They had twenty-four hours' shore leave although it was hard to believe the ship could be made seaworthy again in that time.

The officers were going to a party at the Chancellor's lodge of the Anglican pro-cathedral, whose dramatic shoreside tower they pointed out to each other. The Chancellor, who had a spectacular residence built into the church's seaward side, was apparently a cousin of the skipper's mother. Hearing the officers chat lightly, discreetly adjusting their uniforms as they spoke of family, architecture, the history of the beleaguered island and of the wiliness of the Chancellor in laying down plentiful stocks of sherry, claret and whisky before hostilities broke out, it was hard to believe these were men who had just emerged from prolonged and bloody battle. How did public schools instil this insouciance? In classrooms or on playing fields? And was it real for any of them, or was the apparent calm a game, obliging each to maintain a poker face for the morale of all?

They had no sooner arrived on shore and clambered – *you first, sir* – up a slippery flight of stone steps than an air-raid siren sounded.

'Bloody hell,' said the skipper. 'Follow me, men.'

He somehow knew to lead them to what seemed to be a wine cellar, deep beneath an old honey-coloured house. Where barrels and bottles would once have been stacked, perhaps a hundred people were already huddling – men, women, ragged children – the space lit by just two cobwebbed light fittings. Far more than had the Spanish of Gibraltar, they all looked hungry, dusty and exhausted, the young aged before their time, the old, impossibly weary. And yet their faces lit up on seeing the officers' brilliantly white uniforms, presumably because they represented the arrival of longed-for fuel and food. To Charles's astonishment, several of them, led by the older men, burst into applause until bombs began to fall, showering them all with ancient dust and leaving the only sounds in the shelter the fervent rosary-telling of the women and the outraged weeping of a startled toddler.

Then the all clear sounded. The officers went off to their lunch party at the Chancellor's Lodge, dusting off one another's shoulders, and the Maltese to check on their shops and houses. Charles, dazed, was left to wander.

The last thing he wanted was the bars of Strait Street and a heaving mass of drunken servicemen. What he really craved was to drink a pot of tea at Mother's kitchen table with a plate of her bread and butter, then to climb between clean white sheets and lose himself in sleep. He might find an approximation of that – without the bread and butter – in a small hotel or rooming house later. He had done so on shore leaves before, in Londonderry and Freetown, simply for the luxury of a quiet, louse-free bed in a silent room after days of interrupted sleep at sea. For now, he wandered away from the harbour and up the steep hill through Valletta, taking the place in and relishing being back on land.

Conditioned by long exposure to Gibraltar, he had pictured Valletta as being little bigger, so was taken aback to find it a proper city, however blasted by months of air raids. It was handsome and dramatic, with tall houses and a rigid grid system imposed on the sharp rises and ravines of the limestone. As in Gibraltar, newer houses had been built on older ones, but here they often seemed to have truly ancient foundations. Just up the road from where they had been sheltering, he saw another air-raid shelter emptying. Maltese were emerging from what looked like a catacomb – a tunnel deep into solid rock in the rough base of what, at a higher street level, became a small palazzo. At every turn there were unexpected changes of level, often glimpses of bright blue water at the end of a street, or unnerving craters where a bombed house had tumbled in on itself and down into a cavern beneath that.

Charles had heard the officers say that water was scarce on the island and, sure enough, trees and gardens seemed rare; there were only the pots of herbs and scarlet geraniums on windowsills and doorsteps he knew from Gibraltar. Charles had only seen photographs of the blitz damage in Plymouth, Bristol and London in out-of-date papers from home. Seeing it at first hand, from street level, terrible little mountains of rubble with, here and there, an ironing board, bedstead or rag of bright curtain to show people had lived, and probably died there, was far more shocking. And yet the urge for order, or the urge to fight back against ugly chaos, was clearly deeply ingrained, for he saw an old woman carefully tending her plants with dirty dishwater and there were already teams of men and older boys at work with shovels and barrows, even household brooms, clearing streets blocked with rubble from the latest raid.

Charles wandered as far as a grand square and the cathedral, admired the remains of ramparts and a terrific old wall, then instinctively turned back into the warren of streets in the old part of town. If Valletta had an architectural signature, he perceived it was big, glazed-in balconies, often several to a building, for all the world like glass-fronted wardrobes jutting out from the stone. Presumably they gave sheltered sun in winter and somewhere to catch a badly needed breeze in high summer. Most of their glass was broken now, of course, and most had their internal shutters closed against further damage. Some had been blasted open and revealed perilously balanced furniture or a glimpse of bedroom or grandly marbled saloon.

As he walked, Charles composed a card to Mother in his head. Knowing how dust was her enemy, how to dust each room anticlockwise so as to miss nothing was an article of faith in her, he imagined how all her Vallettan sisters must be suffering in their daily effort to keep the dust of conflict at bay. *I passed a woman who might have been the older Miss Jackson, but with a farm labourer's tan and a crucifix,* he wrote in his head, *dusting the few lemons and apples outside her shop one by one, as though they weren't fruit but pieces of family silver.*

Deeply weary, he took refuge in a church that seemed tiny from the street but became cavernous within. He sat and stared at the gloomy paintings, the guttering candles and cheap grandeur in which the statues had been dressed, and felt extremely Cornish and far from home.

He must have fallen asleep because the next thing he knew was being nudged by a sacristan, who tapped at her

289

watch, shook her bunch of keys, and glanced at the door, which she wanted to lock.

'Oh. I'm so sorry,' he told her, getting up and rediscovering solid ground beneath him.

'English,' she said.

'Yes,' he told her.

'Good,' she said. 'Now go fight, Bulldog!' and she let out a cackling laugh as she ushered him back on to the street and bolted the door behind him.

The light had changed and was casting long shadows. Charles glanced at his watch and saw it was now early evening. He climbed the steep little lane from the church to regain a grander street. Turning on to this, he saw a cluster of sailors ahead, including one he thought he recognised.

The explosion seemed less deafening than the ones he had been experiencing at sea. It came from above him and slightly behind him. He saw pieces of stone and plaster-work landing in the road all around him then, in quick succession, heard Cushty shout his name from far off and was hurled savagely to the ground and pinned by a great weight, his arms flung out, his face ground into the dusty stone. It was only then he realised the blast had deafened him, because he saw pieces of masonry and two of the big window structures crashing to the ground in a soundless explosion of wood, dust and glass. There was a sharp pain in the forearm flung out in front of him and he saw a shard of glass had gone into it. Trying to move his other hand to pick the glass out, he realised it was pinned down by a person, not masonry, that someone was flattened over his back, one of their arms stretched out in an attempt to shield his. He could feel their breath hot against his ear, their heavy legs hard against his. Were it not for the pain in his arm, it would have been oddly comforting.

Soon there was a crowd around them: sailors, Maltese, the sacristan from the church. Something had to be lifted off the man on top of him first and only then was Charles able to shift at all. He immediately reached his freed hand to pull the shard of glass out of his arm and regretted it as the wound then began to bleed heavily. It was Cushty who had been on top of him. He must have sprinted to flatten Charles on the pavement just after the bomb detonated. The explosion had left him so creamy with stone and plaster dust that only his grin was recognisable; Charles could make out nothing he was saying. The sacristan revealed herself as a woman of authority in the district. He saw, and slowly began to hear her barking orders and pointing, and soon four burly Maltese were helping him and Cushty into her undamaged house nearby while she hurried ahead to fling open doors, shoo cats and drive the helpers away again.

Cushty was slumped in a cane chair. Like Charles, he was dripping blood, which showed ruby bright against all the dust on his skin and hair. Charles remained standing at first, then felt wobbly so sank on to a nearby bench. Luckily the floor was tiled. The sacristan returned with a basin of water cloudy with disinfectant and a pile of clean rags and bandages. She muttered in what Charles took to be Maltese as she showed him how to dip a cloth and wring it out, as though he had never seen such things before, and left them, shutting the door behind her.

'Cushty?' he asked hesitantly. 'Am I shouting? I still can't hear very well for the ringing in my head.'

Cushty just grinned and shook his head, then winced.

'I'm going to clean you up a bit,' Charles said. 'This might sting a little,' he added, thinking of the times Mother had said that before picking gravel from an elbow or a splinter from a palm. In fact he wiped and bound his own wound first, as best he could, so as not to drip blood all over his friend. He wiped Cushty's face, carefully teasing two chips of glass from his broad brow. Then he wiped around his ears and neck, where he found another, larger piece of glass that left a bubbling in its wake but had mercifully not reached an artery. He set the pieces of glass carefully on an ashtray. Then he noticed that the back of Cushty's shirt was wet and purple where it should have been blue. There were several more shards of glass embedded there. 'Brace yourself,' he said, and picked them out.

Cushty didn't cry out but merely gripped the arms of the chair a bit tighter.

'I'd better clean there as well,' Charles said.

Cushty stood, suddenly huge beside him in the small room. He started to lift his shirt but was defeated.

'Shall I?' Charles asked, and Cushty nodded and raised his arms.

Wincing as though the pain were his own, Charles carefully peeled the shirt off him, then he wrung out another flannel and washed the wounds on his back, glad they weren't as deep as he'd feared.

'Here,' Cushty said. 'You've no idea. That bandage is too loose to work.'

He gestured to where repeated movement had caused the bandage on Charles's arm to unravel, so that blood was soaking through once again.

'Sit,' Cushty told him, and gently pushed him to sit on the bed, whose springs jangled. He took off and discarded Charles's bandage, then his shirt, which was stained with blood from them both. Charles could smell his distinctive musk as he bent over him to clean his arm again and apply a tidy pad, which he fastened with a fresh, tighter bandage.

The sacristan knocked and came in again, bearing a tray with bread, cheeses, sausage, a bottle of red wine and an icy jug of precious water. She waved away their thanks, muttering something in Maltese, then picked up their shirts and tutted.

'I clean these,' she said. 'Bring back early morning. What time your boat?'

Charles began to protest but she was adamant.

'My daughter do laundry. Salt for blood. Here not my house,' she added. 'Dead brother. Just you. Eat. Sleep. Bye-bye.' Then she was gone.

'Well, that's us told,' said Cushty, and they laughed.

'What if she doesn't come back?' Charles asked.

'Depends what size the dead brother was,' Cushty said. 'Or we go shopping. Wine?'

'Yes, please, but . . .'

Cushty poured two large glasses, held one out. 'What?' he asked.

'Don't you want to be with your mates down in Strait Street?'

'Not especially. Not after I saved your life.'

'You did, didn't you?'

'Reckon so.'

'Thanks, Cushty.'

'Cheers, Jan. Your turn next.'

'Why did that bomb not go off before?'

Cushty shrugged. 'It happens. Back home, Mam said, there've been kids getting killed playing on bomb sites weeks after a raid. It was just luck I spotted you in that second. One of the lads, Catholic boy, wanted to know the way to the cathedral and it was easier to show him than tell him, and then there you were.'

'I'd just been to church myself,' Charles said.

'State of grace! Really?'

'Not to pray. To sleep. It was her church. I mean she sort of looks after it. And I was still half asleep when . . .'

Charles raised his glass and his teeth chattered noisily against it so that he could only take a sip with a conscious effort. The wine was rich and dark and slightly sweet. It might have been vino sacro from the sacristan's holy cellar.

'Last night, or this morning, was terrible,' Charles said, remembering.

'Bad as it gets.'

'Did you lose anyone?'

'Puppy and Chalky,' Cushty said.

'But . . . they're your mates. Cushty, you've worked with them for ever.'

'Yup.' Cushty tore apart the bread, carefully sliced the sausage and the cheese. 'At least it was quick,' he said. 'They wouldn't have known what . . . I was fetching up more rounds from down below. The blast threw me down the ladder but it passed me by. One foot to the left and the ammo would have gone up and me and the whole ship with us, I reckon. Cheese first? Or sausage? They both smell strong.'

'Oh, cheese, I think.'

He passed Charles a hunk of bread with cheese on it, then went to light a candle as the room was now almost in darkness. It had no window but one over its door, Charles realised now. The only natural light came from the door and window on to the street, which had lit the rudimentary kitchen and bathroom they'd passed on the way in. It was not a house but an apartment and a very small one. A converted cave, basically. It made him think of the tenement where they had lived when he was tiny and Father still alive. There had been a place below theirs, he remembered, little more than a cupboard for the storage of the very poor. Cushty made himself a sandwich with the garlicky sausage and clambered on to the bed past Charles so he could sit with his back against the wall. But then he remembered the wounds on his back and lolled on an elbow instead, like a rather hairy Roman senator at a feast.

'It needs grapes,' Charles told him.

'Huh?'

'Nothing.'

'I should take my boots off, shouldn't I?'

They looked at his boots, which were already leaving marks on the sacristan's dead brother's sheets.

'You should really,' Charles said.

295

'Go on then,' Cushty told him. 'Be a love.' He cheekily raised one foot towards Charles.

Charles set down his glass and cheese, loosened the laces and slid off the boot, then did the same to the other. Then he topped up both their glasses as the bread was stale and nerves were making it hard to swallow.

'You know those men we took on board?' Charles began.

'Yeah?'

'The one we had in the Signals mess, with the really bad burns, he died in the night.'

'Probably for the best if the burns were on his face.'

'Yes, but . . . none of us noticed him die. We were right there. All around him. Eating breakfast or playing Convoy or whatever.'

Charles grew suddenly breathless and realised he was about to cry, for the first time since childhood, and that he couldn't hold it back.

It took Cushty a moment or two to realise. At first, he just carried on talking, about death and how it seemed to be easier to die in company or something. Then he must have heard Charles's gasps or seen his tears in the candle-light, and he let out a kind sigh.

'Hey,' he murmured. 'Hey, lad. It happens. It happens. You weren't to blame.'

And as Charles couldn't seem to stop weeping, not just for the nameless, bandaged boy now, but for Ginger and Joe and other friends so in the way of danger they might already be dead or maimed, far from home, Cushty slid forward to join him on the edge of the mattress and put a heavy arm across his shoulders.

'Hey,' he said again. 'Hey, lad.' And he planted a very definite kiss in Charles's still dusty hair as one might kiss a child. And then another, pulling him closer.

Charles broke off weeping to sniff and look at him. Cushty had never been so close to him except once when they were briefly in the back of a tiny truck in Freetown.

'Do you mind?' Cushty mumbled, and to kiss him back, on the lips this time, seemed the most natural response.

Soon after that it was Cushty's turn to unlace Charles's boots. Probably sensing Charles's complete lack of experience from the way his hands kept shaking, he was scrupulously polite at every turn. 'Do you mind?' he asked, and, 'Can I?' and, 'Tell me if it hurts, lad, and I'll stop.'

Charles was so overwhelmed he could never reply, or not with words. Only when they were both spent, and took it in turns to use the rudimentary bathroom, did they think to lock the door before returning to the bed and the rest of their supper.

Charles knew himself for a chatterbox when nervous or relieved, yet found he continued to be struck dumb and he fell asleep with Cushty wrapped about him like a cross between a rug and the perfect guard dog. The bed was narrow and they could only fit on it tightly spooned either towards the wall or the room, and its springs or their various bruises and cuts, woke them regularly until the sacristan returned with their beautifully cleaned and mended shirts as the nearby bells were ringing for morning prayers.

They were still well within the twenty-four hours before they had to report back for duty, so Cushty suggested they

297

find breakfast. There was no discussion, not even an acknowledgement of how they had just passed the night, but Charles felt lightheaded with possibility.

Cushty led him past the ruins of the opera house to a little café by the war-torn palm trees of the Upper Barrakka Gardens, whose terraces overlooked the Grand Harbour. They drank two scorchingly strong coffees apiece and wolfed a plateful of custard buns.

'So, what next?' Charles dared to ask at last.

Cushty shrugged. 'We go where we're sent,' he said. 'Word is it's Alex next.'

Charles didn't like to say he hoped to be sent back to Gibraltar.

'I suppose you're hoping to go back to your cushy number in Gib?' Cushty said with a grin.

'I...I...' Charles stammered. 'Well,' he admitted. 'I want to sit the exams to apply for promotion and you can only do that on shore.'

'Petty Officer Causley?'

'I can dream.'

'There'd be no asking you to take my boots off then.'

Charles felt himself blush, but it was Cushty's sole reference to their night together. Soon he was leading them down the hill, past cascaded buildings, which children picked over for trophies or toys, and an undamaged British postbox, where Charles posted Mother a postcard of the Anglican pro-cathedral, with little faith it would ever reach her. They headed on towards Strait Street, where they would run into some of the others and recount a careful version of their close shave with an unexploded bomb and, somewhere between the Piccadilly Bar and the Old Vic ('Cabaret Every Evening'), they were served a late cooked breakfast by a magnificently impervious male imperson-ator, who appeared to have been working all night.

CAPTAIN'S CHAIR – 1943

'Face the front, boys. It's rude to stare. Especially in church.'

'But they're black. All of them!'

'As God made them. You must have seen black men plenty of times in London. Especially around the docks near you.'

'Yeah, but not smart like these.'

'Ssh, Terry. Face the *front*! There's a good boy.'

Nice, quiet, no-bother Gertie had been replaced after a matter of weeks with Terry and Jerry, a pair of nine-year-old twins from Limehouse, not identical, thank goodness, but comparatively exhausting. They were sturdy little things, one dark, one fair. They were polite enough, ate everything put before them and often made Laura laugh with their jokes and cheeky impersonations. Only one of them had ever wet the bed they insisted on sharing at first, and they were almost worryingly unbothered to be so far from home and their mother. However, they did make her appreciate how quiet and studious Charles had been at the same age, even with all the piano practice. If they weren't eating, asleep or in school, it seemed they had to be in constant motion, either kicking or tossing a ball or a can, chasing each other around (enacting dogfights was a current, very noisy favourite) or riding Charles's old bicycle back and forth along Underlane, often both of them at once. All spring and summer, Laura had been very grateful for the house's proximity to the Jubilee Baths as the boys could play there for hours and come back clean(ish) in one fell swoop. With the school filled to bursting point with extra children there was no lack of playmates for them in all the usual spots, up and down Old Hill, in St Thomas Water or spooking each other around the churchyard. Greater numbers had generated conflict as well, and there were regular fights, one street against another, locals versus evacuees. She gathered there were even one or two little East End gangs, imported and re-established on new territory.

When Charles had been this age, a blackened eye or a bloodied knee represented a major drama, but with Jerry and Terry these were nearly weekly occurrences. Laura had been obliged to restock her first-aid tin twice and now kept it permanently to hand, alongside the bread bin. They never read, unless you counted the *Beano* and *The Hotspur*. They could not be tempted by jigsaw puzzles. Wet weather was a challenge. Happily they had joined the Cub Scouts and there were regular outings organised by Sunday school, the Liberal Club or the WVS. And now that the town had effectively become a garrison one, there were often football tournaments or film shows laid on in the various army camps, half the thrill of which was being transported out of town and back, in army Jeeps and trucks.

In a matter of months Launceston had gone from feeling like a town that workers were abandoning, where key employers were going bust and which only the arteries of two railway lines kept alive, to having its population more than doubled in size. Near the start of the war there were some British soldiers, of course – the Glorious Glosters – and occasionally airmen and mechanics from the RAF base up near Davidstow, rumoured to be almost permanently lost in fog and cloud, but once America joined in it was as though Devon and Cornwall became an American colony or an extra state. Every sizeable town had its camps of GIs. Launceston had two on the edge of its housing, one out at Pennygillam and one defacing the lovely park at Werrington, and there were others a little further out. The castle grounds where Charles had loved to dream and play as a child were covered over with Nissen huts and canvas tents, and, at a time when people with cars had all but stopped using them because of petrol rationing, the lanes were never without Jeeps and lorries, which often stopped to give locals lifts.

At first, the arrival of the Americans had excited everyone. Apart from those old enough to have fought in the last war, most had never met an American before and, knowing them only from the versions of them they saw on screen, briefly had the odd sensation of meeting fictional characters sprung to life. Laura heard fools stop them in shops to ask them to repeat things just for the pleasure of hearing their accents. Shopkeepers and pub landlords loved them because they had so much spending money compared to the cash-strapped locals, and girls loved them for the same reason, and because their uniforms were much better cut than the rough, baggy ones the Tommies had to wear. The children, local and evacuee alike, followed them in packs wherever they appeared on the streets because they always had sweets, chocolate and gum to spare. But all of this led to resentment of them from the British soldiers. And they were brash, the Tommies said, and rude. There were regular scuffles in the town centre, especially around closing time, when the white-helmeted military police on either side were kept busy holding the peace between factions.

Laura had heard little resentment voiced, however, until the arrival of the black GIs. These, mainly tasked with organising camp sanitation and building ammunition dumps, were welcomed as warmly as their white brothers had been, but with an extra interest, in this case, because they were so unlike the black men everyone had seen at the cinema. Unless they were singing and dancing, black characters in films always seemed to be either servants, slaves or shabbily poor. These GIs, by contrast, were as smartly uniformed as their white counterparts and just as ready to turn the heads of girls and spoil children. So people were shocked to discover that Americans not only had a segregated army, with black soldiers confined to the camp at Pennygillam, where the facilities were known to be very basic, and white soldiers at Werrington and else-where, but clearly expected the local populace to accept their imposing segregation on Launceston's pubs and dances. They even tried, and failed, to impose segregation at the cinema. Laura had heard that soldiers from the Glorious Glosters had taken to walking black GIs around with them at night, as much for the excuse to pick fights with white GIs as out of any urge to protect. With no black population of its own and with Padstow encouraging locals to smear on bootblack once a year to celebrate Darkie Day, Cornwall was hardly in a strong position to pass judgement, and yet suddenly everyone was talking about the Colour Bar the way they used to discuss the price of pork.

The vicar came out to announce the first hymn.

'And we welcome amongst us the choir from the 581st Ordnance Ammunition Company, who have kindly come to boost our numbers. Please stay to make them welcome afterwards as they're a long way from home.'

St Thomas's choir had never been especially good, even when Miss Bracewell had been training it. The sound was unblended – you could easily pick out the voices of the singers who thought most highly of themselves – and it had suffered with the onset of war as all but the most wavery male singers had gone off to fight.

The American choir was a revelation, producing so rich a tone and with such relished harmonies that the rest of the congregation all but stopped singing the hymn to turn on the spot to enjoy them. When the children were summoned for Sunday school as usual, Terry and Jerry weren't the only ones to dawdle in the aisle and look back, loath to miss another note. And they did miss a treat, because the second hymn was 'Be Thou my Vision'. The anthem, when it came, was a rather uncertain stab at a ladies' voice setting of Psalm 23, its confidence undermined perhaps by the presence of a better, rival choir at the back of the church. When the children had filed back in after the sermon, they enjoyed a good view of the black soldiers and their uniforms as they were the last in the queue for Communion, and there was much smiling and whispering. One of them, a handsome, older soldier with silver at his temples, surreptitiously passed the boys a handful of toffees, which Laura only just stopped them opening noisily there and then.

'He's a captain,' Jerry said at full volume. He prided himself on having learned army stripes and badges, just as his brother could read the silhouettes of distant aircraft on the rare occasions they saw any.

Laura saw the older soldier have a discreet word with the vicar at the altar rail. In place of the final hymn the vicar then invited the soldiers back to the front to sing for everyone. There was spontaneous applause, and some angry shushing, then they sang two spirituals: 'Go Down, Moses' and 'Nobody Knows'.

Laura knew little about music and wished Charles were there to hear it, but she could tell there were more than simply bass and tenor voices singing. There were high tenors and extra low basses and, here and there, a line that sounded almost like a woman. It was wonderful. Even Terry and Jerry, who fidgeted for England, sat still. Applause broke out again as the soldiers walked back down the aisle to their pews.

There was a little gathering in the sunny churchyard afterwards, while children raced around letting off the energy suppressed for two hours of good behaviour. Laura tended to use the excuse of getting on with lunch to break away after thanking the vicar and exchanging a few quick words with any friends or relations who were there. But today she was invited, with the boys, to Em's for lunch, so had no excuses. There was a cluster of people around the black soldiers, thanking them for the singing, presumably or, in the case of the children, charming Hershey bars out of them.

She jumped when a deep voice behind her said, 'Please don't be offended, ma'am, but are they your grandsons?'

It was the older soldier who had given the boys toffees in church. She explained that they were no relation but evacuees, far from home like him.

'That was a proper treat, by the way,' she added. 'The singing.'

'Thank you, ma'am. If I'm honest it was partly an excuse to get the boys out of camp for a couple of hours. We were locked in one camp after another during training back home and while preparing to ship out. Turns out it's not much better here.'

'Oh, but I've seen some of you in town.'

'The lucky few,' he sighed. He was a good head taller than her and his voice had the kind of rumble to it that made her need to lean on something. 'Your padre just suggested the parish throw a little dance for us, which is kind. When we do get passes, the only pubs they're letting us into are the King's Arms and the Ring o' Bells, and they're a bit quieter than what the boys are used to.'

'Not much room for dancing either,' she said, although she only knew those places from the outside.

'Shall I see you there?'

He began to walk towards his men, and she found she was walking with him.

'I've never been a dancer,' Laura said, 'but I dare say I'll be manning the tea urn.'

'Not even a very careful waltz?'

His eyes were on her, playfully searching her face. They were the colour of khaki buttons.

'I don't even know your name,' she said.

'Sorry, ma'am. I'm Captain Amos Barnes. I hope I didn't offend you.'

'Not at all, Captain. Welcome to Launceston, and I'll see you at the dance.'

Laura watched in the little crowd as he marshalled the soldiers into tidy lines of three, then marched them smartly out along Riverside and on to the road back up to Pennygillam, with him at the rear. She had to call sharply to the twins to stop them joining the little gang of children cheekily attempting to march behind him.

Because nobody knew for sure how long the soldiers would be there for, not even the soldiers themselves, no time was lost in organising a dance. The church hall was far too small. The Snowdrops, as the twins told Laura the military police were called, felt that an event out of town would be less likely to attract undesirable attention from the white GIs. So a farmer just beyond the Pennygillam camp lent the use of a barn that was still empty at that early stage of the summer. Passes were negotiated and a dance band was booked – the second, sprightlier of the two Charles had played with. The barn was swept, fairy lights hung where they wouldn't break blackout rules and straw bales set around the edges as seating. There were buckets of sand for all the inevitable cigarette butts. An army tent was put up along one side for the bar, which Laura volunteered for, once Mrs Netley impressed on her there might not be much call for cups of tea.

It had been a beautiful day – what Laura always thought of as wedding weather – and she found herself becoming quite as keyed up that afternoon as if she'd been a young thing coming to the dance to be whirled around by soldiers. By the time she had finished setting up the bar and ensuring the beer and cider barrels had been allowed enough time to settle, there was already quite a crowd including, happily, lots of young women who never darkened the door of a church and quite a handful of British soldiers. When the black GIs arrived, strolling up in a friendly gaggle rather than marching as they had to church, a pair of Snowdrops was following them slowly in a Jeep, almost like a sheepdog herding. Laura thought it was a shame as it made it look as though they could not be trusted, but then the vicar gravely pointed out that the military police were there to ensure there was no trouble from white GIs.

The soldiers were greeted with cheering and the all-girl band struck up 'The Star-Spangled Banner' before segueing into some Glenn Miller. In no time, Laura's bar was overwhelmed. The beer, cider and ginger beer, all locally brewed, had been sold to her at cost and all profits were going to the Red Cross. She was glad she had not dressed up but wore a simple summer dress, as the heat from the press of eager bodies and the humidity from the grass underfoot built up in the tent as rapidly as the noise levels. There were three of them behind the bar – with Laura, the vicar and one of the church wardens, who had actually run a pub once, but was flustered because he claimed not to understand what the GIs were asking for. There were only three drinks on sale but inevitably the glasses started to run out. Laura had in place a very rudimentary system of washing up behind them, with a tin bucket of soapy water and a baby bath of rinsing water, but both men seemed to think it beneath them to use it.

And then there he was behind the bar with them, face aglow from the heat, smelling of himself and soap.

'Evening, ma'am,' he said, and he took off his jacket.

'There is a queue, you know,' the church warden told him.

'I think Captain Barnes is here to help,' Laura said.

'I am,' he told her. 'Wash, serve or empties?'

'Empties!' they all told him, so he headed off around the tent and barn and returned with a stack of glasses, which he washed and rinsed for them.

There was another great surge when the band took a badly needed break for beer and sandwiches in the farmhouse, and all four of them served on until even the ginger beer bottles had run out and Amos Barnes was obliged to point out to complaining soldiers that it was a table on a tent at a farm, not a bar at a well-stocked pub in town.

While the vicar and his warden took the stuffed cash boxes indoors to count the takings, Laura and Amos washed and stacked whatever glasses they could find before she produced the ginger beer bottles she had slyly hidden under a flap of tent canvas. They sat on a couple of straw bales to drink and enjoy the dancing. She was glad the Snowdrops had done their work and the evening had passed without ugliness. The dancing was like nothing she had seen before. Girls were shrieking and laughing as GIs whirled them around and showed off fancy footwork, even in army boots. Cornishmen never danced if they could simply drink. Charlie hadn't taken her dancing once, even when he still had the strength.

'They'll be spoiling them for local lads,' she told him.

'What?' He put a hand to his ear.

She repeated herself, leaning in close to be heard above the hubbub and he rested a hand on her shoulder as she spoke.

'How about you?' he asked. 'Can you be spoiled?'

'Oh, I'm long past spoiling,' she said. 'Old woman like me. Anyway, I've had my fun. My Charlie died soon after the last war.'

'I'm sorry.'

She shrugged and looked away at the dancers. Even after all these years it was hard to be matter of fact about it, perhaps because she so rarely met new people and had to tell them.

'How about you? Is there a Mrs Barnes?' He was fifty or so, she assumed, around her age. There must be a woman waiting for him back in Chicago.

'Shall we . . .?' He gestured away from the noise and they headed out into the relative peace outside where men were smoking in contented huddles, canoodling with girls or making friends with the steers who had wandered up to peer over a nearby fence.

'There was,' he told her. 'She took off with our two girls

310

ten years ago for another man. They're out in California. Or they were. Not great letter writers.' He pulled a mock regretful face, so she knew he was hurting still.

'I can't imagine,' she said. 'What are you in civilian life?'

'I always wanted to be an engineer but, well, our local black college specialises in teacher training and that's what I became. Teaching very basic science to very reluctant kids. Still, at least they're getting science lessons; black schools in the South are so underfunded they barely have books.'

'But that's awful.'

'No. What's awful is that it's legal and normal. So normal even black parents shrug and accept it as the way life is. It's good for the men to have come here and seen how shocked you Limeys are by it. There've been riots at home since the war started, not that anyone's reporting them.'

'About the black schools?'

'About a lot of things. Injustice. How the Army treats us like dirt, regardless of civilian qualifications. I'm serving under white officers who didn't finish high school. Still,' he raised his eyebrows, 'at least I'm finally learning some engineering, even if it's building ugly ammo dumps and not beautiful bridges.'

He stepped away from her and held out a hand.

'What?' she asked.

'They're playing a home-you-go waltz,' he said, 'and you promised me.'

'I did no such thing. No, no, no!' she laughed, but he meant business and took her hand to draw her back inside the barn and into the slowly turning crowd.

Laura had momentarily forgotten how much taller than her he was. She worried at first about looking stupid, but as Amos held her close, her face had nowhere to go but to sink against the warm, khaki wall of his chest. She worried she might tread on his feet, or he on hers, but the barn floor was too crowded now for anyone to be doing more than hug and shuffle and that was all right with her. She just breathed in the scent of him and thought fondly of Aggie and how they'd laughed about the coy way library romances said things like, *she felt his urgent need*. It was only when she felt him press a discreet kiss on the top of her head that she realised he'd had his face in her hair and must have been breathing her in as she had him. She barely had time to register this than the music ended, and everyone broke apart to applaud and whoop the band.

'Thanks for all your help tonight, Amos,' she said.

'Least I could do, ma'am.'

Now that they no longer had the excuse of waltzing to touch her, his hands had let go of her and were hanging by his side. Having felt them warm and dry on her skin she had to make an effort not to look down at them, but to meet his gaze.

'You do know that in this country only the Queen gets called ma'am?'

'I'm sorry.'

'Don't be. It's one of the reasons your lot are so popular here.'

She said this as they watched amorous, sometimes tearful scenes playing out in the balmy shadows now stealing around the barn.

'I must get these boys back before curfew,' Amos said, 'but I wonder . . .'

'Yes?'

'Might I buy you dinner one evening? Since dancing isn't really either of our thing. I'd like to carry on talking.'

'Yes,' Laura said, although no one had bought her dinner in her life and she wasn't even sure where in Launceston one could do such a thing. 'That would be lovely.'

'I'll see if I can get a pass for Tuesday, shall I? When it's a less popular night for men in the other camps. Call for you at six thirty?'

'Yes.'

He turned to go, blew a shrill whistle for attention and called, 'Company? Fall in!'

All around them temporary couples were parting, some stupid girls giggled and saluted Amos. Ignoring them, he turned back to Laura, remembering something.

'I didn't ask,' he began.

'Tredydan Road,' she told him. 'Number twenty-three. Just before the forge. It's the turning before Riverside, where you came to the church.'

She had a lift back with the church warden in his delivery van, in return for helping return the crates of glasses to their cupboard in the church hall. He was a bit giddy from how much money had been raised and regretting some of it couldn't be diverted from the Red Cross to the church's repairs fund.

'Nothing to stop you organising another dance for the church,' she told him. 'People just want beer and cider and

313

somewhere to dance; I don't think they care where the profits are going.'

She retreated into thinking about her dance with Amos. It was a paltry, fleeting thing by most women's standards, quite possibly pathetic, given that she was a widow in her fifties and he a soldier who had just been showing an old woman a kindness, but, for the week that followed, the dance stayed with her, its every small detail polished to brightness.

The week's routine unfolded its usual rituals for Laura of queuing for food, laundry, ironing, cooking for the boys and doing her best to keep them out of trouble, but the thought of the hasty half-arrangement she had made with Amos began to prey on her mind. What she should wear was easy enough, as she only had two good summer dresses, so could wear the one he hadn't seen. But the question of where they should go gnawed at her. She never ate out, ever, unless picnics counted. She had a pretty strong idea of what the options were in Launceston – there wasn't a great range as it wasn't an eating-out sort of place, not like Teignmouth had been – but she knew the Americans' Colour Bar had complicated everything. Men liked to organise things, or expected to, but she didn't see how Amos could very well organise anything if he was locked in the camp until the evening they were due to meet.

Finally, calling in to collect a bale of laundry from her friend, she blurted it out to Aggie. With only very primitive rivals, Aggie's boarding house was doing extremely well out of all the soldiers, whose business, now the American dollar was in town, eclipsed the busiest of market days. She had her two oldest daughters working with her and had been seen wearing a fur coat to midnight mass the previous Christmas. Laura collected laundry from her three days a week now, and had noticed the bed linen no longer had repairs. She had deep respect for how hard Aggie worked and was grateful that laundering for her meant she no longer needed to get on her knees to clean for anybody.

Aggie chose to misunderstand, of course, being a tease.

'I am not *walking out* with him,' Laura insisted. 'He just very kindly asked me out for supper and . . . Aggie, where on earth do we go?'

Aggie laughed.

'The White Hart,' she said. 'The food's good, even with rationing, and Matty Clemo's a regular here since his wife spent all that time in St Lawrence's. I'll put in a word and have him reserve one of the private dining rooms for you. You don't want to share your evening with a load of shouty soldiers or have half the town gawping through the window. Is he . . .?' She broke off to grin. 'Tell me, girl, is he *very* black?'

Laura pictured Amos against the flapping canvas of the army tent. 'Hush now. He's very . . . courteous. I told you, Aggie, he's just being polite to an old widow woman.'

'Of course he is. Why else would any red-blooded male want to spend an evening with an old baggage like you?'

Aggie laughed and nudged the biscuit tin at her. Laura declined because just thinking about Amos was giving her jitters.

The day dawned wet and miserable. She had a hamper of Aggie's bedlinen to wash and starch, which took her mind off the evening ahead. The postman brought a long letter from Charles, all written on postcards from Gibraltar with funny comments about the apes and buildings and people they showed.

Terry and Jerry were out playing five-a-side football all afternoon and Laura had arranged a babysitter for them. She was counting on the football to wear them both out for once, so they'd eat their supper and be quite happy reading comics and listening to the radio until their bed-time. She finished work in time to enjoy a nicely cooling bath with some of the Spanish lavender essence Charles had, half-mockingly, given her for Christmas. Hoping it made her smell fresh rather than old ladyish, she brushed her hair, which the laundry steam had left more unruly than ever, and put on her newly pressed dress and her blue glass beads. The boys came home ravenous and filthy, so she fed them and ran a bath for them.

Then everything unravelled. There was no sign of the babysitter when Amos knocked at the door. Laura had no sooner introduced him to Wang and shown him to the parlour with a glass of lemonade than there were shouts from Terry overhead, because Jerry had started one of his nosebleeds.

'I'm so very sorry,' she told Amos, but reassured about supper arrangements, he was quite happy sitting on the sofa to read the local paper and told her not to fret. By some miracle Laura managed not to get Jerry's blood on her dress, though he'd splashed it all over a towel and the bathmat by the time she had him pinching both nostrils shut with the day's handkerchief. Then she had to see him through his bath and into his pyjamas and still the babysitter hadn't come.

The boys were delighted to have Amos in the house, of course, and he coped manfully with all their questions about did he have a gun and what were the grenades and shells his men were putting into storage, and were they dangerous and did anyone ever drop them. Finally, mindful of the time, Laura suggested he go on ahead of her.

'I'm sure she'll be here soon,' she said. 'She's normally so reliable.'

'Can't I wait, too?' he asked.

But she was now fretting that they'd be putting Matty Clemo out by not showing up for a reserved dining room someone else might want.

'Well, if you're sure,' he said.

She was half-tempted, because the boys were having such fun with him, to suggest they forget going out at all and simply eat the remains of the rabbit stew, which was what she'd be eating the next day otherwise. She didn't want to hurt his feelings, however, and knew other people's children could feel burdensome, so she gave him directions to the White Hart and said he was to ask for Matty Clemo and say he had a room reserved for supper.

The boys fought tiredness long enough to listen to the latest instalment of *Appointment with Fear*, although Laura was sure the lurid story would give them nightmares, then she made them say their prayers for their parents and friends, and tucked them into bed.

Finally, just as Laura was wondering if she dared leave them alone and deciding she didn't in case they suddenly woke up again and wreaked havoc, the babysitter arrived, having thought she was asked for seven, not six. Laura quickly checked she still looked respectable and hurried out.

It wasn't so late. She checked her watch and realised Amos would only have been there twenty minutes or so without her. She was sure he would have ordered himself something to drink while he waited, so she made herself slow her pace a little so that she didn't arrive unappealingly flushed.

An ambulance left the market square as Laura came into it. She rarely had call to visit the centre of town of an evening so was, irrationally, taken aback by the number of soldiers on the streets. Some were British – even had they not been talking, the boys had taught her to recognise the Glorious Glosters' regimental badge – but most seemed to be American. Many were sitting around the war memorial but there was also a tremendous commotion around the White Hart. Perhaps that was just men drinking? It was probably like that most evenings. She felt sorry for people who lived nearby and had that sort of ruckus night after night. The hubbub and crowd was concentrated around the public bar, where she saw a cluster of military police and not a single black face. Aggie had instructed her to enter on the other side and avoid the two bars entirely.

The private dining room was a small, oak-panelled room off to one side across the corridor from the bars. There was just one round table laid for two in there, and a flattering light cast by a shaded lamp shaped like a candle. One of the napkins had been shaken out then dropped on the table. She guessed that marked Amos's chair so sat in the other one to wait for him to return. Cooking smells reached her and made her feel hungry. She never normally ate so long after stopping work and it was leaving her lightheaded.

A waitress came in, a woman Laura knew by sight only, so a Methodist or Catholic, perhaps, or not a churchgoer. She was thin-faced, birdlike. Laura always assumed that waitresses, like cooks and barmaids, needed to look as though they routinely enjoyed what they were selling, to inspire confidence and lead by example. The waitress seemed startled to find Laura sitting there.

'Oh,' she said. 'Can I help you, madam?'

'Yes. I'm here for supper with Captain Barnes. From the American camp out at Pennygillam.'

'Oh. You mean the coloured chap?'

'That's right. He had to come here ahead of me because I was—'

'Oh. Oh dear. Well, let me fetch Mr Clemo. Would you like a menu? Or probably not now? Wait there.'

Losing her composure entirely, the waitress fled, oddly taking Amos's discarded napkin with her. Laura left her napkin where it was; these were napkins she washed and ironed, after all, so she knew the work that went into getting them so stiff and neat.

There was a surge of male laughter from the bars. She wondered what had caused it; it didn't sound remotely amused or friendly. Where on earth was Amos? Her appetite withered as swiftly as it had grown and she was just thinking this had all been a huge mistake from which she should quietly slip away when Matty Clemo joined her.

They had been at school together, though she doubted he would remember as they moved in such different circles and he was on the council now. He was as smartly dressed as ever, in his usual moss-coloured jacket and tie and with a spotless dark green apron on. He must be doing as well from the war as Aggie was, Laura thought. He certainly wasn't going short of food. But something was wrong. He wasn't his usual ebullient self.

'Mrs Causley?' he asked, surprised, so he did remember her or perhaps simply knew her as one of his hotel's laundresses.

'Hello, Mr Clemo,' she said. 'I'm here for supper. As Captain Barnes's guest.'

'Yes,' he said. 'Yes. Ruth said,' and he took her aback by sinking into Amos's chair. 'The most terrible thing,' he said. 'I can't believe they're all still in there, drinking as though nothing had happened.'

'But what . . .?' Laura began.

'I was serving behind the bar. It's very busy tonight as two of the outlying camps have issued passes. Anyway, as you probably know, they – the Americans, that is – claimed this place as one of theirs. For the white soldiers. I don't hold with that. Nobody does. But the Snowdrops say it saves trouble to go along with it and keep black and white apart. Anyway, your Mr Barnes—'

'Captain Barnes. He's an officer.'

'Is he? Well, he suddenly appeared at the bar right in front of me – he's a tall man, as you know – saying he'd booked a room for dinner – and I knew, as I'd had his name from Aggie, not that she said he'd be . . . Well.

Anyway. And he said could he have a pint while he was waiting as his guest was going to be a bit late and he'd a thirst on him. So of course I said yes, sir, but to go back in here and one of us would bring it to him and . . .'

He fell silent, reliving the moment apparently.

'What?' she prompted softly. 'Tell me, Matty.'

He looked up, almost as though he had forgotten she was there listening.

'It came out of nowhere,' he said, staring at the tabletop again. 'One of those really solid captain's chairs we have in there. The handsome oak ones. Built like tanks, they are. Someone in the crowd had thrown it at him and it caught him on the side of the head and down he went. No shouting. No warning. None of the ugly language I've heard in there, God knows, these few months. Just the chair. Out of the air. Well, all hell broke loose then, of course. People shouting and protesting and that, but nobody coming close. Backing off, if anything. By the time I'd lifted the flap in the bar and got round to him, he was gone.'

'You mean . . .?' she asked.

Matty Clemo simply swallowed and nodded, meeting her gaze again.

'The floors are slate,' he said. 'He must have hit his head a second time when he went down. Blood everywhere. I called the police but the Snowdrops said it was a military matter and not to meddle. They took him off in an ambulance and they took the chair and mopped the floor. They asked a few questions, but nobody was going to own up, were they? Though a few said he had no business in the bar. I wanted to shut up there and then, but the Snowdrops said that'd cause more trouble and just call last orders a bit early. Makes me sick to my stomach. Every time I serve from now on until they go, I'll be thinking: Was it you? Was it you?'

Laura's mind was reeling, unable to accept what she had just been told. 'I'm so sorry,' she said. 'That wasn't a good thing to have to see.'

'Did you know him well?' he asked.

He was sitting in my front room half an hour ago, she thought, chatting with the boys.

'No,' she said. 'Not really. We threw a dance for his men at church and this was going to be his way of saying thank you.'

'Does he have family back home?'

'Yes. Chicago. He was a school teacher in Chicago. A wife and daughters,' Laura told him. She knew people would ask him and it was good to say anything that made them see a person like themselves had been killed. Details mattered. She didn't add that his wife had long since left him for someone else.

She stood, tucked her chair back under the table and left. Two military policemen were leaning against the hotel wall watching the men starting to leave the bar to climb aboard a truck. She heard they were Americans.

'Excuse me,' she said.

The one with his foot propped against the wall stood politely upright.

'Ma'am?'

'I was meeting Captain Barnes, the man who was killed just now.'

'Now we don't know he was killed, ma'am.' The word sounded different in the mouth of a white man. 'That's how rumours start.'

'Mr Clemo said he was. And Amos was there in front of him.' She felt herself start to shake and worked to keep her voice steady. 'Anyway, my name is Mrs Causley. From Tredydan Road. If anyone needs to ask me questions, that is. I'm assuming there'll be questions asked.'

The second man stepped forward.

'The best thing you can do, Mrs Causley,' he said, 'is to go quietly home and not talk about this. There are enough misunderstandings as it is.'

'But—'

'I'm sorry for your trouble, ma'am. Truly.'

And he tapped his white helmet in a ghost of a courteous hat-tap, dismissing her.

She said nothing to anyone. There was no inquiry. No questions were asked. Nothing was reported in the local paper. What she did do was write a careful letter to his wife and children. She addressed the envelope to him, of course, and trusted that a system as laborious as the one that sporadically transferred letters between her and Charles would eventually see that it reached them in California. Knowing there were censors at work she said nothing of what had happened to him, only that he had arranged beautiful singing in church, helped out at the dance, been the soul of courtesy and tact, and that he had told her how much his family and his teaching meant to him as he prepared to go to war for his country and for freedom. Something comforting like that. She couldn't bear the thought of his wife, who

323

would surely harbour feelings for him, if only of guilt, not regret, receiving nothing but a curt, official telegram with a lie about an accidental death in service. She had no doubt she would be told the death had been a mishap, nothing more.

The following weeks brought a tremendous patriotic celebration of the anniversary of the Battle of Britain. There were Union Jacks everywhere, marching bands, pompous speeches, a choir, parades of Home Guard, Boy Scouts, Girl Guides, local troops, even Land Girls. Laura knew it was to boost morale, that such celebrations were being held, by order, across the land, but it felt to her like tempting providence in a country still at war, still with sons and daughters far away risking their lives, so she sent the boys off with their friends and stayed at home.

Only days after the flags had been taken down again, Aggie told her that there had been a sort of armed uprising among the black GIs, furious at being confined to their camp for days on end while white Americans had the freedom of the town and its modest pleasures. Late in the evening, Aggie said, a group of black soldiers had somehow armed themselves, presumably with ammunition hoarded from work, and marched on the square where shots had been fired. The only damage sustained had been a couple of bullet holes in the war memorial and a white soldier with a nasty wound to his leg – nothing as shocking as a man killed for being the wrong colour – but fourteen black GIs were driven to Paignton to face a court martial, which the Americans failed to keep out of the British press. All were found guilty and imprisoned, although it was said the case against them was confused at best.

Laura had never been as keen or as omnivorous a cinemagoer as Charles, but after this she found she had no appetite left for films from Hollywood, however escapist, and for the months that remained until black and white camps alike emptied for the Normandy landings, she regarded any white Americans she encountered around the town as members of an occupying force, and not a civilised one.

PORTRAIT OF AN OLDER WOMAN
TAKING TEA – 1944

The Americans had gone at last, and in the lull that followed there had been a sense of the town waking up from a dream and shaking itself back to the hard realities of rationing, shortages and absent loved ones. Many businesses had become the richer for the interlude, and quite a few bellies were the rounder. Aggie joked with Laura about the handful of older men – romantic no-hopers for various good reasons – suddenly being fairly rushed to the altar by girls anxious it should not be too obvious their first-borns arrived early. Considering that there was still a war on, albeit one that was finally turning in the Allies' favour, it was surprising how many young women seemed to be off on prolonged visits to upcountry relatives. Aggie's first grand-baby had arrived, born to Heppy, with no acknowledged father, and was being adored and dandled by all who were allowed to meet her, shame not being a word in the Treloar vocabulary.

Some of the Nissen huts were dismantled and sold on, the churned-up grass in Werrington Park and the castle grounds rolled and reseeded, but not all the camps stood empty for long. The one at Pennygillam was repurposed to house prisoners of war, badly needed for farm labour as there weren't enough Land Girls to go round. Italians came first, after the

North Africa campaign, many of them already skilled at farming tasks. And then truckloads of Germans began to arrive. Pennygillam could not hold them all and a second camp was taken over at Scarnecross.

These newcomers were not in a position to spend money in the pubs and dances. They were 'paid' for their work but in cigarettes or, depending on where they were set to labour, in cream, cheeses, eggs and bacon, for which local housewives would have fought them. The Italians who went to church were led up the hill to the Catholic one nearer to St Stephen's, but Laura had become used to small groups of Lutheran POWs being escorted into services at St Thomas's. Both groups remained in uniform, or an approximation of it, instantly recognisable, even had they not also had bright red fabric circles stitched on to the backs of their jackets. Terry insisted this was a target to make them easier to shoot if they escaped, but Laura imagined it was for simple humiliation, a revenge for the badges they had forced Jews and other groups to wear. It was hard to think of these flesh-and-blood men as the enemy for long, although some tried hard and there were loud complaints in the local papers when film shows were organised for them or picnics laid on. The truth was that people were tired of the war, of the grim news stories, the grainy photographs of flattened cities and devastated countryside. Now there were no longer nightly raids on Plymouth and army Jeeps rushing in and out of Market Square, the war was beginning to feel a long way off.

Many farmers had been struggling to cope and, with any Land Girls assigned to essentials, had fallen behind with tasks like hedging and ditching, for which teams of POWs, mostly grateful to be doing wholesome work out of the line of fire, were ideally suited. Like the departed Americans, many of them were the age of missed and longed-for sons so naturally were smiled at, chatted to and often befriended.

Like many in the neighbourhood, Terry and Jerry swung between wild over-excitement at the *Enemy* being there, enjoying play-stalking them from behind hedges or on Charles's bicycle, and uncomplicated hero worship. They had recently spent hours enchanted by a gang of Italian workers clearing mud and weeds from the leat that fed both the Jubilee Baths and the mill. Having left the house after breakfast full of plans to spend their Saturday catching the Fascist spies passing on secrets or poisoning the baths to murder schoolchildren, they came home happy and weary, showing off the scraps of Italian they had been taught and model planes the men had made them from Spam tins.

This month there was great excitement as German POWs, spared the fields now that the late harvest was finally in, were not yet needed for the backbreaking work of harvesting winter greens so were coming to work directly across from the house. There was a patch of rough ground there where nobody had found the time or energy at the war's outset to clear the brambles and carve out more allotments. Now there was a ready workforce at the council's disposal, the plan was to clear the ground to create a safe playground with a slide and swings and room for boys to kick a ball back and forth with no more danger than breaking someone's window. With army trucks speeding about the place there had been all too many near-misses – American drivers not being used to narrow Cornish lanes – and there was a move to discourage children from playing in the streets quite so much in future.

Laura was happy at the prospect, although some of her neighbours seemed to think a playground would bring nothing but trouble and vagrants. When she allowed herself a short break between washes, she stole a glance from an upstairs window. There were only four of them, plus the Tommy who was presumably acting as their guard and foreman, so she made them up a tray of tin mugs of tea, with some heavy-cake she feared was not terribly exciting as dried fruit had become scarce.

It was cold out, the first properly frosty day of autumn, and the men seemed grateful, even though she had heard that Germans mainly drank coffee. The foreman had the easy, warmer job, feeding the bonfire they had started, but the Germans were clearing and uprooting brambles and blackthorn. Laura feared their gloves weren't nearly thick enough, as two were bleeding from the thorns when they took mugs from her.

'*Danke*,' they said, and one, tasting the heavy-cake, carefully told her, 'Good. It's very good, missus.'

'Thank you,' she said, adding, 'This'll be nice for the children. I'm glad you're doing it.' And she indicated where her house was, so one of them could drop the tray back with the mugs when they were done with them.

As she could have predicted, the children were fascinated by them once school finished for the day. Bonfires

329

were always a magnet, so a bonfire with real German soldiers was doubly so.

There was a knock on her door shortly after she had stopped work to start making supper. It was one of the POWs returning the tray and mugs. Over his shoulder she could see a gang of children, Terry and Jerry among them, ringing the fire, mesmerised by the clouds of sparks it sent up when something was added. The POW was the nice one with some English, who had enjoyed the cake, or been polite enough to say he had. She didn't think she could ever warm to a man with no appetite for cake; it might mean he had no appetite for tenderness. This man had a large, rather round head with his blond hair cut very short, so that he looked a bit like an overgrown child. He followed her gaze over his shoulder to the bonfire.

'We will tip water from the mill before we go,' he said, 'so nobody burns anything they shouldn't. May I wash up for you?'

'Heavens, no.'

'You are sure?'

'Yes,' she said.

'I'm quite safe.' He said this with a grin.

'Yes,' she said. 'I can see you are, but it's only mugs. I'll wash them with our supper things later.'

'Very good.' He handed her the tray and she felt she had been abrupt with him.

'How is it, then,' she asked, 'up at Pennygillam?'

'Not so bad,' he said.

'I had a friend who was there when it was the American Army's. He said it was very . . . basic.'

'Yes. The bunks are hard and the huts get cold. But it's better than battle. Or sleeping in tents.' He glanced again to where the children were booing as the Tommy tipped water on the remains of the fire, raising a plume of steam. 'I must go,' he said. '*Guten Abend.*'

'Evening,' she said, then called for the boys to come in.

The men were back the next day and finished clearing and burning the thicket, revealing a couple of trees that had hardly been noticeable before. She took them tea again, because it was no trouble and she was grateful for what they were doing. Their overseer told her he called them all Fritz as that was easiest, but he seemed nice enough to them otherwise. He was little older than they were, she guessed, and must have been similarly grateful to have ended up serving so far from any front line.

Once again, the one who spoke English returned the tea tray. This time, Laura was kneading bread, so she let him come in and wash up the mugs while she carried on at the kitchen table.

'My name is Helmut,' he told her. 'Not Fritz.'

'Hello, Helmut,' she said. 'I am Mrs Causley.'

'How do you do? That smells good. Like beer. My mother makes bread.'

'Do you miss her cooking?'

'*Ja.* Very much!'

They both chuckled at that. He should be going, she thought. She did not want to get him into trouble. Instead he took a little notebook out of his back pocket and showed her charcoal drawings he had made in their tea break, of the terrace of houses, including hers, of the newly unchoked saplings. He had used a piece of charcoal from the bonfire, he said. She was impressed. He confessed he had attended art school before joining his father's building firm.

'My son plays the piano and now he writes poems,' she said. 'I can't do anything really.'

'I'm sure that is not true,' he told her. While she continued kneading, he thoughtfully admired the china on her dresser, in particular an old teapot and teacup Miss Bracewell had given her when the last of the other teacups had been shattered by the dog jumping up.

'It's Rose Lustre Staffordshire,' she told him. 'Quite old, I think. An antique. Too good for me to use, but I like to look at it.'

'But you should use it,' he said. 'It was made to be used, although it is beautiful.'

She sighed, despite herself, as she folded the dough into its tin to prove.

'I always used to dream about being, not rich, never that, but, oh, I don't know, the kind of woman who has time to change into a better dress in the afternoon and just sit down for a quiet hour to drink tea.'

He looked a little confused. Perhaps she had spoken too fast or mumbled.

'I should go,' he said. 'Thank you again, Frau Causley.'

He left just as the overseer was coming looking for him, so she hoped she hadn't landed him in trouble by chatting.

After that they spent a few days building a very tidy brick wall to mark off the new playground from the road and to make it a little safer, with just a small space for a gate. Building a wall was less enthralling than feeding a bonfire, so the children lost interest and were resentful that the new play area was roped off to stop them walking where grass had been sown. There were only three of them now: Helmut, the one actual Fritz and their overseer, Bob. Helmut and Fritz were both builders in civilian life so had the skills. The other men were being used elsewhere, digging ditches. From what Laura could see Helmut was effectively in charge now, while Fritz fetched and stacked bricks and mixed cement with stream water. Bob was good for nothing but standing over the others as they worked with quiet efficiency and she fancied he was looking cross about it.

With only three of them, Laura felt more self-conscious for some reason than she had when they were a little gang, and didn't linger to chat when she took out their tea.

The accident happened one afternoon, when the wall was about two courses of bricks high. It had turned into a fine, dry afternoon, though cold, by the time the boys came home from school full of pent-up energy as usual after hours of sitting still in class and, as Jerry resentfully put it, 'being good'. The wall building didn't interest them but, after wolfing some bread and margarine, they raced out on Charles's bike, leaving Laura to her ironing pile.

On weekdays it was not much quieter than her mother's old cottage round the corner had been, in daylight hours at least. There was always noise from the trains, the sawmill, animals heading to the abattoir. There were always bells ringing or a whistle shrieking. Yet her ear still caught any sound out of the ordinary: music, breaking glass or, in this case, the screech of brakes followed by shouting. She was working on a fiddly pleated bodice that would be all too easy to scorch so didn't drop everything to hurry out and see what had caused the noise. Not that she was one of nature's curtain-twitchers anyway. The boys would tell her soon enough if she had missed some excitement.

But then Terry burst in through the front door shouting, 'It's Jerry. I think he broke his ankle.'

Laura was still on her stool, unplugging the iron from the light socket, when Helmut followed him with a very wan-looking Jerry in his arms.

'Where am I going?' Helmut asked her, and for a moment she had an odd sense of reliving something.

'This way.' Laura led him upstairs to Charles's bedroom, where Jerry had taken to sleeping once the twins had settled in.

Terry explained all as they were climbing. 'We were on the bike,' he said.

'I thought I told you only to ride that poor old bike one boy at a time,' she told him.

'Yes,' he said. 'I know. And the brakes failed and we swerved to avoid the Germans' lorry and both came off. Jerry went flying and landed badly.'

'Are *you* all right?' she asked.

'Of course,' he said dismissively. Along with their hair colour, one of the chief differences between the twins seemed to be that Terry was bombproof.

'Good boy. Run down and fetch me the first-aid box, will you?' She didn't need to tell him where it was; they had it out so often.

It was still a shock coming into Charles's room to find its old extreme tidiness overlaid with Jerry's discarded clothes and comics, model aeroplanes, balls and games. Under strict instructions from Charles, she had moved his precious typewriter, which the boys might have found irresistible, to the space under her bed. He kept the desk's drawers locked and had, she assumed, hidden the key in the room somewhere. Helmut laid Jerry on the bed and watched anxiously as Laura removed the shoe and sock of the damaged ankle. It wasn't broken – he could still waggle his toes – but it was sprained and swelling up fast. She gave him an aspirin for the pain, bound his foot and ankle with a bandage and put three pillows under his foot to raise it.

'You're not to try walking on it until tomorrow, and maybe not even then,' she told him. 'There's a potty under the bed and if you need the bathroom, shout for your brother and he can help you there. All right?'

Jerry was being very brave about the pain. She hoped the painkiller might help him sleep in a while.

Laura thanked Helmut and the other men who had gathered downstairs. The driver of the truck was relieved there was no worse harm done and insisted he'd take the bike away overnight for attention in the camp's workshop. It needed new brake pads, apparently, and the front wheel would need straightening. Laura offered them all tea and sat them around the kitchen table, thinking it was a good opportunity to make Terry play host and show some manners. She could tell he was a little shaken by the accident and it was good to see him regain some of his cocky spirit with these uniformed men to pass bread and margarine to.

He introduced them to the very Cornish delight of golden syrup dribbled over the bread, which she had introduced him and Jerry to on their first night with her, but she felt she must point out it should properly be clotted cream, not margarine, to count as thunder and lightning.

'*Donner und Blitzen,*' Helmut translated for the others, and they laughed. They weren't bad men, she decided, just men with bad leaders. Then Helmut insisted she drink her tea from the Rose Lustre teacup, although it was too late to use the pot. He was scribbling something in his notebook as they sat around and humoured the boy's chatter. It took Laura a while to realise he was sketching her or the teacup.

They did not linger – they had work to finish across the way – but the golden syrup made them all a little merry, as though she had served them beer, and the Germans made little bows to her as they said goodbye. Fritz even clicked his boot heels together.

There was a small heap of things Laura was planning to give to the WVS ladies for other evacuee households. On the top was a little paint set, barely touched.

'May I see?' Helmut asked, and opened the wooden box to inspect the brushes, tubes of paint and bottle of turpentine inside. 'Do you paint?' he asked her.

'Lord, no. I'd been given it for the girl we had here before but she'd no interest. I'm going to give all that pile away again. Would you like it, Helmut? Since you draw. I think it's only a toy, really.'

'No, no. These are good paints. Small tubes only but the paint is a good brand.'

'Well, take it. I insist. Go on.'

And she waved aside his protest, pressing the paint box into his mortar-dusty hands, realising as she did so that he had got under her skin by reminding her in passing of her brother, Stanley. It wasn't his face, although his expression was just as kind and humorous, but his size and way of carrying himself as though wary of his own strength.

The next day Laura paid the men little heed as she was run off her feet with laundry and with keeping an eye on Jerry, whom she'd held back from school so as to keep him from putting weight on his bad ankle, but who proved as hard to make lie quietly in bed as a spring piglet, especially once he decided he had read every comic in the house. By the time his brother came home from school, she had relented to the extent of letting him lie on the sofa to listen to *Workers' Playtime* and the like, and noticed the men had made great advances and their wall was nearly done. The day after that it rained so heavily they stayed in camp. But the following day, they brought back the mended bike, finished the wall, hung a little gate in it and took delivery of stout steel poles they cemented into the ground at various carefully paced-out points.

The following morning, happily while the children (including Jerry) were in school, they came with a bigger team and a bigger lorry so as to unload and install three swings – one with a little wooden bracket around the seat like a high chair to make it safe for smaller children – a steel slide with a ladder and a seesaw. The grass seed was only just beginning to germinate and would surely be trampled in no time, but grass was tough stuff and would soon be holding its own if a wet winter kept little boots at bay.

And that was that. The playground was a success. Even though the twins declared it babyish at first, they soon discovered the pleasure of having swings right on the doorstep on which they could dare each other to swing standing up and of using the seesaw so roughly as to bounce each other out of their perches on it.

⚓ ⚓ ⚓ ⚓ ⚓ ⚓

After over a year of absence, Charles had a brief leave. Promoted to petty officer (coding) to Laura's immense pride, he was transferred back to England, though almost immediately posted north to train other sailors to do what he did. He was brown and healthy, which was good to see, though guarded and careful around her, Laura thought, as though shielding her from bad news. He couldn't say where in England he'd be working, though he did say it was too far to slip back easily.

She had worried, with his fastidious ways, that he'd find the twins a bit much and would regret having nobly given up his peaceful bedroom for a bed on the sofa, but he was unexpectedly brilliant with them. He was full of jokes and limericks for them and ghoulish stories, which had them hanging on his every word and hanging off him, literally. He took them for walks around the town to teach them its history so that they came home full of talk of Norman soldiers, dungeons and gallows, and housemaids having their throats cut out on the moor. Watching them on the sofa on his last night, a twin on either side of him as they listened to *Appointment with Fear* together, the boys leaning comfortably into him as though they had known him all their lives, she saw what a brilliant father he would make, and wondered why an odd sadness stole over her at the realisation.

A week, maybe two, after Charles had left again, looking so smart in his officer's uniform, and with a heavy-cake and a jar of her blackberry and apple jam tucked into his kitbag, there was a day of torrential rain. It was the kind of downpour to make a drumming on the roof tiles and bring St Thomas Water close to bursting its banks. Laura was obliged to go out to deliver laundry to Aggie, an oilcloth tightly laced over her hamper to keep everything dry and tidy, and to pick up another load. Her scarf, coat and hair were wet through by the time she came back. She had hung coat and scarf to dry by the range and was actually towelling her hair when there was a loud knock on the door.

Nobody she knew would wait outside in such weather; they all knew she left the door on the latch when she was home. So she was cursing mildly under her breath as she hurried to make herself not wild, at least, before opening it.

It was Helmut, soaked through despite wearing hat and scarf.

'Helmut,' she said. 'Will you come in?'

'*Guten Abend*, Mrs Causley,' he said. 'I am too dirty and wet. We have been harvesting *Wirsing* on a farm and the truck is waiting. But I wanted to give you this, please. To thank you for your kindness.'

He passed her a parcel, thickly wrapped against the wet.

'Oh. Thank you,' she said, flustered. 'Er, *danke*.'

'It is nothing. Just to amuse. Oh. And here is a *Wirsing*

for you.' He handed her a dripping Savoy cabbage. 'Now I must go.'

'Yes, but. Yes. Goodbye.'

He hurried back to an idling truck full of POW farm workers, which then had to execute a lumbering back-and-forth manoeuvre to get around the corner.

He had fastened the wrapping so tightly with string and with so many layers, including an old pillowcase, that it took her a while to undo it all. It was a little oil painting of a woman drinking tea. She sat alone and thoughtful at a table covered with a spotless tablecloth and set with not just the teapot, cup and saucer Helmut knew her to own, but a matching sugar basin, cake plate and side plate. The cake was a peculiarly small Victoria sponge, which would have won no prizes. There was also a jug of anemones and a toasting fork. There was no sign that the woman expected company, but she seemed at peace and had the consolation of a view through a glazed door into a beautiful garden. It was Laura's china, though not her kitchen but a dimly lit, elegant drawing room. And though the woman was clearly meant to be her – so clearly that Laura felt a vain little pang at how old she must now seem to younger people like Helmut – she was wearing an elegant, ladylike navy-blue dress and pearls, unlike anything Laura owned.

She propped it up in a corner, unsure quite what to think of such a present. It was so entirely unlike anything she possessed. When she realised the school would be letting the children out any minute, she took it upstairs and laid it on her bed, not wanting to have to explain or discuss it. Much later, however, when she finally brushed out her hair for the night and said her prayers for Charles and the others, she took the painting up again to lean it on her dressing table so she could see it from her pillow. The picture was a present, but she understood now that its deeper generosity lay in the way Helmut had handed her a quite different version of herself and her story.

LIVERPOOL – 1944

He did me kindness, sir; drew on my side;
But in conclusion put strange speech upon me.
I know not what 'twas but distraction.

Charles was transfixed by Nova Pilbeam's luminous face, which truly was heart shaped, almost like Betty Boop's, and her low, penetrating voice, so well suited to Viola pretending to be a boy. He had seen her on screen, of course, in all sorts of silly films, but it was a revelation to see her on a stage where her voice and gestures alone had to work their charm, unassisted by dewy-eyed close-ups and a surging studio orchestra. The Old Vic Company was in residence at the Liverpool Playhouse, where the two of them had already enjoyed her tragically idealistic Nina in *The Seagull*. Well, Charles had enjoyed it; on both occasions his companion, Bucknall, had fidgeted.

Bucknall was fidgeting beside Charles now, crossing and rearranging his long legs, which did not fit comfortably into the space because boredom was making him slouch down in his seat. Charles strove to tune him out and lose himself again in the drama. People were giggling, determined to find Shakespeare's clear-eyed acceptance of ancient comic conventions funny. Charles had always found Antonio's devotion to Sebastian touching and was

glad the actors were playing him as a man with a real
emotional attachment and not as a hoary old seadog
showing loyalty. Charles watched Antonio unquestioningly
take Viola in disguise for her adored brother and found he
was anticipating the underwritten but surely intended
poignancy of his then being made to stand by as both
siblings were married off. Like *As You Like It*, the play
appealed to Charles because it wove a thread of alteration,
death and solitude through the bright fabric of a love story.
Twelfth Night was a play in which straightforward love
and happiness were constantly dodged or deferred.

Bucknall sighed heavily and crossed his legs yet again,
his long thigh bumping Charles's.

Charles leaned sideways, close enough to feel the
warmth of him.

'Not long now,' he whispered.

'Thank fuck for that,' Bucknall said, not bothering to
whisper and was furiously shushed by the outraged woman
in front of them, whose victory roll was turbaned in a
glittery headscarf almost as distracting as Bucknall's thighs.
'Oh, I'm so sorry,' Bucknall told her, even louder, earning
himself a glare and threatening to make Charles giggle.

They would not ordinarily have been friends and on
several levels they still weren't. They were both instructing
officers at HMS *Cabbala*, a stone frigate in a camp a few
miles outside the city near a place called Lowton. It was a
camp of H blocks on requisitioned farmland, built at the
start of the war to house munitions workers from Risley
Moss. Back then HMS *Cabbala* was in an ugly Victorian
pile on the dirty fringe of the Cotswolds, requisitioned

from an aristocrat absent in Australia. Bucknall had been trained there and said it was 'enormous fun, like boarding school, really' and claimed the new site was a prison by comparison. Still, the place offered a cinema, a chapel, a library, NAAFI canteen and ample playing fields, as well as hosting weekly lectures and dances.

Recruits were now trained in five and a half weeks flat, of which four were the coding course Charles ran or the visual signals one taught by Bucknall. Bucknall's course included instruction in semaphore flags, signals projectors and Aldis lamps as well as teaching the international sig-nalling code, so involved him taking recruits out of doors, which suited him as he was innately sporty. He also led football, rugby and hockey games among both the Wrens and sailors there.

Compared to the questionable charm of the windswept Skegness chalets, the H blocks were cosy to the point of fug-giness. Each housed ninety-four, in cabins divided into port and starboard watches, with just eight baths and sixteen basins. The crossbar of each H was a sitting room with chairs, gramophone and wireless. As officers, Charles and Bucknall enjoyed the relative luxury of having a cabin apiece and being in the marginally less crowded, but otherwise identical officers' quarters. The Nissen hut where Charles taught was similar to the one where he had learned at HMS *Royal Arthur*, complete with school desks, dim lighting and the stove at its centre, which he dubbed the Censor.

Each day began with everyone gathered on the parade ground, regardless of the weather, for largely inaudible morning prayers and the raising of the White Ensign while

MOTHER'S BOY

a marines' band played the National Anthem. For those in the know, the arrangement of signals flags on the mast told whether raincoats were to be worn on parade, carried or left at home. Bucknall said that at Tortworth the commanding officer had been so convinced of the presence of German spies in South Gloucestershire that the Ensign was raised and lowered on a mast erected in the house's three-storey hall.

Charles had first come to Bucknall's attention because of a book – which he would later learn was entirely a pretext, as Bucknall was not a reader. He found Charles enjoying a slim volume of Sassoon's poems at breakfast.

'Don't let the CO see you reading that,' he said.

'Why not?' Charles asked. 'Because of the stand he took against the Great War?'

This was precisely what had drawn him to Sassoon's work at first – a decorated war hero standing up to condemn senseless slaughter presented a compelling contrast to the unquestioning acceptance of war they had been taught to idolise at school.

'No,' Bucknall said. 'Everyone's used to that, and I don't believe that story about him throwing his medal in the Thames; man's as vain as any published author. No, it's his, er, home life. At least until his hasty marriage. Didn't you know? He was involved with that arch pansy Tennant. Not that it's common knowledge but . . . the CO's so anti I often wonder if he isn't a bit of a Baden-Powell himself.'

'Baden-Powell's . . .?'

Charles must have looked gratifyingly shocked as Bucknall grinned and introduced himself before sitting down across from Charles with his laden breakfast tray. 'What a lot I have to teach you,' he said.

After that first, slightly baffling conversation, which had been abruptly cut short by one of the WRNS officers joining them, Bucknall had sought Charles out regularly, always at moments when he could catch him on his own. His interest was so unlikely that it reawakened in Charles the long-buried fear and sense of physical inadequacy he had felt in the hectoring presence of school athletes. It soon became clear that Bucknall was one of those officers – he had never been other ranks, like Charles – for whom enlisting had enabled a reassuring continuity of his days at public school. He called Charles by his surname, of course, and once they became friends, permitted him to call him Bucknall instead of sir, at least when they were alone.

Although he had a reputation as a ladies' man, always the debonair life and soul at dances and regularly taking different Wrens out on dates, Bucknall often complained to Charles that somehow women 'ruined the atmosphere around the camp' and said that it was 'not the same'. As school, Charles presumed. In odd, clumsy ways he kept steering their conversations back to how much better it was when they could be 'all chaps together'. His questions soon exposed the dramatic differences between their upbringings and the disappointment on his handsome face (a face, Charles had come to realise, exactly like an illustration in a *Boy's Own Annual*, complete with square jaw and untameable cowlick) when Charles had said that, yes, his school had been all male but non-boarding, made Charles laugh out loud at him. But there were the Jubilee

Baths, Charles told him then, where there were no women, more often than not, and he said how his friend Ginger had taken him to the men-only, nudist section of the Plymouth Lido.

'Your friend Ginger,' Bucknall pursued, interest piqued.

'Oh, yes. At least I think so,' Charles answered the unasked question. 'He certainly was that afternoon, and not very discreet about it.'

'Discretion is key,' Bucknall said solemnly.

'Yes,' Charles agreed.

'The stuff I got up to at school,' Bucknall went on. 'Unrepeatable, probably. Though I find I often think about it. Especially, you know, in a rugby tackle.'

'Of course,' said Charles, who had managed never to execute a rugby tackle or been tackled in his life to date, but who had found himself becoming almost breathless when watching the games in camp, their fearless, muddy embraces, their odd blend of violence and intimacy, in which the one seemed to license the other.

Before long, Bucknall approached Charles to ask if he'd like to come into Liverpool with him one evening.

'What, just us?' Charles asked in his surprise.

'Well, we could ask a couple of Jennies along if you'd prefer the camouflage, but yes, just us, I thought. There's usually a play on somewhere. You can educate me. You know I know nothing.'

The Old Vic Company was presenting a season of classic drama at the Playhouse. Happily for Bucknall their first trip was to a Restoration comedy, a nimble production of Vanbrugh's *The City Wives' Confederacy*, which he appeared to enjoy immensely, laughing when the rest of the audience laughed, and sometimes when they didn't, and unmistakably letting his knee first bump then lean into Charles's. In the bar in the interval, when Charles bought the drinks as Bucknall had bought the tickets, Bucknall spoke loudly about how pretty one of the actresses was and how surprisingly gamey the jokes seemed to be, but when they were back in the darkness, there was his knee, his thigh, indeed, sometimes with his hand resting on it, pressing into Charles's as though testing to see if he'd withdraw. Which, blood racing rather, Charles hadn't.

Afterwards, because there was still plenty of time before they needed to be back in camp, he steered Charles to the elegant bar of a nearby hotel. He left him at a quiet table with their beers and Charles assumed, because neither of them had eaten, that he had kindly gone to ask about sandwiches. But when he returned, he was holding a key, barely concealed in the palm of one hand. His manner when he sat back down was invigorated, as Charles had seen it after hockey matches and as he imagined it in the sickening din of battle. He was at once on heat, it seemed, and confidential.

'Now I think I know you well enough,' he said, 'for you to understand and say nothing if I'm barking up the wrong petty officer here, but I've just taken a room and I'm hoping you'll join me there. Say in ten minutes? After I've appeared to leave, and you've finished your quiet pint.'

'Er. Yes,' Charles said. 'Yes.' He heard his voice wobble.

'It's quite safe. Other ranks never come in here and it's the sort of place you'd meet your wife or mother, not a floozie.'

'Oh,' said Charles, confused and wondering what that made him in the circumstances. 'Good.'

'Good man. Room twenty-eight. I'll leave the door unlocked.' He stood. 'Night, old man,' he said louder, and shook Charles's hand before leaving the bar by the street door.

Alone, Charles made himself drink most of his pint, then nerves meant he must visit the gents. Bucknall was correct. There were hunting prints everywhere, and quiet, inter-changeable landscapes. He had a moment of panic that he might have to pass a reception desk and be challenged about his business but there was a staircase directly outside the bar and he took that, wondering what on earth he would say if he met a fellow officer coming down it. *Good evening*, he decided. He would say that and nothing more.

He found room twenty-eight on a blessedly deserted landing and took a deep breath before letting himself in. Bucknall was already undressed and sitting up in bed, his big, athlete's body as smooth as sanded oak.

'Good man,' he muttered. 'Key's in the lock.'

Charles turned the key and shot the bolt as well for good measure.

Since then they had seen *The Seagull*, *Uncle Vanya* and an instantly forgettable new thing by Noël Coward. Bucknall seemed practised in his cunning. He made no secret of their play-going to the others in the mess but instead made a small joke of it.

'Causley's educating me. I've said I'll teach him to catch in exchange.'

He also continued to be the life and soul at camp dances,

in which Charles would often take a familiar kind of refuge by playing the piano with the band – and to steer the
better-looking Wrens out on the town occasionally. And
he encouraged Charles to bring a girl of his own a couple
of times. Charles invited Edna, a thoroughly pleasant
WRNS officer, a clever but physically awkward woman he
could imagine as a country librarian or headmistress, who
was glad of the change of scene and did not appear to
think herself short-changed when he did no more than
dance with her and then shook her hand at the evening's
end. She reminded him of Mother – not of Mother herself,
of course, but of when he had started playing in dance
bands and going around with their high-spirited young
women. The limit of her sex education had been to say,
'Now, Charles, I'll trust that you're a gentleman and we'll
say no more about it.'

Shamelessly, after the second of these double excursions, Bucknall had put the two, mismatched women in
a cab, claiming, in a blatant kind of truth-telling, that
'Causley and I have to go on where ladies aren't welcome,'
then steered Charles smartly to the hotel for more of what
he called 'urgent business'.

The time they spent alone in various rooms of the same
hotel was so unrelated to anything else in Charles's life
that he was coming to see how men had mistresses, or even
second marriages. It required a mental sleight of hand. His
heart, he found, remained quite uninvolved, which possibly was how he was able to continue breaking the law
both civilian and martial, with the equanimity of a
practised killer. Bucknall had a hold over him, all the

same; had only to wink at him in the NAAFI queue or pass him, bruised and sweaty and dressed only in a towel on the way to his bath after a match, for Charles's thoughts to be as scrambled as a poor radio signal.

The sex they had was probably little more sophisticated than the things Bucknall had got up to at Marlborough, though they kissed a lot. Apparently the lack of kissing had been a point of honour at school, and had been what reassured boys it was only a phase. He also liked them to stand together in front of a mirror in the middle of things. Charles found this almost unbearable for the dissimilarity between their bodies, but Bucknall found it hugely stirring, which in turn was compensation for Charles's embarrassment.

'Look!' Bucknall would tell him. 'Just look at how much you want me!'

Charles always took his glasses off and set them on the bedside table, partly to protect them, partly because he assumed they were unattractive. *Men seldom made passes at men wearing glasses.* But Bucknall sometimes broke off whatever they were doing and made him put them on again, which seemed absurd to Charles, like wearing nothing but garters, but it excited Bucknall almost as much as the business with the mirror. Perhaps there had been a significant boy at school with round tortoiseshell specs? Charles never asked but enjoyed the sip of erotic power it gave him.

He could not separate his pleasure in these illicit meetings from the equally intense one of going to see really good professional theatre after months of cultural starvation. Bucknall was not given to introspection – it appeared to have been trained out of him, as it had from so many officers – but the release at the end of each meeting, when they both collapsed back on to the pillows, the heady, pears-on-the-beach smell of sex all around them, and when Charles often felt compelled to laugh at the essential silliness of the very dangerous thing they had just done, loosened Bucknall's thoughts a little. Of course he would get married, he told Charles at such a moment, once the war was over and things had stabilised, because he wanted a family. He was surprised and even indignant – like a man hoodwinked – when Charles confessed, only realising the truth of the thought as he voiced it, that he could never live a lie. That evening had ended abruptly with Bucknall washing and dressing in a sort of sulk.

Charles was grateful to Bucknall, however, even though he often thought him absurd, for all his pink and blond handsomeness, and privately christened him the Anticushty for being everything Cushty wasn't, and not for the better. He was grateful to him because Bucknall's cynical attitude towards women in general and the Wrens in particular had made Charles realise how much he liked their company and that he relished teaching these often inexperienced girls and making them laugh even as he instructed them. More importantly, the energy released by their meetings seemed to have unlocked something in his writing. He had written and polished quite a sheaf of poems now, all of them relating to the war and the life at sea and, in a moment of madness, had dared to write a letter to Siegfried Sassoon, praising his work and admitting to feeling his way as a poet himself. To his amazement Sassoon had written back, a proper, thoughtful and encouraging letter. He wrote:

The interesting thing about the poem for me is that there's always a subtext. The skin of the poem is never what it's really about. A poem is much more than what lies on the page in front of you.

Charles was now paralysed by indecision over whether to send him anything to read and, if so, what. Nobody in the mess had any idea he was writing poetry; they thought him oddball enough merely for reading it.

For all Bucknall's fidgeting and impatient thigh grinding, the end of *Twelfth Night* cast its wintry spell and Charles was briefly transported. The last pages of good novels and last scenes of good plays invariably left him with a kind of sorrow that they were nearly over, and a childlike frustration at being left outside the story and returned to his own life. Having tasted, in a small way, the pleasure of being on the stage and receiving applause, he also found himself imagining being an actor in this production, in a small role, of course, like Sebastian's, and returning to shared digs with the others, picking over small things that might be improved in the next performance, dreading the gruelling prospect of a day with a matinée as well as an evening show. He imagined becoming Miss Pilbeam's special friend and confidant. He imagined quite another life than the one awaiting him, and resented Bucknall insisting they slip out before the applause had ended.

'Christ! I thought it would never end,' Bucknall said as they reached the foyer. 'Come along, matey. We've urgent business. I've been thinking about it since the interval.'

Charles had almost hoped the play would have gone on

too long for a hotel tryst afterwards, but Bucknall would not do without and officers had some leeway regarding curfew. He was always mocking Charles for still thinking like other ranks.

As always, they went to the elegant little bar first, whose pink-shaded lamps cast everyone in a flattering light. While Charles was sitting with his beer and looking at the programme to give Bucknall time to settle in upstairs, an elderly couple came in, also clutching programmes.

'Wasn't it marvellous?' the woman said, as she sat at the neighbouring table. 'I think it's my favourite Shakespeare comedy. Even more than *As You Like It*. It allows room for the darkness.'

'Yes,' Charles agreed. 'Not everyone is consoled.'

'And some are cast out of Eden. I find entirely happy endings are almost alarming, like very tidy houses.' She cast a shrewd blue eye over his uniform. 'Are you staying here as well?'

'Yes,' he said. 'Briefly. Ah, well. Good night.'

'Perhaps we'll see you at breakfast.'

Bucknall was particularly passionate and demanding that evening, perhaps because he sensed Charles's thoughts were elsewhere, churned up by Shakespeare in a way they hadn't been by Coward or Chekhov, and his self-love was piqued. It was a deep difference between them that beforehand, Bucknall made a great show of cynical detachment, as though their coming together were purely a matter of animal release, but afterwards he liked to lie there a while smoking, with Charles in his arms, betraying a kind of tenderness as he softly chatted about things he would never have spoken of in uniform. Charles, by contrast, required a degree of tenderness beforehand but itched to be washed, dressed and away once they were through. He could blind himself only so long to their lack of common ground, the radical differences in their politics and natures, and these were all too evident once the only reason for their meeting was out of the way. He found, too, that fear of exposure stole up on him the moment lust was spent. He would lie there, inwardly flinching like an unwilling cat, as Bucknall took drags on his cigarette and stroked Charles's hair, imagining the military police bursting in, inquisitive hotel guests in dressing gowns peering over their shoulders.

He tuned out of Bucknall's sleepily inconsequential chat, though enjoying the rumble of his voice in his chest, and imagined Mother's response to his disgrace. Profound embarrassment would prevent her ever asking for details, would quite possibly prevent her ever even speaking of it, but her disappointment would be the bitter seasoning to every meal she served him thereafter and would congeal like custard skin over her every mention of cousins married or born. But then a word Bucknall spoke snagged Charles's attention and made him sit up.

'That was the name of your ship, wasn't it?'

'Yes,' Charles said.

'Thought so.' Bucknall frowned. He took a last drag on his cigarette, sucking so hard Charles fancied he heard it crackle like a tiny bonfire, then stubbed it out. 'I didn't like to bring it up earlier. Didn't want to spoil your evening, as I know how much you were looking forward to Nova Pilbeam and company.'

'Where were they?'

'You know I can't tell you that. I shouldn't have told you anything.'

'You know I'm not a spy, for God's sake.'

Bucknall frowned again. At unexpected moments he could be a terrible prig. He made a move to show he was getting up so Charles rolled off him.

'Off the Greek coast, let's say. But you don't know any of this. They're keeping quiet about it for morale.'

As usual he pissed carefully, and at length, down the plughole before filling the sink and washing himself.

'What the hell were they doing there?' Charles asked.

'How should I know? Don't shoot the messenger. Anyway, they reckon it was a sub got them. Boat split clean in two. None of them would have suffered for long.'

'You didn't tell me earlier because you knew I wouldn't have felt like coming up here.' Charles detested the querulous tone in his voice.

Bucknall always dressed with impressive speed.

'What?' he asked. 'Don't be stupid. I didn't think you'd be so upset. I thought you'd be pleased, actually, to have dodged a bullet.'

Charles washed too, quickly, avoiding his reflection in the mirror over the sink.

'I'll make my own way back,' he said.

'You sure?' Again that frown. Bucknall was almost comically unused to not getting his way.

'I just need some time alone, Bucknall. Nothing personal.'

'Ah. Right you are, old man.'

Bucknall thought Charles hadn't noticed that he always

pocketed the hotel soap just before leaving, a small piece of meanness that would make it that much easier to defer their next outing until one or both of them received a fresh posting.

'Better take this,' Charles said, drying the little cake of soap on a corner of his towel and handing it to him. Bucknall frowned again but pocketed it. In the past he had admitted it excited him to be fully dressed, back in uniform, while Charles was still naked, to the point where, on two occasions, he had ended by removing at least half his uniform again. Tonight he simply pocketed the soap and cleared his throat.

'See you at breakfast, then,' he said.

'Yes,' said Charles. 'Thank you for the play. I really loved it.'

'No accounting for tastes,' Bucknall said, shot back the little bolt and slipped quietly from the room.

The usual drill was to leave five minutes or so apart and to meet half a mile away beside a rowdy pub popular with all ranks, where it was easy to pick up a taxi. Tonight, Charles found himself climbing back into bed, pulling up the bedding that was so much heavier and more comforting than what they had in camp, and imagining Cushty's last moments.

He hoped it had actually been an attack from another ship or from a plane, and not a sinister torpedo that had sunk the *Starburst*. That way there was a chance he'd have died as Cushty's fellow gunners had on their crossing to Malta, blown to oblivion with no time to anticipate the end.

There could be nothing worse, he thought again, than the mad, terrifying scramble as a ship sank, its lights flickering and going out, the panicky chaos of men racing to free lifeboats before the icy blackness rushed up to envelop them, everyone trying to believe there was a chance, most knowing there was none.

How on earth had the message come through that the boat had been broken clean in two? From a spy, perhaps? He assumed there were spies on the English side as well as on the other.

He touched the small bumpy scar he still had on one forearm. I bound your wounds, he thought, and you bound mine.

Then he was startled to catch himself nodding off and jumped up rather than risk a late return. He dressed swiftly and hurried out, as always leaving the key in the door rather than risk the night porter's smirk as he handed it over. If he ran, he could still catch Bucknall and share a taxi after all. They wouldn't be doing this again, but it was better to avoid a new awkwardness between them that might have to be explained to others.

'Sorry,' he would tell him. 'You weren't to know but I had some good mates on that ship.'

TEIGNMOUTH AGAIN – 1945

Apart from a couple of brief visits to Maggie in Trusham, it was the first time Laura had crossed the Tamar since the outbreak of war. As they pulled into Okehampton, she let her knitting sink into her lap. The view of ships on the water far below always made her dizzy but she couldn't not look. She loved the dramatic sense it gave that Corn-wall was its own country, a sort of island, fortified by rocks and water.

They entered the outskirts of Plymouth and she bent down discreetly to loosen the ankle straps on her shoes. They were a smart new black pair, with a slight heel, broken in around the house and on a couple of trips across to church but not yet worn out properly until today. She regretted her vanity in thinking she should dress up for Aggie who, after all, was a friend and would not have judged her if she'd turned up in a housecoat and curlers.

Since the German surrender the previous month, the town had seen a succession of departures. The evacuees went home first. She was not the only surrogate mother needing to blow her nose on the station platform and pre-tend it was hay fever. Not every evacuee had landed in a loving household – far from it, she suspected – but four or five years was long enough for children to start to feel like family. And not every child would be returning to homes as comfortable or as friendly as the ones that had taken them in. Jerry and Terry had heard from their mother on birthdays and at Christmas, once Laura had managed to get her number to her, but otherwise not at all, which shocked her. They never spoke of her without prompting but Laura had always made a point of encouraging them to speak of home regularly so they didn't forget it. They seemed almost hurtfully calm as the WVS got in touch and the day of multiple departures drew near, but then, on the platform at the last minute, they had each hugged her so hard that it made her weepy.

'I'll miss you two,' she told them. 'You've been a pleasure to have around.'

They promised to write, though she knew this was highly unlikely.

'Your mum won't know you, you've grown so much,' she said. She didn't like to add that their voices had come to sound more Cornish than Cockney. There was little packed in their small suitcases of what they had brought with them; they had outgrown all their clothes, including the earliest jerseys she had knitted them.

She had heard of households that had moved to adopt their evacuees when news of parents' deaths had come through. She had also heard a horror story of a childless couple who had arranged to adopt an evacuated daughter but sent her brother, who they didn't want, back to his family.

'People astonish me,' she often said to Charles.

'So you're forever saying,' he'd always reply.

Because it's true, she thought now. People could be very strange.

She was knitting a jersey for Charles again, having kept a careful note of the stitch count and measurements used in the last one she had made him. When she wrote to announce her plan to make it and asked his preferences his reply had been 'anything but navy blue!' She returned to knitting it as they pulled past Devonport into Plymouth proper. She had settled on a nice warm russet colour and was daring to make him a cardigan, fiddly buttonhole strip and all. Even with narrow needles and slender wool it would certainly be ready by Christmas, although she hardly dared hope that he'd be home by then. All she knew was that he was somewhere in the Pacific and that the war was still raging there.

She didn't like to be thought unpatriotic (though she had never been a flag-waver) or miserable, but she had felt quite unable to join in the noisy celebrations in early May. Secretly, she felt almost disgusted by them after so many deaths and so much destruction, and was sure there were many families of sailors still serving, or of prisoners in Japanese hands, who felt the same way.

The second wave of departures from Launceston had been the POWs, although some seemed curiously reluctant to leave. Just as she knew of cases where young evacuees were effectively becoming Cornish, so she knew there were prisoners who had fallen for local girls. Shy, unofficial courtships were only just edging into the light and many of the men involved in them would be making new Cornish lives rather than returning to whatever the Allies had left of their German ones. She had not seen Helmut again, though she had written him a short letter care of the camp to thank him for the painting. The POWs were leaving and, in dribs and drabs, the sons and daughters the war in Europe had spared were returning in time for a peacetime harvest, and the rude shock of living under civilian rationing.

Laura could not help thinking how the war would have altered Charles; not just the terrible things he must have seen but the excitement, too, and the spending five years far from Launceston among utterly unCornish people, foreigners even. She had caught a glimpse of it in his newly shielded manner towards her in his last leave before shipping out to the Pacific. She knew she had to be ready for change, had to accept that he might not want to return to his nice, quiet job with the Electricity Board – although his place there was guaranteed against his return. (She had checked this detail but known better than to tell him.) She could see, when she was feeling brave, that these aching years of his absence had readied her for his deciding he needed to live far off in a big city once he came home. His letters home continued to have a studied avoidance in them of the future, or even the laying of tentative plans, so perhaps he was readying himself as well.

The third departure, which she should have had the sense to predict, was Aggie's. Within days, it felt, of hosting a noisy all-night celebration of the victory in Europe, Aggie had shut up shop. When Laura took her round a batch of ironed and starched laundry one day, she said there was no bundle of dirty stuff to take away in return. It was like when you clumsily took an extra step at the top of some stairs for a tread that wasn't there.

Aggie had accepted a handsome offer for her dilapidated house from the council, who were hungry for the generous plot it occupied. They were going to demolish it to build a clutch of smaller council houses on the site, just as they planned to build council housing on two sides of the new playground. Aggie's plan was to move away, out of Cornwall, and to somewhere with a sea view where she could help her children start again where they were not known, where their surname would not give rise to winks or their resemblance to other women's husbands to gossip. Heppy had been at once prized and notorious among the soldiers, who nicknamed her the Black Bomber. The youngest, who, Laura was coming to realise, were quite possibly grandchildren, not children, were young enough to benefit from regular school and clean slates. The older clutch would similarly benefit from all the work they had put in during Launceston's army occupation.

'I'll miss you,' Laura told her simply.

'Oh, you've a ton of friends,' Aggie insisted.

'Not really,' Laura said, not wishing to sound self-pitying. 'I know a lot of people through church but that's not the same. I've never been very good at making friends. It's probably why Charles can be so prickly.'

'Well, that's not true,' Aggie told her. 'But you've never allowed yourself much time, have you? I don't know a woman who works so hard.'

'Oh, well, work's work,' Laura muttered, knowing the statement was meaningless but needing to say something as she was surprised to be so upset and needed to hide it. 'I've appreciated all the work you've given me, though.'

'My filthy sheets? You won't miss those!'

She would miss the income they represented, though, and the simplicity of earning most of it from one person. Now Charles had grown up she could probably survive on her pension and savings, but she retained a lifetime's dread of poverty.

As she walked home, empty hamper swinging at her side by its creaking leather handle, she thought about her friendship with Aggie and realised that the fact that it consisted almost entirely of conversations over tea at Aggie's kitchen table, and went unwitnessed and unrecorded, and wasn't shared with others, were what lent it value for her. She had known other men and women just as long, but known them outside in the world, in church, shop queues, or at Sunday school picnics. She was very fond of many of them, felt a kind of love for them even, would rejoice at their grandchildren's christenings and shed a tear at their funerals, but she knew none of them saw her for herself the way Aggie always had, but always by the light of who her siblings were, or her son, or her mother.

The final departure would probably be noticed by nobody but herself. Characterful and funny, quite without his aristocratic mother's imperiousness and territorial instincts, Wang had lived into his teens and gamely done his best to keep up with the rough and tumble games favoured by the twins, but she had noticed him slowing up sharply in the weeks since their departure. He stopped asking to be taken out and had to be woken with a little start for his walks and coaxed out of his bed by having his lead clipped on and given a gentle tug, which felt cruel.

Laura realised his heart must have been failing and had finally given out as he slept, or while she slept at least, for she found him cold and stiff in his bed when she came down to riddle and wake the range in the morning.

Douglas, Ginger's father, buried him for her. She had buried the last cat in the little garden, and Charlie's terrier, Jack, so she was worried it was a bit crowded already. And she didn't like the thought of consigning Wang's larger body to somewhere she now grew vegetables. Douglas suggested they bury him in a verge on Underlane, beyond the baths, which had, after all, been one of his favourite walks.

Poor Douglas had returned from the war earlier than some, and had to spend time shut up in St Lawrence's, the asylum at Bodmin. He had been broken by the trauma of happening to be watching from another ship as Ginger's was torpedoed and sunk with only three survivors. Since his release he had taken to wandering the parish, a lost soul eager to be given tasks, however menial, rather than face more time than he had to alone in the little house Ginger had worked so hard to make a home for them.

As they walked along the lane on their sad mission, he with his spade, she with Wang's bony body wrapped in a blanket, she mentioned something about plans for a peace festival at St Thomas's and he quietly confessed that God had died for him with Ginger. She did not rush to comfort or challenge him, the way she knew others in the congregation might, but let his words speak and have their space between them.

'I can understand that,' she said at last. 'If I heard that Charles's ship was lost, I'm not sure church would be any

comfort. I don't know what I'd do. Go a little mad probably.' She pulled herself up short, remembering Douglas
had not long left the asylum. 'How about here, Douglas?
Near this oak? The ground looks soft and it's not too near
the ditch.'

Watching him dig Wang's grave, the tendons flexing in
his lean arms as he gripped the spade, she thought back to
when Charles finally consented to become poor Ginger's
friend, when Douglas was long enough a widower for
people, including her own family, to start matchmaking
the two of them. Back then she had thought herself long
past a second marriage – Aggie had simply called her
independent, of course – but now she realised she had only
been in her thirties. It was disorienting trying to imagine
herself having shared at least half a life with this tragic,
unassuming man now labouring on her behalf. It had only
been since his return from the asylum that they had fallen
to using one another's Christian names.

He leaned his spade into the mossy bank and held out
his palms to her for Wang.

'Shall I?' he asked. 'Or would you rather?'

'Oh. No. Thank you, Douglas,' she said, and passed
Wang to him, having made sure the dog was still tightly
shrouded.

'Dear little thing,' he muttered by way of an epitaph and
lowered the bundle into the hole.

She had not fully appreciated how much of a presence
Wang had been, even in slumbering age: his snuffling
welcome if she woke in the night and came to the kitchen
for a drink, his way of sensing when she had finally sat

with a view to staying put for a while and coming then to lean against her feet, the muted barks and paw skitterings of his ageless dreams. The little house that had so often felt unbearably full with the twins rampaging through it on bad weather days now seemed shockingly empty and still. Never easy with idleness but without enough work to fill her days now she didn't have mouths but her own to feed or Aggie's mounds of laundry to see to, Laura threw herself into work around the house. She turned mattresses. She washed and starched curtains. She took rugs out into the yard to beat them with Charlie's old cricket bat. She tidied cupboards, then made jams and chutneys to fill them that she would never get around to eating and would probably sell through the Women's Institute. But all this industry seemed only to emphasise the stillness when she stopped. When the telephone jangled and it was Aggie suggesting she come and see her new house she had jumped at the chance.

Aggie met her on the platform, hugged her warmly as nobody else in her life ever seemed to, and asked after her journey. Her strapping oldest boy, Tobey, insisted on taking Laura's overnight case and trundled it behind them on a little trolley he had brought along for the purpose.

'Training him,' Aggie explained. 'I thought we could offer a porter service for our guests. It's not far but it's nice not to have to carry anything. It'll make people feel their holiday has started already.' She saw how Laura was looking about her. 'Is it all coming back to you?'

'Yes,' Laura said. 'I haven't set foot here since I first married Charlie, you know.'

'Has it changed?'

'Don't make me feel older than I am, girl.' They laughed and walked on to Hollands Road and then down Esplanade. Teignmouth had suffered its share of bomb damage near the start of the war, infinitely more than Launceston, mainly from bombers circling back from the strategic target of Plymouth. Here and there a whole terrace had gone, usually where a bomb had caused a gas explosion. In some places just one house had vanished, like a rotten tooth. Shockingly, Aggie told her, the hospital had received a direct hit, which nobody chose to believe was accidental. Rebuilding was already underway and so, apparently, was tourism. Deck chairs and benches on the prom were crowded with people sunning themselves and there were gangs of half-naked children at play.

'And here we are,' Aggie said as they turned on to Courtney Place.

Laura looked up at the handsome, double-fronted house before them, its bay windows capturing a full view of the seafront and a raised ground floor ensuring both sunlight, and privacy from passers-by.

'Oh, Aggie,' she said. 'How on earth . . .?'

'Had it for a song at a bankruptcy sale,' Aggie said proudly. 'It needs work, mind.'

She led the way up the steps and through the big glazed porch, where there were two little benches where people could sit to sun themselves or brush the sand off their shoes.

'The great thing is it was already a hotel, so we don't have to knock the rooms about. And we got it furnished.

The children are having a great time trying on different bedrooms for size.'

Heppy and her sister greeted her as warmly as Aggie had, which was touching, and showed their first non-paying guest to her room, while Tobey continued to play porter, carrying her case to set on a folding frame at the foot of the bed. Left in peace to settle in, she visited the room's little bathroom, imagining the luxury of living with a bathroom only feet from her bed and not down a chilly corridor or flight of stairs. She stood a while in the bay window admiring much the same view that she and Charlie had enjoyed on their honeymoon.

Then she surrendered to being given a tour, not of every room, of course, but of the best ones, and the dining room and sitting room, and the surprisingly sunny kitchen at the front of the basement to one side. On the other side there was a laundry, and behind that a warm drying room with a high rack for hanging sheets on and there was a fair-weather drying yard at the back.

At last, while Tobey and the girls returned to the task of painting bedrooms, Aggie sat Laura in the sitting room's window, where they could enjoy the view, and brought her tea and a luxurious cherry cake. She had never asked but had long suspected that Aggie had contacts who slipped her ingredients for which no coupons changed hands.

'What do you think?' Aggie asked.

'It's wonderful,' Laura told her. 'I mean, it'll be a lot of work but then there are plenty of you. Will you get in any help at all?'

'Well . . . I did remember you once saying how your Charlie had always wanted to run a place like this.'

'Oh, he did,' Laura sighed, remembering. 'He'd have loved it. Mind you, I think he had little idea how much work was involved. He'd have enjoyed dressing up and fetching people and their bags from the station and playing host in a smart waistcoat, and you-know-who would have ended up all hot and red-faced in the basement, cooking and laundering and cursing people who didn't wipe their shoes to spare the carpets.'

'So . . .' Aggie fiddled with her teaspoon. 'I couldn't persuade you?'

'To work here?' Laura realised she was in earnest. 'Oh, Aggie, I couldn't up sticks like you.'

'What's to keep you? And don't you come over all Cornish and tell me Launceston's where you long to be.'

'Well . . .' Laura thought. 'Apart from my earliest memories in Langore, it's all I've ever known, I suppose. It's where most of the family is, or near there. But mainly I think I need to keep a home for Charles to come back to.' Even as she said this, she thought of Douglas, driven half mad by an empty house. 'Everything else will have changed so much for him I think he'll need some things to stay the same. At least until he's found his feet again. It's lovely to have the sea just outside the window, though. So fresh! No tanneries or gasworks smells!' She looked out at the wheeling seagulls following a late fishing boat that was returning to harbour.

'I'll miss our chats,' Aggie said. 'I could picture you in a nice little cottage here. There are some beauties just around from the front, where the fishermen are. Too small for my tribe but they'd be perfect for you and Charles. Or even over the bridge in Shaldon, if you wanted somewhere quieter.'

'Shaldon's a bit prinked up for an old washerwoman,' Laura said. 'Both my parents were workhouse-born, remember.' They laughed, and she felt stirred through with sorrow that Aggie was the only friend she could confidently expect to laugh at such a thing. 'You'll have more than enough help. There's no great mystery to laundry. It just takes hot water, time and elbows and you're well set up. Is there a good boiler?'

Aggie nodded. 'Big oil-fired thing,' she said, 'with a tank out the back. Tobey has already claimed that as his department. That's why the drying room's so toasty.'

'Well, assuming you've a good-sized ironing table, I could teach one of the girls in a day everything she needs to know to be your laundress. Cookery's harder. Do any of you cook much? I mean I know you make good cake.'

Aggie pulled a face. 'Only basics,' she said.

'But basic is all you need. It's only breakfasts. Bought bread. Good Devon butter and bacon.'

'What about evening meals?'

'I wouldn't offer anything you're not happy to offer, Aggie. But what would I know? Only stayed in a hotel once in my life, girl!' And they laughed again. 'I suppose,' Laura went on, 'you could always keep it very simple. No choice. Call it family supper or whatever, then just have the same five or six things you cook in rotation. Fish on Fridays – that's quick and easy. Crab another night as

371

people coming here will expect that. Roast chicken, lamb hotpot, beef stew and you're done. Cook gets Sunday and Monday night off. How's that?'

'Laura?' Aggie reached out to touch Laura's forearm with a finger.

'Yes?'

'How many nights did you say you could stay?'

SURRENDER – 1945

Charles had not felt properly seasick for months. It turned
out that his former captain's pronouncement that he was
'unsuitable for small ships' was quite right and a much
larger vessel suited him better. The *Glory* was to the
Starburst as a city to a hamlet. An aptly named Colossus-
class aircraft carrier, she had been brand new, fresh from
her makers at Harland and Wolff, when he joined her on
this, her maiden voyage from Belfast. She still pitched in a
high sea, of course, and the first days on the Atlantic saw
him once again obliged to work with a gash bucket hooked
under his coding desk, but the movement was far slower
because of her incredible size, with none of the violent
pitching or frightening noises he had endured on the
Starburst. Her size was a help psychologically as well,
making her feel unsinkable and making it easier to forget,
as the Signals office was so far from the waterline, that one
was even at sea. Her purpose and capacity also meant that
as well as her crew, and the air squadrons on board to fly
the Barracudas and Corsairs, she was frequently taking on
or dropping off soldiers, airmen, military bigwigs. There
was none of that intimacy of a smaller ship but, more than
ever, the Navy's mess and watch system meant that each
man lived in her vastness ever mindful of his department's
particular village.

Even after months of teaching raw recruits at HMS *Cabbala*, Charles found it odd to have moved up the chain of command and to have men under him calling him 'sir'. Not many men, admittedly – he was only a petty officer – but that, and the youth of the coders on his team, made him conscious that he would soon turn thirty.

The technology of the work had changed, the business of coding having greatly speeded up with the introduction of the Codex machine. This noisy beast, whose clattering quite drowned out the quick-fire tapping of the telegraphist, was like an electrically powered typewriter, only a system of adjustable gear wheels meant that messages received or sent could be rapidly put out of, or into the day's chosen code without the need to consult cipher books. It changed the rhythm of Charles's work and the noise of it meant he was no longer able to play with lines of poetry as he coded except, occasionally, as a sort of intellectual challenge to himself.

Victory in Europe was declared less than a month after they'd left Belfast and by the time they'd had the incredible experience of sailing into Sydney Harbour, all Allied energy had turned to the routing of the Japanese. This had been done with savage effectiveness, not just in the obliteration of Hiroshima and Nagasaki – when he had felt quite unable to join in his messmates' cheers – but in the stamping-down of pockets of resistance dotted across the islands of the Pacific.

There was a theatricality, a kind of retributive flair, to the way the Americans drew out the Japanese surrender. General MacArthur accepted the principal surrender in

Tokyo Bay, insisting it be done just below the framed American Union Jack once flown on his ancestor Commodore Perry's flagship, and with the *Missouri* anchored at the self-same spot. There was angry impatience, particularly among the Australians on board, that MacArthur allowed no other formal surrenders in the Pacific until after that one. Men were desperate to liberate internment camps where every Australian Charles spoke to seemed to have friends or family imprisoned in what were said to be barbaric conditions.

Three days after that surrender, preparations were in place to take POWs on board at the first opportunity, but first the airmen, the entire ship's company and all the soldiers on board were required to muster on deck. They were gathered smartly, by mess, on every available yard of the main runway but also informally draped around gun turrets and around the bridge. The atmosphere was chatty and festive while they waited. It felt, Charles imagined, like the crowd awaiting the hanging of a notorious murderer, although no blood was to be spilled.

As in Tokyo Bay, a theatrical humiliation was being laid on. First the Japanese leaders were to be brought up from the launch with their guard by the longest possible outside route, and then their path to the signing table had been lined with the biggest and tallest men available – to Charles's eyes, several of the Australians seemed to be well over six foot four. There had been torrential rains and the air was oppressively humid, even though the sky had cleared, and the combination of its electric blue, and the searing white of so many tropical uniforms, blasted the eye.

They were anchored off Rabaul, which the Japanese had made their principal base of operations in the area, only to be steadily hemmed in to the point of powerlessness as island after surrounding island had been blasted into Allied control. Charles had pored over maps and an old guidebook in the mess and could see it might once again be a place of beauty, but this morning it seemed only utterly alien. The Japanese had been cut off from any supplies for months and he wondered if their leaders would appear ragged and hungry. As the Australians took control, the rank and file Japanese were to remain here for a while at least, interned in a camp they would be made to build themselves. He could not voice such thoughts, but Charles felt the obliteration of whole cities was punishment enough, and found the constant calls for revenge repellent. Far more than the Italians and the Germans, he felt, the Japanese had been purposefully mythologised as a foe, made to seem not merely inhumane – which they undoubtedly had been – but unhuman.

The pipe shrilled to bring all sailors to attention and the soldiers and airmen received a corresponding command, then the imposing skipper, the wonderfully named Wass Buzzard, marched out along the corridor of the tall to a table set out for the purpose. He had a cardboard tube under his arm from which he took out and unfurled a document, which Charles could see was covered in ornate script. At the end of such a proudly modern war, a war of typewriters, radio, coders and ever more advanced communications machines, it was strange to see it was being brought to an end with a piece of pseudohistorical quaintness of a sort he could imagine the mayor and worthies of Launceston approving, when honouring some visiting dignitary.

'What's that, then, sir?' a young rating asked Charles.

'That is the Instrument of Surrender,' Charles murmured, because they weren't really supposed to be talking at attention. 'Everyone signs it and then control is given to the Australian Army.'

'What? Just of New Britain, sir?' asked the boy's neighbour.

'And New Ireland, the Solomons and New Guinea. There are a lot of Japanese troops around here. Over a hundred thousand. Shush now. Here we go.'

There was another whistle for attention and Lieutenant-General Sturdee and Brigadier Sheeran emerged and joined the skipper at the table as, in a neat piece of choreography, an armed escort led Admiral Kusaka and General Inamura and their guard on to the deck. From where Charles stood, it seemed that the crowd of men didn't break ranks exactly but distinctly leaned towards the defeated leaders, who stood in for every Japanese soldier who had shot, bombed, bayoneted or imprisoned their friends. The weight of so much attentive loathing must have been unbearable, but Kusaka bore himself proudly, kitted out in ceremonial whites no less splendid than General Sturdee's. Only Inamura – Hitoshi Inamura, Charles had learned he was called – looked defeated, his shoulders hunched, but then his army uniform, baggy and open at the neck to a white shirt, was far less operetta princeling than Kusaka's. There was a studious lack of bowing or greetings. The captain produced a fountain pen – Charles immediately wondered if it had been acquired especially or was the one he was given on starting boarding school and which he now used to write home to his wife – passed it to Sturdee, who handed it to Admiral Kusaka and showed where he was to sign. Fascinated by Japanese lettering, Charles wished he could see the pen at work but any view was blocked in a general craning of necks, and by the time he could see again, Inamura had also signed and the two men were once again being escorted to the start of the long climb down to their waiting launch.

Judging from the things he had heard men say over the last few days, ever since word had arrived of MacArthur's accepting the principal surrender in Tokyo Bay, and people had begun to mock Emperor Hirohito's understatement in his pre-surrender broadcast for saying, 'the war situation has developed not necessarily to our advantage', he had assumed that this final gratification for the victors would be met with ugliness. Charles felt sure someone would shout an obscenity, which would lead to others. He had imagined one of the more hot-tempered Australians might even muscle through to block the admiral and general's path, and spit. But, clearly, he had watched far too many American films on board, and there was no such break in decorum. The stare of the many as the two were led away was worse than any hurled tomato, the disciplined silence more contemptuous than any insult. And the intensity of the whoops and shouts when the command came to fall in was unlike anything Charles had ever heard.

There was no cheering when they finally took on their first band of POWs later that day. The shock and disgust were too great for that. As the men were brought on board, so many shuffling skeletons and many too weak to walk at all, marked by disease, parasites and cruelty, it was clear why the surrender had been signed first; decorum in the face of the enemy leaders would now have been impossible to maintain.

With the POWs, by some bureaucratic anomaly, arrived a delivery of post. On a ship the size of *Glory* letters took hours to sort and be delivered, and Charles was only handed his during a noticeably numbed supper; the sight of their starved and beaten brothers in filthy rags had taken the edge off everybody's appetite for roast pork and boiled carrots.

There was an unwritten naval rule that, though a man clearly had news to share, he was accorded a cushion of incuriosity when handed letters in company. Charles was particularly glad of this tonight. There was a letter from Mother, short as hers often were, but containing an unintentionally funny clipping from the local paper that made him smile as she had known it would. There was a card from Aunt Maggie, which touched him and made him feel bad for not having thought to write to her directly rather than always relying on Mother to pass on any news to her. And then there was a letter from Bucknall. Charles had written to him a while ago, when *Glory* stopped to refuel at Gibraltar, and immediately regretted that his letter had been riskily indiscreet and, to Bucknall's cynical eye at least, unappealingly needy and nostalgic.

He didn't recognise the handwriting because Bucknall had always been at pains never to write him even the most innocuous note when they were both at *Cabbala*. Now he wrote:

Dear Charles,

Your letter went to my home address, of course, as that was all you had and was forwarded to me on my ship by Sylvia, my wife. That's right. Sylvia the Jenny who was so keen on the Andrews Sisters. I can only hope she didn't open it first, knowing her inquisitive nature as I now do. It was very good to hear from you, but you must understand that my life has changed now that I'm a respectable married man etc. I greatly enjoyed our shared time at, (or is it on?) HMS *Cabbala* and I shall always be grateful for your friendship and for the many things you taught me and encouraged me to try. I suspect our lives will take rather different paths now but do keep in touch, Charles. Just be a little more discreet in what you write in future, matey. There are things the Little Woman would never understand.

All good wishes, yours, Edgar

As the meal progressed, he shared the funny newspaper clipping with his neighbours, making sure it made them laugh. He folded Bucknall's letter away and experienced a flush of anger, of which none of these new friends would have thought him capable. He would never make the mistake again of contacting Bucknall, but he would keep his letter always, he decided, long after this anger had passed, as a kind of insurance and reminder. Possibly, over the years to come, he would reserve the right to send him oddly intimate postcards at random, unsigned, purely to unnerve.

MR CAUSLEY – 1948

It was a bitterly cold, wintry Friday afternoon, so Laura was making a fish pie for their supper, one of those comforting recipes she knew so well she could make it with no need for checking details in her notebook. She had been taught it long, long ago by Mrs Ashbridge in the high-windowed kitchen at Teignmouth. She had already boiled two eggs and left them to cool and had now brought the pan of milk to a simmer with a bay leaf, peppercorns and some parsley stalks beneath a piece of salmon and one of smoked haddock. She set the egg timer for three minutes, then took the pan off the heat and used a fish slice to lift the two fish pieces on to a plate to cool. If they still had a cat it would be wreathing around her ankles by this stage. She missed having a pet keenly but felt getting a new one should be a decision taken by them both, and Charles had been too preoccupied by his writing and teaching recently for her to have much of his attention. She knew him so well she could read his moods like a farmer read weather, knew when to ask for favours or decisions and when it was better to hold her peace and bide her time.

The new portable wireless he had given her for her birthday was chattering on, her near-constant companion in the kitchen by day now that she was no longer laundering. The Labour government's exciting reforms were pressing ahead although Launceston remained as stuck-in-the-mud Tory as ever. Free good health and good education for all and cheaper housing were wonderful things Laura had never thought to see brought in, and yet the attitudes she heard expressed when waiting to be served in the shops of the town sometimes brought her home clenching her fists in indignation. Charles loved this and called her his firebrand.

Now the fish pieces were cool enough to handle, she used a blunt knife to tease the thick skin off them and on to a saucer, which she carried out to the yard. There was a feral cat out there sometimes, and she had taken to feeding it without telling Charles. It was a female, a scrawny, blotchily marked thing with a badly chewed ear. Laura had little hope of taming it. It would take the food she left down for it but yowled if she made any move to approach. It hissed at her fiercely even as she was setting down food for it. It was there now and darted away as she came out, only to turn round, smelling fish. All cats loved fish skin, she knew. Sure enough, the stray darted forward and rose up on its back paws in a kind of beseeching motion even as it hissed warnings at her.

'Silly thing,' she said, and set down the saucer. It made short work of the skin, tugging each piece off a little way from her, purring loudly as it chewed it down but breaking off to throw ungrateful glares Laura's way.

She checked the small amount of washing on the line. It was as dry as it would get outside at that time of year so she unpegged it, draping the clothes over her shoulder as she went and dropping the pegs into the gingham peg bag she had sewn long ago and which must be past thirty now, as old as Charles. Inside, she hung the laundry on the wooden rack near the range. She could iron it in the morning.

Charles had surprised her by taking up one of the further education grants for returning servicemen to spend a year away in Peterborough training as a teacher, then delighted her by taking up a junior post at the old National School just up the hill from their front door. He said he had nearly set by enough now to take out a mortgage so they could own the house rather than continue renting it, and he had insisted she stop working and retire. Or stop working for others, at least.

She realised he had, in effect, made her the kind of wife she had never been able to be for Charlie, whose work was entirely for her loved ones: cleaning, shopping, cooking, ironing and the rest. Laura could never have been a woman who sat there and did nothing, or who had another woman in to do work she could do better herself, but it meant that her days now were easy compared to what they had been. Charles settled all the bills and tucked money into her purse every Saturday morning: money for housekeeping and for herself.

'But shouldn't you be saving?' she asked him. 'For when you want to settle down?'

'Hadn't you noticed?' he teased her. 'I am settled, or as settled down as I'll ever be.'

He said it with one of his slightly shy gestures of affection, a touch to her shoulder as he passed her armchair to fetch more coal for the fire.

There was a pattern to their weekdays now. Breakfast together was followed by his heading off to school, looking smart and respectable in jacket and tie, yet far more approachable than the teachers of his she remembered. Laura then cleaned the house and shopped, and went to the Women's Institute if it was a WI day. When Charles returned late in the afternoon, he had tea with her and heard about her day and told her funny stories about his. Sometimes his stories were sad, of course; some of the children were still so poor or neglected, and compassion could make him quite angry. Then he swiftly did any marking he had to do before retiring to his room to write.

He was writing stories and poems. Mainly poems. She had learned to regard the clatter of his typewriter as a good sign as it meant he had finished something and was making a fair copy. If the typewriter lay silent, he would become moody and she would tread with care. She would no sooner have asked about his writing than she would have tried to stroke the feral cat. They spoke about his teaching – he often asked her opinion about this or that child or family, as he liked to say she had a village postmistress's ability to retain local family histories – but she sensed his writing was mattering more and more to him.

He had never courted in earnest, to her knowledge, and she was coming to feel that was now impossible, for the writing demanded an intense emotional attention, a devotion almost, he could now never spare for a person. There was no more talk of plays. The silk dressing gown phase had passed, apparently. Sometimes, when dusting his room, she read whatever lay on top of the various piles on his desk. If it wasn't covered, she felt this was allowed. She didn't understand much modern poetry. She had tried and abandoned his copies of T. S. Eliot. What he was writing, though, didn't feel like that. It felt as direct and arresting as someone seizing your cuff to tell you something as you were leaving church. It excited and unsettled her, but she had no idea what would happen to it all. She knew writers of romantic novels made a handsome living, but it was hard to believe poetry would ever pay the bills as securely as teaching did. The need for the one was so evident compared to the need for the other.

On Saturdays, Charles often took himself off on excursions, visits to old churches or long walks across Bodmin Moor or out along the coast. Sometimes he took her too, but not always. On Sundays, Laura had church, of course, to which she could never predict his coming. (He said he felt nearer God when a church was empty, which was perhaps just his clever way of letting her down gently.) She never challenged him about this; if ever tempted to, mildly humiliated at the sight of people attending in big family groups when she came all alone, she remembered Douglas saying how the war had killed God for him, and held her tongue. She was fairly sure Charles had seen terrible things in the war, things that gave him bad dreams that would have him shouting out in his sleep or pacing the house in his dressing gown at night, but which she dreaded him sharing with her. They always had a good Sunday lunch together after church, often with friends or family, which was worship of a kind.

They rarely argued. They could have done all the time, because their temperaments were so alike, but she had learned when to step back. Occasionally she mis-stepped,

though, and there were, by his fastidious standards, fire-
works. One day, she had been reading the local paper, as he
read the national one, and she read him out a court report
because he liked lurid stories about murders and the like.
It concerned a group of men being sent to prison for com-
mitting acts of gross indecency just outside Callington on
Kit Hill. She was genuinely baffled. Whatever could they
have been doing, she wondered aloud, to merit such savage
prison sentences?

'Nobody was hurt,' she told him. 'It doesn't mention
any victims here.'

'Mother, if you really don't understand,' he said, 'I am
the very last person who's going to explain it to you.'

His words had been mild enough. He hadn't sworn,
which he sometimes did, like the sailor he had been, when
something truly angered him. But the tone he used had
been withering in a way that frightened her into an awkward silence, which was only broken when he mercifully
turned on the wireless for a discussion programme he was
keen to catch.

She was halfway through carefully straining the fishy
milk for the pie's sauce when there was a knock at the
door. She was on her way to answer it when she remembered she was still in her housecoat. She swiftly unbuttoned
it, hung it on the back of the kitchen door, checked in the
little kitchen mirror that her hair wasn't wild, then went to
see who it was.

A sailor stood there, his uniform just visible beneath his
regulation duffel coat. He was a big man, perhaps a bit older
than Charles, though with a blue-eyed, open countenance

that let you immediately see the trusting boy within the weather-beaten man. He doffed his hat as she opened the door, revealing a fuzz of close-cropped auburn hair, and stepped back a little.

'Hello?' she said.

'Mrs Causley?' His accent wasn't local.

'Yes,' she told him.

'You don't know me, though I feel I know you from all Jan's stories. I'm his friend Cushty. We sailed on the *Starburst* together.'

'Cushty, hello. Come in. I'm afraid he's still at work, but come in and wait in the warm. He won't be long.'

'Are you sure? He's not expecting me.'

He was so much bigger than Charles that he fairly loomed over her, but she felt entirely unthreatened.

'He'll be delighted. And so am I. He's never had any of his navy friends visit and nobody's ever exactly passing Launceston.' She waved him past her. 'Let me take your coat.' It was heavy and smelled of man and tobacco. She had not long persuaded Charles to drop the smoking habit the Navy had encouraged with all its free cigarettes, but it was still a smell she quite liked out of doors. 'You're a petty officer like Charles was,' she said, seeing his uniform.

He glanced down at his sleeve. 'He got there well before me.'

'But you're a proper sailor. I mean—'

'I'm in it for the long haul,' he agreed. 'I've been in the Navy since I left school.'

'Goodness! Don't your family miss you?'

'They're used to it.' He shrugged. 'Plenty more where I came from. Where's Wang?'

She told him Wang had died two years ago and was surprised he knew of his existence.

'Oh, we often laughed about his name,' he said, and cleared his throat.

She led him to the front room where he sat in the armchair across from hers, Charles's chair. She sat too, waiting for the kettle to boil.

He asked about Charles's teaching and was amused at the thought of his working just up the road in the same school he'd gone to as a little boy.

'It's very Cornish of him,' she told him. 'Men here travel the world but then they come home and don't budge much. Cornish roots run deep and hold fast. How long is your leave, Cushty?'

'A whole two weeks this time,' he said, 'as we've been away so long. I thought I'd look Jan up before I head back up to Liverpool to see my folks again. I feel bad leaving it so long, but I've been away so much and, well, he never gave me his address.'

'However did you find us, then?'

'Took a while,' he said, 'as I didn't know Lanson and Launceston were the same place.'

She smiled at his attempt at an upcountry accent.

'But once I realised my mistake and got a train here from Devonport, all I had to do was say the name and there was fairly a rush to betray you. Funny, though, hearing Jan called Mr Causley, like he was a bank manager or a doctor.'

'Why did you call him Jan?'

389

''Cause of Janner, I suppose. Officially. London ears hearing no difference between a Cornish accent and a Plymouth one but, well . . .'

'Yes?'

He looked at her to gauge her reaction.

'Jan suits him,' he said with a grin. 'He could be a bit prissy sometimes.'

She laughed at her own mischief. 'He still can!' she said. 'You should have heard him at sixteen, though.'

He chuckled. 'I can imagine.' He paused, looking at her, his blue eyes shining. 'You are so exactly as he described you, you know.'

'Oh dear.'

'No, in a good way. He thinks the world of you. Your strength and, what's that word, stoicalness? I used to get quite jealous, homesick too, hearing him talk about you and this place. If you can miss a place you've never been. I'm very sorry about your little dog.'

'Well . . . Wang was a good age and he went very fast, which was kind. I hate to see old dogs dragging themselves around when their back legs go.'

The front door opened and shut, and Charles called out a brisk hello as he always did.

'In here,' Laura called, adding, 'You've a visitor,' as she knew he disliked surprises. She stood to meet him, thinking to give him her chair as she gathered the tea things.

She had always thought it just a figure of speech, but when he came to the doorway and saw Cushty, she truly saw the blood drain from his face. She half-thought he might faint.

'Hello, Jan,' Cushty said. 'Or is it Mr Causley now?'

Charles just stood there. 'I . . . I thought you were dead,' he said.

'Charles!' she rebuked him.

'But I did,' he snapped. 'I was told the *Starburst* was blown in two and all hands lost.'

'You never told me that,' she protested.

'Yes, well, there's a lot of horrible things I never told you, Mother.'

'She was,' Cushty said. 'Blown in two. But I wasn't on her, was I? After Alex, I was promoted and transferred and . . . well.' His words ran dry on seeing Charles again.

'I'll make tea,' Laura said quietly, and slipped out past Charles as Cushty stood up.

In the room behind her she heard mumbles and a back-slap as the men finally greeted each other. There were tears in Charles's voice as he said, 'I thought I'd seen a ghost. I swear, all this time . . .'

She decided she would give them tea on their own. She made up a tray with the second-best teapot (the best having only one cup that matched), and a plate of bread and butter and another of gingerbread. Cushty definitely looked like a man who liked cake. When she took the tray in, they had an armchair each. Cushty stood but she waved him back down.

'Stay,' she said. 'I need to get on with finishing supper.'

'No,' Charles told her strangely. 'Don't leave us.'

'I'm just out there if you need me, Charles,' she said. 'You've catching up to do.' She smiled reassuringly at Cushty, who must also see that his behaviour was a bit odd. If her funny, prickly boy had survived the war and come safely back to her, it was thanks to gentle giants like him. She closed the door behind her so they could talk freely and got on with boiling potatoes in one pan, and in another making a white sauce with the herbed, fishy milk.

She turned the wireless back on to some music to improve their privacy but, as the sauce began to thicken up, she became increasingly aware of their voices. Were they arguing? And then, quite clearly, she heard Charles say, 'Don't you see it's completely impossible now?' and heard him fling open the front-room door and thunder up the stairs.

'Charles?' she called out, and turned off the wireless. 'Charles?'

She tugged the sauce off the heat. Charles could be so rude sometimes. She stepped out of the kitchen and heard his typewriter going. Behind her, Cushty appeared. He had the tea things neatly back on the tray.

'Delicious gingerbread, Mrs Causley,' he said.

'Oh, but you've hardly touched a thing. And . . .' She threw a glance upstairs. 'I'm so very sorry. I don't know what got into him.'

He smiled with a kindness that made her immediately picture him with a fretful child against one shoulder. 'It was a shock, is all,' he said. 'If I'd known he thought I was dead, I'd have written first.'

'Only you didn't have our address.'

'No.'

'Let me take that,' she told him.

'It's fine.' He stepped past her with the laden tray and

set it carefully down on the kitchen table. 'Will he come down for your fish pie?' he asked.

'Not until he's finished typing,' she said. 'I've become a specialist in food that won't spoil . . .'

He took down his duffel coat from where she had hung it and pulled it on.

'You're not travelling all the way to Liverpool tonight?' she asked, wondering whether Charles would be very angry if she offered his old friend the spare room.

'No,' he said. 'Plymouth tonight. I've a bed at Mrs Weston's. Then home in the morning.'

'Ah, that's good. But you'll take something for your journey?'

'It's only forty minutes, if that.'

'No, but for tomorrow.'

'Really?'

'Cushty, I'm afraid I insist.'

There was some good ham left in the meat safe. She swiftly made him two rounds of ham sandwiches with the remaining bread and butter and, in a second greaseproof bundle, packed him three slices of the gingerbread.

'I can see why he missed you,' he told her. As if she had known him for years, quite as though he were a son of her own, she found herself standing on tiptoe to hug him. And she was not a woman who hugged.

'Bye, Cushty. Come back soon, now you know where we live.'

'Yes,' he said, but as she walked him to the front door and watched him stride off up the dark lane towards the trains, she was suddenly quite certain he would never return, and she dimly understood that something had passed of whose significance Charles would never speak to her.

Charles typed hard for nearly twenty minutes longer. Perhaps it wasn't a poem but one of his strange stories? When he came down he was bright and hungry, warmly appreciative of the fish pie, full of chat about a troubled girl in his class and clearly indicating that he did not wish to speak of the visit or his bad behaviour earlier. He ate a piece of her gingerbread with some stewed apple for pudding, though, which she took as a coded apology.

The delivery arrived the next morning, off the eleven o'clock train. The junior porter from the station was wreathed in smiles as he handed it over to her. 'Reckon you'll have your work cut out with this one, missus,' he said as she signed for it.

It was a small wicker hamper, fastened with leather straps and carefully addressed to her in the hand of someone to whom writing did not come readily. It was lined with a folded-up blanket and contained a kitten so small it looked barely weaned. It was quite black, without even the usual white tuft somewhere. As she set down a saucer of milk for it and it fell to eagerly feeding, she saw that its paws were huge and had an extra toe each. Happy but bemused, Laura moved the hamper, thinking it would make a good basket until the creature grew a little, and she spotted a note pushed down one side of the old blanket.

'Dear Mrs Causley,' the same uncertain handwriting began, 'Here is a Janner kitten to replace your Wang. Thank you for my picnic. All good wishes, Cushty.'

By the time Charles returned from school, the kitten

had made itself thoroughly at home, eating well, visiting the garden, touring the downstairs rooms and sensibly electing to sleep in its wicker hamper, from which she'd removed the lid, close to the range, in Wang's old spot.

'But he's a true Janner,' Charles exclaimed. 'Look at those paws!' He had lifted the kitten and laughed as he let it scramble across the tweed of his jacket. 'They're famously popular with sailors because the extra toes make them good mousers and give them extra good balance on a rolling deck. Wherever did you find him, Mother?'

Rather than risk the challenge of saying Cushty's name out loud, she simply handed him his old friend's note to read. She turned to carry on preparing supper and soon afterwards heard him head upstairs to his room to work. Almost immediately his typewriter began to clatter. Laura noticed he had taken the kitten with him.

AUTHOR'S NOTE

Many readers will have noticed that this novel is a very loose retelling of the early life of the Cornish poet Charles Causley and his mother, Laura. After the point where I leave them, Laura and Charles continued living together for the rest of her life, moving, as he settled into his teaching job, to a more out-of-the-way cottage called Cyprus Well, on the precipitous slope of Angel Hill. It's no exaggeration to say she was the love of his life. After her death in 1971 his prolonged grief became a kind of nervous breakdown but also a path to liberation. He retired from teaching to become a full-time poet, travelling the world and providing one of the few authentically Cornish voices on Radio 4. He left Cyprus Well only when frail old age demanded, but remained in Launceston until his death in 2003.

I have honoured most of the established facts and included plenty of others I stumbled on in my research, but I'd want nobody to mistake this for a scholarly biography of a great man, not least because I have shamelessly used fiction and conjecture to fill the gaps in stories that history and discretion had left blank. All the other characters beyond Laura, Charles and Charlie and the historical ones are either entirely made up or amalgams of real-life friends depicted in Charles's minutely scribbled diaries. I purposefully left Charles's numerous relatives on the margins of the story, out of respect for their living descendants.

Charles did, indeed, come first in class with a markedly antisemitic poem called 'The Jew'. There is not a trace of antisemitism in his later writing (private or public) so this can safely be set down to the dubious tenor of the times when he was at school. In the characters' references to race, I used the anachronistic term black rather than risk causing offence with other terms then in common use.

If Charles's work is not yet known to you, I urge you to discover it. He deserves a place in the pantheon alongside Stevenson for his children's poetry, but his poems for adults are often astonishing. Some are written in a ballad voice that has endeared them to the Cornish and folksingers alike, but many, like 'Timothy Winters' or 'Bridie Wiles', have a plain directness to them that will never age and is, as my Laura has it, like having someone catch your cuff on your way out of church. He is one of the few great poets of the Second World War, that novelists' war, scarred for life by the loss of multiple friends, and by survivor's guilt at not having gone down with his boat (in real life HMS *Eclipse*) but also having had his horizon immeasurably broadened by war's ambiguous adventure. He is a great visionary poet often co-opted by active Christians, but his vision is far more interesting and ambivalent than that might suggest. And he wrote many marvellously funny poems tenderly evoking his family and boyhood in Launceston.

His early collection of short stories, *Hands to Dance and Skylark*, and his abandoned novel, *Other Men's*

Poison, were invaluable in helping me recreate his experiences in the Navy while his diaries and papers, preserved for all in Exeter University's Special Collections (and currently awaiting the writer of a full, critical biography), gave me confidence in piecing together a version of his character more challenging and prickly than the saintly teddy bear to which his admirers threaten to reduce him.

Whenever asked why he hadn't written more of a memoir than his numerous short autobiographical pieces, Causley always said, 'It's all in the poems.' And it is, up to a point, but the true ambiguous nature of the man and his life is, I think, often carefully encoded there. I was inspired to write this novel by a handful of his poems where his love, and his pain, seem to be hiding in plain sight. Notably 'Eden Rock', his meditation on the prospect of joining his parents in death and 'Never Take Sweets from a Stranger', which I quote at the front and which, I think significantly, he chose to withhold from publication. But my chief inspiration was the haunting ballad I quote with permission here, in which the narrator is visited by and, St Peter-like, denies the tender claims of a former messmate who may, or may not, be dead.

Angel Hill

A sailor came walking down Angel Hill,
He knocked on my door with a right good will,
With a right good will he knocked on my door.
He said, 'My friend, we have met before.'
No, never, said I.

He searched my eye with a sea-blue stare
And he laughed aloud on the Cornish air,
On the Cornish air he laughed aloud
And he said, 'My friend, you have grown too proud.'
No, never, said I.

'In war we swallowed the bitter bread
And drank of the brine,' the sailor said.
'We took of the bread and we tasted the brine
As I bound your wounds and you bound mine.'
No, never, said I.

'By day and night on the diving sea
We whistled to sun and moon,' said he.
'Together we whistled to moon and sun
And vowed our stars should be as one.'
No, never, said I.

'And now,' he said, 'that the war is past
I come to your hearth and home at last.
I come to your home and hearth to share
Whatever fortune waits me there.'
No, never, said I.

'I have no wife nor son,' he said,
'Nor pillow on which to lay my head,
No pillow have I, nor wife nor son,
Till you shall give to me my own.'
No, never, said I.

His eye it flashed like a lightning-dart
And still as a stone then stood my heart.
My heart as a granite stone was still
And he said, 'My friend, but I think you will.'
No, never, said I.

The sailor smiled and turned in his track
And shifted the bundle on his back
And I heard him sing as he strolled away,
'You'll send and you'll fetch me one fine day.'
No, never, said I.

ACKNOWLEDGEMENTS

Research for this novel was greatly helped by the support of the Charles Causley Trust, of which I'm proud to be a patron. The chairman, Ian Tunbridge, furnished invaluable documentary evidence of Charles's family tree and of Charlie and Stanley's war records, and the director, Kate Campbell, let me spend a hugely inspiring week living in Cyprus Well, the final house where Charles and Laura lived, surrounded by their possessions, including the unattributed painting of the woman drinking tea and the ghosts of several cats. Mike Cooper repeatedly alerted me to archived Causley snippets he'd come across during his MA research into Charles's naval career. And she won't remember, but it was thanks to the repeated hospitality shown by another trustee, Fiona Colville, at Penheale Manor when I was in my twenties, that I first became aware there was a famous poet still living up the road.

Another boon was having frequent access to Charles's fascinating archive in Exeter University's Special Collections maintained by Dr Christine Faunch and her endlessly patient staff. Without having been able to squint over his letters, diaries and manuscripts for myself I should never have had the courage to make up the things I did. (Bucknall's letter has a real-life counterpart, carefully kept by Charles until his death.) My research trips there were partly funded by a writer's residency at Exeter's Custom

House Museum awarded by Literature Works, for which I was immensely grateful.

Thanks also to the archivists at the Teign Heritage Centre, the curators of the Teignmouth and Shaldon Museum and the archivists at the Imperial War Museum. Thank you David Smart, for making my exploration of Trusham such a delight; sometimes it really helps to have a second pair of eyes to see through. Thanks to the press office at Butlin's Skegness for letting me cheekily stroll among their unsuspecting holiday-makers. Thanks to Horatio Clare and his hugely distinguished naval uncle, Roy, who between them helped open so many crucial doors to me, not least that of the museum and site director, Richard Holdsworth, who generously gave up a whole morning to take me on a brilliantly vivid tour of HMS *Cavalier* at Chatham Historic Dockyard.

My research in Gibraltar was greatly assisted by an inspiring stay with the then Governor, Lieutenant General Ed Davis and his lovely wife, Lorraine.

Major Dominic Collado, the staff at the Garrison Library, Jean Paul Latin and Brian Reyes were also a great help there, as was Sally Dunsmore of the Gibraltar Literary Festival. In Valletta, meanwhile, the Reverend Canon Simon Godfrey, Chancellor of Malta's Pro-Cathedral, showed marvellous hospitality and was a fount of good stories at the Chancellor's Lodge.

Thanks to Clive Smith of the De Vere hotel at Tortworth Court, for the light he shed on the first home of HMS *Cabbala*, to the Science Museum for finally enabling me to examine one of the few surviving Codex machines and to Clive Kidd, David White, Ken Sutton, Ron Hawkins (of

Cornwall's National Maritime Museum) and Godfrey Dykes for helping a mere crossword solver understand more about naval coding in general and 'the Black Monster' in particular. Thanks to Dr Sophie Ratcliffe, who so kindly helped track down and scan the Bodleian Library's copy of Charles's 'Never Take Sweets from a Stranger' for me.

Thanks to the friends and admirers of Charles who so boosted my enthusiasm. His fellow poet, Kate Clanchy, first showed me 'Eden Rock' and made me start asking questions. The film maker Jane Darke's encouragement and beautiful documentary *The Poet Charles Causley* made me brave. Charles's lifelong friend, Arthur Wills, one of the children who used to crouch below the window to hear Charles play the piano brought Charles's childhood brightly to life for me. Stephen McNeff and Renee Smithens, friends of Charles's later years, brought home to me how deeply Charles valued the company of women.

Finally, thank you to Ken Stanton for letting me reproduce this evocative drawing made of Charles by his friend Stanley Simmonds when they were both stationed in Gibraltar.

ACKNOWLEDGEMENTS

Illustration of Charles Causley by Stanley Simmonds,
reproduced by permission of Kent Stanton